Praise for *New York Times* bestselling author RaeAnne Thayne

"[Thayne] engages the reader's heart and emotions, inspiring hope and the belief that miracles *are* possible."

—#1 *New York Times* bestselling author Debbie Macomber

"RaeAnne Thayne is quickly becoming one of my favorite authors.... Once you start reading, you aren't going to be able to stop."

—*Fresh Fiction*

"RaeAnne has a knack for capturing those emotions that come from the heart."

—*RT Book Reviews*

Praise for *USA TODAY* bestselling author Patricia Davids

"Patricia Davids pens a captivating tale.... *The Color of Courage* is well researched, with a heartwarming conclusion."

—*RT Book Reviews*

"*A Matter of the Heart* is a touching and wonderful story that's not to be missed."

—*RT Book Reviews*

RaeAnne Thayne finds inspiration in the beautiful northern Utah mountains, where the *New York Times* and *USA TODAY* bestselling author lives with her husband and three children. Her books have won numerous honors, including RITA® Award nominations from Romance Writers of America and a Career Achievement Award from *RT Book Reviews.* RaeAnne loves to hear from readers and can be contacted through her website, www.raeannethayne.com.

Patricia Davids has led a storied life, so it is no wonder she enjoys writing books. She has been in turn a Kansas farmer's daughter, a nurse, a pen pal to a lonely sailor, a navy wife, a mother, a neonatal transport nurse, a champion archer, a horse trainer, a grandmother times two, a widow, a world traveler and finally an award-winning, bestselling author. Pat now lives on the Kansas farm where she grew up. She loves to hear from readers. You can contact her through her website at www.patriciadavids.com or follow her on Facebook at Author Patricia Davids.

New York Times **Bestselling Author**

RAEANNE THAYNE

REUNITED IN WALNUT RIVER

HARLEQUIN® BESTSELLING AUTHOR COLLECTION

If you purchased this book without a cover you should be aware that this book is stolen property. It was reported as "unsold and destroyed" to the publisher, and neither the author nor the publisher has received any payment for this "stripped book."

ISBN-13: 978-1-335-46996-0

Reunited in Walnut River

Copyright © 2019 by Harlequin Books S.A.

The publisher acknowledges the copyright holders of the individual works as follows:

Reunited in Walnut River
Copyright © 2008 by Harlequin Books S.A.
First published as A Merger...or Marriage? by Harlequin Special Edition in 2008

This edition published 2019

A Matter of the Heart
Copyright © 2008 by Patricia Macdonald

All rights reserved. Except for use in any review, the reproduction or utilization of this work in whole or in part in any form by any electronic, mechanical or other means, now known or hereafter invented, including xerography, photocopying and recording, or in any information storage or retrieval system, is forbidden without the written permission of the publisher, Harlequin Enterprises Limited, 22 Adelaide St. West, 40th Floor, Toronto, Ontario M5H 4E3, Canada.

This is a work of fiction. Names, characters, places and incidents are either the product of the author's imagination or are used fictitiously, and any resemblance to actual persons, living or dead, business establishments, events or locales is entirely coincidental.

This edition published by arrangement with Harlequin Books S.A.

For questions and comments about the quality of this book, please contact us at CustomerService@Harlequin.com.

® and TM are trademarks of Harlequin Enterprises Limited or its corporate affiliates. Trademarks indicated with ® are registered in the United States Patent and Trademark Office, the Canadian Intellectual Property Office and in other countries.

PLEASE RECYCLE
THIS PRODUCT IS RECYCLABLE
Recycling programs for this product may not exist in your area.

Printed in U.S.A.

CONTENTS

Also available from RaeAnne Thayne

HQN Books

The Cliff House

Haven Point

Snow Angel Cove
Redemption Bay
Evergreen Springs
Riverbend Road
Snowfall on Haven Point
Serenity Harbor
Sugar Pine Trail
The Cottages on Silver Beach
Season of Wonder

Harlequin Special Edition

The Women of Brambleberry House

A Soldier's Return
A Soldier's Secret
His Second-Chance Family
The Daddy Makeover

**Don't miss *A Haven Point Christmas*,
coming October 2019 from HQN Books.**

For a complete list of books by RaeAnne Thayne,
please visit www.raeannethayne.com.

REUNITED IN WALNUT RIVER

RaeAnne Thayne

Chapter 1

So this was what it felt like to be a pariah.

Anna Wilder tilted her chin slightly higher, tightened her grasp on her briefcase and walked firmly past the two gray-haired biddies at the information desk in the lobby of Walnut River General Hospital.

She didn't need to keep them in view to feel the heat of their glares following her to the gleaming elevator doors. She also didn't need to fully hear their whispers to catch enough to make her ulcer go into overdrive.

It's her, Anna Wilder.

The traitor.

James and Alice must be rolling in their graves.

She did her best to ignore them—and the hurt that settled like greasy black bile in her stomach. Still, to her great shame, she wasn't quite able to control the slight tremble of her hand as she pushed the elevator button to go up.

One of the two cars appeared to be permanently stuck on the second floor but the other one at last began creeping downward in what felt like excruciatingly painful slow motion.

She prayed the blasted thing would hurry up and arrive—not only to allow her to slip inside and escape the stares and whispers but, more importantly, because she was late.

She really hated being late.

The elevator stopped on the second floor and paused there for a few moments before continuing its descent. Suddenly a new apprehension fluttered her ulcer.

Why hadn't she been smart enough to take the stairs? The only thing worse than being late for her meeting would be the social discomfort of encountering one of her siblings in the elevator during her first few minutes at the hospital.

She didn't know which one would be harder to face right now. Ella? Peter? David? It probably didn't matter. They were all furious with her and would no doubt love a chance to let her know.

Just before the elevator arrived, one of the two volunteers at the information desk raised her voice in what had to be deliberate malice so Anna couldn't miss her words.

"She might have the Wilder name," she said in a carrying voice, "but she's not a true Wilder. How can she be, since she's in bed with those who are trying to sell out this hospital and this town?"

Anna inhaled sharply. Apparently the doctors weren't the only ones at Walnut River General who could wield a scalpel. The words effectively sliced straight to where she was most vulnerable.

Her hand tightened on the briefcase as she ruthlessly tried to ignore the hot tears burning behind her eyelids.

It didn't matter what a couple of dried-up old prunes had to say about her. Why should it? They had nothing better to do with their time than sit around gossiping and watching all the human suffering march through their lobby.

She knew she was doing the right thing—the *best* thing—for Walnut River and its citizens. She just had to convince everybody else in town.

No problem.

At long, long last, the elevator car arrived and the doors whooshed open. She considered it nothing short of a miracle that it was blessedly empty. Not a Wilder in sight.

Only after the doors slid shut did she close her eyes and slump against the wall of the elevator, pressing a hand to her stomach before she dug in the pocket of her suit jacket for an antacid.

She did not want to be here. In Walnut River, at the hospital her family had all but founded, in this blasted elevator.

It helped nothing that she had expected the reaction she had received from those two volunteers and she expected much more vitriol in the days ahead.

She had read the reports and knew the merger she had been sent here to expedite wasn't popular among the staff at WRG. Not that she had needed reports. Her family's unreasonable opposition was all the evidence she needed. They had all made no secret that they were furious at her.

Traitor.

Not a Wilder.

She screwed her eyes shut. Focus on the job, she chanted to herself. That was all that mattered. Move in fast and hard and wrap things up so she could return to New York.

She had no choice, not if she wanted to keep her job. And she certainly did.

She loved working for Northeastern HealthCare, one of the fastest growing health care conglomerates in the region. She was on the fast track there and had great hopes of making vice president within the next five years. That goal would be even closer if she could pull this deal off.

Mercifully, though the elevator stopped on the second floor to pick up a couple of nurses, she didn't recognize them and they didn't seem to know her. One of them even gave her a friendly smile.

So maybe David hadn't yet gotten around to plastering up wanted posters throughout the hospital of her wearing devil horns.

Beware of the evil HMO-mongerer.

She wouldn't put anything past her second-oldest brother, a gifted plastic surgeon who had recently returned to Walnut River as well. Unlike her, he had come back to a warm welcome, embraced by one and all—the prodigal son giving up a lucrative career in L.A. as plastic surgeon to the stars to share his brilliance with patients in his own hometown.

On the fourth floor, the nurses exited with her. Anna stood for a moment, trying to catch her bearings.

This part of the hospital had been renovated in the

past few years and she was slightly disoriented at the changes.

She remembered it as slightly old-fashioned, with wood-grained paneling and dark carpeting. Now everything was light and airy, with new windows and a far more modern feel.

"Do you need help finding something?" one of the nurses asked, noticing her confusion.

"Yes. Thanks. I'm looking for the administrator's office."

"Down the hall. Second door on the right," she said.

"Thank you." Anna gave a polite smile, grateful for any help she could find here in this hostile environment, then headed in the direction the woman indicated.

The receptionist's nameplate read Tina Tremaine. She greeted Anna with a friendly smile, her features warm and open.

"Hello. I'm Anna Wilder. I'm here for a three-o'clock meeting with the hospital attorney and the administrator."

The instant she heard Anna's name, the woman's smile slid away as if a cold breeze had just blown through the room.

"I'm here for a three o'clock meeting with the hospital attorney and the administrator."

"Phil Crandall, the hospital attorney, is not here yet, Ms. Wilder. But Mr. Sumner and your attorney are in the boardroom. They're waiting for you."

Though she spoke politely enough, Anna thought she saw a tiny sliver of disdain in the woman's eyes.

She fished around in her mind for something she might say to alter the woman's negative impression, then checked the impulse.

She was working hard to break the habits of a lifetime, that hunger for approval she couldn't quite shake. Did it really matter what J.D.'s receptionist thought of her? It certainly wouldn't change anything about her mission here in Walnut River.

"Thank you," she answered, mustering a smile she hoped was at least polite if not completely genuine. She headed for the door the receptionist indicated, tilting her chin up and hoping she projected confidence and competence.

This was it. Her chance to cinch the promotion at NHC and cement her growing reputation as a rainmaker there.

Or she could blow the merger, lose her job, and end up begging on the street somewhere.

Think positive, she ordered herself. *You can do this. You've done it before.* As she pushed open the door, she visualized herself handing over the signed deal to her bosses, both her direct supervisor, Wallace Jeffers—vice president for mergers and acquisitions—and the NHC chief executive officer who had given her this assignment, Alfred Daly.

It was a heady, enticing image, one she clung to as she faced the two men at the boardroom table, papers spread out in front of them.

Two men sat at a boardroom table talking, papers spread out in front of them. She knew both of them and smiled at J. D. Sumner and Walter Posey, the NHC attorney.

"I'm sorry if I've kept you waiting. I didn't realize there would be so much construction surrounding the hospital."

J.D. nodded. "Walnut River is growing. You just have to walk outside to see it."

"Which is one factor that makes this hospital an attractive opportunity for NHC, as you well know."

J.D. had first come to Walnut River as an employee of NHC. He had ended up falling—literally—for her sister, Ella, resigning from NHC and taking the job as hospital administrator.

She didn't know all the details but she knew Ella had treated J.D. after he was injured in a bad tumble on some icy steps when leaving the hospital. Something significant must have happened between them to compel a man like J.D. to fall for his orthopedic surgeon and leave a promising career at Northeastern HealthCare to take the reins of Walnut River General Hospital.

She couldn't imagine giving up everything she had worked so hard to attain for something as ephemeral as love, but she had to admit part of her envied her sister. J.D. must love Ella very much.

She could only hope his relationship with Ella had turned him soft. Judging by his track record at NHC, Anna feared he would be a formidable foe in her efforts to make the merger happen.

"Our attorney was caught up in the traffic snarl as well," J.D. answered. "He just called and was still parking his car but he should be here any moment."

Though he spoke cordially enough, there was a reserve in his voice she couldn't miss.

She had only known him casually when he worked for NHC, but their interactions as coworkers had always been marked by friendly respect. Now, though, they were on opposite sides of what was shaping up to be an ugly fight over the future of the hospital.

He didn't seem antagonistic, as she had feared, only distant. She had to admit she was relieved. He and Ella were engaged, from what she understood. This was bound to be awkward enough between them without outright antipathy.

"I'm going for some coffee before we get started," the NHC attorney announced. "Can I get either of you anything?"

Anna shook her head at Walter, whom she had worked with before on these due diligence reviews. "None for me, thanks."

"Sumner?"

J.D. shook his head. "I'm good."

As soon as Walter left the room, J.D. leaned back in his chair and studied her carefully, until Anna squirmed under the weight of his green-eyed gaze.

"So how are you? I mean, how are you *really?*"

She blinked at the unexpected personal question and was slow to answer, choosing her words carefully. "I'm managing. I suppose you heard I tried to stay out of this one, obviously without success."

He nodded, his brow furrowed. "I heard. Does Daly really think your family connection will make anyone happier about NHC's efforts to take over the hospital?"

"Hope springs eternal, I suppose," she muttered.

J.D. laughed. "Alfred Daly obviously doesn't know your stubborn siblings, does he?"

If her boss had any idea what he was up against, Anna had a feeling he never would have initiated the merger proceedings at Walnut River General.

"How's Ella?" The question slipped out before she could yank it back.

J.D.'s eyes widened with surprise for just an instant

that she would ask before they softened into a dreamy kind of look that filled her with no small amount of envy.

"She's great. Wonderful. Except the wedding next month is making her a little crazy. I told her to just leave the details to someone else, but she won't hear of it." He paused. "She misses you."

I miss her, too. The words tangled on her tongue and dried there. She couldn't say them, of course. She could never tell J.D. how she hated this distance between her and her sister.

They used to be so close—best friends as well as sisters, only a year apart. They had shared everything—clothes, secrets, friends.

She remembered lying on her stomach in their backyard, daydreaming and giggling over boys.

"You're going to be my maid of honor," Ella declared more than once. "And I'll be yours."

"One of us will have to get married first," she remembered answering. "So one of us will have to be a matron of honor."

"That sounds so old! Like one of the gray-haired ladies at the hospital! How about we'll both still be maids of honor, even if one of us is already married?"

Anna remembered shaking her head at Ella's twisted logic but in the end, she had agreed, just like she usually did.

That had always been their plan. But now Ella and J.D. were getting married in a month and Anna wasn't even sure she would receive an invitation.

Especially not if she successfully carried out her objective of making this merger a reality.

Her career or her family.

A miserable choice.

"You should talk to her," J.D. said into the silence, with a sudden gentleness that made her want to cry again.

"I wish this were something that a little conversation could fix," she murmured. "I'm afraid it's not that easy."

"You never know until you try," he answered.

She didn't know how to answer him, and to her relief she was spared from having to try when the door opened.

She looked up, expecting Walter with his coffee, then she felt her jaw sag as recognition filtered through.

"Sorry I'm late, J.D. That traffic is a nightmare," the newcomer said. He was tall and lean, with hair like sunlight shooting through gold flakes. His features were classically handsome—long lashes, a strong blade of a nose, a mouth that was firm and decisive.

The eight years since she had seen Richard Green had definitely been kind to him. He had always been sexy, the sort of male women always looked twice at. When they were teenagers, he couldn't seem to go anywhere without a horde of giggling girls around him, though he had barely seemed to notice them.

Now there was an edge of danger about him, a lean, lithe strength she found compelling and seductive.

J.D. rose and shook his hand. "I appreciate you filling in for Phil at the last minute."

"No problem."

The attorney looked over J.D.'s shoulder and she saw shock and disbelief flicker across the stunning blue eyes that had lost none of their punch even after eight years.

"Anna!"

In a different situation, she might have rushed to hug him but he was sending out a definite "back off" vibe.

"You two know each other, obviously," J.D. said.

She managed to wrench her gaze away from Richard, wondering how she could possibly have forgotten his sheer masculine beauty—and how she ever could have walked away from it in the first place.

The reminder of how things had ended between them sent a flicker of apprehension through her body. He looked less than thrilled to see her. Could this merger become any more complicated? Her family was fighting against her tooth and nail, the hospital administrator was marrying her sister in a month's time, and she and the hospital attorney had a long and tangled history between them.

How was she supposed to be focused and businesslike around Richard when she couldn't help remembering exactly how that mouth had tasted?

"Richard lived only a few blocks away from the house where we were raised," she finally answered J.D., and was appalled to hear the husky note in her voice. She cleared her throat before continuing. "We went to school together and were…good friends."

Friends? Is that what she called it?

Richard listened to her with a mixture of anger and disbelief.

He supposed it wasn't strictly a lie. They had been friends through school. Both had been on similar academic tracks and had belonged to many of the same clubs and after-school organizations. Honor Club, Debate, Key Club. Even later when they went off to different universities, they had stayed in touch and had gotten together as often as possible with their other friends.

Yeah, they had been friends. But there had been much more to it, as she damn well knew, unless she'd somehow managed to conveniently wipe from her memory something that had certainly seemed significant—earthshaking, even—at the time.

What the hell was she doing here? Why hadn't somebody—J.D. or Peter Wilder or Phil Crandall, his absent partner—warned him?

He had heard from Peter and Ella that Anna was working for Northeastern HealthCare, their dreaded enemy. He just had never dreamed she would be a part of the conglomerate's efforts to take over Walnut River General.

She had changed. She used to wear her hair down, a long, luscious waterfall. Now it was tightly contained, pinned back in a sleek style that made her look cool and businesslike. Her features were just as beautiful, though some of the bright, hopeful innocence he remembered in the clear blue of her eyes had faded.

How could she sit across the boardroom table, all cool and gorgeous like some kind of damn Viking princess, acting as if her very presence here wasn't a betrayal of everything her family had done for this hospital and for this community?

The depth of his bitterness both shocked and disconcerted him. What did it matter if the NHC executive was Anna Wilder or some other mindless drone they sent?

Either way, the outcome would be the same.

NHC was determined to purchase the hospital from a city council eager to unload it and a solid core of doctors and administrators was just as determined to prevent the deal.

Richard numbered himself among them, even though he was here only in a fill-in capacity for his partner.

Yeah, he had been crazy about Anna once, but it had been a long, long time ago.

That fledgling relationship wasn't significant in the slightest. It hadn't been important enough to her to keep her in Walnut River and whatever might have been between them certainly had no bearing on the current takeover situation.

"Shall we get started with the hearing?" he said icily.

She blinked at his tone—and so did J.D., he noted with some discomfort.

Richard had built a reputation as a cool-headed attorney who never let his personal feelings interfere with his legal responsibilities. He supposed there was a first time for everything.

After a long awkward moment, Anna nodded.

"By all means," she replied, her voice matching his temperature for temperature.

Chapter 2

Two hours later, Richard understood exactly why Anna Wilder had been brought into this takeover.

She was as cold as a blasted icicle and just as hard.

While the NHC attorney had been present to vet the information offered by the hospital side, all of them recognized that Anna was truly the one in charge.

She had been the one leading the discussion, asking the probing questions, never giving an inch as she dissected their answers.

Richard had certainly held his own. Anna might be a tough and worthy opponent but he had one distinct advantage—he was absolutely determined to keep NHC from succeeding in its takeover efforts while he was still alive and kicking.

"Thank you, everyone." Anna stood and surveyed the men around the boardroom table with the sheer aplomb of a boxer standing over the battered and bloody body of an opponent.

"We've covered a great deal of ground. I appreciate your forthrightness and the hospital's compliance with the municipal council's disclosure order. You've been very helpful. I'll take this information back to my superiors and we can go from there."

Richard gritted his teeth. Until they could find a way out of it, the hospital administration had no choice but to comply with the municipal council's strictures.

For now, city council members controlled the purse strings and they appeared eager to escape the costly hospital business that had been a drain on taxpayers for years.

Even the NHC contretemps a few weeks ago involving charges of corporate espionage hadn't dissuaded them.

The only bright spot in the entire takeover attempt was that the municipal council seemed genuinely committed to listening to the opinion of the hospital board of directors before making a final decision to move forward with the sale of the hospital to NHC.

Right now, the board members were leaning only slightly against the sale, though he knew the slightest factor could tip that ultimate decision in either direction.

Who knows? Maybe the NHC bigwigs would take a look at the hospital's tangled financial and personnel disclosures and decide another facility might be more lucrative.

Though he was committed to doing all he could to block the sale, Richard was nothing if not realistic. He wasn't even the hospital's lead attorney, he was only filling in for his partner, who had called begging the favor only an hour before the meeting.

Before he knew Anna Wilder was on board as the NHC deal-closer, he would have jumped at the chance to step up and handle the merger discussions. Seeing her at the board table with her sleek blond hair yanked ruthlessly into a bun and her brisk business suit and her painfully familiar blue eyes changed everything.

He sighed as he gathered his laptop and papers and slipped them into his briefcase. He was zipping it closed when Anna managed to surprise him yet again, as she had been doing with depressing regularity since he walked into the boardroom.

"Richard, may I speak with you for a moment?"

He checked his watch, his mind on the very important person waiting for him. "I'm afraid I'm in a hurry," he answered.

"Please. This won't take long."

After a moment, he nodded tersely, doing his best to ignore the curious glances from J.D. and the NHC attorney as they both left the room.

Anna closed the door behind the two men and he was suddenly aware of the elegant shape of her fingers against the wood grain and the soft tendrils of hair escaping her pins to curl at the base of her neck.

She had changed perfumes, he noted. In college she had worn something light and flowery that had always reminded him of a sunwarmed garden. Now her scent was slightly more bold—and a hell of a lot more sexy, he had to admit. It curled through the room, tugging at his insides with subtle insistency.

She turned to face him and for an instant, he was blinded by the sheer vibrancy of her smile. "Richard,

I know I didn't say this before, but it's really wonderful to see you again! I've wondered so many times how you were."

He found that hard to believe. She had to know where he was. If she had wondered so much, she could have found out as easily as sending a simple e-mail or making a phone call.

"I've been fine. Busy."

Too busy to spend time mooning over the only woman who had ever rejected him, he wanted to add, but managed to refrain.

He was an adult, after all, something he would do well to remember right about now.

"Rumor has it you got married," she said after a moment. "Any kids? I always thought you would make a wonderful father."

"Did you?"

She either missed the bite in his tone or she chose to ignore it.

"I did," she answered. "You were always so great with the neighborhood children. I can remember more than a few impromptu baseball games with you right in the middle of the action. You didn't care how old the players were or anything about their ability level. You just tried to make sure everyone had fun."

He was trying really hard to ignore the softness in her eyes and the warmth in her voice.

She had walked away from everything he wanted to offer her, without looking back. He had a right to be a little bitter, eight years later.

"So do you have any children?" she asked. She seemed genuinely interested, much to his surprise.

"One," he finally answered, not at all pleased with

her line of questioning. He didn't like being reminded of old, tired dreams and newer failures.

"Boy or girl?"

"Boy. He's just turned five."

And he would be waiting impatiently for his father to pick him up if Richard didn't wrap things up quickly and escape.

"I do the best I can with him, especially since his mother and I aren't together anymore. The marriage ended right after he was born. I have full custody."

He wasn't sure why he added that. It wasn't something he just blurted out to people. If they hadn't been friends so long ago, he probably would have kept the information to himself.

Shock flickered in the depths of her blue eyes. "Oh. I hadn't heard that part. I'm so sorry, Richard."

He shrugged. "I'm sorry she's chosen to not be part of Ethan's life, but I'm not sorry about the divorce. It was one of those mistakes that make themselves painfully clear minutes after it's too late to be easily fixed."

"That doesn't make it hurt less, I would imagine," she murmured softly.

"No, it doesn't," he answered, his voice short. He regretted saying anything at all about Ethan and especially mentioning his failed marriage that still stung.

He gripped his briefcase, desperate to escape this awkwardness, but her words stopped him before he could do anything but put his hand on the doorknob.

"Can I ask you something?"

He eased his hand away, flashing her a wry look. "You haven't seemed to have any problem asking questions for the last two hours. You're amazingly good at it."

"That was different. Business. This is…not."

For the first time since the meeting she seemed to reveal her nerves weren't completely steel-coated. Wariness flickered in her eyes and she appeared to be gripping a file folder with inordinate force.

He ought to just push past her and get the hell out of there but he couldn't quite bring himself to move.

Instead, he shrugged. "Go ahead."

"I just wondered about this…hostility I'm sensing from you."

Apparently he wasn't as good at concealing his inner turmoil as he'd thought. "I'm sure you're imagining things."

"I don't think so," she answered, her voice pitched low. "I'm not an idiot, Richard."

Abruptly, suddenly, he was furious with her, as angry as he'd ever been with anyone. She had no right to come back, dredging up all these feelings he had buried long ago. The rejection, the hurt, the loss.

He had thrown his heart at her feet eight years ago. The hell of it was, he couldn't even say she had stomped on it. That might have been easier to handle, if she had shown any kind of malice.

But he supposed that would have been too much bother for her and would have required her to care a little. Instead, she had politely walked around it on her way out the door.

And then she dared to stand here now and ask him why he wasn't thrilled to see her!

This wasn't personal, he reminded himself. Or if some part of him couldn't help making it so, he shouldn't let everything between them become about their shared past. He couldn't afford it, not in his temporary role as hospital counsel.

"Why would I be hostile?" he said instead. "You're only the point man—or woman, I guess—for a company trying to destroy this hospital and this community."

She blinked a little at his frontal assault, but it only took her seconds to recover. "Not true. I would have thought as an attorney you could look at this with a little more objectivity than…" Her voice trailed off.

"Than who? Your family?"

She sighed. "Yes. They won't listen to reason. Peter and David think I've betrayed the family name and Ella…well, Ella's not speaking to me at all."

He didn't expect the sympathy that suddenly tugged at him, fast on the heels of his own anger. Her family had always been important to her. Sometimes he thought she placed *too* much importance on their opinions. She had always seemed painfully aware that she was adopted and struggled hard to find a place for herself among the medicine-mad Wilders.

As a single child himself, he could only imagine what she must be feeling now—alienated by her siblings and bearing the brunt of their anger over her role in the NHC takeover attempt.

On the other hand, he instinctively sided with her siblings in this situation, not Anna.

He pushed away the wholly inappropriate urge to offer her comfort. "How did you expect them to react, Anna? This hospital is in their blood. Your family is basically the heart of Walnut River General. Everyone here knows that. And the soul, the essence, of this place is the sense of community—neighbors reaching out to help neighbors. That's what has made this hospital such an integral component to the quality of life in Walnut River. No one likes to go to the hospital, but the ordeal is made a little easier here when you know you'll be treated with respect and dignity, often by someone who has known you all your life."

She blinked with surprise. "Times change," she answered. "The health-care industry is changing. Independent community hospitals just don't have the competitive edge anymore."

"Nor should they. It's not about making money. It's about helping people heal."

"Exactly! And if Northeastern HealthCare can help them heal in a more efficient, cost-effective way and provide better access to cutting-edge procedures not currently available in this market, don't you think that will be better for everyone in the long run?"

"Will it?"

"Yes!" she exclaimed. "Walnut River would be part of a powerful consortium of health-care providers. With that backing, the hospital can afford to bring in state-of-the-art equipment and the newest procedures. NHC is already talking about building a cancer treatment center so patients don't have to drive twenty miles away for radiation treatment! And they're talking about an entire renovation of the labor and delivery unit and an after-hours Instacare facility for parents who work during the day to bring their children to see a doctor...."

Her voice trailed off and color brushed her cheeks like the first hint of autumn on the maple trees along the river. "I didn't mean to ramble on. I'm afraid I get a little...passionate sometimes."

She obviously believed the NHC takeover would truly be best for the hospital. Richard had to admire her passion, even if he disagreed with it.

"You certainly are free to believe what you want," he said. "And I'll do the same."

After a moment, she nodded. "Fair enough. But that doesn't really answer my question."

"What question would that be?"

She opened her mouth to answer but before she could, the boardroom door opened and Tina Tremaine, J.D.'s receptionist, stepped through.

"Oh. I'm sorry. I thought everyone was gone."

"We're just on our way out," Richard answered.

"You don't have to rush. Take your time. I only needed to make sure things were straightened up in here for a meeting J.D. has first thing in the morning."

She smiled at Richard but he was surprised to see her smile disappear completely by the time she turned to Anna.

Anna didn't seem to miss the sudden disdain in the other woman's eyes. Her shoulders straightened and her chin tilted up slightly but she said nothing.

"We're just leaving," Richard said again.

"Fine." Tina closed the door behind her, leaving behind a sudden awkward silence.

"Look, would you like to go somewhere? Grab an early dinner or something?" Anna asked.

He gazed at her, stunned that some tiny part of him was actually tempted, even though the more rational part of his brain recognized the absurdity of the impulse.

"That's not a good idea, Anna."

Somewhere in the depths of her blue eyes he thought he saw a shadow of vulnerability, just the barest hint of loneliness. But she mustered a brittle-looking smile. "Really? Why not? What could possibly be the harm in it? We're just two old friends catching up over dinner."

"Two old friends who happen to be standing on opposite sides of a corporate battlefield."

"Oh, for heaven's sake. That doesn't mean we can't be civil to each other! You were one of my closest friends, Richard. I told you things no one else in the world knows about me."

You said you loved me and then you walked away when something better came along.

His bitterness again seemed to sweep up out of nowhere, taking him completely by surprise.

He thought he had dealt with all this years ago. He never would have guessed seeing her would dredge up all those feelings and make them fresh and raw all over again.

He chose his words carefully, not at all eager to reveal too much to her. "I'm sorry, Anna. Even if not for the gray area regarding conflict of interest ethics in seeing you socially, I have other plans."

She froze for an instant and color climbed her cheeks. "Some other time then, perhaps. It was…great to see you again."

She headed for the walnut-paneled door. As she reached out to pull it open, he thought she paused slightly. Her gaze met his and if he hadn't known her so well years ago, he probably would have missed the flash of trepidation there.

He wondered at it for only an instant before he realized what must lie beneath her hesitation. Judging by Tina's reaction in the boardroom just now, he was willing to bet Anna wasn't at all popular at Walnut River General Hospital. The antimerger forces were vocal and vociferous in their opposition.

Again that unwanted sympathy surged through him.

He might not agree with her position but he couldn't argue with her convictions. She was only doing her job and she didn't deserve to be mistreated by employees of the hospital who might oppose her mission here.

"I'll walk out with you," he said impulsively.

Her lush, delectable mouth opened a little with surprise, then she rewarded him with a glowing smile that made him far too aware of how the years between them had only added to her loveliness.

Much to his dismay, he suddenly felt a familiar clutch of desire twist his insides. He wanted to reach across the space between them and capture that mouth with his, to see if her skin was as silky as he remembered, if she still tasted heady and sweet.

He had been far too long without a woman. Between Ethan and trying to build his practice, he had little time or inclination left for extracurricular activity.

Maybe he needed to make time—especially since the one woman who stirred his interest in longer than he cared to remember was Anna Wilder.

It was ridiculous for her to be so grateful Richard was walking beside her. What did she expect, that she would need a bodyguard to help her safely make it through the hospital?

She might be persona non grata around the hospital right now, but she couldn't quite believe anyone would physically assault her to keep NHC at bay.

Still, she couldn't deny she found great comfort from Richard's calm presence as they headed for the elevator. She always had, she remembered now. He had been a source of strength and comfort through high school and college—the one she always turned to for advice, for counsel, for encouragement.

And more.

She pushed the memories away, refusing to dwell on them. She couldn't think about them right now, when he was only a few feet away looking blond and dangerously gorgeous.

They paused at the elevator to wait for a car and stood in silence, watching the numbers rise. She was just about to ask him about his other clients when she heard a commotion down the hall.

"Hold the elevator. The trauma lift isn't working."

Anna sucked in her breath as the familiar voice rang through the hallway. Her insides knotted with dread but she had no choice but to turn her head.

She wasn't at all surprised to see her sister working an oxygen pump as a team of medical personnel pushed a gurney down the hall. Anna had a quick impression that the patient was a middle-aged woman with her face covered in blood.

Ella faltered for just a moment when she saw Anna but she didn't break her stride. "Have the ER hold trauma room one," she told a nurse running beside them. "And alert the surgical team that we've got a femoral compound fracture and possible head trauma."

She snapped out other commands firmly in a crisp, focused tone that reminded Anna painfully of their father, leaving no doubt exactly who was in charge of the situation.

She had never seen her sister in a professional capacity, Anna realized, as a mixture of pride and awe washed through her.

She always knew Ella would kick butt as a doctor.

Seeing her in action was all the confirmation she needed. Ella was cool, composed and completely in control—all the things Anna couldn't quite manage during her single year of med school.

Anna and Richard stepped aside to allow the team access to the elevator. Just before the doors slid closed, Anna's gaze met her sister's for only a millisecond.

Everything on the periphery seemed to fade, and for a moment Anna was ten years old again, snuggling in her sleeping bag in a tent in their big backyard next to her sister and best friend while the stars popped out, sharing secrets and popcorn and dreams.

Oh, Ella. I miss you so much, she wanted to whisper, but she could never say the words tangled in her throat, and in an instant, the doors closed and the moment was gone.

She fought back tears, praying her emotions wouldn't betray her in front of Richard.

"Wow," he said after a moment. "Hurricane Ella, as usual."

"Right." She didn't trust herself to say more than that as a thousand different regrets pinched at her.

Their rift was largely her fault, one that had been widening for eight years since she left Walnut River, and it had become an unbreachable chasm these days.

If she had told Ella and their brothers about her job with NHC, her involvement in the merger might not have come as such a shock to the other Wilders. Instead, for two long years she had chosen the coward's way, avoiding their questions when they asked about her work, offering them half-truths and evasions.

She had suspected exactly how they would react. She

supposed that was the reason she had deceived them for so long.

"Not a good time for sisterly conversation, obviously."

She wrenched her mind away from her guilt to Richard, who was watching her with entirely too much perception in his blue eyes.

She forced a smile past her aching heart. "Ella runs a mile a minute. She always has. When we were kids, she was always on the go. You remember what she was like."

"I do. There was never a quiet moment with the two Wilder girls around."

She forced another smile, though she had a feeling it was probably as transparent as it felt. She could only hope he didn't see the hurt washing through her in fierce waves.

"You never asked your question," he said.

She blinked at him. "Sorry. What question was that?"

"I don't know. You said you wanted to ask me something and then we were sidetracked."

She frowned, replaying their conversation of the past few minutes in her mind. Suddenly she remembered the direction of her thoughts and she could feel herself flush.

If not for the encounter with Ella, she might have made some laughing remark and changed the subject. But her emotions were too raw for equivocation and for some strange reason she decided to be blunt.

"I did ask you, but you didn't give me a straight answer. I'm just wondering if it's business or personal."

"What?"

"The...hostility. Coolness, antipathy, whatever you want to call it. I'm just wondering if you're angry because I work for NHC or if there's something else behind it."

A strange light flickered in his eyes for just an instant before his handsome features became a mask once more. He opened his mouth but before he could say anything, the elevator arrived.

Only after they stepped inside and he pushed the button to return to the main floor did he turn to answer her.

"I suppose a little of both," he said. "We were friends. You said it yourself. And for one night, we were far more than that. I guess I'm trying to figure out how a woman I considered a friend could turn her back on her family and this town."

I didn't, she wanted to cry. But she was already so tired of defending herself and her choices to everyone in Walnut River. Didn't anyone think it was possible—just maybe—that she might have the community's best interests at heart?

Richard certainly didn't. She could see the censure in his eyes. She couldn't argue with him. That was the hell of it. He had the right to his opinions and she suspected nothing she said would convince him her motives were anything other than crass profit.

The elevator arrived at the main floor and the doors sprang open. He walked with her through the lobby, past the censorious eyes and out of the hospital.

She wanted to thank him for providing a buffer, but she couldn't figure out just how to put the words together.

"I'm parked over there," he pointed.

"Oh. I'm on the other side. I guess I'll see you around, then."

"Probably not. I was only filling in temporarily today in the meeting. My partner is usually the one at our firm who represents the hospital. He should be back on the job tomorrow."

She should be relieved, she told herself. The prospect of spending more time with this prickly, distant Richard who had once been so very dear to her was not appealing.

"Well, in that case, it was…good to see you today."

"Right," he answered.

She walked to her car, wondering why she felt worse leaving the hospital than she had going in.

Chapter 3

Twenty minutes later, Anna walked into her duplex apartment and was instantly assaulted by a miniature dynamo.

Her dark mood instantly lifted as if dozens of sunbeams had followed her home.

"There's my Lilli-girl."

Her tiny dog gave one short yip of greeting then did a standing leap on all four legs, jumping almost to Anna's knees. She laughed at the dog's antics and bent to scoop Lilli into her arms, all five pounds of her.

"Did you have a good day, sweetheart? I hope those two big monsters didn't run you ragged."

Lilli—short for Lilliputian—yipped again and wriggled in her arms, maneuvering so she could lick eagerly at Anna's chin with her tiny sandpaper tongue.

Anna smiled and cuddled the dog closer. What a

blessing this duplex had turned out to be, one of the few bright spots in her life since she had been ordered by the NHC CEO, Alfred Daly, to come home to Walnut River to wrap up the hospital merger.

She hadn't been able to find a single hotel in town that would allow pets, but then she'd stumbled on this furnished place near the river that would allow a temporary lease for the short time she expected to be in Walnut River.

The duplex itself wasn't anything fancy, just bare bones lodging with little personality or style. But it had a good-sized backyard for Lilli to play in, and the landlady had two gentle yellow labradors who already adored her little Chihuahua-pug mix and kept her company all day.

Yeah, Anna was paying an arm and a leg above her per diem for the few weeks she expected to be here. But she figured it was worth it if she didn't have to kennel Lilli during her time in Walnut River or confuse her with a temporary placement with one of her friends or coworkers back in Manhattan.

She adored the dog and had from the moment she heard her tiny whimpering squeaks from a Dumpster near her subway stop in the financial district. Anna had been on her way back uptown on a cold dank January evening after working late and only heard the puppy by a fluke when she had paused for a moment to fix a broken heel on her shoe.

Another night, she might have been in too big a rush to investigate the sound. But that night, something had sparked her curiosity and she had dug through the Dumpster until she found Lilli, bedraggled, flea-infested, half-starved. The tiny puppy had looked at her with pleading dark eyes and Anna had been lost.

That had been six months before, just after her father died. She freely admitted that while dog ownership had been an adjustment, especially with her hectic schedule and the added complications of city life, she had never once regretted her decision to rescue the puppy. Lilli had brought boundless happiness into her world.

Not that her life hadn't been fulfilling before, she reminded herself. She had carved out a comfortable life for herself in New York. She enjoyed her job and found it challenging and interesting. She had good friends in the city, she volunteered at an after-school mentoring program, she enjoyed a full and active social life.

Still, somewhere deep in her heart, she sometimes yearned for the comfortable pace and quiet serenity of Walnut River and she couldn't deny that she missed her family, especially Ella.

She remembered the heated anger that had flashed in her sister's eyes earlier at the hospital and hugged Lilli a little closer to her. She had ruined her chance for any kind of reconciliation with her family by deceiving them for two years.

Understanding and accepting her own culpability in the situation somehow didn't make it any easier to endure.

She sighed. "I need a good ride to clear my head. What do you say, Lilli-girl?"

The dog gave a yip of approval and Anna smiled and set her down, then hurried into her temporary bedroom. The dog followed on her heels, then danced around the room impatiently as Anna changed from her business suit to lycra bike shorts and a matching shirt. The transformation only took a few moments, with a few more needed to change her work chignon to a more practical ponytail.

A short time later, they set off with Lilli in her safety harness, watching the world pass from her perch inside a custom-made basket on the front of Anna's racing bike.

Almost instantly, Anna felt some of the tension leave her shoulders. Even in the city, this was her escape, riding along her favorite trails in Central Park, exploring new neighborhoods, darting around taxis and buses.

Rediscovering the streets of her hometown had been a particular pleasure these past few days, and she could feel herself relax as the bike's tires hummed along the asphalt.

Early summer had to be her favorite time of year, she decided, when the world was green and lovely. As she rode down one street and then another, she savored the smells and sights, so different from her life the past eight years in Manhattan.

The evening air was thick with the sweet smell of flowers, of meat grilling on a barbecue somewhere, of freshly mowed lawns.

She pushed herself hard, making a wide circuit around the edge of town before circling back. By the time she cut through the park near her duplex, she felt much more centered and better equipped to tackle the mounds of paperwork still awaiting her attention that evening.

The trail through the park took her past a baseball diamond where a game was underway. Because it seemed like such a perfect ending to her ride, a great way to celebrate a June evening, she paused to watch for a moment in the dying rays of the sun.

The players were young. She had never been very

good at gauging children's ages but since many of them still had their baby fat and seemed more interested in jabbering to each other than paying attention to the game, she would have guessed them at five or so.

She smiled, watching one eager batter swing at the ball on the tee a half-dozen times before he finally connected. The ball sailed into right field, just past a player who ran after it on stubby little legs.

"Run for it, bud. You can catch it. That's the way."

Anna jerked her head around at the voice ringing from the stands and stood frozen with dismay.

When Richard claimed another commitment, she had assumed he meant a date. Instead, he sat in the bleachers looking gorgeous and casual in jeans and a golf shirt, cheering on the towheaded little outfielder she assumed was his son.

For just an instant, she was tempted to ride away quickly so he didn't think she was stalking him or something, but Lilli chose that inopportune moment to yip from her perch in the basket.

Drawn to the sound, Richard turned his head and she saw his eyes widen with surprise as he recognized her.

For one breathless instant, she thought she saw something else flicker there, something hot. But it was gone so quickly she was certain she must have imagined it.

She raised a hand in greeting and then—mostly because she didn't know what else to do amid the awkwardness of the chance encounter—she climbed from her bicycle, propped it against the metal bleachers then scooped Lilli out of the basket before joining him in the stands.

"That must be Ethan out there," she said.

"It is. We're up one run with one out and just need to hold them through this inning and it will be all over."

He turned his attention back to the game in time to cheer as the next player at bat hit the ball straight at the shortstop, who tossed it to first base. The fielder on first base looked astonished that he actually caught the ball in time to pick off the runner.

"I have to admit, I'm a little surprised to see you here," Richard said after a moment when the crowd's wild cheers subsided. "I wouldn't have expected a T-ball game to be quite up your alley."

Anna gave a rueful smile. "I only stopped on a whim. We live just a block away from here and have ridden through the park several times. This is the first game I've stopped at."

"We?"

She held up Lilli and Richard raised one of his elegant eyebrows. "Is that a dog or a rat with a bad case of indigestion?"

She made a face. "Hey, watch it. This is the queen of my heart. Lilli, this is Richard Green. Say hi."

The dog deigned to lift her paw but Richard only blinked.

"You're kidding."

Anna shook her head, hiding a smile. "I'm afraid not. She'll be offended if you don't shake."

With a sigh, he reached out a hand to take the dog's tiny paw in his, which was all the encouragement Lilli needed to decide he was her new best friend. She wriggled with delight and gazed at him out of adoring eyes.

This wasn't the first time Anna had noticed her dog had a weakness for handsome men.

"So you said the center fielder is your son?"

Richard nodded. "He's the one picking dandelions," he said wryly.

Anna laughed. "Correct me if I'm wrong, but I see three kids picking dandelions out there."

He smiled and she wondered how she could possibly have forgotten the devastating impact of his smile. "Mine's the one in the middle."

As if on cue, the center fielder began to wave vigorously. "Hi, Daddy! Can you see me?"

Richard nodded. "I see you, buddy," he called out. "Watch the ball, okay?"

Ethan beamed at his father and obeyed, turning his attention back to the game just in time as a pop fly headed straight for him.

"Right there!" Richard exclaimed. "You can do it!"

Ethan held his glove out so far from his face it seemed to dangle from his wrist but the ball somehow miraculously landed right in the sweet spot with a solid thud.

Caught up in the moment, Anna jumped to her feet cheering with delight, along with Richard and the rest of the onlookers on their side of the bleachers.

"That's the game," the umpire called. "Final score, sixteen to fifteen."

Anna held tight to Lilli as the little dog picked up on the excitement of the crowd, yipped with glee and vibrated in her arms, desperate to be part of the action.

"Great game," she said after a moment. "Be sure to tell Ethan congratulations for me."

"I'll do that. Or it looks like you can tell him that yourself. Here he comes."

An instant later, a small figure rushed toward them, his features bright with excitement as he launched himself at his father.

"Did you see that, Dad? I caught the ball right in my glove! Right in my glove! I won the game! Did you see?"

Richard hugged his son with enthusiasm. "Nice work! I'm so proud of you, bud. You're getting better every game."

"I know. I am." He said it with such blatant confidence that Anna couldn't help but smile.

Lilli, never one to sit quietly when hugs were being exchanged and someone else was getting attention she thought rightfully belonged to her, gave another of her love-me yips and the boy quickly turned toward her.

"Wow! Is that your dog?" he exclaimed to Anna, the baseball game apparently forgotten.

Anna set Lilli down, careful to hold on to the retractable leash while Lilli trotted eagerly to the boy. He instantly scooped her into his arms and giggled with delight when the dog licked the little-boy sweat from his cheek.

"What's his name?" Ethan asked eagerly.

"She's a girl and her name is Lilli," Anna answered.

"I like her!"

She smiled, charmed by how much this darling boy resembled his father. "I do, too. She's a great dog."

"My name is Ethan Richard Green. What's yours?"

She sent a swift look toward Richard, not at all sure if he would approve of her engaging in a long conversation with her son. He returned her questioning look with an impassive one of his own, which she took as tacit approval for her to answer.

"My name is Anna. Anna Wilder. Your dad and I knew each other a long time ago."

"Hi." He set Lilli on the ground carefully and held

out a polite hand to her, a gesture that charmed her all over again.

She shook it solemnly, tumbling head over heels in love with the little boy.

"I'm very pleased to meet you, Miss Wilder," he said, obviously reciting a lesson drummed into him by someone.

"And I'm very pleased to meet you as well, Mr. Green," she answered in the same vein.

His solemnity didn't last long, apparently, at least not with Lilli around. He knelt to pet the dog, giggling as she tried to lick him again.

"Would you like to hold her leash?" Anna asked.

"Can I?"

"If it's okay with your dad."

Ethan looked at his father, who nodded. "You can take her once around the bleachers but don't go farther than that."

The little boy gripped the leash handle tightly and the two of them headed away.

"I wouldn't have pegged you for a dog person," Richard said after a moment.

"Why not?"

"I don't know. Just seems like a lot of responsibility for a single executive living in the big city."

Though his words echoed her own thoughts of earlier in the evening, she still bristled a little that he apparently doubted she might possess the necessary nurturing abilities.

"It's not always easy, but I make it work," she answered. "What about you? I wouldn't have pegged you for Little League games and car-pool duty. Talk about responsibility, Mr. High-Powered Attorney."

One corner of his mouth quirked into a smile. "Point taken. Just like you, it's not always easy but I make it work."

She didn't doubt it was a major juggling act—nor did she doubt Richard handled it with his typical elegant competence, just as she remembered him doing everything.

Both of them turned to watch Ethan and Lilli make their way through other onlookers and players back around the bleachers.

Richard sighed as the boy and dog approached. "You know this is going to be one more salvo in our ongoing, occasionally virulent we-need-a-puppy debate."

She laughed at his woeful tone. "Sorry to cause more trouble for you. But Ethan is welcome to borrow Lilli anytime he'd like while I'm still in Walnut River."

He looked less than thrilled at the prospect, which only made her smile widen.

"That was super fun," Ethan exclaimed. "Can I do it again?"

"You'd better give Lilli back to Anna now, bud. Remember what I promised you after the game?"

"Oh yeah!" He handed the leash over to Anna. "We're gonna get a shaved ice," he exclaimed. "My dad promised I could have one if I was a good sport and didn't get mad if I didn't get on base again. Hey, do you and Lilli want a shaved ice, too?"

She slanted a look at Richard, who was again wearing that impassive mask.

Common sense told her to pick up her dog and run. She didn't need to spend more time with either of the Green males, both of whom she found enormously appealing on entirely different levels.

On the other hand, all that awaited her at her place was more paperwork. And she couldn't escape the sudden conviction that Richard wanted her to say no, which conversely made her want to do exactly the opposite.

"I'd love a shaved ice," she proclaimed. "It's thirsty work carrying a huge dog like Lilli around. Wears me right out."

The boy giggled as he eyed the miniscule Chihuahua. "You're super funny, Miss Wilder."

She hadn't heard that particular sentiment in a long, long time. She couldn't remember the last time anyone had thought she was anything other than a boring numbers-cruncher. She decided she liked it.

"You know what? You can call me Anna, as long as I can call you Ethan. Is that okay?"

"Sure."

"Ethan, would you mind holding Lilli's leash while I walk my bike?"

He nodded eagerly. "I won't let go, I promise," he said.

"Okay. I trust you."

She slanted one more look at Richard, who was watching their exchange with only a slight tightening of his mouth showing his displeasure. She almost apologized for forcing herself into a family event but then gave a mental shrug.

They were only sharing shaved ices, not spending the entire evening together.

This was completely unfair.

Richard barely had time to adjust to the idea that she was back in town and here she was again, crowding his space, intruding in his carefully constructed life, making him think about things he had put on the back burner.

A casual observer probably wouldn't be able to imagine that the coolly competent executive he had spent two hours with earlier in the day could be the same woman as this softer, far more approachable, version.

This Anna looked sleek and trim and sexy as hell, with all that gorgeous blond hair pulled back in a ponytail and her skin glowing with vitality.

She looked much like he remembered his old friend from eight years ago—bright and vibrant and so beautiful he couldn't manage to look away for longer than a minute or two at a time.

She seemed completely oblivious to her allure as she walked beside him, pushing her bike. And he would have bet she had no idea how hard it was for him to fight down the surge of pure lust.

The evening was one of those beautiful Walnut River summer evenings and the park was full of families taking advantage of it. He greeted several people he knew on the short walk to the shaved ice stand but didn't stop to talk with any of them.

"Do you know every single person in town?" Anna asked after a few minutes.

"Not quite. There are some new apartment complexes on the other side of town and I believe there are one or two tenants there I haven't managed to meet yet. I'm working on it, though."

He meant it as a joke but she apparently didn't quite catch the humor. "Are you running for mayor or something?"

He gave a rough laugh. "Me? Not quite. I've just lived

here most of my life. You can't help but come to know a lot of people when you're part of a community."

"Why did you stick around Walnut River?" she asked him. "You always had such big plans when you were in law school. You were going to head out to the wild frontier somewhere, open your own practice and work on changing the world one client at a time."

He remembered those plans. He had dreamed of heading out West. Colorado, maybe, or Utah. Somewhere with outdoor opportunities like skiing and mountain biking—all the things he didn't have time to do now that he was a single father.

"Things change. Life never quite turns out like we expect when we're twenty-two, does it?"

He didn't think he had ever confided in her the rest of those dreams. He had been desperately in love with Anna Wilder and wanted to bundle her up and take her into the wilderness with him.

She was quiet, her eyes on his son, who was giggling at her little rat-dog. "Maybe not. But sometimes it's better, though, isn't it?"

The fading rays of the sun caught in Ethan's blond hair and Richard's heart twisted with love for his son.

"Absolutely." He paused. "And to answer your question about why I'm still here, mostly it's because this is where my mother lives. She takes Ethan most days when I'm working and they're crazy about each other. She's a godsend."

"Is Ethan's mother in the picture at all?"

He wasn't sure he could honestly say Lynne had ever really been in the picture. Their relationship had been a mistake from the beginning and he suspected they both would have figured that out if not for her accidental pregnancy that had precipitated their marriage.

"Is that the wrong question?" Anna asked quietly and he realized he had been silent for just a hair too long.

"No. It's fine. The short answer is no. The long answer is a bit more…complex."

He wasn't about to go into the long and ugly story with Anna, about how Lynne hadn't wanted children in the first place, how she had become pregnant during their last year of law school together, that she probably would have had an abortion if she hadn't been raised strict Catholic.

Instead, he had talked her into marrying him.

Though she had tried hard for the first few months after Ethan was born, Lynne had been a terrible mother—impatient, easily frustrated, not at all nurturing to an infant who needed so much more.

It had been better all the way around when she accepted a job overseas.

"I'm sorry," Anna said again. "I didn't mean to dredge up something painful."

"It's not. Not really."

She didn't look as if she believed him, but by then they had reached the shaved ice stand. Ethan was waiting for them, jumping around in circles with the same enthusiasm as Anna's little dog as he waited impatiently for them to arrive.

"I want Tiger's Blood, just like I always have," Ethan declared.

Richard shook his head. His son rarely had anything else but the tropical fruit flavor. "You need to try a different kind once in awhile, kiddo."

"I like Tiger's Blood," he insisted.

"Same here," Anna agreed. "You know what's weird? It's Lilli's favorite flavor, too. I think it's the whole dog-cat thing. Makes her feel like a big, bad tough guy."

Though Ethan looked puzzled, Richard felt a laugh bubble out as he looked at her tiny dog prancing around at the end of her leash.

His gaze met Anna's and for just an instant, he felt like he was back in high school, making stupid jokes and watching movies together and wondering if he would ever find the courage to tell the prettiest girl in school he was crazy about her.

They weren't in high school anymore, he reminded himself sternly. She might still be the prettiest girl he had ever seen but he certainly wasn't crazy about her anymore. The years between them had taken care of that, and he wasn't about to change the status quo.

Chapter 4

The line was remarkably short and they had their icy treats only a few moments later.

"I saw a bench over there," Anna said. "Do you want to sit down?"

Richard knew he ought to just gather up his son and head home. But he couldn't quite force himself to sever this fragile connection between them, though he knew damn well it was a mistake to spend more time with her.

He was largely silent while they ate the shaved ice. For that matter, so was Anna, who seemed content to listen to Ethan chatter about his friends in kindergarten, his new two-wheel bike, the kind of puppy he wanted if his dad would ever agree.

Though Richard wondered how he could possibly have time to eat around all the never-ending chatter, Ethan finished his shaved ice in about five minutes flat then begged to play on the playground conveniently located next to the stand.

"Not for long, okay? It's been a long day and you need to get home and into the tub."

Ethan made a face as he handed Lilli's leash back to Anna then raced off toward the slide.

"He seems like a great kid," Anna said after a moment.

"He is. Seeing the world through his eyes helps keep my life in perspective."

"He's lucky to have you for a father."

She paused, her eyes shadowed. "My dad's been gone for six months and I still can't believe it."

Her father's opinion had always been important to Anna. Maybe too important.

He had respected her father—everyone in town had. James Wilder had been a brilliant, compassionate physician who had saved countless lives during his decades of practicing medicine in Walnut River. He doubted there was a family in town that didn't have some member who had been treated by Dr. Wilder.

But he didn't necessarily agree with the way James had treated his children. Even when they were younger Richard had seen how James singled Anna out, how hard he tried to include her in everything and make her feel an integral part of the family.

From an outsider's standpoint, Richard thought James's efforts only seemed to isolate Anna more, reminding her constantly that she was different by virtue of her adoption and fostering resentment and antipathy in her siblings.

"I tried to find you at the funeral to offer my condolences but you must have left early."

She set her plastic spoon back in the cup, her features suddenly tight. “It was a hard day all the way around. My father’s death was such a shock to me and I’m afraid I didn’t handle things well. I couldn’t wait to get out of there and return to New York so I could…could grieve.”

He found it inexpressibly sad that she hadn’t wanted to turn to her siblings during their moment of shared sorrow.

“Have you seen Peter or David since you’ve been back?”

“No. Only Ella, today at the hospital.” Her brittle smile didn’t conceal the hurt in her eyes. “I’m quite sure they’re all going out of their way to avoid me.”

“They may not even be aware you’re back in town.”

“You know better than that, Richard. They know I’m here.”

She was quiet for a moment, then offered that forced smile again. “It’s not exactly a secret that NHC has sent me here to close the merger after six months of problems. I might not have received an angry phone call from holier-than-thou Peter or a snide, sarcastic email from David, but they know I’m here.”

He didn’t want to feel this soft sympathy for her but he couldn’t seem to keep it from welling up, anyway.

She had created the situation, he reminded himself sternly. Why should he feel sorry for her at the estrangement with her siblings when she had done everything possible to stir up their wrath?

She shrugged. “Anyway, I’m sure J.D. spread the word he was meeting with me today.”

She rose suddenly and threw her half-eaten shaved ice in the garbage can next to their bench. He had the distinct impression she regretted letting her emotions filter through.

"Which reminds me, I'd better go. I've got a great deal of paperwork to file after today's meeting."

He didn't think the reminder of their adversarial roles in the takeover was at all accidental.

She picked up her little dog and set her in a carrier attached to the handlebars of her bike. In bike shorts that hugged her trim, athletic figure, she looked long and lovely and so delectable she made his mouth water.

"It was nice bumping into you and meeting Ethan. Thank you for letting me share a little of your evening together."

"You're welcome."

She gave him one more small smile then, to his surprise, she stopped at the playground to say goodbye to Ethan. She even went so far as to take the dog out of her carrier one last time so the petite creature could lick at Ethan's face.

Their interaction touched something deep inside him. In his experience, most women either completely ignored his son or went over the top in their attentions, fawning all over Ethan in an effort to convince Richard how maternal they could be.

Anna's interest in Ethan seemed genuine—and it was obvious his son was smitten by her.

Or at least by her little rat-dog.

After a moment she gave Ethan one last high five, settled Lilli in her carrier again and rode away with one last wave to both of them.

He watched her go—as he had watched her go before. He sighed, his mind on that last miserable day when she had left Walnut River.

He still wasn't sure exactly why the hell she had left—or, more importantly, why the memory of it still stung.

They had been good friends through high school and he could admit to himself now that he'd always had a bit of a crush on her, though he hadn't fully realized it until college.

They went to different universities for their undergraduate work. He was at Harvard, but since she had only been a few miles away at Radcliffe, they had seen each other often, but still only as friends.

Though he could sense his feelings for her deepening and growing, they had both been running in opposite directions. He was headed for law school while she was busy preparing for med school.

But one summer night after their first year of graduate work everything had changed.

By a happy coincidence, they had both been home in Walnut River temporarily for the wedding of a friend. Since neither of them had dates, they had decided to go together—again, strictly as friends.

But he had taken one look at her in a sleek, pale-blue dress he could still remember vividly and he hadn't been able to look away.

They had danced every dance together at the wedding reception and by the time the night was over, he'd realized he had been hiding the truth from himself all those years.

He was in love with her.

Deeply, ferociously in love.

And she had returned his feelings—or least, she had given a good imitation of it.

After the wedding festivities were over, they had gone to his house for a late-night swim. His parents were gone and he and Anna had stayed up long into the night, sharing confidences and heady kisses, holding hands while they looked at the stars and savored being together.

And then they had made love and he still remembered it as the single most moving experience of his life, except for Ethan's birth. She had given him her innocence and had told him she was falling in love with him.

And then in the morning, everything had changed.

The memory seemed permanently imprinted into his head, of standing on the front porch of her parents' house just hours after he had left her there, those stars still in his eyes.

He'd expected to find the woman he had just realized he loved.

Instead, he'd found chaos. Anna was gone. She must have left soon after he had dropped her at her doorstep, with one, last, long, lingering kiss and the promise of many more.

Both of her brothers were living away from home at the time but Richard clearly remembered the reaction of the three remaining Wilders. Her father had been devastated, her mother baffled and Ella had been crushed.

He couldn't really say she had left without a word. She'd mailed him a letter that had arrived the next day—a terse, emotionless thing.

What kind of fool was he that he could still remember the damn thing word for word?

Dear Richard.

I can't do this with you right now. I'm so sorry. I meant everything I said last night about my feelings for you, but after I've had a few hours to think about it, I realize I can't string you along while I try to figure out my life. It wouldn't be fair to you and to be honest, I'm not sure I have the emotional strength for it. You deserve so much more.

I have to go, Richard. I can't live this lie anymore. Being with you last night only showed me that more clearly. I'm being crushed by the weight of my family's expectations and I don't know any other way to break free of them. I only wish, more than anything, that I didn't have to hurt you in the process.

She had signed it with love and, while he had wanted to believe her, she had made no other effort to contact him.

That had been eight years ago. Another lifetime. Then had come Lynne and Ethan and his world had changed once more.

But his heart had never forgotten her.

He sighed, acknowledging the truth of that rather grim realization.

Some part of him still had feelings for Anna Wilder, feelings he didn't dare take out and examine right now.

It was a damn good thing his partner was representing Walnut River General in the whole NHC matter.

Richard wasn't sure his heart—or his ego—could handle being screwed over by Anna Wilder again.

Two days later, Richard sat in his office rubbing the bridge of his nose and trying to fight back the odd sensation that the walls of his office had suddenly shrunk considerably.

"Say that again. Where are you, Phil?"

His partner gave a heavy sigh, sounding not at all

like his normal affable self. "Wyoming, at the Clear Springs Rehab Center. It's supposed to be one of the best in the nation."

"Rehab, Phil? Is this some kind of sick joke?"

"I wish it were that easy."

"I'm stunned!"

"You shouldn't be," the other man said wearily. "You covered for me enough the last six months that you should have seen the clues. Peggy's gone. She moved out two weeks ago and took the kids with her."

Those walls seemed to crowd a few inches closer. "You didn't say a word to me!"

"What was I going to say? I was too ashamed. My wife left me, my kids aren't talking to me. I've only held it together at work by luck and a hell of a good partner."

Okay, Richard had to admit he had suspected something was going on. With all the sick days and missed meetings, he had wondered if Phil was fighting a serious illness he wasn't ready to disclose.

In retrospect, he wondered how the hell he possibly could have missed the signs.

"I'm an alcoholic, Richard. I can't hide it anymore. I've tried to stop a dozen times on my own and I can't. This is the only way I know how to straighten out my life."

All the pieces seemed to fall into place with a hard thunk and again Richard wondered where his own head had been to miss something so glaring in his partner and friend.

Yeah, there had been mistakes the past few months—a couple of serious ones that Richard had been forced to step in and mend. But he had just assumed Phil would tell him what was going on when he was ready. He hadn't minded the clean-up work. Phil had been a mentor and a friend since he came to the practice straight out of law school, green in more than name and a single father of an infant to boot.

"How long will you be there?" he finally asked.

"As long as it takes. I wish I could be more specific than that but I don't know at this point. The average stay is two months."

Two months? Richard fought down a groan. They had too much work as it was and had discussed adding another partner to the practice to help ease the burden.

"What about your clients?" he asked.

"I'm sorry to dump them on you. But my two junior associates have been basically carrying everything for the last few months, anyway. They can bring you up to speed on the major cases. I'm not worried about anything but the hospital takeover attempt. I'm afraid you'll have to step in and handle that. My files are copious, though. You should find everything you need there."

"I'll take care of everything on this end," Richard assured him. "You just focus on what you're doing there."

"Thanks, man. Entering into a partnership with you was the smartest move I've made in years."

Richard hung up a few moments later and let out a long, slow breath. He was concerned about his friend, first and foremost. But he was also suddenly overwhelmed with the weight of more responsibilities.

The hospital merger had been Phil's project for six months. Richard had helped a little but getting up to speed on all the intricate details was going to take days, if not weeks.

Talk about a complication. Just when he was thinking he wouldn't have to have anything more to do with

Anna Wilder, circumstances had to go and change dramatically.

He would have no choice now but to work with her, on a much closer level than he was sure made him completely comfortable, given their shared past.

Amazing how a day could go from rough to truly miserable in the space of a few moments.

Anna stood in the cafeteria line in the basement of Walnut River General, wondering why she was even bothering to grab a salad when her appetite had abruptly fled and the idea of trying to force down lunch was about as appealing as walking back through the halls of the hospital and encountering another of her testy siblings.

She sighed, moving her tray along the metal track, one step closer to the cashier.

Blast David anyway.

Of all her siblings, she would have expected him to at least be civil to her—not because they had been the best of friends but because she had a tough time thinking he would bother to involve himself in the political side of things at the hospital.

Peter had at least tried to be brotherly to her, but because he was so much older than she, their lives had always seemed on slightly different tracks.

Ella had been closest to her, in age and in their relationship. If not for the distance she herself had placed between them after she dropped out of medical school and moved away from Walnut River, she imagined she and her sister would still have been close.

David, though, had always seemed a challenge. She'd always had the vague sense that he resented her. He had never been deliberately cruel, had just treated her with somewhat chilly indifference, making it overtly obvious he didn't want to be bothered with a whiny little sister who wasn't even really related to him.

She supposed nothing had really changed. Rather blindly, she pushed her tray one person closer to the cashier, replaying the scene outside the cafeteria doors just a few moments earlier.

After spending all morning going over records the hospital refused to allow her to take off-site, she had been tempted to go somewhere in town for lunch. Maybe Prudy's Menu downtown or a fast-food place somewhere.

But since she was looking at several more hours of analyzing patient accounts, she had decided to save time by eating in the cafeteria.

Big mistake. She should have considered the possibility that she might encounter one of her testy siblings.

Sure enough, when she reached the cafeteria, the first person she had seen had been David, looking relaxed and happier than she'd seen him in a long time.

Becoming engaged and moving back to Walnut River apparently agreed with him. He had lost the edgy restlessness that had seemed so much a part of him for so many years.

She had smiled and opened her mouth to greet him, forgetting for just an instant where things stood between them.

Before she could say anything, he looked straight through her, then turned around and walked out of the cafeteria, leaving his food behind, as if he'd just stumbled into a leper colony.

No, not quite right. David was a compassionate, caring physician. He would rush right in to help anyone who was ill, especially if they suffered from a potentially life-threatening condition.

Apparently, she ranked somewhere well below a colony of lepers in her older brother's estimation. He couldn't even manage to bring himself to say hello to her.

Anna sighed. She had to stop being so maudlin about her siblings. She had made her choice when she had suggested Walnut River General as a possible acquisition target to her superiors at NHC. She had created this situation and she had no business moping about it.

"Looks like you're up," someone said behind her and Anna realized with some chagrin that while she had been sitting brooding, the line had moved forward and she was next to check out.

She jerked her tray forward along the metal rails then watched with horror as her diet soda toppled sideways from the jolt. In her distraction after the scene with David, she apparently hadn't fastened on the plastic lid securely. As the cup fell, the contents splashed out—directly on the woman standing behind her.

Anna's face burned and she wanted nothing more than to leave her tray there and just escape. Still, she forced herself to turn to the other woman and found an elegant, pretty redhead wearing a pale green Donna Karan suit and a white blouse that now sported a golfball-sized caramel-colored stain on the front.

The woman looked vaguely familiar but Anna was quite certain she had never met her.

"I am so sorry," Anna exclaimed. "I'll give you my card. Please send me the bill for the dry cleaning."

The woman's smile was remarkably gracious. "Don't worry about it. This was my least favorite blouse, anyway."

"I'm sure that's not true."

The woman laughed. "Well, maybe second least-favorite. I've got an orange thing in my closet that's really a disaster."

She narrowed her gaze, her smile slipping just a fraction. "You're Anna, aren't you?"

Anna's stomach clenched. She really wasn't sure she could handle another confrontation right now. The woman was liable to dump her entire lunch all over her.

"Yes," she said warily. "I'm sorry, have we met?"

"No, though I was at your father's funeral. And I've just seen a picture of you in Peter's office."

"You…you have?"

"It was a picture taken at your father's last birthday party and has all four of you together. I've been wanting to meet you for a long time. I'm Bethany Holloway."

Bethany Holloway? *This* was Peter's fiancée?

Here was another stark reminder of the rift between her and her siblings. Her brother was marrying this woman in a few weeks and this was the first time Anna had even met her.

"Your total is six dollars and twenty-three cents," the cashier said pointedly. "You can go ahead and get another soda if you want."

Anna realized abruptly that she was holding up an entire line of hungry people. "Let me at least pay for your lunch," she said to Bethany.

"You don't have to do that."

"I do," Anna insisted. The cashier gave her a new total. Anna handed her a twenty and pocketed the change.

"That was not necessary, but thank you, anyway,"

Bethany said, moving with her out of the way so others could pay for their lunches.

"You're welcome," Anna replied. "I mean it about the dry cleaning."

Bethany shook her head. "I've got on-the-go stain removal stuff in my office. Soda should come out in a flash. If nothing else, I always keep a spare shirt in my office and I can change into that one after lunch. Please don't worry about it."

Anna had to admit, she was astonished. Bethany Holloway was actually smiling at her. She couldn't quite figure out why. Not only had Anna dumped soda all over her, but Anna would have assumed Peter's fiancée would be firmly on the opposite side of the family divide.

"I was supposed to meet Peter for lunch but he had an emergency. I guess I need to get used to that if I'm marrying a doctor, right? I hate to eat alone, though—are you meeting someone for lunch?"

"Uh, no."

In truth, she had planned to take the tray up to the tiny little hole in the wall office J.D. had begrudged her to go over the accounts.

"Good," Bethany said. "We can sit together and you can tell me all of Peter's secrets."

Her warm friendliness left Anna feeling off kilter, as if one of her heels was two inches shorter than the other, and she didn't know quite how to respond.

"I'm afraid I don't know any. Of Peter's secrets, I mean. I've been away from Walnut River for a long time."

Bethany smiled. "That's all right, then. You can tell me all of your secrets."

Bethany headed for a table without looking to see if

Anna followed or not. Anna again fought the urge to flee to the relative safety of her borrowed office.

But she wasn't a coward. For some strange reason, her brother's fiancée wanted to talk to her and Anna didn't see that she had much of a choice but to comply.

Chapter 5

Anna slid into the booth opposite Bethany, wondering how she was possibly going to be able to swallow with these nerves jumping around in her stomach.

It was silly, really.

She had no reason to be apprehensive around Peter's fiancée. By all appearances, Bethany was kind and gracious. Anna didn't know many women of her acquaintance who could handle having a soda slopped all over them with such aplomb—especially when the one doing the slopping was on the outs with her fiancé.

She tried to focus on what she knew about Bethany and remembered that at one point she had been in favor of the merger, identified by NHC as a definite vote for their side. She decided there was no reason to talk around the issue.

"I understand you're an efficiency expert here at the

hospital," she said when they were both settled. "And you've been on the governing board of directors for a little over a year."

Bethany raised a slim auburn eyebrow. "NHC has a good research team. I suppose you have complete dossiers on every board member."

Anna toyed with a piece of lettuce, refusing to feel like a corporate stoolie. "You know how it works. It pays to know the players. At one point you were considered firmly on our side."

"I was. Absolutely."

"But you've gone on record opposing it now," she said. "Is that because of Peter?"

It was a rude question and one she regretted as soon as the words came out. To her vast relief, Bethany only laughed.

"Oh, he would love to hear you say that. No, I didn't change my vote because of my relationship with your brother. From an efficiency standpoint, the merger still makes sense. I won't deny that."

She paused and appeared to be considering her words with delicate care. "From a human standpoint, though, I'm not convinced Northeastern HealthCare has the best interest of our patients at heart."

Just like that, Anna automatically slid back on the defensive. "If you look at the statistics, you'll find we have a great track record at other hospitals of improving patient access to care while saving money at the same time."

"I know all the arguments, Anna. I promise, I've read the reports on NHC. We could debate this endlessly and I'm not sure we would get anywhere. There are compelling arguments on both sides but right now I have to go with my gut, that this deal isn't right for Walnut River General at the moment."

She lifted a slim hand to forestall any further arguments. "Let's talk about something else, okay? I'm sure you get enough arguments from everyone and I'd really like us to be friends."

Anna wasn't sure that was possible, given the current situation, but she found she desperately liked the idea of having Bethany as a friend.

"I hate to be a bridezilla," Bethany continued, "but can we talk about my wedding?"

Anna gulped. She would almost rather stage a public debate on the merger right there in the cafeteria than talk about her brother's wedding. Short of getting up and leaving her food there at the table in her rush to escape, she wasn't sure how to wiggle out of it.

"Okay," she said slowly.

"You're coming, aren't you?" Bethany asked. "Last I checked you hadn't sent an RSVP. You did receive the invitation, right? I sent it to your New York apartment and was hoping it didn't miss you on your way here."

Yes, she had received it. She had pulled out the elegant sheet of calligraphied vellum and had stared at it for a long time, sorrow aching through her at the distance between her and her siblings.

In the end, she had slipped the invitation into her briefcase, though she had absolutely no intention of accepting.

"Yes. I got it," she admitted.

"And? You're coming, aren't you?"

"Does Peter know you sent me an invitation?"

Bethany blinked but not before Anna was certain

she saw a little glimmer of uncertainty in the depths of her green eyes.

"Of course," she answered, but somehow Anna was certain she wasn't telling the whole truth.

The vague suspicion, that tiny hesitation on Bethany's part, was enough to remove any lingering doubt in her mind about whether to attend the wedding.

"I'm really happy for you and Peter," Anna said. "But… I don't think I can make it."

"Why not?" Bethany asked bluntly.

The other woman might look as soft and fragile as puff pastry but that impression was obviously an illusion. She was glad for it, Anna thought. Bethany Holloway appeared more than a match for her oldest brother, who could sometimes be domineering and set in his ways.

"The last thing you need on your wedding day is to have a simmering family feud boil over and explode all over the place. It would be better if I stayed away."

"Oh, don't be ridiculous!"

If Bethany hadn't sounded so sincere, Anna might have taken offense. Instead she merely shook her head.

"It's not ridiculous. None of them are even talking to me right now. I ran into David ten minutes ago just outside and he looked right through me as if I wasn't even there. I got the same treatment from Ella last week when I bumped into her on the fourth floor."

Compassion flickered in the depths of Bethany's green eyes. "That must have hurt."

For half a second, she thought about shrugging off her sympathy but the sincere concern in Bethany's expression warmed somewhere cold and hollow inside her.

"Like crazy," she admitted quietly. "Ella used to be my best friend. Now she won't even talk to me."

"I'm so sorry."

"I knew they would be upset that I'd chosen to work for Northeastern HealthCare. I guess I'd hoped they would at least try to hear my side of things."

"You Wilders all feel passionately for the things you care about," Bethany said.

"I'm not one of them," Anna said quickly.

As far as she was concerned, that was the crux of the problem. She didn't have the Wilder medical gene and she didn't have their dogmatism.

"I'm sure Peter told you I was adopted," she said when Bethany just looked puzzled.

A strange, furtive look flickered in those green eyes. Bethany opened her mouth to respond then closed it again, as if she had suddenly reconsidered her words.

"I've heard the story," she finally said. "Peter told me he was ten years old when your father brought you home and claimed he found you on the steps of Walnut River General. It was a defining moment in his life."

She stared. "In Peter's life or my father's?"

"Well, I'm sure in your father's life as well. But I meant Peter."

"How?"

"As the oldest son he felt responsible for the rest of you, and for your mother's feelings as well. I know she… wasn't well those few years before you came into the family."

A polite way of saying Alice Wilder had suffered deep depression and had ended up medicated in the years before Anna's adoption.

"Yes," she answered warily. Her relationship with her mother had always been complicated. She had loved Alice, as every child loves her mother, but their relationship had always felt strained. Cumbersome. Deep in her heart, she had wondered why her mother didn't quite seem to love her as much as she did Peter, David and Ella.

James had more than compensated for any coolness from Alice but the pain still lingered.

"Your father worked a great deal," Bethany said. "As the oldest son, Peter always felt responsible for everyone's happiness. His mother's. David's. And then when you and Ella came along, for yours as well. I don't know that that has changed much over the years. He loves you very much, Anna. And he misses you. They all do."

She might find it a little easier to believe if she hadn't experienced firsthand the compelling evidence that none of the Wilders was thrilled to have her back in town.

"He might be angry with you right now over the merger," Bethany continued, "but that's because he feels as if your father's legacy is threatened."

Anna's frustration erupted. "It's a hospital! It's walls and a roof and medical equipment! What kind of legacy is that? James's legacy ought to be the children he left behind. Children who have grown into four fairly decent adults who are doing their best to make the world a better place for others. That's a legacy to be proud of, not the hospital where he spent every waking moment he should have been spending with kids who needed their father!"

She was mortified the moment she heard the heat and lingering bitterness behind her own words.

She thought she had gotten over all that when she walked away from medical school—the secret fear that her father would only love her if she became a doctor like he was, if she devoted all her energy to the hospital where he had rescued her.

How many times had she heard that story about finding her on the hospital steps? Too damn many.

You were the only infant ever left at Walnut River General. I knew the minute I saw you that you belonged in our family. James always used to say that with pride in his eyes—whether for the hospital he loved or for her, she was never quite sure.

She couldn't help wondering what might have happened to her if she had been left somewhere else besides the hospital—an orphanage, a garbage can, even James's and Alice's own doorstep.

Would he have wanted her at all?

"From what I've heard of your father, I know he was very proud of each of his children," Bethany said.

Each of the three physicians in the family, perhaps. As for her, Ella and their brothers wondered why she'd kept her job with NHC a secret for two years. She could just imagine what James's reaction would have been if he had known before his death that she had gone to work for a corporate entity he would have considered the enemy.

The shock alone would have brought on that fatal heart attack.

She forced a smile. "I'm sure you're right," she murmured, though the lie tasted like acid.

"Peter is your brother, despite your current…estrangement. He will feel your absence at the wedding deeply, no matter what he might say. Will you at least think about coming?"

Anna shook her head. "You're a very persistent bride, aren't you?"

Bethany smiled. "That's a polite way to say stubborn

as a one-eyed mule, isn't it? I can be, when the situation demands it."

She might not be the woman Anna would have expected her brother to fall for, but she decided she very much liked Bethany Holloway. Somehow she had a feeling they *would* become good friends. It was a comforting thought.

"I'll think about it," she answered. "That's all I can promise right now. The wedding is still three weeks away. A great deal can happen in three weeks."

Bethany opened her mouth to respond, but before the words could escape, Anna's attention was drawn to a trio of men entering the cafeteria—J. D. Sumner, new chief of staff Owen Mayfield, and Richard Green.

Richard spotted her and Bethany at almost the exact same instant. She saw something bright and luminous flash in his eyes for just an instant before it faded.

A moment later, he excused himself from the other men and made his way toward their corner booth.

Anna was aware of several things simultaneously—the funny little dip and shiver of her stomach as he approached, the clean, elegant lines of his summer-weight charcoal suit that made him look as gorgeous as if he had just stepped out of a gentlemen's magazine, the faint lines of fatigue around his blue eyes.

Most of all, she was aware of how her heart seemed to tremble just at the sight of him.

"Good afternoon."

He smiled freely at Bethany, but his light expression faded when he turned his attention to Anna.

She tried to ignore the shaft of hurt piercing through her at the contrast, aware of how very tired she was becoming of fighting battles with everyone she encountered at Walnut River General.

"J.D. was just telling me you were working here this morning," Richard said.

"Yes. The hospital's legal counsel apparently won't give permission for me to take any records off site," she said pointedly.

"All in one more effort to make your life more difficult, I'm sure," Richard said dryly.

She made a face. "It certainly does. But the administration has been kind enough to give me a temporary work space. I suppose I should be grateful they stopped short of blocking access completely."

"Since the municipal council has approved your inquiries, legally there's nothing the hospital can do to stop you."

His hard voice stopped just shy of outright hostility but it was enough to make Bethany blink and Anna bristle.

"No. I don't suppose there is," she said evenly. "Short of tackling me in the parking lot and tying me to a bench somewhere."

Something warm and slightly naughty sparked in his eyes for just an instant, then it was gone. Still, her insides shivered in reaction.

"I was trying to reach Alfred Daly but perhaps you can give him a message for me."

She gazed at him warily, wondering just how many other people from her past would she alienate before NHC succeeded in its efforts to absorb Walnut River General into its family of hospitals.

"All right," she answered.

"Please let him know I will be representing the hospital for the foreseeable future. My partner is taking an indefinite leave of absence."

She thought of the attorney she had met only a few times since coming to Walnut River. He had seemed very nice, if somewhat distracted. Never once had he looked at her with anything resembling scorn, unlike others she could mention.

"Everything's all right, I hope?"

His expression registered surprise at her concern and he hesitated for just a moment before answering. "I'm sure it will be."

He said he was representing the hospital for the foreseeable future, which must include the NHC merger negotiations. The jitters in her stomach became a sudden stampede. There was no escaping the grim realization that she would have no choice but to work closely with Richard Green if she wanted to pull off this merger.

"I will let him know," she answered coolly, pleased her voice didn't reveal any of her inner torment. "I should tell you in the interest of disclosure that your partner asked for copies of the reports I'm working on. Our legal team agreed to provide them as a show of good faith to demonstrate our willingness to cooperate as fully as possible. I can have them ready for you first thing in the morning."

He frowned. "No chance they'll be ready before then? I'm going to be in court the rest of the week. Tonight would be the best chance for me to find time to look at them."

She quickly considered her options.

She could be an obstructionist and tell him no, that she couldn't possibly finish the financial study until the next day. But that wasn't exactly true. She was close to being done and with a little accelerated effort, could have things wrapped up in a few hours.

"I can try to finish them tonight and run them over to you at home."

Again, the flicker of surprise in his expression frustrated her. Once they had been close friends. He had known her better than just about anyone in her life, except maybe Ella. Did he really have to register such astonishment when she tried to be cooperative and do something nice?

"That would be perfect. Thank you."

Still annoyed, she gave him a cool, polite smile. "You're welcome. Give me your address and I'll run them by when I'm done."

"You don't need an address. I'm living in my parents' house. It was too much upkeep for my mother so I bought it from her after my father died. She lives in a condo just a few blocks away."

Anna had always liked Diane Green. She had been warm and gracious, always willing to open her home to Richard's friends. His house had been the high-school hangout, with its huge game room and built-in swimming pool.

It would be a lovely place to raise a son, she thought.

"I don't know what time I'll be finished. It might be late."

"That's fine. I'll be up late prepping for court in the morning."

She nodded and managed to hang on to her polite smile when he said a cool goodbye to her and a much warmer one to Bethany before he returned to J.D. and Dr. Mayfield.

She watched his elegant frame walk away for just

a moment longer than she should have. She knew it as soon as she turned back to Bethany and found Peter's fiancée watching her with upraised eyebrows.

"I'm sorry. What were we talking about?"

"My wedding." Bethany grinned suddenly. "But that's not important right now. I would much rather hear what's going on with you and sexy Richard Green."

"Going on? Absolutely nothing."

She cursed her fair skin as she felt heat soak her cheeks. She couldn't bluff her way out of a blasted paper bag, the way she turned red at the slightest provocation.

Bethany didn't look at all convinced. "Are you sure about that? There was enough energy buzzing between the two of you to light up the Las Vegas strip."

"We grew up together. His house is just a few blocks away from where we grew up and we were always good friends."

"And?"

She could feel her blush deepen as she remembered that last night together and the kisses and touches she had never been able to forget.

For one shining moment she had held paradise in her hands.

He had offered her everything she'd ever dreamed of. He had told her he was in love with her. She could still remember her giddy joy, how she had wanted nothing more than to hold on tight and never let go.

She had wanted so much to grab hold of what he was offering—but she hadn't been able to figure out a way to break free of her family's expectations while holding tight to Richard at the same time.

Seeing him again, learning more about the man he

had become, made her see how immature a response that had been for a girl of twenty-two years.

She had been so certain she had to take all or nothing, to sever all ties to Walnut River if she wanted to escape the immovable path her family expected her to take.

But Richard had never placed the kind of unrealistic expectations on her that her father had. He had even told her if medical school wasn't for her, she needed to decide earlier, rather than later.

What would have happened if she had decided she could still drop out of medical school and pursue her business career while maintaining a relationship with Richard?

It wasn't at all helpful to speculate on the hypothetical, she reminded herself harshly. The truth was, she had turned her back on Richard when she had turned her back on her family. That ship had sailed, and all that. She would never know, so there was absolutely nothing to be gained by speculating on what might have been.

"There's nothing between us," she assured Bethany. "I haven't seen him in eight years and now we're on opposite sides of the hospital merger."

Which might as well be a twenty-foot high fence topped with another five feet of razor wire for all the chance she had of breaching it.

Chapter 6

"Dad! You shut my door! You know I can't sleep with my door shut all the way!"

Ethan's voice echoed down the hall, drawing nearer with each word, and Richard sighed as he straightened and closed the oven door where he'd just set his dinner to warm.

Here we go, he thought.

He turned and, just as he expected, he found Ethan in the doorway wearing his Buzz Lightyear pajamas, his little mouth set in a disgruntled expression.

"Sorry, bud. I forgot."

"You forgot everything tonight! You forgot to give me an Eskimo kiss and during bathtime you didn't even ask me my five fun things."

Guilt pinched at him and he wished that he could split himself into two or three people to get everything in his life accomplished. His court appearance in the morning weighed heavily on his mind—but his son always had to come first.

"I'm sorry. It's been a long day," he said. "I'll do better tomorrow, okay? Come on, let's get you back into bed and you can tell me your five fun things."

"Okay."

It was a tradition they had started as soon as Ethan learned to talk, where each evening they would share five interesting things they had seen or done that day.

Ethan's list usually consisted of games or toys he and his nana had played with that day. It was sometimes a scramble but Richard usually tried for a little creativity in his own contributions to the game. Today he was afraid he was running on empty.

"You said that yesterday," Ethan exclaimed when Richard tried to use the colorful clown that stood outside the local hamburger joint with a signboard and a pleading expression as one of his five interesting things to report about his day.

"But this time he had on one of those crazy rainbow wigs," Richard said. "I didn't tell you that yesterday."

Much to his relief, his five-year-old accepted his logic and climbed into bed obediently.

They exchanged hugs and the obligatory Eskimo kisses then Richard tucked him in for the second time that evening. "This time I'm spraying glue on your pillow so you can't get out again."

While Ethan giggled he pretended to spray an aerosol can around his son's bed, his hair, behind his back. "There. Now you're stuck. You're not going anywhere."

"Okay. But don't forget to come unstick me in the

morning before you leave. Nana said we can go to the park after breakfast and I don't want to miss it."

He smiled and kissed his son on the nose. "I will. I've got magic un-stick spray just waiting for morning, I promise."

This time, he left Ethan's door slightly ajar and returned to the kitchen. His stomach rumbled at the delicious smells starting to emanate from the oven. A quick check of the timer on the oven revealed he still had twenty minutes before his mother's lasagna would be finished. That should be long enough to go over his opening argument one more time—that is, if he could hang on to his limited concentration long enough to do the job.

He sighed again, all too grimly aware of the reason he had been so distracted all evening.

One word.

Anna.

Since bumping into her at the hospital cafeteria earlier, he hadn't been able to shake her from his mind. The curve of her cheekbones, the little shell of her ear, the fragile vulnerability in the set of her mouth he wondered if anyone else could see.

She said she would drop off her report that night and he felt as if he had spent the entire evening in a state of suspended animation, just waiting for the doorbell to ring.

He knew damn well those feelings swirling through him were entirely inappropriate, but he couldn't seem to move beyond them.

He couldn't wait to see her again, foolish as he knew that was.

He had absolutely no sense when it came to Anna

Wilder. It was a rather depressing thing to acknowledge about himself.

Just how long did he have to carry a torch for her? If someone had asked him a week ago if he still had feelings for Anna, he would have busted up laughing at the very idea. He never even thought of her anymore, he would have answered quite smugly. How could he be foolish enough to think he still had feelings for the woman?

He thought he had done a pretty good job of purging her from his thoughts. Eight years was a long time to burn for a woman who had made it plain she didn't want him.

But now she was back in Walnut River and every single time he saw her, she seemed to become more and more entangled in his thoughts until he had a devil of a time thinking about anything else.

Did he still have feelings for her? He certainly wasn't about to admit something so dangerous, even to himself. Sure, he was still attracted to her. He certainly couldn't deny that, especially since he wasn't able to stop himself looking at his watch every five seconds and had even gone out once to check that the doorbell was working right.

He needed to get out more. He could count on one hand the number of dates he'd had in the years since his marriage imploded.

Richard sighed, wishing again for a clone or two. When, exactly, was he supposed to find time for a social life? Between working to establish his practice and trying to be the best father possible to Ethan, his time was fragmented enough.

What if Anna hadn't blown him off eight years ago

and left town? If she weren't here representing NHC? If they didn't have diametrically opposing goals regarding Walnut River General Hospital?

What was the point in wasting time with useless hypotheticals? Richard chided himself. He had too damn much to do tonight to indulge in fantasies of what might have been.

The fact was, she *had* walked away, she *did* work for NHC and he would need to keep all his wits about him to keep her and her corporation from taking over the hospital he cared about.

He would do well to remember all those things, Richard thought as he forced himself to turn back to his laptop, angled on a corner of the kitchen table where he had been working earlier while Ethan played with trucks on the floor.

The screen had just come out of sleep mode when he heard a car engine out front. The swirl of anticipation he'd tried so hard to tamp down became a wild cyclone. So much for the little pregame lecture, he thought ruefully.

A click of the keyboard sent the monitor back to sleep, then he hurried to the front door. He reached it just an instant after she rang the doorbell.

"Oh!" she exclaimed when he opened the door, her hand still half raised to the bell. "Hello."

"Sorry to startle you. I was trying to catch you before you rang the doorbell so you didn't wake Ethan. I have a tough time getting him back down to sleep if something disturbs him."

"I'm so sorry. I didn't even think. I should have knocked."

"No. It's fine. I doubt he's even asleep yet."

The words had barely escaped his mouth when Ethan popped his head out of his bedroom, his hair tousled but his eyes not at all sleepy. They lit up with excitement when he saw Anna.

"Hi!" he exclaimed brightly. "I heard the doorbell but I didn't know it was you."

"Hi, Ethan!"

Richard tried to steel his emotions against the soft delight in her eyes as she looked at his son.

"I thought you were glued to the bed," he said dryly to his son.

Ethan giggled. "I guess the glue must have worn off. When I heard the doorbell, I was able to climb right out. I don't know how."

"What a surprise," he muttered.

Anna sent him a sideways, laughing look that stole his breath.

"Anna, can you read me one more story?" Ethan wheedled. "If you do, I promise, I'll stay in my bed this time for good."

"I guess that's up to your father."

"Daddy, can she?"

He didn't want her to feel obligated, but if the anticipation on her features was any indication, she was excited at the prospect.

"All right. Just one story, and then to bed this time to stay. You have to pinky swear."

Ethan had to hold down his other four fingers with his left hand in order to extend the little finger on his right, but his features were solemn and determined as he interlocked with Richard's pinky.

"I swear. I won't get out again, Daddy, if Anna can

read me one story. Oh, and if she can give me one more Eskimo kiss, too."

"Deal," she said quickly, before Richard could even think about negotiating different terms.

She reached for Ethan's hand and the two of them headed for his son's bedroom. Richard followed, unable to resist leaning against the door jamb and watching as they carefully selected the right story.

He wasn't sure what he felt as he watched Anna slip off her heels and sit on the edge of Ethan's bed. His son cuddled up to her as if they were best friends and after a moment, she slipped her arm around him, their blond heads close together.

She read the story, about a worm keeping a diary about his life, with pathos and humor. When she turned the last page, Ethan sighed with satisfaction.

"I sure do wish I could have another one. You're a really good story reader."

"You made a pinky swear, remember," Anna said with a smile. She slipped her shoes back on then leaned in and rubbed her nose against his.

"You smell good," Ethan declared, and Richard wondered how his son had possibly become such a lady killer with the lousy example he had for a father in that department.

Anna laughed. "So do you. Now go to sleep, okay?"

Ethan snuggled down into the covers, his eyelids beginning to droop. "Okay. Will you come to another one of my baseball games? I only have two more."

She glanced at Richard, then back at his son. "Sure," she answered. "I'd love to."

"You have to promise or else I can't go to sleep."

She laughed again. "You're a born negotiator, Ethan, my man."

"What's a go-she-a-tor?"

"Negotiator. It means somebody who works out deals with people. You agree to do something as long as I do something else in return."

"I just want you to come to my baseball game."

"I said I would."

"Is that a promise?"

She shook her head. "All right! I promise."

He grinned with satisfaction. "Thank you for the story, Anna."

"You're very welcome, sir."

"Will you come back and read to me again sometime?"

She paused for just an instant and Richard thought he saw a faint brush of color on her cheeks before she tugged Ethan's covers up to his chin. "We'll have to see about that one. Good night."

"Good night," Richard added. "This time I mean it."

"Okay. 'Night, Dad."

He closed the door behind Anna—remembering just in time to leave it slightly ajar.

"I'm sorry you had to do that."

"I'm not." She smiled softly. "He's darling."

"He's a manipulative scoundrel who's going to end up behind bars someday."

"It's a good thing his father is a lawyer, then."

And his mother, Richard thought. The blunt reminder of Lynne and all the mistakes he had made was like jumping into a mountain stream in January.

Anna picked up her briefcase and riffled through it for a moment, pulling out a slim maroon folder.

"Here's the report I promised you. I'm sorry I didn't get it here earlier. I meant to have it done two hours ago but I, uh, had a bit of a tough time getting some of the information I needed."

Translation: Those who opposed the NHC takeover were making life as difficult as possible for Anna. He didn't need her to spell it out for him when he could see the exhaustion in her eyes and the set of her mouth.

A twinge of pity flickered through him. None of this could be easy for her.

"Have you had dinner?" he asked. The moment the words were out, he regretted them but it was too late to yank them back.

She stared. "Dinner?"

"You know, that meal you traditionally eat at the end of the day?"

"Oh, that one." She smiled. "I guess my answer would have to be no, not yet. That's next on my agenda."

"I've got some of my mom's lasagna in the oven. You're welcome to join me."

Surprise flickered over those lovely features. "It does smell delicious. But I've got Lilli out in the car. Since my place is on the way here, I stopped on the way to check on her and she begged me to bring her along."

He should let her use the excuse as a way to avoid the meal but he found himself reluctant to give up that easily. "She's welcome to come inside while we eat. I don't mind."

"Are you sure? I wouldn't want to provide Ethan more ammunition in the Great Puppy War."

"He'll never know. Besides, maybe having Lilli underfoot during dinner, begging for scraps, will shore up my sagging resolve to wait a few more years before we enter pethood."

She raised an eyebrow. "Excuse me, but my dog is extremely well-behaved. She never begs. She just asks nicely."

Anna was so beautiful when she smiled, he thought, and cursed himself all over again for the impulse to invite her to stay—an impulse, he admitted, that had probably been simmering inside him all evening. Why else would he have thrown an entire lasagna in the oven instead of just grabbing a TV dinner?

He had absolutely no willpower around Anna Wilder and no common sense, either. He had a million things to do before court in the morning. He certainly didn't have time to spend the evening entertaining a woman he had vowed to keep at a distance.

Despite the knowledge, he found he couldn't quite bring himself to regret extending the invitation.

Not yet, anyway.

He wanted her to have dinner with him? Anna wouldn't have been more surprised if Richard had met her at the door doing the hula in a muumuu and lei.

A wise woman would tell him to forget it and get the heck out of there. She had very few defenses left against Richard Green and his adorable son, and she was very much afraid she was in danger of falling hard for him all over again.

"Go and get Lilli and by the time you come back in, the lasagna will be on the table."

She paused for only half a second before surrendering. How could she do anything else, when this was the most amiable and approachable she'd seen Richard since coming back to Walnut River?

"All right," she said. "I'll admit, my mouth has been watering since I walked in the door."

And not just because of the delectable smells of lasagna wafting from the kitchen, she was forced to admit to herself. Richard Green in his charcoal business suit was gorgeous, in a dangerous, formidable kind of way. Richard Green in his stocking feet, faded Levi's and a casual cotton shirt with the sleeves rolled up was completely irresistible.

She quickly collected Lilli from her car and juggled the excited dog and her umbrella as she hurried back up the walkway to his house. He stood in the open doorway waiting for her and her stomach gave a funny little tremble at the sight of him.

"Behave yourself," she ordered as she set Lilli down on the tile of the entryway, the stern reminder intended for her own benefit as much as her dog's.

"I'll do my best," Richard answered dryly. He reached for her umbrella and Anna slipped off her heels, lining them neatly by the door.

Lilli's tail wagged like crazy as she trotted around the house, sniffing in corners and under furniture. With the excuse of keeping a close eye on her inquisitive little dog, Anna managed to assuage her own curiosity about Richard's house.

Their group of friends had spent many hours at his place through high school. With the built-in swimming pool and the huge media and game room in the basement, it was a natural teen hangout. She remembered pool parties and study sessions and movie nights.

Seeing it now after years away was rather disconcerting. Little was as she remembered.

"Your house has changed."

He smiled. "Just a bit. When I bought the place after my dad died, I had the interior completely redone. New paint, new carpet, took out a wall here or there to open it up. The house had great bones but everything was a little outdated."

"Diane didn't mind?"

"Are you kidding? My mother loved helping oversee the redecorating, as long as it was my own dime."

"It looks great," she assured him as Lilli investigated a cluster of houseplants climbing a matte black ladder in the corner.

The house was elegant but comfortable, with solid furniture that looked as if it would stand up well to a busy five-year-old.

"I'm just going to throw together a salad," Richard said. Do you want to come back to the kitchen?"

"Sure."

With Lilli close on their heels, she followed him down the hall. Here were the most dramatic renovations she had seen in the house. She remembered the kitchen as a rather small, cramped space with dark wood cupboards and a long breakfast bar that took up most of the space.

This must be where he had talked about knocking down walls because it was about twice the size as she remembered. Rain clicked against skylights overhead and in place of the breakfast bar, a huge island with a sink and second stovetop dominated the space.

The colors reminded her of a Tuscan farmhouse, warm red brick floors, mustard yellow walls with white accents. It was a dream of a kitchen, airy and welcoming and vastly different from the tiny sliver of a kitchen in her apartment in Chelsea.

"Would you like a glass of wine?"

"Yes, please," she decided, perching on one of the stools at the island.

He seemed very much at home in his own kitchen and she knew darn well she shouldn't find that so sexy.

She sipped her wine and watched him work while Lilli sniffed the corners of the kitchen. The silence between them was surprisingly comfortable, like slipping into a favorite jacket in the autumn.

"So who was giving you a tough time today?" Richard asked after a moment.

She flashed him a quick look. "How do you know somebody was?"

"You never turned an assignment in late in your life when we were in school. If I remember correctly, you always turned everything in at least a day or two early. I figured the only reason you would be late with anything must have more to do with external forces."

"Clever as always, counselor."

"So who was it?"

She sighed, some of her peace dissipating at the reminder of the hurdles in front of her and their clear demarcation on opposite sides of the NHC front. "No one. Not really. I just had a…difficult time getting some of the information I needed. I don't blame anyone. I completely understand there are mixed feelings at the hospital about the merger."

His laugh was dry. "Mixed feelings is one way to put it."

"Believe it or not, I do understand why not everyone likes the idea of an outside company coming in and messing with the status quo. I understand about tradition and continuity and about safety in the familiar. But I wish people could approach this with an open mind. If people would look beyond their preconceptions, perhaps they might see how Northeastern HealthCare is looking at innovative changes that would benefit both the hospital and the community in general…."

She caught herself just before launching into a passionate argument once more. "I'm sorry. I really don't want to talk about the hospital tonight. After living and breathing this merger from the moment I awoke this morning, I could use a break. Do you mind?"

He stopped mixing the salad, watching her with an unreadable expression for a moment before he suddenly offered a smile she felt clear down to her toes.

"Excellent idea. I wouldn't want to ruin by mother's delicious lasagna by launching into a cross-examination."

He grabbed the salad and carried it through an arched doorway to the dining room.

Out of old habit, she grabbed plates from the cupboard where they had always been stored, finding an odd comfort that they were still there.

The silverware was also still in its familiar spot and she grabbed two settings and carried the utensils into the dining room.

Richard raised an eyebrow but said nothing as she helped him set the table. A moment later, he carried in the lasagna and placed it on the table then took a seat across from her.

Lilli stopped her wandering and curled up, her body a small warm weight on Anna's feet. The next few moments were busy with filling plates and topping wineglasses.

"If we're not going to talk about the hospital, what's

a safe topic of conversation, then?" she asked when they were settled. "Baseball? The weather?"

"Who says it has to be safe?" The strangely intent look in his eyes sent a shiver ripping down her spine. A strange undercurrent tugged and pulled between them.

"All right. Something dangerous, then. Your marriage?"

He gave a short laugh as he added dressing to his salad. "Not what I had in mind, but okay. What would you like to know?"

She had a million questions but one seemed paramount, even though she hardly dared ask it. "What happened?"

He shrugged, his expression pensive. "The grim truth is that it was a mistake from start to finish. I met Lynne at Harvard. She was brilliant, ambitious. Beautiful. In our last year, we started seeing each other, mostly just for fun. Nothing serious. In fact, we both planned to go our separate ways after graduation."

"But?"

He sighed, sudden shadows in his eyes. "A few weeks before we were to take the bar exam, she found out she was pregnant."

She tried to picture a younger version of Richard as she remembered him, perhaps with a few less laugh lines around the corners of his eyes. The Richard she knew always took his responsibilities seriously. She wasn't at all surprised that he would step up to take care of the child he fathered, only that he and Ethan's mother would make things official.

"Marriage is a huge leap of faith for two people who were set to go their separate ways, even with a child on the way."

"I think we both badly wanted to believe we could

make it work. On paper, it seemed a good solution. We were both attorneys, we had shared interests, we enjoyed each other's company. I think we both tried to convince ourselves we were in love and could make it work. But Lynne wasn't ready for a family. She tried, but I could see what a struggle it was for her. She…wasn't really cut out for motherhood. When Ethan was four months old, she received an unbeatable job offer overseas. Her dream position as lead counsel for an international shipping conglomerate. We both decided there was no good reason for her not to take it."

She heard the casual tone he tried to take but she also picked up the subtle sense of failure threading through his words.

He had always been competitive—captain of the debate team, a star on the baseball diamond, school valedictorian. He hated losing at anything and she imagined this particular failure would have hit him hard, especially with the loving example he had of marriage from his own parents.

The urge to touch him, to offer some small degree of comfort, was almost overwhelming. But they didn't have that kind of relationship, not anymore, so she curled one hand in her lap and picked up her wineglass with the other.

"I'm sorry," she murmured. "That couldn't have been an easy situation for you."

"We've done okay. My mother has been a lifesaver. I would have been lost without her."

They were quiet for a moment, the only sound Lilli's soft huffs and the rain clicking against the skylights.

"What about you?" he asked after a moment. "Any relationship mistakes in your past?"

Besides leaving you? The thought whispered through her mind unbidden and she had to shift her gaze away from his so he wouldn't read the truth in her eyes.

"Not really. Nothing serious, anyway."

"Why not?" Richard asked.

She decided to keep quiet about the fact that she hadn't had enthusiasm for dating in a long time, if ever. She had been too focused on her work, in making a success of herself—okay, in proving to her family that she could have a successful life outside medicine.

"I don't know. It hasn't really been a priority for me, I guess."

"I suppose it's a little tough having a long-term relationship when you travel so much."

"Something like that."

She really didn't want to discuss her love life—or decided absence of such a thing—with Richard Green.

"Okay, I just came up with the first dangerous topic of conversation. It's your turn."

"I thought I just asked you about the men you've dated. That's not dangerous enough for you?"

"Not at all. Trust me. The men I date are usually a boring lot. Accountants. Stockbrokers. Mild-mannered, one and all."

Not like you, she thought. Richard radiated a raw masculinity, even during a casual dinner at his home with his five-year-old sleeping only a few dozen feet away.

He studied her for a moment, and she had the vague impression of a lean and hungry wolf moving in for the kill.

"All right. You want dangerous? Why don't we talk about why you broke my heart eight years ago?"

Chapter 7

Anna stared at Richard across the table, his mother's delicious lasagna congealing into a hard, miserable lump in her stomach.

The noises of the kitchen seemed unnaturally loud in the sudden tense silence, the whir of the refrigerator compressor sounding like a jet airplane taking off.

She wanted to scoop up her dog and race away from the awkwardness of his question and the guilty memories she couldn't escape.

"I didn't break your heart," she mumbled.

He lifted his wineglass in a mocking salute. "Excuse me, but I think I'm a little better judge of that than you are. You haven't seen me or my heart in eight years."

Though his words were light, she saw the barest hint of shadow in his eyes. She thought of all her reasons for leaving. What seemed so compelling eight years ago now seemed like a coward's way out.

"You couldn't have been too heartbroken," she pointed out. "You were married a few years later."

She didn't want to remember how she had holed up in her tiny shared apartment in New York City and wept for an entire day when Ella had called her with the news.

He was quiet for a moment and then he sent her a quizzical look. "Would you like to see a picture of Lynne?"

His question threw her off stride, especially in the context of their discussion. Why would he possibly think she would want to see a picture of his ex-wife right now?

She shrugged, not quite sure how to answer, and he slid away from the table and moved to a mantel in the great room off the kitchen. Through the doorway, she saw him take a picture from a collection on the mantel and a moment later he returned and held it out for her.

A younger, chubbier version of Ethan's winsome face filled most of the frame but just in the background, she could see a stunning woman with blond hair and delicate features. She looked at her son with love, certainly, but also a kind of baffled impatience.

"She's very beautiful."

"You don't see the resemblance?"

"I can't really tell. Ethan certainly has her eyes."

"You don't think she looks at all like you?"

Shocked to the core, she stared at the woman again. Is that the way he saw her? Cool and lovely and…distant?

"Her hair and her eye color, maybe," she protested. "That's all."

"You're absolutely right. That's where the resemblance ends. She's not you. Not at all. But here's the funny part. I asked her out for the first time because she looked a bit like you. Since I couldn't have the real deal, I tried to convince myself an imitation was just as good. It was an idiotic mindset, one I'm ashamed I even entertained for a minute, but what can I say? I had been abruptly dumped by the only woman I ever loved."

Anna froze, reeling as if she'd just been punched in the stomach.

"Richard—"

"I didn't mean to say that. Withdrawn."

She had no idea what to say, to think. He had said that night he was falling in love with her but she had always attributed it to the heat of their passion.

After a long, awkward moment, he gave a rough laugh. "Dangerous is one thing when it comes to topics of conversation. Excruciatingly embarrassing is quite another."

She had to say something. She knew she did, especially after he stood up and returned his plate of half-eaten lasagna to the kitchen.

She rose, shaky inside. Lilli scampered ahead of her into the kitchen.

"I convinced myself it wasn't real," she finally said quietly when she joined him there. "What we shared that night. It was magical and beautiful and…miraculous. But I tried to tell myself we were just carried away by the night and…everything. You were my friend. Maybe my best friend. I couldn't let myself think of you in any other way or I wouldn't have been able to…to do what I knew I had to."

"Leave medical school and basically cut things off completely with your family."

"Yes," she admitted. "I loved my family. You know

that. But you also know what things were like for me with them. In my father's mind, there was no other possible career for any of his children. He refused to see how I was struggling that first year. How much I hated it. I tried to talk to him—all summer I tried! His advice was only to stick it out, that the second year would be better. *Wilders aren't quitters.* I can remember him telling me that as clearly as if he were sitting right here with us."

"He wanted you to follow in his footsteps."

"That's what *he* wanted. Not what *I* wanted. I was suffocating in med school. I hated it. The blood, the gore. The unending stress. Especially knowing I couldn't help everyone."

She could clearly remember the first time a patient whose care she had been observing had died. It had been a woman in her late fifties with end-stage breast cancer. She could remember the dispassionate attitude of the attending and the residents, in sharp contrast to the vast, overwhelming grief of the woman's husband and teenage daughters.

She had left the hospital that day feeling ill, heavy and ponderous, as if she carried the weight of that grief and the responsibility for their pain. Ridiculous, since she was only a first-year med student who hadn't even really been involved in the woman's care, but she hadn't been able to shake her guilt and the cries of the survivors that haunted her dreams.

"I knew if I made it through the second year, I would be trapped. I had to go, Richard. I didn't see any other choice."

He shrugged. "You could have stayed and stood up for yourself, fought for what you cared about."

Including him, she thought. She should have stayed and fought for what they could have shared.

"I missed you like crazy those first few months in the city," she confessed. "I think I missed you even more than I missed my family."

He leaned against the kitchen counter. "Forgive me if I find that a little hard to believe. At any point that year you could have picked up the phone or sent off an e-mail. But you cut me off completely. What the hell was I supposed to think? I just figured I was crazy and had imagined everything that happened that night."

"You didn't," she whispered, more miserable than she had been those first early days after she left.

"It doesn't matter now. Eight years ought to be long enough to get over a broken heart, don't you think?"

Something shifted between them, a subtle tug of awareness. "Yes," she managed.

"I thought I had done a pretty good job of putting you out of my head. Of course, then you had to ruin everything by coming back and making me remember."

"I'm sorry," she murmured.

His long exhalation stirred the air. "So am I."

Before she realized what he intended, he stepped forward and pulled her into his arms.

She caught her breath, unable to focus on anything but the blazing heat in his eyes as his mouth descended on hers.

The kiss was raw and demanding and she tasted eight years of frustration in it. Despite the undertone, everything inside her seemed to sigh in welcome.

Oh, she had missed this. Missed *him*. No other man had made her blood sing through her veins like Richard.

She knew she shouldn't return his kiss. If she were

smart, she would jerk away right now and leave this house that contained so many memories for her.

She couldn't do it, though, not with this heat and wonder fluttering through her.

Her hands were trapped between their bodies and she could feel his heart pound beneath the cotton of his shirt, rapid and strong.

She spread her hands out, marveling at the taut muscles under her fingers. He might be an attorney but Richard still had the lithe athleticism of the baseball player he had been in high school.

His mouth deepened the kiss and she leaned into him, lost to everything but this moment, this man.

She wanted him. Just as she had eight years ago, she wanted him with a wild hunger that stole her breath.

He was the first one to pull away, wrenching his mouth free of hers and stepping away with such abruptness that she could only stare into the blue of his eyes, turned dark by desire.

He studied her for a long moment while she tried to catch her breath and catch hold of her wildly careening thoughts.

"Aren't you going to say anything?" he asked after a moment.

She might, if she could manage to string more than two words together in a brain that suddenly seemed disjointed and chaotic.

"That was…unexpected."

He lifted an eyebrow. "Was it?"

"Richard, I…"

He shook his head with a rough-sounding laugh. "Don't. Just don't. I was trying to remember what you tasted like. My curiosity has been appeased so let's just leave it at that."

That's all it had been? Curiosity? Not the kind of stunned desire that still churned through her body?

"Look, it's late. I'm due in court early tomorrow."

She drew in a shaky breath, mortified at her wild reaction to what had been purely experimentation on his part. "You're absolutely right. I never meant to stay so long."

If she had left fifteen minutes ago, none of this would have happened. She wouldn't have the taste of him on her lips or the scent of him, masculine and sexy, on her skin or the memory of his kiss burned into her brain.

She scooped up Lilli, absurdly grateful for the comfort of the dog's tiny, warm weight in her arms. He walked her to the door and helped her into her jacket, careful not to touch her more than completely necessary. He then held her umbrella while she slipped on her shoes.

"Thank you for dinner," she finally said.

"You're welcome," he answered, as formally as if they were two strangers meeting for coffee instead of lifelong friends who had just shared a moment of stunning passion.

She should say something more, but for the life of her, nothing else came to mind. "Good night, then."

He held the door open for her and she walked out into the night. She didn't bother with her umbrella, hoping the rain might cool her feverish skin and douse the regret that burned through her like a wind-whipped wildfire.

Richard stood at the window of his house watching her taillights gleam on the wet street before they disappeared.

So much for his intention to remain cool and composed around her. He had been about as calm as a blasted typhoon.

What had he been thinking to kiss her? It had been a mistake of epic proportion. Catastrophic.

He should have known he would skate so close to losing his control. She'd always had that effect on him. What was it about Anna that revved his engine like that?

She was beautiful, yes, with that shimmery blond hair and those luscious blue eyes and skin that begged for his touch....

He jerked his mind away from all of Anna's many attractions. Beautiful as she might be, he had been around lovely women before, but Anna was the only one who ever tempted him to forget every ounce of common sense.

A few more moments of their embrace and he didn't know if he would have been able to stop—and that was with his son sleeping only a few rooms away.

She could break his heart again, if he let her.

Richard sighed. He wasn't about to let her. Not this time. He had learned his lesson well. Anna Wilder wasn't a woman he could count on. She had made that plain eight years ago. His foolishness over her had led him to some fairly disastrous mistakes.

He couldn't afford to lose his head over Anna again—not only for his own sake but for Ethan's.

He couldn't forget his son in this whole situation. Ethan had suffered enough from Richard's poor choices. If Richard had kept his wits around him, he would have known what a disaster his marriage to Lynne would be, that his choices would leave his son without a mother.

Richard's own mother did her best but she was now

in her sixties and didn't have all the energy needed to keep up with a busy five-year-old boy.

For Ethan's sake, Richard couldn't afford to risk an involvement with a woman who already had a track record for leaving the things she cared about in pursuit of her career.

Hadn't that been exactly what Lynne had done? She had tried the whole family and motherhood route but had fled when the responsibility had become too constricting.

Richard just had to use his head when it came to Anna Wilder. He was fiercely attracted to her and apparently that had only intensified over the years, so the only smart course would be to minimize contact with her as much as possible.

He couldn't avoid her completely. The NHC negotiations made that impossible, but he had to do everything he could to make sure their interactions in the future were formal and businesslike and as brief as he could manage.

It was the only way he would get through her temporary stay in Walnut River without hurting himself again.

The resolve managed to last more than a week.

Though he never lost focus of the hospital's fight for autonomy, other clients' legal issues took precedence for the next several days. He was busy, first with a trial date then with several evidentiary hearings.

He might not have seen Anna during that time, but unfortunately she was never far from his thoughts.

At random moments he found himself remembering the silky softness of her hair or the way her mouth trembled when he kissed her or her hands smoothing against his chest, burning through the fabric of his shirt.

He blew out a breath on his way to an appointment with J.D. to discuss strategy for the final board of directors' vote coming up in less than a week.

He supposed he shouldn't have been surprised when he walked into J.D.'s office to find Anna sitting in one of the office chairs, but the sight of her still stopped him in his tracks and he fiercely wished he could just turn around and head back out of the hospital.

She looked prim and proper again in a black jacket and skirt and he was furious at himself for the instant heat that jumped in his stomach.

Her eyes flashed to his and he saw an edge of discomfort, but not surprise. She must have had a little advance warning that he would be joining them.

Lucky her.

J.D. rose from his desk and shook his hand. "Hi, Richard. When I told Anna I was meeting with you this morning, she decided to steal a few minutes of our time so she could ask a couple of questions about our vendor accounting practices, since I told her I couldn't respond without legal counsel present."

J.D. met his gaze with a meaningful look and despite his unease, Richard had to hide a smile. Just the afternoon before, he had lectured the administrator about that very point—to avoid giving any information to NHC they weren't legally obligated to provide under the conditions the municipal council had set forth.

There were three chairs across from J.D.'s desk. As Anna sat in the middle chair, Richard had no choice but to sit beside her, where he was unable to escape her scent, fresh and lovely and sensual, or the heat shimmering off her skin.

"Anna, you're the one with the questions," J.D. said. "Where would you like to start?"

She opened her mouth, but before she could speak, Richard heard voices in the outer office through the open door.

"Hey, Tina," he heard someone greet J.D.'s assistant. "I just need to drop off some paperwork. I won't disturb him for long."

Richard recognized the voice and saw by the way Anna's features paled that she did as well. A moment later, her oldest brother stuck his head in the doorway.

Dr. Peter Wilder always commanded attention wherever he went, with his dark hair and eyes, handsome features and the undeniable air of authority that seemed to emanate from him. He was very much like his father in that respect.

His gaze sharpened to a laser point when he saw his sister and the room suddenly buzzed with tension.

Richard wondered if Peter had seen the love that leapt into Anna's blue eyes when she had first seen him, before she quickly veiled her expression into cool indifference.

"Sorry. I didn't mean to interrupt."

J.D. rose from his desk and gestured to the vacant chair. "No, it's all right. We were just getting started. Why don't you join us? Anna had some questions about our patient accounting. As the former chief of staff, you might have some insight into that."

Peter looked as if he would rather shove a scalpel down his throat, but after a long, painfully awkward moment, he complied.

"You know I'm always happy to share my insight with NHC. Anything I can do to help," he drawled, and Anna's mouth tightened at his sarcasm.

"And NHC certainly appreciates your cooperation, Peter," she replied sweetly.

J.D. moved to referee before Peter could voice the heated response brewing in his dark eyes.

"So what are your questions?" he asked, interjecting.

She sent another swift look at her brother then seemed to stiffen her shoulders, becoming brisk and focused.

"My analysis of your records shows an unusually high percentage of patient accounts the hospital deems uncollectible compared to hospitals of similar size and community demographics. Can you explain a reason why that might be the case?"

"I can." Peter broke in before J.D. could answer—or before Richard could vet either man's response.

"We're a local hospital that cares about the community. We refuse to turn anyone away and don't give a damn whether our patients are in the highest tax bracket or not. Our mission is to save lives, not bilk people out of their life savings."

"But according to my analysis, the hospital is losing a hundred thousand dollars a month and most of that is in uncollectible patient accounts," she pointed out. "How long do you think the taxpayers can continue to cover those losses?"

"Some of us care more about our patients' health than going after their wallets," he snapped.

"A noble sentiment, Peter. Exactly what I would have expected you to say. Just what Dad would have said."

Peter bristled. "What's that supposed to mean?"

She sighed and seemed to have forgotten both J.D. and

Richard were there. "Nothing. It's all well and good to ride that high horse about focusing on patient care and battling back the evils of HMOs like some kind of league of superheroes with stethoscopes. But what's the alternative, Peter? For the hospital to just keep going deeper and deeper in the hole? Budgets are tightening everywhere. The city council has to do something. What if they decide to close the hospital instead of continuing to try in vain to plug the endless revenue drain?"

"So what you're saying is our patients are screwed either way. Better to get substandard care than none at all."

Anna's blue eyes flared. "NHC is not about substandard care! That's a simplistic argument. Our ultimate goal for all our member hospitals is to find more efficient, cost-effective ways to provide the same level of patient care."

"You really buy that company line? I thought you were supposed to be some hotshot business genius. I would have thought you were smarter than that."

Anna paled a shade lighter and J.D. moved to intervene but she cut him off. "Why can't you at least try to look at what NHC has to offer the hospital with a little rational objectivity?"

"I know what NHC is offering," her brother bit out. "Cut-rate services, increased patient load on physicians. Every day they play money games with people's health care, with their very lives! I can't believe you would pander to these bastards, Anna! What happened to your sense of decency?"

"You're as sanctimonious as ever. There's absolutely no reasoning with you. Yet another way you're just like Dad!"

"Leave him out of this! What do you think Dad would

say if he knew you were doing this? Working for the enemy? Doing everything you can to destroy his legacy?"

Her mouth trembled just a bit before she firmly straightened it. While he had to admit he agreed with Peter, Richard still had to fight the urge to comfort her. A hand on her arm, a touch on her shoulder, whatever might ease the pain he couldn't believe her brother missed.

"I'm sure Dad would probably say the same thing you and David and Ella are saying about me. I'm a disgrace to the Wilder name. Isn't that what you all think?"

"Right now, hell, yes," Peter said. "You've always had a chip on your shoulder but I never dreamed you'd take it this far, by trying to destroy something this family built nearly singlehandedly."

"Why don't we get back to your question." J.D. finally stepped in—about five minutes too late in Richard's opinion—but Anna ignored him.

"I imagine it's a huge comfort to you all that I'm not really a Wilder, then."

Peter's expression changed instantly and something very much like guilt flickered in his eyes.

"You are," he muttered.

"I'm not, Peter. We both know it."

J.D. cleared his throat. "Can you show us the figures that concern you in your report?"

She seemed to drag herself back to the meeting and Richard saw color soak her pale cheeks as she must have realized the detour the conversation had taken.

She took a deep breath and turned back to gaze blankly at the pages in front of her for a moment before she collected herself and rose. "I…yes." She looked flustered and Richard again fought the urge to rest a comforting hand on her arm.

"You'll see I've highlighted several pages in section eight of my report. I would appreciate if you and your legal counsel would formulate a response and get back to me."

"We can discuss it now. Richard's here to make sure I don't speak out of turn."

She twisted her mouth into a facsimile of a smile. "I don't want to take any more of your time, especially since I just remembered I've got a conference call."

She glanced briefly at her brother. "You know. With those bastards I pander to. If you'll all excuse me, gentlemen."

She picked up her briefcase and walked out of the office and Richard wondered if either of the other men saw the way her fingers trembled on the handle—or the determined lift of her chin as she left the office.

Chapter 8

After Anna left, the three men sat in silence for a long, awkward moment.

J.D. was the first to break it. He gave Peter a long look. "Next time give me some warning when you're going to beat up on your little sister and I'll make sure I have someone from the E.R. standing by to mop up."

Peter shrugged. "Anna gives as good as she gets. She always has."

His nonchalance about the pain that had been radiating from Anna suddenly infuriated Richard. She was vulnerable in ways her family refused to see. She always had been.

As hospital counsel, he knew he ought to stay out of the Wilder family squabbles. It was none of his business. But he cared about Anna—he always had—and he couldn't quite force himself to stay quiet.

"She's only trying to do her job," he finally said. "I know the fact that she has that job infuriates you but you didn't have to make it personal, Peter. You did that, she didn't."

Surprise flickered in Peter's gaze at Richard's defense of Anna, then quickly shifted to guilt. "You're right. You're absolutely right."

"This whole takeover attempt would be much easier to fight if Northeastern HealthCare had sent someone else—anyone else—to do their dirty work," he continued. "Anna's presence makes everything feel personal, like the corporation is waging a war against the whole Wilder family, not just the hospital. I'm afraid I got a little carried away. I'm sorry."

"We're not the ones you need to apologize to," J.D. pointed out to his future brother-in-law quietly.

Peter sighed. "I know. Things are just…complicated with Anna. They have been for a long time. But you're right. She didn't deserve that."

He stood and studied Richard with an odd look in his eyes. After a moment he seemed to come to some decision. "Rich, when you're done here with J.D. would you mind stopping by my office for a moment? I need to talk to you about something."

Still annoyed with him for his casual oblivion when it came to his sister's feelings—and even more annoyed with himself for caring so much about something that wasn't any of his business—Richard wasn't in the mood to be cooperative.

"Sorry. I don't do prenuptial contracts."

Peter gave a bark of surprised laughter. "That's not what I needed. Just stop by if you have time."

* * *

An hour later, his curiosity at fever pitch, Richard made his way through the hospital to Peter's office.

"He's with a patient," the receptionist told him. "Do you mind waiting for a few minutes?"

He had a million things to do but was too curious to leave without some clue as to what Peter could possibly want with him.

Only a few moments passed before Peter joined him. "Thanks for stopping in. I could use some advice."

"You do know I don't handle malpractice cases, either, right?"

Peter laughed. "Wrong again. What I really could use is a little insight from a friend."

Richard raised an eyebrow.

"Specifically, I need advice from a friend of Anna's," Peter added, further confusing him.

He shifted in his seat. "I haven't seen Anna in years, until she came back to town a few weeks ago."

"Neither have I. Not really. But you were friends with her before she left town, right?"

More than friends, but he wasn't about to confide that little detail to her older brother. "Yes," he said warily.

"And Bethany said she saw the two of you together the other day and you still seemed…friendly."

He wracked his brain trying to remember his encounter with Anna the day she had been having lunch with Bethany. "Since she's been back in Walnut River, I've had some interactions with her in an official capacity," he finally said. *Mostly official, anyway.* "I'm not sure how much help I'll be, but I can certainly try."

Peter blew out a breath. "If nothing else, I know I

can at least trust you to keep what I'm about to tell you confidential."

"Of course. What's this about, Peter?"

Peter hesitated for a moment then reached to unlock a desk drawer. He pulled out a slim black folder, from which he extracted a legal-sized white envelope.

"I have a letter to Anna from our father. I received it as executor of his will and I've been trying to figure out what to do with it ever since."

Richard might not have seen Anna until recently, but just from their few interactions, he could tell she still grieved for James. He knew she regretted the stilted relationship and the unresolved business between them before his death.

"Your father has been gone for six months. Why haven't you given it to her before this?"

"When would I have the chance? Anna has done her best to stay away from Walnut River and the family during that six months. Hell, she barely stayed long enough for the funeral. I didn't receive the letter until after she left, and I was still trying to figure out what to do with it when we found out Anna was working for Northeastern HealthCare."

He said the last words like a bitter epithet. Richard remembered how Peter had goaded her earlier in J.D.'s office and the disdain he hadn't bothered to conceal, and his temper heated up a notch.

"What does it matter who she works for? If your father wanted her to read that letter, you have no right to keep it from her, either legally or morally."

"I wish it were that clear-cut. My father didn't make it that easy on me. He left the decision completely up to me. In the cover letter he included with it, he said if I felt she was better off not knowing what it contains, I should burn the letter."

The heat of his temper cooled slightly at Peter's obvious turmoil, though his curiosity ratcheted up another level. "But you haven't burned it, even though Anna works for, in your words, the enemy."

"I haven't burned it. No. Some part of me knows she needs to read it. I just… I don't know how she's going to react. I barely know her anymore, Richard. I wonder if I ever did."

Richard had wondered the same thing about his own relationship with Anna. But he was stunned to realize as he sat in her brother's office that his feelings for her hadn't died. They had only been lying dormant inside him, like spring crocuses, waiting for a chance to break free of the frozen ground.

What the hell was he supposed to do with that? He didn't want to care about her. What possible good would ever come of it, when he was certain she couldn't wait to return to New York and the brilliant business career waiting for her there?

"What's in the letter?" he finally asked.

Peter stared down at the envelope for a long moment and his reluctance was in direct contrast to the vocal, outspoken man who had taken on his sister earlier in J.D.'s office.

"I need your vow of confidentiality first. No matter what, you cannot tell a soul."

"Of course."

"I'll read you the cover letter. That explains everything."

* * *

Five minutes later, Richard sat back in his chair, reeling from the information in the letter, from James Wilder's confession that Anna was truly his daughter, conceived during a brief affair with a nurse years ago.

"You have to tell her," he said into the long silence. "You can't keep this from her. She has a right to know."

"You know her, Richard, at least better than I do. How do you think she'll react?"

He thought of Anna and the vulnerability she worked so hard to conceal from the world. "I can't answer that. Stunned, certainly. Overwhelmed. Perhaps angry. Wouldn't you be?"

"Yes. It's a shocker, all right. I've known for six months and I still can't believe it." Peter paused. "I know I probably sound like a cold-hearted bastard here but I have to consider the timing and the possible fallout. In light of the bid to take over the hospital and the vote next week, how do you think this information might impact Anna's role in that bid?"

"I have no idea!"

"What's your best guess? I see things happening one of two ways. Either she might lean more toward our side or, being Anna, she might be more determined than ever to win in some kind of twisted payback against our father for not telling her."

Richard thought of the woman he was coming to know—a woman who could read bedtime stories to a five-year-old with sweetness and affection and then turn shrewdly determined about her career.

She was complex and intriguing, which was a big part of her appeal, he realized.

"I honestly can't answer that, Peter. Why would you

think I would have any idea what Anna will do? I told you I barely know her."

"You've got an uncanny knack for gauging people's behavior. I've seen you in action as you've helped Phil with hospital legal issues. I figured since you and Anna were friends before, you might have a guess."

"Our friendship was over a long time ago. We're both different people now."

"But taking history into account and judging by what you've observed since she's been back, what's your gut telling you?"

"I think none of that matters. It's irrelevant. You need to tell her what's in that letter, regardless of how it might impact the merger. This isn't about the hospital. It's a family matter."

Peter gazed at Richard for a moment then sighed. "I was afraid you would say something like that."

"She deserves to know, Peter. You know she does."

"You're right. I need to tell her as soon as possible. I've put it off too long."

He sighed again, looking not at all thrilled by the prospect. "I don't look forward to it. A hell of a mess my father left, isn't it?"

"Yes. He should have told her himself. This shouldn't be your responsibility."

Peter's laugh was gruff. "An understatement. He took the coward's way out. The only time in his life, I think, that he didn't step up and do what had to be done. I guess my biggest mistake the last six months has been following in his footsteps, at least where Anna is concerned. Thanks, Richard, for the time and for the advice. You have definitely helped put things in perspective for me."

"No problem. Consider it an early wedding gift."

Peter gave a distracted smile and showed him out. As Richard walked through the hospital and to his car he was still stunned by the revelation—and even more stunned by the baffling mix of emotions churning through him toward Anna.

He definitely still had feelings for her. Why else would he be consumed with this warmth and sympathy and something else, something soft and fragile that scared the hell out of him?

Anna was finally back in her rented duplex, wearing her most comfortable jeans and a T-shirt, barefoot, with Lilli curled at her feet, chewing her favorite squeaky toy.

Unfortunately, instead of relaxing, she was getting berated by her boss.

Alfred Daly was hundreds of miles away in Manhattan, probably gazing out the vast window of his office at the peons below who walked the city streets. But despite the distance between them, the man still had the power to make her feel as if she had shrunk several inches since the moment the phone call began.

"Tell me, when are you presenting your report to the hospital board of directors?"

She knew he knew such a significant detail, probably right down to the second, but she played along with him.

"Wednesday at five. They're expected to vote Thursday and give their final recommendation to the mayor and city council later that day."

"And you still believe the vote is too close to call?"

"The board is evenly split, as it has been since we first presented our offer. I believe we're making some progress, though. I think at least one or two of the maybe's have moved toward our camp."

Not without a great deal of wheeling and dealing on her part, but she left that unspoken.

"I certainly hope so. That's why you're there, Miss Wilder."

"Yes, sir."

He didn't mention the threat that had been hanging over her head since the day he had ordered her to come to Walnut River and make the merger happen, though it was uppermost in her mind.

If she failed—if the merger vote did not go their way—Anna knew she would be scrambling to find a new job. Not the end of the world, maybe, but she would find it devastating to start over elsewhere. She had worked too hard at NHC to see it all trickle away because of her stubborn, idealistic family members and their behind-the-scenes opposition.

By the time Daly finished his diatribe fifteen minutes later, Anna realized she had downed half a roll of Tums.

"I want that report no later than noon tomorrow. It's too important to send via e-mail so I want you to upload it directly onto my private server," he snapped.

He gave her a password and username, then hung up with one more dire warning about what would happen if she failed to close the deal.

No pressure, Al. Geez.

Anna hung up the phone and gazed into space, feeling as if she stood at the foot of Mount Everest.

She was on her own here and had been charged with achieving the impossible. Worse, she had just been forcefully reminded that her career hung in the balance if she failed.

Alfred Daly had begun to take the Walnut River General merger personally. She wasn't sure why it was so important to him but she sensed he would not take defeat well. He wanted this hospital and was pulling out all the stops to make it happen.

Suddenly, the doorbell rang, and Lilli bounded to the door, yipping away and jerking Anna from her grim contemplation of an unemployment line in her immediate future. She was not at all in the mood for unexpected company.

After twenty minutes on the phone with her boss, what she really needed was a stiff drink and a long soak in the tub.

Or perhaps both.

The doorbell rang again and Anna jerked the door open, ready to blast away, but the words died in her throat.

Of all the entire population of Walnut River, the last two people she would have expected to find standing on her doorstep on a Friday night were her brother Peter and his fiancée, especially after her altercation with him earlier.

Her day only needed this to go from lousy, straight past miserable, into sheer purgatory.

"Peter… Bethany… What brings you here?"

She could barely even look at her brother. All she could think about was her own immature reaction to him earlier. All her plans to be cool and in control around her family had dissolved with a few harsh words from him. Instead of showing off her logic and business acumen, she had ended up running away like a twelve-year-old girl escaping to the bathroom during gym class to hide her tears.

She wanted to come up with some glib comment,

something cool and nonchalant, but the impulse died when she saw his solemn expression.

She instantly forgot about their altercation. “Peter! What is it? What’s wrong? Has something happened to David or Ella?”

Peter shook his head. “No. Nothing like that.”

“What is it, then?”

For the first time in her memory he appeared to be at a loss for words as he gazed at her mutely.

“May we come in?” Bethany finally asked.

“Oh. Of course. Come in.” She held the door open and they walked inside.

Lilli sniffed their ankles for a moment then returned to her chew toy.

“What a darling dog,” Bethany said with a smile, and Anna decided she had been right to instinctively like her brother’s fiancée. She seemed to have a definite knack for putting people at ease in difficult circumstances.

In fact, right now Anna was quite certain she liked Peter’s fiancée more than she liked her brother.

“Come in. Sit down.”

“I hope we weren’t disturbing you.”

“No.”

She didn’t think Peter would appreciate knowing that she had just finished talking to her boss at NHC so she decided to keep that particular bit of information to herself, especially in light of Peter’s obvious unease.

“Can I get you something to drink?” she asked, doing a mental inventory of the meager contents of her larder.

“Nothing for me,” Bethany said.

Peter sighed. “I could use a drink right now, but it’s probably better if I keep a clear head.”

Anna narrowed her gaze at him. "All right, what's going on, Peter? You're freaking me out."

"I'm sorry. I just… Now that I'm here, I don't know how to start."

"I've always found the beginning's as good a place as any," Anna answered.

It was advice they'd all heard from their mother many times and Peter must have recognized one of Alice's familiar axioms. He gave a fleeting smile and she was struck again by his resemblance to their father.

"First of all, I owe you an apology."

She blinked, not at all used to seeing her self-assured oldest brother look so wary.

"I was out of line today at the hospital. Richard Green ripped into me after you left for making things personal and he was exactly right. I said things I shouldn't have today and I apologize. It's just…a little hard for me to watch the little sister I love taking the other side on an issue I care so passionately about."

Warmth soaked through her and Anna didn't know what stunned her more—that Peter said he loved her or that Richard would stand up to defend her.

He had taken her brother to task? She would have liked to have seen it, even though she had a tough time believing it.

"Your apology is not necessary, Peter, but thank you," she said. "You came all the way over here just to tell me you were sorry?"

"Not completely."

He glanced at Bethany and some unspoken signal passed between them, something private and personal that made Anna feel excluded—and envious. She didn't miss the way Bethany slipped her hand in his, or the way Peter seemed to grow a little calmer at the gesture.

"I have something for you," her brother finally said. "Something I should have given you months ago."

He appeared to be empty-handed and Anna gazed at him, baffled. "What is it?"

Peter slid a hand to the inside pocket of his jacket and retrieved an envelope. "Um, Dad left you a letter. It came to me since I'm executor of his estate."

Instantly, joy and anger warred within her—joy that she might have one more message from the father she missed and anger at her brother's high-handedness. "You're just getting around to giving it to me? Dad's been gone for six months!"

"You make it sound so easy. I wish it were. Dad left it up to me whether to give it to you or not, which was a hell of a position to find myself in, especially when you were making yourself scarce."

He held the letter still and she had to fight the urge to snatch it out of his hand and order him out of her house.

"You knew how to find me."

"I did. But you didn't seem to want to have anything to do with us. You couldn't leave fast enough after the funeral. You wouldn't even let me give you a ride somewhere. And then we found out you were working for Northeastern HealthCare. You should have told us, Anna."

"Don't make this about me and my choices, Peter. Yes, I should have told you about my job. I was wrong to keep it from the family. But that didn't give you the right to withhold something like this from me."

"No. You're right. I should have given the letter to you long ago. I should have driven to the city and tracked you down at your office if I had to, and I'm sorry I didn't. But I'm here now. Do you want it or not?"

"Peter." Bethany said his name, only that, but it appeared to be enough to center him.

He drew in a deep breath and dragged a hand through his hair in a gesture that again reminded her of their father.

"I'm sorry," he said again. "Here it is. Whatever you want to do. It's out of my hands now."

Chapter 9

Anna's stomach suddenly clenched with nerves and she wasn't at all sure she wanted to take the letter from Peter's outstretched hand.

What would her father have written in a letter that he couldn't have told her to her face?

Did she really want to know?

The three of them froze in an awkward tableau and the moment dragged out, longer and longer. Finally she drew in a breath and took it from him, though she was still reluctant to open it.

Her name was written on the front in her father's sloping, elegant script. By the weight of the envelope, she guessed it was maybe two or three pages long. No more than that, but it felt oddly heavy, almost burdensome.

She had the strangest premonition that once she read what her father had written in the letter, her life would never be the same. This was one of those before-and-after moments—everything after would be different than it was right at this instant.

She had no idea why she was so certain—maybe the gravity in Peter's eyes.

"Do you know what it's about?" she asked, though she thought she knew the answer.

His mouth tightened and he nodded. "I haven't read it but he included another letter to me explaining what was in it. I think it's safe to say what he has to tell you is…unexpected."

She nodded but still couldn't bring herself to open it.

"We can wait while you read it," Peter said after another moment. "You might have questions. Scratch that. You will have questions. I can't answer many of them but I'll do what I can."

Finally she knew she couldn't sit much longer, putting off the inevitable. She carefully slid a finger under the flap of the sealed envelope and pulled out the sheets of paper.

The lines of her father's handwriting turned wobbly and blurred for a moment. She blinked quickly, horrified that she might cry in front of her brother.

She thought she had come to terms with his death—and the distance between them the last few years. Though she did her best to contain it, a single tear slid past her defenses. She swiped at it, hoping Peter didn't see. But to her surprise, a moment later, he sat next to her on the sofa and Bethany sat on her other side.

"Take your time," Bethany murmured, with a comforting arm around her shoulders. She didn't know what might be in the letter but she was suddenly enormously grateful for their presence and the strength she drew from having them near.

They had taken time from their wedding preparations to be here for her, she realized with some wonder.

She drew in another shaky breath and smoothed a hand down the paper.

"My dearest Anna," her father's letter began.

I have written this letter in my head a hundred times over the years. A thousand. Each time, the words seem to tangle in my mind and eventually I stopped trying. This time I must press forward, no matter how difficult I find the task.

I must first tell you how very proud I am of you for what you have done with your life. I may not have agreed with your decision to leave medical school—I still believe you would have made an excellent physician. You were always so compassionate and loving.

But over the years I have come to accept that you had to chart your own destiny, and I will say now what I should have said eight years ago. I believe you made the right choice to leave medical school. Your heart was never in it, something I refused to see back then. One of my biggest regrets in life is that I was not the sort of father I should have been to you. I should have listened to your worries and fears instead of trying so hard to crowd you onto the path I wanted for you.

I did try to be a good father to you. Perhaps I tried too hard. I wanted so much for you to feel you belonged. I know things were not always easy for you. I could see the lost look in your eyes when you would see one of your siblings on your mother's lap or having a bedtime story with her and I always tried to rush in to fill the void.

My dear, I ask you not to judge Alice too harshly. She was a wonderful woman who endured more than you can ever guess, more than any woman should. I always suspected she had guessed the truth about you, the truth I dared not tell her.

She never said anything and I know she loved you in her way but surely you sensed she treated you differently than Peter or David or Ella.

Neither of us ever spoke of it—afraid, I think, to upset the fragile peace we had achieved. But time is no longer my friend. When a man reaches a certain age, he must come face to face with his own mortality. I don't want this secret to die with me.

I only ask that as you read this, you do not judge me too harshly. Please remember how much I have always loved you.

The truth is, I have lied to you for all these years about how you came to be part of our family. The story about finding you on the steps of the hospital is true. But missing in that tale are certain significant details.

She paused to turn the page, still vaguely aware of Peter and Bethany on either side of her, bolstering her.

I was the one who "found" you, yes, but only because that was the prearranged plan between me and your mother. Your birth mother.

I'm sure it will shock you to find out I knew all along who she was. It wasn't some unknown mys-

tery woman who left you, but a nurse at Walnut River General. See, Anna, you are my daughter. Not only through adoption but in every other way.

She inhaled sharply and lifted shocked eyes to Peter, who was watching her through her father's solemn eyes. She jerked her gaze away from him and focused on the letter again.

Please, I beg you again, don't judge me too harshly. I had one moment of indiscretion during the depths of Alice's depression, when she had retreated to a dark and terrible place. Monica, your birth mother, showed me great kindness and compassion and in a moment of weakness, I went against every standard I have ever believed in. She was not at fault, the blame was wholly mine. I cannot regret it. I know I should, but without that moment of weakness, I never would have had the great honor and privilege of being your father.

Anna realized she was gripping the letter so hard she was afraid she would tear it. She forced her grasp to relax as she fought back tears. A moment later, a handkerchief appeared in front of her and she took it from Peter but still didn't allow the tears to fall.

I'm sure you're curious about your birth mother and why she would choose to give you up. She was a wonderful woman, kind and generous, but she wasn't at all prepared to be a mother, especially not on her own. I know that leaving you with me was the hardest decision she ever made, but she knew that as a Wilder, you would have opportunities she couldn't provide on her own.

I'm sorry to say she is gone now. She died not long after your birth when the small plane she was flying in crashed, but I am certain her last thoughts were of you.

Our actions were done out of love for you, Anna. Please don't forget that. Even the deception I have maintained over the years was out of love and the enduring hope that you would find acceptance and stability in our family.

I am sorry for the years of deception. I should have told you earlier, I see that now. I only pray that someday you will forgive me for the magnitude of the lie.

I love you, my darling Anna. I have been proud to call you my own every moment of your life.

Your devoted father
James Wilder

She finished the letter and sat stunned for a long moment, the pages dangling from her fingers.

She didn't know what to think, what to feel.

She was not some anonymous orphan, as she had believed for so many years. She was James Wilder's daughter, conceived during a brief affair with a nurse at the hospital.

Her father's daughter, in every possible way.

She felt numb, dazed, and couldn't seem to work her brain around the implications.

"You…knew about this?" she finally said, her jaw so achy and tight the words were hard to get out.

Peter nodded. "I told you, he left me a cover letter explaining everything. I've known for months, I just haven't known how to tell you."

"How could he?"

The words were wrenched from her and she didn't know what she meant—her father's infidelity in the first place or the years of deception upon deception from the man she had always considered the most scrupulously honest she had ever known.

Peter sighed. "You don't remember what Mom went through during those terrible days of her depression, before she found the right combo of meds to control it. I do. I remember it vividly. I was nine and I can remember days when I was afraid to come home from school, because I didn't know what I would find. It was horrible. The medication they gave her made it worse. She was barely there and when she came to herself, she would rage and scream at Dad for hours."

She closed her eyes, feeling battered and achy and still fighting tears. If she let them out, she was afraid she wouldn't be able to stop.

"Do— Do Ella and David know?"

He shook his head. "Bethany knows and I've confided in two others, seeking advice—a social worker and friend at the hospital and more recently, Richard Green."

She stared. "Richard knows? And he said nothing to me?"

"I only told him today after I saw you in J.D.'s office. I swore him to secrecy."

So Richard hadn't betrayed her. She found some solace in that.

"Will you tell them? David and Ella, I mean?"

Peter shook his head. "That's your decision. If you

want them to know, I can tell them but perhaps you should be the one to do it. And if you decide to say nothing, I will back you up."

He paused, appearing to choose his words carefully. "Things are difficult between us all right now. I would only ask that if you tell them, you don't do it out of spite or anger."

His words were a blunt reminder of the rift between her and her siblings, of the chasm she had no idea how to cross.

She forced a smile that didn't feel at all genuine. "Always the protector, aren't you, Peter?"

He studied her solemnly. "Of you as well, Anna."

She didn't know how to respond to that and the tears seemed even closer to the surface. Bethany seemed to sense the fissures in her control. She squeezed Anna's arm.

"The wedding rehearsal dinner is next Friday," she said softly. "It would mean a great deal to us if you would be there. Will you come?"

Would she even still be in town? she wondered. The hospital board of directors was set to vote on Thursday and everything would be decided by then.

Still, she was deeply grateful suddenly for Bethany's freely offered friendship.

"I'll try," she managed.

Bethany gave her a hug. "That's all we can ask," she said.

To her shock, Peter hugged her next. "I would say welcome to the family, but it doesn't seem quite appropriate since you've been my sister for thirty years."

Somehow she managed a smile, though it felt watery and thin. "Thank you for bringing this, even though you didn't want to. I understand your hesitation a little better now."

"Dad never should have kept it from you and I shouldn't have either for this long."

He paused, then embraced her again. "When the shock wears off, I hope you will see this as a good thing. You've always been one of us, Anna. Blood or not. But maybe knowing you share our blood will help you see that more clearly."

She nodded and showed them out.

When they left, Lilli gazed at her quizzically. Anna reread the letter, still fighting tears, while the walls of her bland, boring, temporary home seemed to be closing in on her, crowding her, smothering her.

She suddenly needed to escape from the thick emotions squeezing her chest, stealing her breath, choking her throat.

And she knew exactly where she needed to go.

"Good night, kiddo. You be good for Grandma, okay?"

"Dad!" In that single word, Ethan managed to convey all the disgust of a teenager instead of a five-year-old. "You know I always am!"

Richard smiled into the phone. "Of course you are. I love you, bud."

"I love you, too, Dad."

The sweet, pure words put a lump in his throat, as they always did. "Can you put your grandma on the phone again?"

"Okeydokey."

After a moment's silence, his mother picked up the phone.

"Are you really sure you want to do this, Mom? You've had him all day."

"Absolutely." His mother's voice was firm and not at all as exhausted as he might have expected after she had wrangled Ethan for the past ten hours. "You know we've been planning this sleepover for a week. We're camping out. I've got a tent set up in my living room and the sleeping bags are already up. We're going to roast marshmallows in the gas fireplace after I crank up the air conditioning to compensate and I have all the makings of s'mores ready to go. We're going to have a blast."

That was part of the problem, Richard admitted. He hated being excluded. He hadn't seen Ethan since dropping him off at his grandmother's that morning and he missed his son.

Ethan's absence was part of his restlessness, but not all of it. Some had to do with a particular woman he couldn't get out of his mind.

"Thanks, then," he said. "You two have a great time. I'll pick him up tomorrow morning."

"No hurry. We'll probably sleep in."

"Wishful thinking, Mom. Ethan's idea of sleeping in is waiting to jump out of bed until six-forty-five instead of six-thirty."

His mother laughed. "I'll survive. The question is, what will you do with a night to yourself?"

He was so unused to the idea that he found the prospect of an evening without Ethan rather daunting. "I'm slammed with work right now so I'll probably just take advantage of the chance to catch up."

"Booorrring. Can't you think of something better than work? It's Friday night. Why don't you go out and have some fun? Call up one of those girls on your Black-Berry and head out for a night on the town."

The only females on his BlackBerry were clients or associates, but he decided his mother didn't really need to know that particular piece of information.

"Interesting idea," he murmured. "I doubt it will happen but I'll certainly add it to the list of possibilities."

His mother was quiet for a moment. When she spoke, her voice held a surprising degree of concern. "I worry about you, Richard. You're a wonderful father, but your world has become only about work and about your son. You need to take time for yourself once in awhile. Go have a little fun. Grab a little spontaneity in your life."

Richard frowned. Where was this coming from? Okay, so he didn't have much of a social life. But when, exactly, was he supposed to find the time for one while being a full-time father?

He opened his mouth to answer, but before he could, the doorbell chimed through the empty house.

Relief flooded him at the convenient excuse to end the conversation. "I've gotta go, Mom. Somebody's at the door."

"Oh, good. Maybe it's a hot girl looking for a little action."

A strangled laugh escaped him. "Wouldn't that be an odd twist of fate?"

"Stranger things have happened."

"If I were you, I wouldn't hold my breath. Have fun sleeping on the floor."

He hung up and hurried to answer the door. In light of the conversation with his mother, he couldn't have been more shocked to find Anna Wilder on his doorstep.

"Anna!"

"I…didn't know where else to go."

His initial surprise shifted quickly to concern. Her eyes were hollow and her face looked ashen in the pale glow of his porch light.

She was holding an envelope in her hand and he knew instantly that Peter must have given her James's letter.

He only had about half a second for the thought to register before she launched herself into his arms.

He caught her but the momentum pushed them both back into the room. He heard a strangled gasp and then, like a torrent, she began to weep great, heaving sobs, as if she had been waiting for only this moment to unleash them.

He eased down to the sofa and pulled her onto his lap.

He held her for a long time, until the sobs finally began to subside. She was trembling, little shivers that broke his heart, and he tightened his arms. After a moment, she let out a deep breath and struggled to regain control, and he relaxed his hold a little.

"I'm sorry." Her voice sounded raspy. "I'm so sorry. I didn't mean to… I never intended to come here and break down like this. I just… I had to talk to someone and I didn't know where else to go."

"I'm glad you came here."

"I feel so stupid. I don't know what happened. I saw you and suddenly it all just seemed too much."

He was honored and humbled that she trusted him enough to let him see beyond the cool veneer she showed to the world. "Do you want to talk about it?"

"You mean blubbering all over your shirt for twenty minutes isn't enough torture?"

It *was* torture having her in his arms, but not the way she meant. Despite the toll it was taking on his control, he wasn't about to relinquish this chance to hold her, in any capacity.

"I'm guessing you talked to Peter."

She sighed. "Yes. He said he talked to you earlier today and told you about the letter from my father."

"He did."

"Then you know the truth. That James Wilder is my father. My true father, not just my adopted one."

"A bit of a shock, wasn't it?"

She gave a short, bitter laugh. "It changes everything I thought I knew about myself."

"You're still the same person, Anna. Finding out your genetic blueprint doesn't change thirty years of living."

She was silent for a moment, her cheek still pressed against his chest. She didn't seem inclined to leave his lap and he certainly wasn't in any hurry to let her go.

"I have always believed I stood on the outside of the Wilder family circle. My mother—Alice—didn't exactly push me out but I never truly felt welcome, even though James did everything possible to make me feel I belonged. Now I understand why."

"She knew you were his child?"

"My father said in the letter he thought she must have guessed but they never discussed it."

"It must have been terribly difficult for her if she did suspect. To keep her head high while she raised her husband's illegitimate child."

"Yes. It explains so much about…everything."

To his regret, she finally slid from his lap and sat beside him on the couch, her hands tightly folded on her lap.

Though he knew a little distance was probably a wise thing right about now, Richard couldn't prevent himself from reaching out and covering her clasped hands with his. After a moment, she gripped his tightly.

"You know, I think he tried to tell me several times over the years, in an oblique kind of way," she said. "The summer I…left, when I dropped out of med school and everything, I tried to tell him how unhappy I was. I told him straight out that I was afraid I just didn't have the Wilder gene for medicine. I can remember him saying in that sturdy, no-nonsense voice of his, 'Don't let me hear you say that again. You're as much a Wilder as the rest of my children!' I thought it was simply another effort to make me feel I belonged in the family."

"What will you do now?"

She closed her eyes and leaned against the sofa. Her color had returned, he was pleased to see. Despite the crying jag, she was so beautiful he couldn't seem to look away.

"I don't know. Peter says he hasn't told Ella and David. He seems to think I'll blab it to them out of spite over the hospital merger."

Despite her glib tone, he could hear the hurt underscoring her words and his heart ached for her. He couldn't help himself, and he pulled her into his arms again.

"You'll figure it all out, Anna. I know it must feel like an atomic bomb has just dropped into your lap, but when you think about it, what has really changed?"

"Everything!"

"Maybe you found out your father had some human weaknesses after all. But your siblings are still your siblings, just as they've always been. You might all be going through a rough time right now with the hospital merger but they still love you."

She sighed against his chest. "I feel like everything I thought I knew about myself is a lie."

"It's not, Anna. Not at all. What's different right now than it was a few hours ago? You're still a bright beautiful woman who loves her dog and is kind to little boys and who still makes my heart pound."

Her gaze flashed to his for one breathless moment before he surrendered to the inevitable and kissed her.

Chapter 10

Anna closed her eyes and leaned into Richard, trying to absorb his strength.

She needed him. For comfort, yes, but for so much more. She found a peace in his arms that she had never known anywhere else.

Though she had dated in the eight years she'd been away, she had never cared enough about any of those men to take a relationship beyond the casual to this ultimate step.

This had never felt right with anyone but Richard. He was the only man she had ever made love to.

She wondered what he would say if she told him that and decided to keep the information to herself for now.

She wrapped her arms around his neck with the oddest sensation that this was where she belonged. Right here, with his mouth firm and insistent against hers, his masculine scent filling her senses, his hard strength against her.

Here, in his arms, she didn't feel disconnected or off kilter. It didn't matter whether she was the odd Wilder out or James Wilder's illegitimate daughter. She had nothing to prove here—she knew exactly who she was when Richard Green kissed her. Everything else faded to nothing.

He deepened the kiss, until tiny sparks raced up and down her nerve endings, until her thighs trembled and every inch of her skin ached for his touch.

"You taste exactly like I remember," he murmured.

"How?" Was that breathy, aroused voice hers, she wondered with some amazement. What happened to the brisk and businesslike woman she had always considered herself?

"Like every delicious, decadent, sinful dessert ever created. Sweet and heady and intoxicating. That's you."

His words ignited more heat and she kissed him fiercely, reveling in his sharp intake of breath, in the tremble of his hands on the bare skin above the waistband of her jeans.

He traced designs on the sensitive skin at her waist for long, intoxicating moments, then finally moved to the buttons of her white shirt.

A wild hunger for his touch bubbled and seethed deep inside her and she arched against his hand, needing him with a steady, fiery ache.

He opened the buttons of her shirt and touched her through the lacy fabric of her bra and she found the sight of his sun-browned hand against her pale skin the most erotic thing she'd ever seen.

She arched against him, wanting more. Wanting everything. For long moments, they kissed and touched, until nothing else mattered but this moment.

"I'm going to have to stop." His voice was raspy with need. "I'm afraid I have no self-control where you're concerned."

"Take it from me. Self-control is overrated," she murmured, her voice a breathy purr.

He closed his eyes for a moment. When he opened them again, they were dark with passion. "I can't take advantage of you, Anna. You're upset. This isn't really what you want."

"You couldn't be more wrong. This is exactly what I want."

He looked torn between desire and his sense of duty and she decided to take the decision out of his hands. She kissed him hard, wrapping her arms around him tightly and savoring the strength against her.

He groaned. "I can't fight you and myself at the same time."

"Then don't," she said.

He kissed her again, fierce and possessive, and her stomach trembled with anticipation. It wouldn't be the same magic she remembered from eight years ago, she warned herself. It couldn't be.

She was only half-right.

It wasn't the same. It was better. Much, much better.

They kissed their way down the hall to his bedroom and she had a vague impression of bold masculine colors and a massive bed before Richard began to undress her with a soft gentleness that nearly made her weep.

She was in love with him.

The realization washed through her, not with the punishing force of a tidal wave, but like a sweet cleansing rain on parched desert soil.

It was terribly difficult not to blurt the words out right then but she choked them back. He didn't want to hear them. Not now. She had hurt him eight years ago, he had said as much. He might let her into his arms and his bed but somehow she knew finding her way back into his heart wouldn't be nearly as easy.

She put the fear away for now as she helped him out of his clothes and then she forgot her fears, lost in the sheer wonder of having all those muscles to explore.

They kissed and touched for a long time, until both of them were breathing raggedly, their hearts pounding.

At last, when she didn't think she could endure another moment, he grabbed a condom from the bedside table and entered her, and she again had to choke back her words of love as sensation after sensation poured over her.

She pressed a hard kiss to his mouth, desperate to show him with her lips and her body how she felt about him, even if she didn't quite feel she could say the words yet.

He gripped her hands tightly as he moved deeply inside her and she cried out his name, stunned at her wild hunger. She arched into him, desperate and achy.

She couldn't wait another second, another instant. Sensing how close she was to the edge, he reached between their bodies and touched her at the apex of her thighs and the world exploded in a wild burst of color and heat and sensation.

While her body still shivered and hummed, he pushed even deeper inside her, deeper than she would have thought possible, then groaned out her name as he found his own release.

He held her while they floated back to earth together and she mouthed the words she couldn't say aloud against his chest.

"What did you say?" he asked softly.

She shook her head, her hair brushing his skin. "Wow," she lied. "Just wow."

He laughed softly and pulled her closer and she wondered how she had ever found the strength—or the stupidity—to walk away from this eight years ago.

He awoke to the pale light of early morning filtering through his window and an odd sense of peace.

The sensation was unfamiliar enough that it compelled him to slide a little further into consciousness. Most mornings, he jumped out of bed ready for the day's many battles—from his regular tussle with Ethan over breakfast cereals to pondering the many things on his to-do list.

This morning, his limbs were loose and relaxed, his thoughts uncharacteristically still.

While he was trying to piece together why that might be, a sexy feminine scent drifted through the air from the pillow beside him, and he saw an unfamiliar indentation with a few long blond hairs against the pillowcase.

The memories came flowing back—of Anna in his arms, her mouth eager, her body soft and responsive.

He closed his eyes, reliving the incredible night they had just shared. It had been more than he would ever have imagined. Much more. He had never known such tenderness, such overwhelming sweetness.

They had made love three times and each time had been more intense than the time before.

And now she was gone.

He opened his eyes, not quite sure why he was so certain of it. Her clothes were gone and some instinct told him he didn't need to search his house to know he wouldn't find her.

He couldn't say he was really surprised. Saddened, maybe, but not really surprised.

The bleak inevitability of it still made him want to throw on a pair of jeans and tear off after her, chase her down at her apartment and confront her, but he checked the impulse. What the hell good would that accomplish, besides making him look like an idiot?

He sat up, his emotions a tight hot tangle in his chest. He was in love with her—a thousand times more now, this morning, than he had been eight years ago. Those had been fledgling, newborn feelings.

This, what he felt right now, was powerful and strong.

Too bad for him, but if their history ran true, Anna was likely to whip out a twenty gauge shotgun and blast his heart right out of the sky.

He didn't learn his lesson very well with her, did he? He was either a masochist or he had no sense of self-preservation whatsoever.

Anna just wasn't emotionally available.

She couldn't make it more clear to him if she took out a damn billboard right outside his office.

Even when they made love, he could sense she held some part of herself back, something she hid away from him. He didn't know whether that was a protective mechanism from a childhood where she struggled to belong, or if it stemmed from her dedication to her career, but even in his arms she wouldn't let him through that last line of defenses.

He sighed. So much for the relaxed state he'd awakened to. His shoulders now ached with tension and regret.

It was still early, just barely daylight. He wasn't going to lay here and brood, he decided. He had survived having his heart broken by Anna Wilder before. He could certainly do it again. The trick was returning to as normal a life as possible, forcing himself to go through the motions until the vicious ache in his heart began to fade.

He was getting to be an expert.

When she had left before, the only thing that had saved him had been law school. He had thrown himself into his final two years, until he didn't have room in his brain to think about anything else but tort reforms and trial transcripts.

At least now he had Ethan to distract him.

A good, hard run before he went to his mother's to collect his son for the day would be an excellent place to start picking up the pieces of his world, he decided. A little physical activity would be just the thing to burn off this restlessness suddenly churning through him.

Ten minutes later, dressed in jogging shorts and a T-shirt, he was heading out the front door when he spotted an envelope on the coffee table in the living room.

He saw her name on the front and realized this must be the letter from her father. His mind flashed to the night before, to her coming through the door and into his arms. She had been holding it then. Sometime during the wild storm of emotion that came after when she had wept in his arms, she must have dropped it on the table.

He was going to have to return it to her, which meant he would have to see her again.

Sooner, rather than later.

He grimaced, gazing malevolently at the envelope. Getting over her again would be a hell of a lot easier if he didn't have to face her every damn time he turned around.

She was an idiot.

Anna sat in her living room, Lilli curled up at her feet and her laptop humming on the coffee table in front of her as she tried to focus on work instead of the delectable image of Richard, naked and masculine, as she'd left him a few hours earlier.

Walking away from that bedroom and out of his house had been the single hardest thing she had ever done.

She had stood watching him sleep for a long time in the soft light of early morning, trying to force herself to go.

With one arm thrown over his head, his features relaxed and youthful in sleep, he had been so gorgeous that she had wanted nothing more than to climb right back into his bed and never leave.

She sighed, gazing at her computer until the words blurred.

She was in love with him.

It was one thing to face such a thought when she was in his arms, when his body was warm and hard against hers. It was something else entirely in the cold unforgiving light of morning, when she couldn't escape the harsh reality that they had no possible future together.

She had destroyed any chance of that eight years ago,

when she made the fatal decision that proving herself to her family was more important than following her heart.

It had been a colossal mistake. She could see that now.

Richard didn't trust her enough to love her. Even when he had been deep inside her, she had seen the doubt shadowing his gaze, the edge of distance he was careful to maintain.

She deserved it. She had hurt him by leaving, more than she had ever imagined.

The night she had shared dinner with him at his house, he had told her with blunt and brutal honesty that he had only dated Ethan's mother because she had reminded him of Anna.

He had offered her his heart eight years ago and she had callously refused it. She supposed it was only right and just, somehow, that now she would be the one to bleed.

She stared at her computer for a long time then glanced at the clock. She had promised Mr. Daly her report would be posted on his private server by noon, which gave her only an hour to finish up.

Compartmentalizing her heartache was almost as hard as walking out of Richard's house, but she forced herself to focus on work with the harsh reminder that she only had a few days left in Walnut River. Either way the board voted, her work here would be done by the end of the week and she could return to the city and the life she had created there.

She quickly input the new numbers from the hospital in her report then went online to access Daly's private server via the instructions he had given her the night before.

It only took a moment to upload her report. Just as

she was about to disconnect she spied a folder she had never seen before, labeled WRG/Wilder.

She stared at it for a long moment, a vague foreboding curling through her like ominous wisps of smoke where they didn't belong.

She had no business reading Daly's private files, even if they did have her name on them.

But he had given her the access code to his server, she reminded herself. Surely he wouldn't have done that if the server contained information he didn't want her to see.

Maybe this was some kind of message to her and he meant for her to see it. Maybe if she didn't read it, he would accuse her of not doing her job somehow. The man could be devious that way.

After another moment of dithering, she surrendered to her curiosity and opened the folder. It contained only one file, she saw, with the initials P.W.

In for a penny, she thought, and clicked to open it....

Ten minutes later, she printed out the document after making her own backup copy. Her hands were shaking so much she could barely move them on the keyboard to disconnect from the server.

She shut down her laptop and folded it closed, then eased back on the sofa. Her stomach roiled as the bagel she'd had that morning seemed to churn around inside her. She pressed a hand to the sudden burning there while her mind whirled with the implications of what she had just read.

She wasn't sure which emotion was stronger inside her right now—outrage at what her superiors planned for the hospital or the deep sense of betrayal that she had been used.

P.W. stood for *Peter Wilder.* That had been abundantly clear the moment she opened the file that turned out to be an internal memo between Daly and his three closest cohorts.

She closed her eyes as snippets of the memo seemed to dance behind her eyelids. *Force out old guard. Bring in cheaper labor. Cut costs and services.*

It was bad enough that NHC planned to do exactly as her siblings claimed, sacrifice patient care for the bottom line. Worse was the way they intended to win this battle, by using her to bring down her siblings, primarily Peter.

Peter Wilder leads the opposition, the memo stated clearly. *Take him out and you'll cut the opponents off at the knees.*

The smear tactics outlined in the memo were brutally ugly, ranging from manufacturing malpractice allegations to planting a patient willing to accuse him of sexual misconduct.

Anna pressed a hand to her mouth, sickened all over again as she remembered her own passionate defense of Northeastern HealthCare, how absolutely certain she had been that the company had the community's needs at heart.

How could she have allowed herself to be so blind?

She thought she had been doing the right thing. For two years, she had bought into the NHC philosophy of providing streamlined medical care to reach the masses. She had wanted to believe in their mission. She had nothing but respect for her direct supervisor, Wallace Jeffers. He had always struck her as a man of integrity and honor.

Not everyone at NHC was like him, she had to admit. Now, as she looked back over two years, she could see times she had turned her head away at practices that might have blurred ethical lines.

She hadn't wanted to see them, she acknowledged now. She had wanted only to focus on her career and climbing as high as she could. Wallace had talked about her succeeding him as vice president of mergers and acquisitions, sometime long in the future, and she had wanted it.

She'd been brought into this project not because of any brilliance on her part, she saw now, but because she was a Wilder. Alfred Daly seemed to have an almost pathological need to win the NHC merger. He was frustrated and angry at all the complications and delays the past six months in what should have been a simple process.

Of course he would use any advantage in front of him. No doubt he thought her presence would be enough to distract her family while NHC implemented more nefarious plans.

This memo was dated a few weeks earlier. She read it again, sick all over again. Were the wheels in motion already? Was her brother going to be hit any day now with some kind of trumped-up malpractice suit or an allegation of sexual abuse?

Her honorable upright brother would be devastated by either option.

"Oh, Lilli. What am I going to do?"

Her dog yapped in response, her head cocked and her eyes curiously sympathetic.

The dog held her gaze for just an instant before she suddenly scampered to the door with an excited yip, then sat vibrating with eagerness, her little body aquiver.

As usual, Lilli was prescient. The doorbell rang an

instant later and Anna groaned, tempted to ignore it and pretend she wasn't home.

The doorbell rang again, more insistently this time. Who was she fooling? Her car was in the driveway, and whoever was out there probably knew she was sitting here trying to pretend she was invisible.

"Anna?" She heard through the door and closed her eyes at the sound of Richard's smooth voice.

Who else? She only needed this.

She was even more tempted to ignore the doorbell, but she just couldn't bring herself to do it. Finally she ramped up her courage and forced herself to wrench open the door.

Sunlight gleamed in his golden hair and he looked gorgeous—sexy and casual in jeans and a polo shirt. She had an instant's image of how she had left him that morning, the sheets tousled at his waist and his muscled chest hard and warm.

Awkwardness at seeing him again temporarily supplanted her dismay over the memo.

A few hours ago, she had been in his arms. She had no experience with this sort of thing and didn't know how to face him.

"Hi," she finally said, her voice throaty.

He nodded, though his stoic expression didn't change.

"Would you…like to come in?"

After a moment, he stepped through the doorway with a reluctance she didn't miss. He stopped for a moment to greet Lilli, who hopped around with infatuated enthusiasm.

"I can't stay," he finally said. "I'm picking Ethan up in an hour. I just wanted to return this. You left it at my house."

He held out a familiar envelope and she stared. She certainly hadn't forgotten the stunning news that she was James's daughter but the letter had completely slipped her mind when she was sneaking away from Richard's bed.

"Oh. Right. Um, thank you."

"You're welcome."

They lapsed into an awkward silence. She wished she could read his expression but he seemed stiff and unapproachable.

"Why did you…"

"Look, I'm sorry I…"

They both spoke to break the silence at the same time and Anna gestured. "You first," she said.

He shrugged. "I just wanted to know why you rushed away this morning without a word. You could have at least nudged me awake to say goodbye."

She flushed, not at all in the mood to talk about this right now after the tumult of the past half hour.

Richard made it sound like she had taken what she wanted from him and then left on her merry way without giving him another thought. It wasn't at all like that, but she could certainly see how he might have been left with that impression.

She couldn't very well tell him she had been terrified by the wild torrent of emotions rushing through her, that she had been almost desperate for the safety of a little distance from him.

"I don't know that I can answer that," she finally said, her voice wary. "I was hoping to avoid this kind of awkwardness. I guess I thought it would be…easier that way."

His mouth hardened. "I wouldn't want you to try something hard."

His words were quiet, which only made them that much more devastating.

"What's that supposed to mean?"

"Nothing. Forget it." He looked toward the door as if he regretted saying anything and wanted to escape.

"No. I'd like to hear what you have to say."

"You sure about that?"

She folded her arms across her chest, though she knew that pitiful gesture would do nothing to protect her heart.

"Yes. Tell me."

"I'm just looking at your track record. You quit medical school because it was too tough for you."

"Not true! I had straight A's my first year. I walked out because I hated it!"

"Fine. You're right. It wasn't tough academically, just emotionally, which for you was even harder. So instead of staying and explaining to your family that you hated it, instead of taking a stand, you chose to run. You were so afraid of your family's reaction that you gave up on *us* before we even had a chance. You've got a track record, at least where I'm concerned, so I guess I wasn't really surprised you walked out this morning. It's what you do. You're good at it."

She managed, just barely, not to sway from the bitter impact of his anger. How dare he? she wanted to say, but the words tangled in her throat. She only had to look at her laptop and that damning memo to know he was right. Absolutely right.

She was a blind, self-absorbed idiot whose actions were threatening her family and her community.

She deserved his condemnation and more. Much more.

Chapter 11

He needed to shut the hell up and just leave, pretend the last twelve hours hadn't happened, but Richard couldn't seem to make the words stop coming. "Even as we were making love, I expected you to leave. That doesn't make it hurt any less. That's all I'm saying."

Her features had paled a shade, but in typical Anna fashion, she stiffened her shoulders. "I don't understand. If you have such contempt for me and think I'm such a terrible person, why would you want anything to do with me?"

Though her tone was calm, dispassionate even, he didn't miss the hurt in her eyes, a pain she was trying valiantly to conceal from him.

"I don't think you're a terrible person. Quite the contrary. I wouldn't be—" in love with you, he almost said, but checked himself just in time "—I wouldn't be here if

I did. I think you're a brilliant, capable, beautiful woman who doesn't see her own strengths. You don't see yourself as I do, as someone with the ability to cope with anything that comes along. Because you don't see it, you protect yourself by avoiding things you're afraid you can't handle."

She looked as if he had just punched her in the gut and Richard sighed. He needed to just shut the hell up and leave. He tended to forget how vulnerable she was.

He had no business coming here, twisting everything, making it all about her.

"I'd better go. Ethan will be home soon. I just thought you might be looking for your father's letter."

"Thank you."

She didn't meet his gaze and Richard closed his eyes, furious with himself. "Look, I'm sorry. Forget I said anything. I'm just acting like a spoiled brat. I can't have what I want and so I'm blaming everyone in the world but myself."

"What…do you want?"

"Haven't you figured that out yet? I want you. Still. Always."

She blinked those big gorgeous eyes and with a sigh, he stepped forward and pulled her into his arms.

She stood frozen with shock in his arms for just a moment then she seemed to melt against him, her mouth soft and eager against his. Her arms clasped around his neck and he lost himself to the heat that always flared between them.

Was it only because he knew he couldn't have her? he wondered. Was that why each touch, each taste, seemed such a miracle? As if each time might be the last.

He wasn't sure how it happened but she was backed

against the wall, her body wrapped around his, and he was lost in the overwhelming tenderness, unlike anything he had ever known with anyone else.

They kissed for a long time, until finally she sighed against his mouth and he tasted exactly the moment when she started to withdraw.

She slid her mouth away from his and backed away, her eyes wide, slightly dazed, for only a moment before she seemed to blink back to awareness.

"I wish you wouldn't do that."

"What? Kiss you?"

"Confuse me," she said, her voice low. "Distract me. Richard, I can't do this with you. Last night was..."

A mistake. He heard the words, even though she cut off the sentence before she said them.

"I was confused and upset and I—I needed you. I won't deny that. But I shouldn't have stayed. The lines are too blurred. Surely you can see that. You're the hospital attorney and I..."

"And?"

"And things are so complicated right now. I can't even begin to tell you." Her gaze flashed to her laptop behind him. "*Complicated* is an understatement. Right now, I need... I can't afford to be distracted by you. By this."

The words had a painfully familiar ring to them. She was doing it again, damn her.

"I'm sorry," she murmured. "It's just...my life is a mess. The merger. My family. Northeastern HealthCare. Everything."

When would he stop just handing his heart to her and then sit by watching her twist and yank the poor thing into knots?

"You're right. I wouldn't want a little detail like the

fact that I'm in love with you distract you from all that other important stuff in your life right now."

He hadn't meant to say that, damn it. The words slipped out of nowhere to hover between them, where they seemed to expand sharply, to grow and morph until they filled the entire room.

"Richard!"

"Forget I said that."

"How can I?"

"I'm sure you'll find a way. Especially since you're so focused on what's really important. The merger. Your family. NHC. Everything."

As he headed for the door, he dislodged some papers from the coffee table. Out of habit, he reached to pick them up to replace them—it wouldn't do to leave a mess, after all, he thought bitterly—then his attention was caught by the top page in his hand.

He shouldn't have read it but a few key phrases leapt out and grabbed his attention. Law school had taught him to read briefs rapidly and digest them just as quickly. It took less than ten seconds to read enough to feel like throwing up.

"What the hell is this?"

She stared at the paper in his hand and he saw the color leach from her face like bones in the sun. She grabbed for the memo. "Nothing. Absolutely nothing."

He held it above his head so she couldn't reach it. Her dog, thinking they were playing some kind of game, yipped beside their feet. "Nothing! You call this nothing?"

Panic twisted her features and she looked like she shared his nausea, so pale and bilious that he might have allowed a twinge of pity if he'd had room for anything else around the disgust.

"It's not what it looks like."

"I hope to hell it's not."

He pulled it down and read it again and had to fight the urge to shove the whole thing down her throat. "Because what it looks like is your master plan to win this merger fight, no matter what the cost. You're planning to sacrifice your own brother for the sake of your damn job!"

"I'm not!"

"What else? *Take Peter Wilder down, any way you can.* That's what the thing says. *With Wilder out of the picture, the opposition will crumble.* How could you? What have you become, Anna?"

If possible, her features paled further but she still lifted her chin. "You're jumping to unfounded conclusions, counselor."

"To hell with that! The proof is right here. How could you?" he asked again. "You're willing to destroy Peter—your own brother—just to win. The job at all costs. Nothing has changed with you, has it?"

She ignored his words, holding out her hand. Her fingers trembled, he realized, but the sight gave him no satisfaction. "Give it to me, Richard. That is an internal Northeastern HealthCare memo. You have no legal access to it. You're an attorney. You know that."

"It was here in plain sight."

"Among my private papers, in a private home. You read it without my permission and now you just need to forget you ever saw it."

She was right, damn it. She was right and there wasn't a thing he could do about it. He handed over the document with bitter reluctance, as all his illusions about her shattered into nothing.

"I don't even know you, do I? I was completely wrong. How could I have been so stupid? You aren't protecting your emotions. You've got none. You're a cold heartless woman who is willing to sell your own family down the river to get your way."

"Richard—"

He shook his head, cutting her off. "I've been in love with an image all these years. You never cared about me. I finally see it. I tried to convince myself you were doing what you thought was best to escape your family's expectations. But the truth is, you left without even a backward glance because I didn't matter. My feelings didn't matter. You don't care about anyone or anything but yourself, do you?"

"Not true. So not true." Her voice was low and cool but she fluttered one hand over her stomach like he'd kicked her. Her dog, sensing the tension, seemed to get more excited, dancing around their feet.

"It is. I can't believe I've been so blind. I've been hanging on to this illusion of the girl you used to be in high school and college. But she has completely disappeared somewhere along the way."

"I'm sorry you had to read that."

"I won't let you and those bastards you work for get away with this," he growled. "No way in hell. I'll go to the media. To your family. To anybody who will listen."

"And say what? You have no proof of anything. Just leave it alone, Richard."

She was right. He was certain the incriminating document would be shredded and the memo purged from the NHC system the moment he walked out the door.

"You would love that, wouldn't you? If I just walked out and forgot everything. It's not going to happen. If I can't go to the media, I can at least do everything I can to protect your brother."

She took a deep breath. "That's not necessary."

His laugh was raw and scraped his throat. "Oh, believe me, Anna, as the hospital attorney and your brother's counsel now by default, I think it damn well is. Northeastern HealthCare is running out of time. I'm sure they're going to move fast. But we'll be ready for them."

He headed for the door but her voice stopped him.

"Richard, I… This is not what you think, I swear. Can you just give me a few days to straighten things out?"

"A few days? In a few days, your brother's life could be devastated. He's getting married in a week, Anna. Did you once think of that? A little accusation of sexual misconduct with a patient would be a hell of a thing to have hanging over his head on his honeymoon."

She drew in a shaky breath. "A few days. That's all I need."

"In a few days, this could be a done deal and your bloodsucking company could win. I am *not* going to let that happen."

She closed her eyes for a moment and the vulnerability on her features gave him the absurd urge to comfort her.

"Fine," she said after a moment. "Do what you have to do. And I will, too. Will you excuse me, then? I have a great deal of work to do."

Without another word, he spun on his heels and headed out the door.

He sat in his SUV for just a moment before turning

the key in the ignition. Betrayal tasted like bitter ash in his mouth.

His mind flashed with images. Anna reading to Ethan with his son snuggled against her and her features soft and affectionate. The way her eyes lit up when he kissed her. Making love with her and the tenderness that wrapped around them like a blanket on a cold winter's day…

All a mirage. He couldn't believe he was so stupid about her. So very, very blind.

He jerked the vehicle in gear and backed out of her driveway, hitting the speed dial on his cell phone as he went.

"Hi, Mom," he said when Diane answered. "I need you to keep Ethan a little longer, if you can."

"Is anything wrong, dear?"

What the hell wasn't wrong? He was in love with a woman willing to sacrifice her family for her career.

"Just a few work complications. I've got to run to the hospital. I'm sorry."

"No problem," his mother answered. "We're having a great time, aren't we, kiddo?"

He could hear Ethan giggling in the background and the pure sound of it centered him. He loved his son. He might feel like his legs had just been ripped out from underneath him but he still had Ethan, his mom, his practice. He had to hold on to the good things in his life. There would be time to mourn his shattered illusions later.

Right now, he needed to find Peter Wilder.

Any more shocks in her life and she was going to need a good cardiologist.

Anna sat numbly in her living room after Richard

left. Lilli regarded her quizzically for a long moment then leapt onto her lap. Anna managed to yank herself out of her near-catatonia to pet the dog, while her mind continued to churn.

She felt like she was caught in the throes of a raging tornado for the past eighteen hours. The stunning news about her father, the outrageous discovery about NHC's plans for Walnut River General, making love with Richard and then being forced to face his bitter anger.

Lost somewhere in there had been his stunning declaration that he was in love with her.

I wouldn't want a little detail like the fact that I'm in love with you distract you from all that other important stuff in your life right now.

He couldn't be in love with her. Why would he possibly say such a thing? Still, she couldn't forget the emotion on his face the night before when he had held her, a certain light in his eyes as he kissed her.

I think you're a brilliant, capable, beautiful woman who doesn't see her own strengths. You don't see yourself as I do, as someone with the ability to cope with anything that comes along.

His words seemed etched in her memory, permanently imprinted there, just like the wild pulse of joy that had jumped inside her at his words, only to fade into shock a few moments later when he read that damn memo.

She buried her face in her hands. He couldn't love her. Not really. Obviously his feelings couldn't be very sure if he could tell her in one breath that he was in love with her, then believe her capable of betraying her own brother the next.

She remembered the disgust, the disillusionment in

his eyes and wanted to weep. She could have told him everything, that she had just read the memo herself and was as sickened by it as he. The temptation to do just that had been overwhelming.

But she had known even as she opened her mouth that she couldn't do it. Richard had no legal access to an internal NHC memo, just as she had reminded him. But somehow she had a feeling that wouldn't have stopped him from taking on NHC and its powerhouse attorneys singlehandedly and potentially endangering his own career.

She hadn't wanted him to take that risk. This was her mess and she was obligated to figure a way out of it herself. She wondered what Richard or her siblings would say if they knew she had been the one to bring Walnut General to the attention of her superiors at Northeastern HealthCare.

She had closed her eyes to some of the more questionable practices at NHC. Fury burned through her at her own negligence, her own gullibility. She should have known better. She should have remembered everything James Wilder tried to instill in his children. Things like character and strength and the awareness of greater good.

She had to fix this, and she had to do it on her own, no matter the cost to her job or her reputation.

She would probably face charges—or at least be sued. She had signed a nondisclosure clause when she took the job at NHC and whistle-blowing about an internal memo was in direct violation of what she had agreed to.

She was going to need a good attorney. Too bad she had just ensured the one man she trusted wanted nothing to do with her.

A sob welled up inside her but she choked it down. She had to keep it together. She had far too much to do right now to waste time sitting here feeling sorry for herself amid the wreckage of the life she had created for herself.

She picked up her cell phone and dialed Peter's number, programmed there just like Ella's and David's, though she hadn't used any of them for months.

At first, she was frustrated when she was sent directly to voice mail, but then relief flooded her at the temporary reprieve.

Eventually she would have to explain to her older brother how stupid she had been, but at least for now she could escape with only leaving a message.

"Peter, it's Anna." Her voice trailed off as she floundered for words. "Look, this is going to sound really strange but I have a feeling Richard Green will be trying to get in touch with you. When you hear what he has to say, I would…ask you to withhold judgment for now. I have no right to ask you that. To ask you anything, really. But… I promise, I have my reasons. Just don't rush to conclusions, okay?"

She hung up, feeling even more like an idiot. Would he think she was crazy or would he give her a chance to explain?

She drew in a deep fortifying breath, then picked up her phone again. She had to fix this, no matter what might happen to her as a result. For her family's sake—and for her own—she had to make things right.

Chapter 12

Richard headed immediately to the hospital, where to his relief he found Peter Wilder's vehicle in his assigned parking space.

After checking Peter's office and the cafeteria, he finally found the man on the fourth floor in the administrative boardroom—along with Ella, David and J. D. Sumner.

Ella looked lovely and competent in surgical scrubs, her dark hair held away from her face with a headband, while her brothers and fiancé wore casual clothes, fitting for a Saturday.

Papers were scattered across the table and they all looked deep in conversation.

He hated what he was about to do to the Wilder family.

Not his fault, he reminded himself. He had done nothing. Anna and the bastards she worked for had created all of this. Acknowledging that didn't make his task any easier, though.

They were so engrossed in conversation that none of them noticed his presence for several moments until Peter finally looked up.

"Richard! Come in. Just the man we need to talk to."

"Oh?" He felt vaguely queasy at their eager smiles.

"We've decided we're not just tossing a white flag up in the air and giving in to Northeastern HealthCare without a fight." Animation brightened Peter's features. "We need to come up with another plan for the municipal council to consider. A better alternative."

"Okay," he said slowly.

"What do you think of this? Walnut River wants out of the hospital business. Fine. I understand where they're coming from. With overhead and malpractice insurance costs through the roof, it's tough for public entities to stay viable in today's health-care market. We get it. But what if we could figure out a way to privatize the hospital without a takeover? If we could find local investors with the financial backing to purchase the hospital from the city?"

"That's a big *what if.*"

"Absolutely," David Wilder interjected. "But with just a few phone calls we've found several major players who are interested and I think we could get many of the local physicians to join up on a more limited basis."

"I really think we could make it work," Peter said. "This way the city would be out of the hospital business but decision-making control would still remain in local hands instead of some faceless corporate behemoth."

A corporate behemoth that intends to take you down.

Richard forced a smile. "Sounds like you've thought it through."

"We're just in the beginning stages." Ella beamed with excitement. "But we need to know what legal hoops we'd have to jump through. That's where you come in."

All three of the Wilders were humming with energy and he hated even more what he had to tell them about their sister. He, conversely, was suddenly exhausted. At the same time, he was filled with a fierce desire to do everything he possibly could to beat Northeastern HealthCare any freaking way possible.

"I'm in," he said promptly. "Whatever you need, I'll help you."

It was the least he could do, especially since they would soon be dealing with Anna's latest betrayal.

"I knew you would help us."

Ella smiled at him and for the first time Richard saw a trace of Anna in her smile. How had he missed the resemblance all these years? Was it simply because he had been acting on the assumption that Anna was adopted and hadn't been looking for it?

What else had he missed about Anna Wilder? he wondered.

"So what brings you here on a Saturday afternoon? Was there something you needed?" Peter asked.

Richard could feel his shoulders tense and he forced himself to relax as much as possible. "I need to speak with you," he finally said. "It's about Anna."

"What about her?" Ella asked, and Richard didn't miss her sudden tension or the disgust dragging down the corners of David's mouth or Peter's weary resignation. Only J.D. looked impartial, but Richard was quite confident that would quickly change.

"Perhaps this would be better in private."

"He'll only tell us what you said after you leave," Ella said.

"Not necessarily," Peter murmured, exchanging a look with Richard.

"You can use my office if you need a place to talk," J.D. offered.

"Thanks," Richard said, then led the way down the hall to the administrator's office.

"What's going on?" Peter asked when Richard closed the door behind the two of them.

Richard let out a long weary breath. This was a miserable thing to have to dump on a man as conscientious and upright as Peter Wilder. "I hate to be the one to tell you this, but you need to know what Northeastern HealthCare is planning."

He briefly outlined the memo he had inadvertently read, including their underhanded strategy to defeat the opposition by taking Peter out through any means necessary.

When he finished, Peter's features were taut with fury. "Sexual misconduct allegations? Malpractice?"

He paused and seemed at a loss for words. "What the hell kind of people does Anna work with?" he finally said.

"We knew they would fight hard and possibly fight dirty to obtain such a potentially lucrative hospital."

"Yes, but I never expected something so underhanded. And you're telling me Anna knew about the memo? About what they planned?"

He hated every moment of this. "I'm sorry. I found it at her place. She told me to stay out of it. That it wasn't any of my business."

Peter raked a hand through his hair, his eyes dark with betrayal. "She called while I was talking to a potential investor earlier but I haven't had time to check my messages."

"I have no proof, Pete. Only what I saw. I couldn't take it from her house since I didn't have any legal right to access the corporation's internal documents. It would have been theft."

"Even if it was there in plain sight?"

"It wasn't. Not really. I wouldn't have even seen it except some papers fell when we were…" Fighting. Kissing. What the hell difference did it make? He caught himself just in time from offering either answer. "When we were talking. I went to pick them up and saw the memo."

"My own sister is willing to throw me to the wolves. How could she be a party to such a thing?"

"I can't answer that," Richard answered.

"I thought after last night, maybe we could manage to salvage some relationship with her. Things seemed… different with her after she read the letter."

"I'm sorry." It was painfully inadequate but he had nothing else to offer.

"This is going to kill Ella. As angry as she's been at Anna, she still misses her sister, especially with all the weddings coming up in the family."

"You have to tell them."

Peter nodded, not looking at all thrilled at the prospect. "If we have no proof of what they're planning, how can we fight it?"

"You're getting married in a week. Any chance you might be willing to take a little personal time, reschedule your appointments, to stay away from the hospital?

If you're not seeing patients, they can't entrap you, either through malpractice allegations or anything else."

"I'm not running and hiding! That's not the way my father would handle this and it's not the way I will, either."

He expected exactly that answer. Richard sighed. "I have a few other ideas. None of them easy."

"I don't care," Peter snapped. "I am not going to let them win, no matter what it takes."

Saturday afternoon at Walnut River General brought back a world of memories for Anna: the light slanting through the front doors, the smell inside of cafeteria food, the underlying hint of antiseptic and antibiotics, and the slightly quieter pace.

How many Saturdays of her youth had been spent here waiting for her father while he wrapped up just one more bit of paperwork or attended to one more patient?

Her memories seemed so rich and fresh as she stood in the lobby that she almost expected him to come striding through the halls of the hospital, his stethoscope around his neck, his white coat flapping behind him and that steely determination in his blue eyes.

Oh, she missed her father.

The last eight years had been so strained between them that she couldn't think of him at all without this hollow ache of regret inside her. So much wasted time. She would have given anything if her father had once communicated in person the things he'd written in that letter about being proud of her and supporting her career choices.

Instead, she had always felt the bitter sting of knowing she had disappointed him.

She pushed the familiar pain away and approached the security guard seated behind the information desk.

"I'm looking for my brother, Dr. Peter Wilder. He wasn't at home and his car is parked in his parking space out front. Can you give me some idea where I might be able to find him?"

"Don't know. Sorry."

His expression was cool, bordering on hostile, and she sighed. She had never met this man in her life. The only reason she could think for his pugnacity was that he belonged to the anti-merger camp and knew she worked for NHC.

She didn't have time to play hospital politics. Not today.

"Would you page him for me, then?" she asked briskly.

He went on reading his newspaper as if he hadn't heard her and she nearly growled with frustration.

"It's important," she finally said. "A family emergency."

Though he hesitated, she could see the wheels in his head turning as he wondered whether he might be incurring Peter's wrath by delaying. Finally he picked up the phone and punched in Peter's pager number.

She drummed her fingers on the counter, impatient for her brother to return the page. She was still waiting a few moments later when the elevator doors opened and the absolute last person she wanted to see right now—okay, last five, at least—walked out.

Ella's eyes were swollen and her nose was red, as if she had been crying. Anna had just a moment's advantage since Ella was busy digging through the messenger bag slung diagonally over her shoulder and didn't see her immediately.

Her sister pulled out her cell phone and started to punch in a number when her gaze suddenly caught sight of Anna and her fingers froze on the phone.

Anna was grateful for the tiny window of opportunity she'd had to prepare herself for the coming confrontation. Otherwise, she was certain Ella's vicious stare would have destroyed her on the spot.

In some corner of her mind, she knew her imagination was running in overdrive but suddenly the previously empty foyer seemed filled with people, all of their attention focused on the two sisters.

Every warning bell inside her was clanging, warning her to escape, that she didn't need this right now. But she couldn't do it. Though it was one of the hardest things she'd ever done, she forced herself to step forward, until she was only a few feet away.

"Ella," she murmured, aching inside, wishing she could make everything right again. After that one word, she had no idea what else to say, but her sister didn't give her a chance, anyway.

Ella glared at her. "If we were kids again, I'd be ripping your hair out right now. Literally. Hank by painful hank, until your eyes watered so much you couldn't see."

Under less dire circumstances, Anna might have smiled at the threat and the way Ella's hands fisted on her messenger bag. She wouldn't have put anything past her feisty little sister. Ella might have been the youngest Wilder but she had always been able to hold her own with the rest of them.

Suddenly Anna missed her sister and the closeness they had once shared, with a fierce hollow yearning. She missed late-night gab sessions and shopping trips to the mall and fighting over their shared bathroom.

While Anna was trying so hard to prove herself, her sister had become a beautiful dedicated physician and she had missed the whole process because of her foolishness.

"Don't believe everything you hear, El."

"Are you calling Richard Green a liar? He knows what he saw in that memo and I believe every word he says."

Anna closed her eyes, hurt all over again that Richard had so quickly allied himself with her siblings against her, that he trusted her integrity so little.

With good reason, she reminded herself. She couldn't blame him for this. She had created the mess through her own stupidity and it was up to her to make it right.

The magnitude of the task ahead of her seemed daunting, terrifying, but she had to do it, for her family's sake and for her own.

"I would never call Richard a liar. He saw exactly what he said he saw."

"So you admit it!" If anything, the shadows under Ella's eyes looked darker, almost bruised. "You're part of Northeastern HealthCare's dirty tactics to destroy Peter's reputation! How could you, Anna?"

"I didn't know about the memo, El."

"That's easy to say now that we know about it."

She couldn't argue with Ella. Nothing she said would convince her sister, and in the meantime, she was wasting valuable time.

"I'm not going to stand here in the hospital foyer and have a shouting match with you. You'll believe what you want to believe. Nothing I say will make any difference."

Ella's mouth drooped and she looked as if she might cry again. "What happened to you, Anna? The sister I loved so much would never have been a party to something like this."

Ella's use of the past tense sent a shaft of pain through her but Anna fought it down. She deserved all of this. How could she blame Ella for thinking the worst of her when she had purposely created so much distance between them that Ella had nothing else to judge her by?

"Can you tell me where to find Peter?"

"Why? Have you come to twist the knife a little harder?"

She sighed. "Where is he, El?"

She thought for a moment her sister wasn't going to answer but then she shrugged. "He's in his office with Richard. They're working on strategy."

Great. Not only did she have to face her livid brother but now she had to see Richard again. This was shaping up to be one fabulous day.

"None of us will let you do this to him, Anna," Ella said, her voice fierce and determined. "You need to know that. Whatever friends Northeastern HealthCare has in this hospital won't be on your side for long when word leaks out about these dirty tactics. The entire hospital will mobilize to protect Peter before we let you destroy him."

"Fair enough," Anna murmured.

Knowing any further arguments with Ella were futile and would only deepen the chasm between them, she turned away and headed for the elevator.

As she rode up to the fourth floor, she realized Peter had kept his part of the bargain from the night before. She was certain of it. He was still leaving the choice of telling David and Ella about their father's letter up to Anna. If she had learned about James's indiscretion that had resulted in Anna's conception, Ella would have said something. She would have at least looked at her a little differently.

The last thing any of them probably wanted right now was a closer kinship with her.

The door to Peter's office suite was closed and her hands trembled as she reached to open it.

Forget this and go home.

The thought whispered through her mind and for an instant, she was deeply tempted. Seeing the disillusionment in her brother's eyes would be hard enough. Seeing it all over again in Richard's and knowing she had lost his love forever would be unbearable.

She stood for a long moment, trying to bolster her courage. She had no idea what she would say to Peter but she had to attempt some kind of explanation.

Finally she knocked on the door before she could talk herself out of it.

"Yeah," Peter said gruffly and she took that as all the invitation she was likely to receive.

She pushed the door open and nearly wept with relief to find her brother alone in his office.

"Where's Richard? Ella said he was up here with you." It was the first thing she could think of to say but Peter didn't seem to think it was an odd opening volley.

"He had to leave to pick up Ethan. His son."

"I know who Ethan is. He's a great kid."

She was stalling. She recognized it but this was so excruciatingly hard with Peter watching her out of those eyes that reminded her so much of their father's.

"I guess you're probably surprised to see me."

He shrugged. "I wouldn't have expected you to show your face around here right about now. It's a good thing David had to meet Courtney and Janie downtown or you wouldn't have made it this far."

She laughed bitterly. "Ella threatened to yank my hair out down in the lobby."

"What did you expect?"

The hard edge to his expression made her want to flee but she hardened her resolve and clasped her hands together in her lap.

"I didn't know about the memo, Peter. I swear I didn't. I know you have no reason to believe me, but it's the truth. I found it just minutes before Richard arrived. It was top secret and on a private server I shouldn't have had access to, but my boss gave me his password to upload some documents regarding the merger and it was just…there. I made a backup copy of it for my files and printed it out and was trying to figure out what to do when Richard showed up and saw it."

He was quiet for a long moment, studying her features intently. "And what did you decide to do?" he finally asked, his voice so controlled she couldn't begin to guess whether he believed her or not.

She lifted her chin. "I'm a Wilder. Of course I'm going to do the right thing!"

He smiled with such sudden brilliance she felt a little lightheaded. "Of course you're going to do the right thing."

His certainty washed through her, warm and soothing. He believed her. The rest of the world might think she was a sleazy, sneaky corporate mole but Peter believed her.

To her chagrin, her eyes burned with emotion and a single tear escaped to trickle down her face.

"I'm sorry. I just… I thought you would be as convinced as everyone else that I intended all this from the start."

Peter stepped forward and pulled her into a quick hug. "Richard put forward a convincing argument. But some part of me still couldn't quite believe it."

She leaned against him for only a moment while she struggled to regain her composure.

"I've been a fool. There were other warning signs of NHC's more questionable business practices among the top level of brass but I ignored them. My other boss is a good decent man, so I convinced myself I was imagining things. I was on the fast track there and I convinced myself they were harmless and that I could make a difference when I moved up in management. I never expected these sorts of underhanded tactics, especially not against my own brother. I should have, though. If they make good on any of the strategies outlined in the memo, I'll never forgive myself."

"We're not going to let them get away with it, Anna."

"Neither am I," she said grimly. "It's going to take me some time, though. For a few days, it may seem as if things are continuing normally with the merger negotiations and the board vote Thursday. I know I've given you absolutely no reason, but I have to ask you to trust me, just for a few days."

"Okay."

Just like that.

His faith made her want to weep again but she drew herself together. "In the meantime, listen to Richard.

He can help you protect yourself against whatever Alfred Daly and his cohorts might have up their sleeves."

"He wants me to take this week off before the wedding."

"Not a bad idea."

"I won't run. Dad wouldn't have."

She smiled, sensing a ray of light for the first time since she opened that file on Daly's server earlier that day. "No, he wouldn't have."

"You're more like him than you've ever given yourself credit for," Peter said.

"Not yet," she answered with a shaky smile. "But I'm getting there."

Chapter 13

"Hurry up or we're going to be late, Ethan. Where's your baseball glove?"

"Don't know." His son remained remarkably unconcerned that his last T-ball game was supposed to start in forty-five minutes as he continued playing with his Matchbox cars.

Richard drew in a deep breath. Trying for patience was just about the toughest task he faced as a father—especially since Ethan was easily distracted and usually bubbled over with energy.

The process of encouraging him to stay on task was tougher than facing a whole courtroom full of high-powered attorneys.

"Think. Where did you have it last?"

Ethan zoomed one of his trucks along the edge of the carpet where it met the hardwood flooring. "Outside, I guess. Me and Grandma played catch earlier today. I think maybe I left it there."

"So go look for it, or we're not going to make it to your game."

His snappish tone finally captured Ethan's attention. He dropped his car and gave his father a wounded look. "We have to go! It's my last game!"

"Then go find your glove."

Ethan glared at him but headed for the backyard in search of the missing equipment, leaving Richard with only his guilt for company.

He needed to practice a little more patience with his son. His bad mood wasn't Ethan's fault. Richard knew exactly why he had been irritable and out of sorts for the past four days.

Anna Wilder.

He hadn't seen her since Saturday morning at her duplex but she hadn't been far from his thoughts. He had done his best to push away the memory of making love to her but sometimes random images intruded into his mind, usually at the most inopportune moment.

Despite that little glitch, for the most part his whole world had condensed to two clear objectives—protecting Peter Wilder and beating the hell out of NHC in the merger negotiations. Everything he did was aimed at those goals.

So far, Peter appeared to be safe. No malpractice allegations or harassment claims had emerged out of the woodwork. Since the hospital board vote was scheduled for first thing in the morning, he had to look at the relative quiet as a positive indicator that NHC had reconsidered the strategies outlined in that damn memo.

He wasn't letting down his guard, though, and he wasn't allowing Peter to do so, either. He had been fiercely busy wrapping Anna's brother in as many legal safeguards as he could devise.

To his further frustration, Peter seemed remarkably unconcerned about any possible threat to his reputation or his practice, until Richard wanted to shake him out of his complacency.

"See, Dad? I found it! I told you it was in the backyard."

Ethan still looked annoyed at him for the flare of temper so Richard forced himself to smile. "Good job. We'd better get going."

On the way out to the SUV, he closed his eyes and arched his neck one way and then the other, trying to force his shoulders to relax. He couldn't take his grim mood out on his son. Ethan didn't deserve it. The one person who did deserve it was making herself remarkably scarce.

Ethan jabbered all the way to the park where he played T-ball. When they were a few blocks from the baseball field, he suddenly stopped in the middle of a soliloquy about the playdate he had enjoyed with a friend that afternoon.

"Hey, Dad, Anna said she would come to another one of my games. She promised, remember, the night she read me the funny story about the worm and the spider? This is my last one. Do you think she'll be there?"

Apparently, Richard wasn't the only one who couldn't stop thinking about a certain lovely blond double-crosser.

"Anna's really busy right now," he murmured. *Destroying the hospital her father dedicated his life to, and her family in the process.* "She might not make it."

"She promised," Ethan said, his voice brimming with

confidence. "I wonder if she'll bring Lilli. Do you think she'll let me walk her again? I sure like that dog."

He so hated that his son had to learn the lesson early in life that some people couldn't be trusted to remember things like honor and decency and promises made. He wanted Ethan to hang on to his illusions for a little bit longer.

"We'll have to see what happens. Like I said, Anna is really busy right now."

But to his shock, when they arrived at the ball diamond, she was the first person he saw. She sat on the top bench of the bleachers, looking sleek and elegant even in Levi's and a crisp white shirt.

At the sight of her, his heart gave a slow surge of welcome and his body tightened with longing. How was it that when he was away from her, he always managed to forget how her long blond loveliness took his breath away?

"She's here! I knew she would come. Do you see her, Dad?"

"I see her," he answered, his voice gruff. Fast on the heels of his initial pleasure at seeing her was hot hard anger that racketed through him like a pinball.

Why the hell couldn't she leave him alone? This was hard enough for him, knowing how stupid he had been for her.

Even knowing what she was, what she was part of, he couldn't keep himself from wanting her.

"I'm gonna show her how good I am at catching the ball now." Ethan raced ahead of him and climbed like a little howler monkey up the bleachers to talk to Anna. Richard was grateful for the few minutes to gain control of the wild surge of emotions. By the time he reached them, the careening emotions inside him had faded to a dull ache instead of that terrible, piercing pain.

Her blue eyes held wariness and something else—something elusive and tantalizing that he couldn't quite identify.

"Hi." She pitched her voice low.

He nodded, but didn't quite trust himself not to yell at her all over again so he said nothing.

"I promised I would be here," she said. "I didn't want to let Ethan down."

She was willing to crucify her own brother but she didn't want to break a promise to a five-year-old boy? He gave her a skeptical look and she had the grace to flush.

"Where's Lilli?" Ethan asked. "Did you bring her?"

"Not tonight. She hasn't been feeling good the last couple of days. I think she has a cold."

"Dogs get colds?"

"Sometimes. Or maybe it's just allergies."

He looked disappointed for about half a second, then with rapid-fire speed, his mood cycled back to excitement. "Hey, guess what, Anna? Me and my grandma played catch all day today and now I'm super good. I won't miss another fly ball, ever again. Wanna see?"

"Absolutely. Bring it on."

She gripped Ethan's hand and climbed down from the bleachers, smiling at his son with such genuine pleasure that Richard felt as if his heart were being ripped into tiny pieces.

Ethan grinned back and shoved the ball at Richard. "Dad, can you throw it at me so I can show Anna how good I catch?"

"Sure. Let's step away from the bleachers a little so we don't hit anybody if we miss the ball."

"I'm not going to miss, Dad. I told you, I've been practicing."

"It's not you I'm worried about, it's me. I don't even have a glove."

"I won't throw hard, okay?"

Still doing his best not to look at her, he led Ethan to an open stretch of ground between two playing fields. He tossed the ball to his son and was pleased when Ethan easily caught it in his glove.

"Good job!" Anna exclaimed. "You have been practicing."

"Yep. Now watch me throw it back!" He tossed it back to Richard, harder than he expected and a little to the right. Richard managed to snag it with his bare hands, but it was a near thing.

Anna stood watching them both play catch for several minutes, her features revealing little of her thoughts, until Ethan's coach blew a whistle to call his team into the dugout.

Ethan ran off eagerly, leaving Richard alone with her—exactly the position he didn't want to find himself.

They made their way back toward the bleachers in silence. Just before they reached them, Anna touched the bare skin of his forearm to stop him. She dropped her hand quickly but not before the heat of her fingers scorched through him.

"I'm sorry. I'm sure you're wishing me to Hades right about now. But I did promise Ethan."

"I wouldn't want you to break a promise."

That delicate flush coated her cheekbones and he wondered at it. How could she possibly still have the ability to blush?

"Have you talked to Peter?" she asked after a moment.

"Several times. He seems remarkably nonchalant for a man whose sister is trying to destroy him."

"Has anything…happened?"

"You tell me. You're the one with all the inside information."

Her jaw clenched at his bitter tone. "You're going to believe what you want to believe."

"No. I'm going to believe the evidence. I'm an attorney. That's what we do."

"Maybe the evidence isn't as cut-and-dried as you think."

He opened his mouth to offer a scathing rebuke but she cut him off with a shake of her head.

"I didn't come here to fight with you, Richard. I also didn't want to spoil the game for you. I'll just watch an inning or two and then get out of your way. You'll hardly know I'm here."

He was saved from having to respond by Ethan's team taking the field.

The park had two sets of bleachers and she at least had the courtesy to sit on the other bleachers, several dozen feet away from him. That didn't stop his gaze from drifting in her direction entirely too often.

He knew it was crazy but he could almost smell her from here, that feminine, sexy scent of hers.

He didn't miss the way she stood up and cheered when Ethan caught a fly ball to end the inning half and then again a few minutes later when his son hit a two-run single. When his son crossed home plate, sent home by another player's hit, Richard also didn't miss the way Ethan grinned triumphantly first at his father then turned to aim the same grin at Anna.

Damn her. His heart was already shattered. Did she have to do the same thing to his son's?

She lasted all of an inning and a half—long enough to watch Ethan hit another single—before she couldn't bear another minute.

As she slid down the bleachers, the sun was just dipping below the horizon, bathing the baseball diamond in the pale rosy light of dusk. She closed her eyes, wanting to store up this moment.

It had been foolish to come. Foolish and self-indulgent. She had hoped four days of reflection would have had some kind of impact on Richard, that perhaps he might begin to experience a little doubt about her guilt.

She supposed some optimistic corner of her heart had hoped he'd begun to wonder if he might have been wrong about her.

Obviously, that hadn't happened. He was as angry as he had been Saturday morning when he had seen that memo. More so, maybe. Hearing the bitterness in his voice, seeing the cold disdain in those eyes that had once looked at her with such warm tenderness, had been chilling proof that nothing had changed.

She walked back to her car with one hand curled against the crushing pain in her chest.

Nothing had changed and everything had changed. The wheels she had set in motion couldn't be stopped now.

Now she just had to wait and see what happened.

Richard walked into the hospital the next morning in his best suit and his favorite power tie. He had slept little the night before. After tossing and turning for a couple of hours, he had finally risen well before dawn.

He wanted to think it was diligence to his client that kept him up and not his last glimpse of Anna as she had left the baseball diamond. Unfortunately, he knew otherwise.

He was totally committed to representing the hospital to the best of his ability but the images haunting his fragmented dreams hadn't had anything to do with the hospital. They had everything to do with Anna.

He wanted this hospital board meeting to be over. Though the merger vote was still too close to call, at this point he just wanted a damn decision. Then maybe this sense of impending doom would dissipate. At least Peter would be safe—and maybe Anna would return to New York where she belonged and he wouldn't have to spend a sleepless night every time he happened to bump into her.

He would probably see her this morning at the board meeting. Twisted as he was, he couldn't help the little buzz of anticipation at the prospect.

He sighed as he walked through the lobby. The security guard waved and grinned at him. Richard managed a half-hearted wave, then furrowed his brow when three more staff members beamed at him on his way to the elevator.

Weird.

Though he usually didn't buy into those woo-woo kind of things, he sensed a curious energy in the air. The impression was reinforced when he rode the elevator with Bob Barrett, a physician he knew only casually. The man actually patted him on the back when the elevator stopped at the second floor.

"It's a great day for Walnut River General, isn't it?" he said, before stepping out.

Something definitely odd was going on. He couldn't begin to figure out what.

The first person he met coming out of the elevator on the administrative floor was Ella Wilder. She aimed a thousand-watt smile at him, then went one better, throwing her arms around him.

"Isn't it wonderful?" she exclaimed. "The best news I can imagine. Peter and Bethany's wedding this weekend will truly be a celebration."

Before he could ask her what the hell she was talking about, she released him and jumped into the waiting elevator just before the doors closed, leaving him completely befuddled.

He headed to J.D.'s office, hoping Ella's fiancé could shed a little light on things.

J.D. wasn't alone. Peter Wilder stood in the outer office with him and his assistant, Tina Tremaine, and all of them looked jubilant.

"I knew she would come through for us," Peter exulted when he saw Richard. "She's a Wilder, isn't she?"

He frowned. "Who? Ella?"

"Of course not. Anna!" He grinned at Richard but his smile faded when he took in his confusion. "I'm guessing you haven't read the paper this morning."

"I didn't have a chance. I was too busy prepping for this morning's board meeting." And brooding about Peter's sister. "Why? What did I miss?"

J.D. and Peter exchanged laughing looks. "Maybe you'd better come into my office and see for yourself," J.D. said. "My staff made sure I received a copy."

He opened the door behind him and Richard was

stunned to see every available surface covered with the front page of the *Walnut River Courier.*

The same headline in huge type screamed from all of them: Northeastern HealthCare Drops Hospital Bid.

A subhead read: Municipal Council Considering Options, May Look to Private Investors.

He stared at the headline and then at both men. "They're pulling out? After six months of fighting? Just like that?"

Peter laughed. "No. Not just like that. My brilliant baby sister did it all. In five days, she managed to accomplish what the rest of us have been trying to pull off for months."

He shook his head to clear the fuzziness out, wishing all over again that he'd been able to grab more than a few hours of restless sleep. He grabbed one of the newspapers off the wall and read the first few paragraphs, stopping when he reached the statement released by NHC.

He read,

> Upon further study, we have determined that Walnut River General would not be a good fit for NHC. We regret that we will not have the opportunity to bring our winning health-care model to the citizens of Walnut River but wish the community and hospital personnel all the best.

It was definitely a blow-off quote, leaving NHC very little room to reconsider.

"I'm sorry. I'm lost here. You're going to have to back up a step or two for me. What is this? Why did they pull out? And why do you seem to think Anna had anything to do with it? Last I heard, she was the enemy. What about the infamous memo?"

"That memo is the best thing that's ever happened to the merger opposition," J.D. answered.

"How can that be possible?" he growled.

"Because finding it infuriated Anna and mobilized her to our side," Peter answered.

"What do you mean, finding it? She knew about it all along."

Peter shook his head. "No, she didn't."

"So she says." He couldn't keep the bitterness out of his voice, the deep sense of betrayal.

Peter frowned and gestured to the newspaper headlines blaring across the room. "This is evidence she's telling the truth. Do you really think NHC would have dropped their bid for the hospital if Anna hadn't maneuvered things so they had no other choice?"

"How?"

"She's brilliant," J.D. said. "Savvy and smart. She single-handedly orchestrated what amounts to an internal coup to force them out."

"She knew there was an anti-Daly faction at NHC, shareholders and other top-level executives who weren't happy with some of his tactics," Peter added. "Anna has been working like a demon for the last four days, negotiating with them. She agreed to deliver the memo as evidence against Daly to force him out if they would consent to drop their bid for the hospital. It all hit the fan yesterday. Daly's out at Northeastern HealthCare, a new guard is in and their first action was to issue the statement withdrawing their bid for the hospital, as promised."

Richard felt as if J.D. and Peter had both taken turns pummeling him with an office chair.

He tried to remember Anna's demeanor Saturday morning when he read the memo at her apartment. She had been shaky and uneasy, he remembered. Pale, nervous, edgy. But he had just attributed it to guilt that he had found out about NHC's nefarious plans for Peter.

Was it possible she hadn't known? When she had faced all his accusations, could she have been withholding evidence that would have exonerated her?

He couldn't seem to wrap his head around it. He had been hard, bordering on cruel. *You're a cold heartless woman who is willing to sell your own family down the river to get your way.*

Those had been his words. And she had stood there absorbing them. Why the hell hadn't she tried to defend herself? She had stood there and let him rip into her without saying a thing.

Not quite true, he remembered with growing self-disgust. She had told him he was jumping to unfounded conclusions. She had asked him to give her a few days to straighten things out but he had assumed she was only trying to delay him from taking action until after the vote.

Just last night, she had told him that maybe the evidence wasn't as cut-and-dried as he wanted to believe.

She had skirted the truth but hadn't told him all of it.

She hadn't trusted him. That's what it all came down to. She had taken his criticism without explaining anything at all of substance to him.

And he deserved her lack of trust. He had jumped to conclusions, had based his entire perceptions of her guilt and innocence on past misdeeds that should have been inadmissible.

Because of what happened eight years before, he had been completely unwilling to give her any benefit of doubt. When he saw that memo, he had taken it as damning evidence against her—proof of her perfidy, he now realized, that he had been looking for all along.

Even if she had tried to defend herself a little more strenuously, he wasn't sure he would have allowed himself to believe her.

He had told her he loved her.

It hadn't been a lie, exactly. He did love her. But love without trust was flimsy and hollow.

"So obviously the board vote this morning has been canceled," Peter interrupted his thoughts. "We're moving ahead with our efforts to privatize the hospital. Is your firm still willing to help us through the legalities?"

"Of course," he answered absently.

"Excellent," J.D. said. "We'd like you to draw up a preliminary partnership agreement as soon as possible so we can present it to the city council. I know this is an imposition, but can you work up a rough draft today?"

"No problem. I allocated most of the day to hospital business, with the merger vote and possible follow-up work. I can have it to you by this afternoon."

"Thanks, Richard," Peter said. "I knew we could count on you."

The other man's words scraped his conscience raw. Anna should have been able to count on him, on the man who claimed he loved her. He should have trusted his own heart, not a stupid piece of paper. Instead, Richard had rushed to convict her without any kind of trial.

He would be lucky if she ever wanted to see him again.

Chapter 14

"We're serious about this, Anna. We want you to stay."

Anna watched Lilli chase her favorite toy, wondering why she couldn't manage to drum up a little more enthusiasm for Wallace Jeffers's unbelievable offer. He wanted her to take over his position as vice president of the mergers and acquisitions division of NHC since he was poised to move into Alfred Daly's newly vacated spot.

This was what she had dreamed about for eight years. Wallace had been her mentor at NHC, the reason she had taken the job there in the first place. He had been one of those at the company who predicted a great future for her there and now that he was taking over for Daly, he appeared to be willing to make those predictions reality.

She should be over the moon. She should be doing

cartwheels, sending notice to all the trade papers, ordering new business cards.

Instead, she sat in her rented duplex, watching her dog drool all over a rubber lizard and trying to summon a little excitement. "I appreciate your trust in me, Wallace. I do. But I'm going to have to think about this."

"What's to think about?" He sounded genuinely startled. "It's a no-brainer, Anna. If you take this job, you'll be completely skipping over several rungs in the corporate ladder."

"I know that. It's an incredible offer and I'm grateful. I just need a little time to think about it."

"We need to move fast to reorganize the company if we want to enact the kind of changes some of us have been pushing for a long time. I'm going to need an answer sooner rather than later."

"Can I at least have a few hours?"

She had been thinking for five days that she was going to lose her job and now she was being offered the promotion of her dreams. It was enough to make her head spin.

He sighed. "I want you on board, Anna. Without you having the guts to come forward with that memo we used to push Daly out, none of this would have happened. I want people of integrity and grit on my team. You've earned this promotion. No one in that department works harder than you do or gets my vision more clearly."

She had nothing but respect for Wallace Jeffers and knew that under his leadership, NHC would thrive. She was deeply flattered that he had enough faith in her to believe her capable of replacing him. She ought to just say yes right now and start packing her bags to return to New York, but the words seemed to clog in her throat.

"I appreciate your offer. I'm just… I have to consider my options right now."

"What options?" His voice sharpened. "Have you got another offer I don't know about?"

"No," she assured him. "Nothing like that."

"Then what?"

My heart is here.

She couldn't say the words, not to her boss, a man she respected professionally and personally.

"Give me a few hours, Wallace. I'll call you back by the end of the day, I promise."

"All right. Just make sure you give yourself enough time to pack up and be back here for an 8 a.m. staff meeting so I can introduce the new leadership team of Northeastern HealthCare."

She managed a laugh. "You're so confident I'll say yes?"

"You'd be stupid not to take this promotion, and you are far from a stupid woman, Anna."

Wrong, she thought sadly. She was stupid. A smart woman would walk away from Walnut River and not look back. But these past few weeks had shown her how deeply her life and the person she had become were intertwined with this community and the people who lived here.

She wasn't sure she was ready to leave.

What was her alternative, though? Jobs in her field weren't exactly thick on the ground in Walnut River. And even if she found one, what would she gain by staying? Only more heartache, she was certain.

She sighed. Why delay the inevitable? She couldn't turn down Wallace's offer. She should just pick up the phone right now and tell him yes. What did Walnut River have to offer her?

She even picked up her cell phone, nerves strumming through her, but Lilli suddenly barked with excitement and raced to the door and Anna's hand froze on the numbers.

Richard?

Her heart jumped along with her little dog as the doorbell rang.

It wouldn't be, she told herself, though she couldn't help the little spasm of hope that faded when she opened the door. Instead of Richard Green, she was instantly assaulted by her entire family. Peter, David, Ella and their significant others—Bethany Holloway, J. D. Sumner and a lovely brown-eyed blonde she assumed was David's fiancée, Courtney Albright.

"There's my baby sister," David announced before she could even greet them.

She opened her mouth to answer but the words were snatched away when he scooped her into his arms and twirled her around her miniscule living room until her head spun while Lilli yipped and danced around their ankles.

"David," she exclaimed. "Put me down before you either step on my dog or make me puke."

"You're still motion sick? I would have thought you outgrew that years ago."

"Not completely," she said as her stomach churned.

"Ew," he said, releasing her so abruptly she almost fell.

Peter was there to catch her, though. Before she could even find her breath, he pulled her into his arms, enveloping her in a tight hug.

"You didn't let us down, Anna."

His voice sounded so much like their father's. "I knew you could do it. If anyone could save Walnut River General Hospital, I knew it would be you. You were amazing. Absolutely amazing."

She allowed herself one quick moment to bask in the warm glow of her siblings' approval before she pulled away. She had to tell them the truth, the one she had been withholding from them for months.

"You know my company wouldn't have even looked at Walnut River General if not for me, don't you? I'm the one who proposed the hospital as a possible acquisition target in the first place."

Peter made a face. "Okay, so you're not completely perfect. But we're still keeping you."

She almost cried then, holding her tears in by sheer force of will as Peter gave her another tight hug then released her.

"My turn," Ella said, stepping forward.

Anna stared at her little sister, overwhelmed, for just a second too long. Ella's expression started to cool, her arms to drop, and Anna's tears broke free.

"El," she murmured, just that, then grabbed her sister tightly.

For so long she had lived with a hole in her heart without even realizing it. She had tried to fill it with work, never realizing it would always be empty until she made her peace with her family.

Now she stood and rocked with her arms around her sister, the tears trickling down her cheeks.

"I have missed you so much," Ella said.

"I'm sorry. I'm so sorry."

"No. I'm the one who's sorry. I said awful things to you."

"I deserved them. All of them. I've been so stupid. Incredibly stupid. When I dropped out of med school, I was sure I had failed everyone. I thought I had to choose between my career and my family. If I wasn't in medicine, I felt like I didn't belong with the rest of you."

"You do," Ella exclaimed. "Of course you do. You always have."

Anna saw that now. She was a Wilder. It didn't matter whether she was their half sister or their adopted sister. Either way, she belonged in this family. She loved them and needed them in her life and she had been so very foolish to believe she could take on the world by herself.

"You're our sister and we love you," Ella said. "We have all missed you."

"Oh, Ella." She sniffled again.

Sometime soon she would tell Ella and David about the letter from their father but not today, she decided.

"Cut it out, you two," David interrupted. "This is supposed to be a party. A celebration of good triumphing over evil. No offense, Anna."

She couldn't help but laugh. "Oh, none taken, I'm sure."

"We even have champagne," Bethany interjected.

"And food," the other woman added. "Hi. I'm Courtney. I'm thrilled to finally meet you. You have to come to dinner sometime soon so you can meet my little girl, Janie. She's thrilled at the prospect of another aunt to add to her growing family."

To Anna's surprise, David's fiancée gave her a warm hug, as did Bethany and even J.D.

"You can't get away from them all now," J.D. murmured in her ear. "You Wilders are relentless. You had your chance to escape but now you're stuck."

Anna had been alone for so long that the prospect of all this family was daunting but wonderful at the same time.

She looked around at her siblings and their loved ones and she had to laugh. "I just have one question. If you're all here, who's left to run the hospital?"

"Nobody. We closed down so we could come and celebrate with you," David deadpanned.

"I've actually got to go back on in an hour," Ella said. "So I'm afraid I'll have to skip the champagne."

"Ha. I'm off rotation for five whole days," David boasted.

"Lucky," Ella muttered.

"Just wait. When you're an attending, you'll be able to flaunt it over all the lowly residents, too," he said with a grin.

Anna smiled at their banter. Once she would have felt excluded when the rest of the Wilders talked shop. It used to bug the heck out of her and she would always bite down frustration when family discussions inevitably turned to medicine. Now she realized her annoyance had been a result of her own insecurities.

If she hadn't wanted to talk medicine, all she would have had to do was change the subject instead of simmering in her separateness.

"Bring on the champagne," Peter said, distracting her from her thoughts.

"I'm afraid I don't have enough glasses."

"No problem." Bethany grinned. "We brought our own. Courtney thought of everything."

Out of a wicker basket, they pulled out plastic champagne flutes along with cheese, crackers, several boxes of gourmet cookies and even Godiva chocolates.

"I raided everything I could think of from the gift shop," Courtney said with a warm smile.

She and Bethany poured champagne for everyone except Ella, who filled her glass with water.

"To Anna," J.D. said and she flushed as everyone lifted their glasses to her.

"And may I add," he continued, "I find it slightly ironic that the one Wilder who chose a different path than medicine is the one who ended up saving an entire hospital."

"Hear, hear," Peter said, squeezing her arm.

The next hour would live forever in her memory. As she moved around her tiny apartment talking to first one sibling, then the next—and all three of her prospective in-laws—Anna felt eight years of loneliness begin to heal.

"You're coming to the wedding, of course," Bethany proclaimed. "I'm not taking any other answer but an enthusiastic yes."

"Of course," Anna said with a smile. "I wouldn't miss it."

It would be somewhat humiliating to show up alone when all the other Wilder siblings were conveniently paired up. Richard's image flashed in her head but she quickly shunted it aside.

She had no idea where things stood with him and her heart ached as she thought of his anger the day before.

She wanted to share the triumph of this day with him but he had made no effort to contact her. Maybe he wouldn't. After the past five days, he probably wanted nothing to do with her.

"And now on to business," Peter said suddenly, distracting her from the ache in her chest. "J.D., do you want to do the honors?"

Anna frowned, confused, as they both faced her with meaningful looks. "What business?"

"We have a proposition for you," J.D. said.

"What kind of proposition?" she asked warily.

"Obviously, Northeastern HealthCare has pulled out of talks with the hospital or we wouldn't all be here. But we still need to look to the future. It's only a matter of time before another health-care conglomerate sets its sights on the hospital. We want to head that off if we can so we're moving forward with efforts to privatize the hospital to keep it under local control."

"That won't be easy," she warned. "There are very few freestanding hospitals around anymore."

"Exactly," Peter answered. "That's why we need someone smart and savvy to be our chief financial officer and help us make this a viable enterprise. Somebody who knows the business end of things inside and out and who has ideas for making the necessary economies so we can be profitable while not sacrificing patient care."

She blinked at them, stunned at the offer. After all she had nearly done to destroy the hospital, her siblings wanted her here now to help them save it?

"You think I can do that?" she asked.

"We know you can," Peter said. "We want you to be part of this, Anna. Though I guess we should have asked first where things stand for you at NHC now."

Just a few weeks ago, she would have loved to flaunt her job offer to her siblings. Finally, she would have had proof to show her family that she could succeed in her chosen world. How could they look down on her for dropping out of medical school if she were the mergers and acquisitions vice president of a leading health-care company?

That seemed so petty now.

"I'm still considering my options," she said, content to leave it at that.

"Well, add our offer to the mix," Peter said. "We need you in Walnut River. You belong here, Anna. We can't offer you a high-powered corner office in Manhattan or the salary to match. But we can offer an opportunity to genuinely make a difference, to be part of something with the potential to make life better for everyone in this community."

She gazed at her brothers and sister as a hundred thoughts churned through her mind. They wanted her here with them. The Wilder siblings, united in a common effort to save something so important to the community and to their family. They believed in her and seemed convinced she could actually help them pull this off.

She found the idea heady and exhilarating—and terrifying.

Could she do it? She knew she could handle the challenge. Just thinking about the possibilities filled her with excitement. But how could she possibly just take the plunge straight off the steep career ladder she had been climbing at NHC the past eight years, give up all she had worked for, to stay here in Walnut River with her family to rescue one faltering hospital?

"You don't have to decide right this minute," Peter said into the silence. "It's not fair of us to spring this on you all at once. I can see you're feeling overwhelmed."

"A little," she admitted, deeply grateful they didn't expect an immediate answer.

"It's been a crazy day all the way around. Take some time to think about it. The offer will still be open tomorrow, or even after the wedding if you want to take the weekend and get back to us next week."

"I'll think about it," she promised, astonished that the idea of staying in Walnut River could hold so much appeal. Was she genuinely thinking about taking a job as CFO for a community hospital when she could be a vice president at a major health-care industry player?

"That's all we can ask," J.D. said.

"This has been wonderful but I'm going to have to get back to the hospital," Ella said.

"Of course," Anna said. "Thank you so much for coming. It means the world to me."

"Thank you," Ella said with a hard fierce hug. "I'll call you tonight when my shift ends, okay? I have so much I want to talk to you about."

Anna smiled. "Deal. You know my ear is always here."

It was their secret code. Ear here. Tell me what's on your mind. I'm here to listen.

Ella sniffled again at Anna's words. "I'm so glad to have you back."

"Same, El."

Their sister's departure with J.D. seemed to be the signal to Peter and David and their fiancées to leave as well. In only a few moments, her apartment was quiet once more.

Anna closed the door behind David and Courtney, then slumped against it. She had forgotten how exhausting her family could be, but she wouldn't trade the last hour for anything.

She was still leaning against the door a moment later,

marveling at the abrupt change in her life, when the doorbell rang. Assuming someone had left something behind, she hurried to open it then stopped dead.

Richard stood on the other side, looking wildly sexy in charcoal-gray slacks, a white dress shirt with the sleeves rolled up and a red power tie that was just a little off center.

Her heart seemed to thrum out of her chest and she could do nothing but stare at him, her mind awash in memories of kissing him, touching him, lying in his arms.

"May I come in?" he finally asked, and she realized she must have been standing there staring at him for a full minute or more.

"I…of course," she managed and opened the door for him.

Her duplex apartment had seemed small but still comfortable with her three siblings and their prospective spouses. So why did it seem to shrink immeasurably when Richard walked inside?

She should say something. *Hello. How are you? I love you.*

The words caught in her throat and she couldn't manage to do anything but stare at him.

He was the first to break the silence.

"Why didn't you tell me?" His voice was low and intense, his eyes a heartbreaking shade of blue-green today.

"I tried," she said. Was he still angry at her? She couldn't read anything in those eyes.

"No, you didn't. Not really. You said I was misinterpreting things but you never gave me the full truth. Why didn't you tell me you knew nothing about that memo until right before I found it?"

She chewed her lip. She remembered how desperate she had been to get him out of her apartment after he had kissed her with stunning tenderness and then said such devastatingly cruel things.

"You won't like my answer."

"Try me. It can't be any worse than all the possible scenarios I've been coming up with all morning for why you didn't trust me enough to ask for my help."

She sighed. "It wasn't that. It wasn't that at all, Richard. Of course I would have trusted you if I could. But what would you have done if I'd told you the truth and enlisted your help?"

He shrugged. "I don't know. Maybe go to the media."

"You would have been on extremely shaky legal ground. As I pointed out, you had no right to access internal NHC documents. That was a confidential memo that you shouldn't have seen at all. I was afraid you would be willing to sacrifice your career by going public with what amounted to stolen information."

He stared at her, stunned. She had been trying to protect him? Of all the explanations he had considered, that one wouldn't have even made the top twenty.

"I'm the one who brought Walnut River to their attention," she continued. "I felt like I had to handle the situation on my own. To fix my own mess. If anyone's career was going to be destroyed, I wanted it to be mine, not yours. You could have been disbarred, Richard. I wasn't about to let that happen."

"Was your career destroyed?" he asked carefully.

He knew she had orchestrated the back-door coup

but he had no idea where things stood for her with the new management.

She managed a smile. "I wouldn't say exactly that."

She paused. "The new chief executive officer at NHC just offered me his old job as vice president of mergers and acquisitions."

A chill swept over him and Richard thought for sure he could hear the crackle of his heart freezing solid. All the dreams he had dared let himself begin to spin turned to ice along with it.

"Vice president." He forced a laugh that sounded fake and hollow to his ears. Could she tell? he wondered. "That's amazing. Wonderful news. Congratulations."

She looked a little taken aback, as if she expected some other reaction from him. "Right. Wonderful news."

"Is that why the rest of the Wilders were here? To celebrate?" He tried to inject a little more enthusiasm in his tone. "I saw them all leaving when I pulled up. They must be so proud of you. When do you start?"

"They want me there first thing in the morning," she said, somewhat woodenly.

"What about Peter's wedding Saturday?"

"I…haven't figured that out yet."

He gripped his hand into a fist at his side, doing everything he could not to betray his pain. "Make them wait," he suggested. "If they want you badly enough, they'll have a little patience."

"Will they?" she murmured.

Did her words seem double-edged or was that simply his imagination? Richard studied her closely but her lovely features revealed nothing. He knew he was in danger of losing control in a moment so he edged closer to the door.

"Congratulations again on the job offer. I just stopped by to tell you thank you for what you did for Walnut River General. I'm sorry for jumping to the wrong conclusion before and for the things I said. I should have trusted you."

He turned to leave but she stopped him.

"Richard—"

He didn't know what she intended to say. It didn't matter. When he turned back, he thought he saw a misery in her eyes that matched the pain and loss tearing through him.

He didn't give himself time to think it through, driven only by the need to touch her one more time. He crossed the space between them in two steps and pulled her into his arms, crushing her mouth with his.

After one stunned moment, she made a tiny kind of sobbing sound and her arms slid around him, holding him as if she never wanted to let go.

He kissed her fiercely, pouring all his emotions into the embrace, doing his best to leave no doubt in her mind about how much he loved her. If she was going to leave him again, he damn well wasn't going to make it easy for her.

"Anna, don't go."

She blinked at him. "Wh-What?"

His hands were shaking, he realized with chagrin. He should just leave now before he made a bigger ass out of himself. "I shouldn't have said that. I'm sorry."

"You did, though."

"I did. I know I have no right to beg you to stay after the way I've treated you the last five days. But forget that. I'm going to beg anyway. I love you, Anna. It just about killed me when you walked away last time. I don't think I can bear losing you again. Please stay."

She stared at him, saying nothing for a long, painfully drawn-out moment, then joy flared in those beautiful blue eyes and she wrapped her arms around him again and lifted her mouth to his.

He kissed her with all the pent-up frustration and fear and longing inside him, until his insides trembled and his heart threatened to pound out of his chest.

"I love you," she said. "I love you so much. I have been absolutely miserable without you."

He framed her face with his hands, the lovely serene features he had dreamed about nearly all of his life.

"I want to marry you, Anna. I've wanted it for eight years. Longer, if you want the truth. Since we were kids studying for our calculus tests together. You are the only woman I have ever loved."

Anna closed her eyes at the sweetness of his words, at the sheer sense of rightness she found here in his arms. She had almost missed this, she thought with wonder. If she hadn't taken the assignment to return to Walnut River, she would never have found Richard again, would never have realized how very empty her life was without him.

"Yes, I'll marry you!"

"Ethan and I are a package deal. Are you sure you're okay with that?"

She thought of his darling son, with his cowlick and his mischievous smile. "Better than okay. I already love your son as much as I love you."

He kissed her again and for a long time, she forgot everything else.

"I suppose I'll have to start looking to join a firm in New York," Richard said.

She stared, shocked to her core. "But you love Walnut River."

"Not nearly as much as I love you."

The sincerity of his words humbled her. She had no idea what she had ever done to deserve a man like Richard Green but she didn't care. She was keeping him, whether she deserved him or not.

"My family has asked me to stay on and become chief financial officer for the new privately owned Walnut River General Hospital. I'm going to call them and tell them I'm in."

He looked stunned. "Are you sure? It's a big step down from an NHC vice president."

"I'm positive," she murmured. "I want to stay right here, in Walnut River and in your arms."

He kissed her again while Lilli danced around them, and Anna knew this was one merger that was destined to succeed.

* * * * *

Books by Patricia Davids

HQN Books

The Amish of Cedar Grove

The Wish

Love Inspired

North Country Amish

An Amish Wife for Christmas

The Amish Bachelors

An Amish Harvest
An Amish Noel
His Amish Teacher
Their Pretend Amish Courtship
Amish Christmas Twins
An Unexpected Amish Romance
His New Amish Family

Brides of Amish Country

Plain Admirer
Amish Christmas Joy
The Shepherd's Bride
The Amish Nanny
An Amish Family Christmas: A Plain Holiday
An Amish Christmas Journey
Amish Redemption

Don't miss *Shelter from the Storm*,
the first book in the North Country Amish series
from Love Inspired books.

Visit the Author Profile page
at Harlequin.com for more titles.

A MATTER OF THE HEART

Patricia Davids

That he may incline our hearts unto him, to walk in all his ways, and to keep his commandments, and his statutes, and his judgments, which he commanded our fathers.

—*1 Kings* 8:58

To Lenora Worth, Marta Perry,
Brenda Coulter, Margaret Daley and Jillian Hart.
Working with y'all has been a pleasure.
Thanks for all the help you gave me.

Chapter 1

"Excuse me, where is the patient I'm operating on this morning?" Dr. Nora Blake stood impatiently at the nurses' station in the Pediatric Intensive Care Unit. Two nurses in brightly colored uniforms were laughing about something until they heard her voice. Then they immediately fell silent, their smiles vanishing.

Nora knew she wasn't a favorite with the staff. She didn't possess the people skills many of her colleagues displayed. Her insistence on attention to detail and her intolerance of mediocre work had earned her the reputation of being difficult.

It wasn't that she didn't care what her coworkers thought of her—she did. It hurt to see how quickly their expressions changed from cheerful to guarded, but making sure her patients received the highest quality care was far more important than being popular.

Arching one eyebrow, the slender nurse with short blond hair asked, “Do you mean Cara Dempsey?”

Nora raised her chin. Her skill was saving children with heart defects, not winning popularity contests. Professionalism was the key to getting things done right in the hospital, not sociability.

“I’m looking for the patient who came in from Blackwater General yesterday with transposition of the great arteries. Do you have the chart?” The words came out sounding sharper than she intended.

The ward nurse held out a black three-ring binder. “The patient is in room five. Dr. Kent just finished talking to the parents.”

“Thank you.” Nora nodded, relieved to hear that her partner had arrived first. Peter Kent would have explained the coming procedure to the family. It saved Nora the time and headache of trying to make laypeople understand the complex nature of the upcoming operation.

If she found any fault with Peter, who was ten years her senior and had been her partner for the past two years, it was that he was too upbeat in dealing with the families. As far as she was concerned, he often sugarcoated the truth and offered false hope. She would need to impress on the Dempsey family the risks involved, especially for an infant. Not every patient survived open-heart surgery.

Thumbing through the chart, she paid special attention to the laboratory values and medications being given to the two-day-old infant. Satisfied that everything had been done correctly, she closed the binder and moved to the computer in the corner of the desk area reserved for use by physicians. She pulled up the echocardiogram images of her patient.

She had already studied the scans extensively in her office late last night, but she wanted to make sure that she hadn't missed anything, so she watched the movie of the child's beating heart one more time. As always, a profound sense of wonder and awe engulfed her. The human heart was a beautiful thing.

She quickly focused on gathering the information she would need to repair the child's flawed heart. Operating on a newborn baby was always hard for her. It brought back too many painful memories. She preferred her patients to be at least six months old, but this child wouldn't live a week without surgery. It had to be done now.

The quality of the echocardiogram and tests were excellent, but Nora wouldn't know what she was actually dealing with until she looked inside the patient's chest. If there was one thing that she had learned during her years of training, it was that every heart was unique.

Leaving the desk, Nora walked to room five. Outside, she paused a moment to brace herself. Drawing a deep breath, she pasted a smile on her face, knocked once and then entered.

Inside, she saw a young couple sitting on the small couch at the back of the room with their arms around each other for support. They both had red-rimmed eyes, either from crying or from lack of sleep or both. They looked shell-shocked and barely out of their teens—far too young to be facing what lay ahead.

They both rose to their feet, and their hopeful eyes begged her for help she wasn't sure she could give. For a split second she envied them each having someone to hold on to during the coming hours. She had been in their shoes once with no one to comfort her. The memory of those terrible days haunted her still.

On the warming bed, a baby girl with thick dark hair lay unnaturally still. A white tube taped to her mouth connected her to a ventilator. IV pumps and monitors took up most of the space around her and beeped softly. Drugs kept her from moving and fighting the very machines that were keeping her alive. Even with the ventilator breathing for her, the child's lips were dark blue. It wasn't a good sign.

Nora nodded at the parents. "I'm Dr. Blake and I'll be performing your child's surgery this morning."

The father spoke quickly. "You can make her well, can't you? Doctor Kent, he said you were the best."

"As you know, your daughter was born with the blood vessels leading from the heart in the wrong places. Outcomes are usually good with this procedure, but five percent of the children who have this done don't survive or survive with serious brain damage. You need to be aware of that."

Cara's mother laid a loving hand on her daughter's small head. "God will be with you and with Cara. He will save her. God can do anything."

Nora bit back the comment that rose to her lips. She didn't share this young mother's belief in a benevolent God, but she had learned that revealing her philosophy with families frequently increased their anxiety.

Instead, she said, "I'll meet with you in the surgical waiting room when the operation is over. It will take several hours, but one of the staff will come out to give you updates during that time."

The door to the room opened and the blond nurse looked in. "Mr. and Mrs. Dempsey, would you please step out to the desk? I have some forms for you to sign."

As the couple followed the nurse out into the hall,

Nora found herself alone with her patient. Looking down at the baby depending on her for so much, she experienced a pang of overwhelming compassion. Reaching out, she stroked the child's hair with one hand. The tiny curls were soft as silk.

"If God can do anything, then why am I always fixing His mistakes?" Nora whispered.

She touched the small oval locket that hung on a gold chain around her neck. There was no answer to her question today. There never had been.

Catching her lower lip between her teeth, she closed her eyes and regained the composure she would need in surgery. Intense focus, not sympathy, would save this child.

After leaving the baby's room, Nora headed to the elevators. At the fifth floor, she stepped out and walked quickly toward the operating suites. She passed the pre-op nurses' station without pausing, barely noticing the women in green surgical garbs identical to her own standing in a group behind the tall, black granite counter.

Her mind was already intent on the delicate surgery she would be doing in the next few minutes. She rehearsed each move in detail.

Step-by-step, she visualized the course of the entire procedure, taking into account the obstacles and challenges the walnut-sized heart of this baby might present. Once the operation was under way, timing would be critical. The child couldn't afford to have her surgeon wondering what to do next.

The hallway led her past the family waiting room outside the surgery doors. Nora didn't bother glancing in. The parents would stay upstairs until the OR and PICU staff moved the baby to the surgery. If all went well, Nora would find Mr. and Mrs. Dempsey in about four hours and tell them their baby was still alive.

If all went well? It was a big if. There were so many things that could go wrong.

"Dr. Blake, may I have a word with you, please?"

Startled by the sound of a deep male voice behind her, Nora spun around. It took her a second to place the tall man with wavy dark brown hair who stepped out of the waiting room. When she did, she scowled.

Mr. Robert Dale, persistent reporter for the *Liberty and Justice* newspaper jogged toward her.

He was a man most women would notice. Dressed in jeans and a blue button-down shirt, he exuded confidence. His long stride and easy grace had her guessing that he was a runner, an activity that she enjoyed as often as her work permitted. His rugged features and deep tan made it clear that he preferred the outdoors over a treadmill. His bright blue eyes were fixed on her now with the intensity of a sprinter sighting the finish line.

She didn't intend to become his journalistic prize.

"I'm on my way to surgery, Mr. Dale. I'm afraid I don't have time to answer your questions."

Not bothering to hide her annoyance, she turned back toward the OR and quickened her pace. The wide, gray metal doors were only a few yards away. He couldn't follow her in there.

The man had been practically stalking her in his quest for information about the Ali Tabiz Willis case. The story of a five-year-old war orphan from the Middle East being flown to Texas for life-saving open-heart surgery apparently made a good human interest story. At least, Mr. Dale's paper seemed to think it did.

Or maybe they were so interested because the boy's grandfather was a retired U.S. Army general.

Either way, Mr. Dale had called her office enough times over the past few days that she had finally instructed her secretary to stop taking his messages. It seemed he couldn't take a hint.

A sudden thought struck her—how had he found out that she would be here? She hadn't known until late last night that she would be doing surgery this morning. Annoyance flared into anger at the possibility that her secretary or one of the hospital nurses had informed him of her schedule.

Determined to find out who had leaked the information, she spun around to confront him. Her abrupt change in direction caught him off guard and he plowed into her. The impact knocked her backward.

His strong hands shot out and grabbed her arms to keep her upright. "Sorry about that, Doc."

The feel of his long fingers curled around her bare arms triggered a thrill of awareness that shocked her. She drew a deep breath to steady her nerves. It didn't help. Instead, it flooded her senses with the masculine scent of his aftershave and a hint of caramel coffee.

She focused her gaze on a small damp stain on his pale blue shirt. He must have sloshed coffee on himself just as she walked by the waiting room. The thought that he had been lurking there expressly to waylay her brought her anger rushing back. She used it to suppress the strange and unbidden attraction she felt as she jerked away from him. "Who told you I'd be here this morning?"

His eyes sparkled with mirth and a grin tugged at the corner of his mouth, revealing a dimple in one cheek.

For a split second, she envied his self-confidence and friendly poise.

"Now, Doc, you know a reporter never reveals his sources. Besides, you haven't returned my calls. I wasn't left with much choice except to track you down at work."

She rubbed her upper arms trying to dispel the tingle his touch caused. "How often do you have to hear that I have no comment, Mr. Dale?"

"Call me Rob."

"I prefer not to, Mr. Dale." She turned and began walking away.

He quickly fell into step beside her. "I'd like to know why you object so strongly to being interviewed about Ali Willis's case?"

"Medical information is privileged. I'm sure you are already aware of that."

"I have copies of a release from the boy's guardian as well as from the Children of the Day organization. Would you like to see them?" He pulled several folded sheets of paper from his hip pocket.

Ignoring the missives, she paused long enough to swipe her ID badge in front of a small black sensor on the wall. The OR doors swung open, revealing a flurry of activity as men and women dressed in green scrubs moved patients on gurneys and carts loaded with supplies and equipment through the wide, brightly lit halls.

She paused to glare at the man following her with a small sense of triumph. "I won't help your paper or anyone else profit from a child's suffering. We're done. You aren't allowed in here. If you don't leave, I'll have security remove you."

Granting Rob Dale or any reporter an interview was the last thing she wanted to do. It was their job to pry, to uncover stories and reveal secrets. There were things in her past that were best left undisturbed.

He stepped back as the doors began to close but leaned to the side to keep eye contact with her. "If you won't talk to me about Ali, why don't we talk about the Children of the Day organization? I'll buy you a cup of coffee."

She merely arched one eyebrow and waited until the steel panels clicked shut, eliminating him from her sight.

The man was certainly persistent…and attractive. There was no denying that fact. Not once since her husband's death six years ago had a man affected her so strongly. Her reaction to the reporter was an aberration, but not something she couldn't handle. Rob Dale would have to take no for an answer this time and she wouldn't have to deal with him again.

Closing her eyes, she reached up and curled her fingers tenderly around the locket at her neck. She had more important things to think about than a man with friendly blue eyes, an engaging grin and strong hands that sent shivers down her spine when he touched her.

This is crazy. Get him out of your head. Refocus.

Forcing thoughts of the man out of her mind, she tucked the locket beneath the scooped neck of her top and proceeded into the scrub room. A long morning loomed ahead of her.

Rob admitted only temporary defeat as the doors closed between him and the intriguing doctor with shoulder-length blond hair, a cute upturned nose and intense hazel eyes. Dr. Blake might not want to speak to him, but he wasn't about to give up so easily. His paper had sent him to do a story. It wasn't an earth-shattering feature, but he would have to make do until a better story came his way.

He returned to the waiting room and scooped up his interrupted cup of mocha caramel latte. After taking a sip, he walked back down the hallway. Perhaps he could get what he needed for the story without using Dr. Blake.

At the nurses' station, he paused to speak to the short, friendly brunette who had told him of Dr. Blake's surgical schedule after only the mildest probing earlier that morning.

"You were right," he said, leaning both elbows on the waist-high countertop and gracing her with his best smile.

She closed the chart she was writing on and stuck it in a silver wire rack. "I told you Dr. Ice Princess wouldn't give you the time of day."

An older nurse seated beside her looked up and said, "Traci, that's no way to talk about Dr. Blake. She's an excellent surgeon. Your patient has just arrived in pre-op number two. I think you're needed there."

Traci rolled her eyes and rose with an exaggerated sigh. "I didn't invent the title, Emily, and you know she's earned it."

Rob watched her walk away, then turned his attention and his smile on the woman still seated at a long desk behind the counter. "Emily, it's nice to meet you. I'm Rob Dale. I'm doing a story on a little boy having surgery soon named Ali Willis."

"We aren't allowed to give out patient information."

"Of course, and I wouldn't ask you to do that. I already know that Dr. Blake will be doing the surgery, and I'm interested in finding out more about *her*. I've been told she does quite a bit of charity work. That doesn't sound like an ice princess to me."

Emily sent a wary look his way, but he gave her his most disarming grin.

After a moment, she relaxed and said, "If she does, she doesn't advertise the fact, but then I've never known her to give an interview. She's a very private person."

Or she has something to hide, he mused to himself. In the past he'd often found that the people who didn't want to talk to him were the ones that deserved a closer look. The phone on the desk rang, and Emily excused herself to answer it.

Rob straightened but he didn't move away. With half an ear, he listened in on Emily's end of the conversation. Dr. Blake's reluctance to talk to him had piqued his interest. The fact that she was prettier than any surgeon he'd ever met made him consider trying to interview her again, but his assignment was to do an in-depth piece on Children of the Day, a Christian charity devoted to helping innocent victims of war, not specifically on Dr. Blake. The only reason he was here was because of her work for the organization.

It was a fluff piece, but while he was in the States, he had to go where he was assigned. He glanced down at the red puckered scar on his forearm and flexed the fingers of his left hand. He was as healed as he was going to get. How many more of these feel-good stories would he have to do before he could return to the real action?

"You're not staying home from school unless you're running a fever, young man. Let me talk to your father."

Rob couldn't help but smile at Emily's unsympathetic tone. He and his three brothers had been subjected to the same stern speech plenty of times while they were growing up. How did mothers everywhere know when their kids were faking it? However they did it, it would be a useful trait for a reporter to learn.

Rob's cell phone began to ring. A surge of anticipation shot through him when he recognized the distinctive tone he had set for his boss and friend, Derrick Mitchell, the senior editor of *Liberty and Justice*.

Maybe I'm getting reassigned at last. Please, Lord, let it be the Middle East post that's open.

Rob walked a few steps away from the desk and answered on the third ring.

"Rob, where are you on the Willis story?" Derrick's voice crackled with impatience.

"Hello to you, too, Derrick. I'm still in Austin trying to get an interview with the boy's surgeon, but she's not talking."

An orderly pushing a gurney came down the hall. Stepping aside to let the bed transporting an elderly man pass by, Rob frowned at the silence on the other end of his connection. Maybe Derrick was worried about Rob making the deadline.

Quickly, Rob said, "I don't think she's that important to the piece. I know you said I had until the end of October to get the story in, but I can have the rest of it on your desk in two weeks. A week if you need to rush it. Then I'll be free to take the Middle East assignment that's open. It's my old stomping grounds. With the people I know in the area, I'll be a real asset to the paper there."

Stateside reporting was okay, but nothing was as thrilling as reporting from inside a war zone. He missed it—a lot.

"I'm sorry, Rob. I know how much you want that post, but I'm sending Dick Carter."

Pressing a hand to his forehead in disbelief, Rob said, "You're joking, right? Carter's a greenhorn."

"He's got a nose for a story and he's done some great work for us. You'll want to check out his piece on the baggage handlers at Memdelholm Airfield."

"Memdelholm was my piece."

"Your piece about their special handling of packages to deployed servicemen was good—touching even. Carter's piece about their drug-smuggling ring using phony names and addresses of Americans overseas is dynamite. It's on today's front page."

"What? That's crazy. I know men in charge there. Drake Manns and Benny Chase are both buddies of mine. They wouldn't be involved in something illegal."

"I'm afraid your friends are involved up to their necks. They were both arrested a few hours ago. My sources say they've pled guilty and are each trying to cut a deal."

Thankful that there was a solid wall behind him, Rob leaned back and covered his eyes with his hand. "I can't believe it. I served with Drake and Benny for three years. Benny saved my life. They're great guys. They have so much respect for the men still serving."

"Didn't you have an inkling that things weren't right?"

"They were reluctant to talk about their work, but I thought it was humility. Drake said they didn't want me singing their praises. I trusted them."

Rob couldn't believe how much it hurt knowing someone he had served with had deceived him. How could he have been so easily mislead? That a raw newcomer like Carter had uncovered the story stung even more. "Oh, man. I really blew it, didn't I?"

"You're a good reporter, Dale. People open up to you. You could charm the U.S. Mint out of its gold and my grandmother out of her secret mincemeat pie recipe, but your trouble is that you prefer to see the good in people. You didn't dig deep enough."

"Overseas it was so black and white. We were the good guys, they were the bad guys."

"That's your army mentality speaking. You aren't a soldier anymore. Your obligation is to report all sides of a story, even when it casts some of our servicemen or women in a poor light. The truth needs to be told, even when it hurts. That's what journalism is."

Looking down, Rob shoved his free hand into his front jean pocket. "Am I fired?"

"I've given Carter a monthlong trial assignment in our Middle East bureau. If he does well, I may make it permanent. I haven't decided yet."

"Then there's a chance I can go back?"

"All I'm going to say is dig deeper, Rob. Make every story important. Use your instincts. Don't make me regret giving you this job."

Derrick hung up, and after a second Rob closed his own phone. He stuffed it in his front pocket but didn't move from his place outside the surgical waiting room.

How could he have missed that his buddies at Memdelholm were involved in something shady? The fact that he had been so easily deceived was hard to swallow.

Derrick's right. I wasn't looking hard enough. I thought it was a simple piece and I blew it.

When he had been among the soldiers and marines on the front lines, the best stories had all but fallen into his lap. Over there, his gut instincts were never wrong. He knew that world inside and out.

He needed to be back there, but that wasn't going to happen now. Not until he proved to Derrick Mitchell that he had what it took to get to the bottom of any story.

Lord, I failed to make the most of Your gift. It won't happen again. You sent me here for a reason. I don't know what that reason is, but I'm going to keep looking until I find it.

He glanced toward the surgery doors. His gut told him that Dr. Nora Blake was more than a woman who didn't grant interviews. He had no idea what a woman like her might be hiding, but he was going to find out. He intended to dig deep.

Chapter 2

"You can't be serious!"

In stunned disbelief, Nora sat in the black leather chair in front of Willard Branson, the CEO and chief administrator of Mercy Medical Center, and stared openmouthed at her boss. In the chair beside hers, Rob Dale sat with a smile on his face that wasn't quite a self-satisfied smirk, but it was close.

She had hoped that their confrontation outside of surgery the day before yesterday would have convinced the reporter to leave her alone. Apparently, it hadn't.

His audacity provoked a slow burn of irritation, but it didn't prevent her from noticing how attractive he looked in charcoal slacks, a sage dress shirt that accentuated his lean, athletic body and a tasteful silk tie that made her wonder if a wife or girlfriend had picked it out for him.

"I'm perfectly serious, Dr. Blake," Willard replied,

drawing her attention back to him. "You are free to donate as much time and energy as you wish to Children of the Day, and I applaud your dedication to the organization, but the hospital must weigh the pros and cons of each case. We have already donated many hours of the staff's time and much of our limited resources to helping your cause. It's time we got something back."

"Saving the lives of needy children isn't enough payback for you?" She didn't bother hiding her sarcasm.

Steepling his fingers together, Willard leaned forward on his wide mahogany desk. "I hired you because you had a reputation for being the brightest new pediatric cardiologist to come out of the Cleveland Clinic in years. I hired you because I wanted someone who could grow our program."

"Haven't I done that?"

"You have to an extent. Your surgical success rate is impressive, but the publicity generated by a series of articles like Mr. Dale is proposing could very well increase the number of patients referred to this facility. Patients you will operate on.

"It might even generate substantial donations to us and to Children of the Day. I'm sure I don't need to remind you that *Liberty and Justice* is an international and very well-respected paper. Frankly, I don't understand why you aren't jumping at this opportunity."

Everything Willard said was true, but Nora couldn't abide the thought of someone poking about in her life and in her work.

She tried one last avenue. "I'm sure Dr. Kent would be delighted to have Mr. Dale shadow him on a day-to-day basis."

"But he doesn't do volunteer work for Children of the Day," Rob interjected.

She glared at him. "Dr. Kent has aided me a number of times. If you're so interested in the organization, I suggest you spend your time with Anna Terenkov. She is the founder of Children of the Day. I'm certain she will answer any questions you have."

"I've already spoken to Ms. Terenkov. She's the one who pointed out how frequently your expertise has been utilized even before little Ali Willis's case was brought to their attention."

He pulled a small notebook from his shirt pocket, flipped it open and began to read. "And I quote, 'Dr. Blake is personally responsible for saving the lives of a dozen children in the past year who would otherwise have died of their congenital heart defects in war-torn third world countries.

"'Besides doing these surgeries without compensation, she has been instrumental in convincing Mercy Medical Center to provide the additional care needed at a greatly reduced fee. She oversees the donated medical supplies and has convinced numerous drug companies to donate badly needed medications—medicines that families in these countries would otherwise have to buy on the black market at exorbitant prices.'"

He paused and looked up. "Shall I continue? There's a lot more. Like the fact that you also work part-time at Fort Bonnell Medical Center and have even traveled overseas on a medical mission for Children of the Day. It must be difficult to maintain any kind of private life with this much on your plate."

"I'm well aware of my workload, and my private life is off-limits. Is that understood?"

His eyes brightened. "Then you'll allow me to tag along with you for Ali's surgery?"

She glanced at Willard, the man responsible for hiring her and approving the amount of charity work Mercy did. He nodded slightly. She closed her eyes in resignation. "It seems I have little choice."

"You won't regret it, I promise," Rob quickly assured her.

"Strange, but I already do." She looked at Willard. "Are we done here? I have rounds to make."

She hated confrontations, especially when she didn't emerge the winner.

"We're done, Dr. Blake. Mr. Dale, when would you like to start?"

"There's no time like the present. Care to show me around, Dr. Blake? May I call you Nora?"

She rose to her feet already uncomfortable with his close scrutiny. How was she going to tolerate having him around for days? She had to see that he kept his distance. Cool professionalism was the key.

"You may address me as Dr. Blake. Ali's surgery isn't scheduled for another two weeks. I see no reason for you to hound me until then."

He tucked his pad and pen back in his shirt pocket. "I'll need some background information about how heart surgery is carried out, and the best way would be for me to see a few surgeries for myself."

"I'm not taking you into the operating room."

Turning on her heel, Nora left the CEO's office and walked quickly toward the elevators. She knew Rob was following without looking back.

"Now, Nora, I know that you have students and visiting physicians who observe your surgeries. It won't be any different having me in the room."

For some reason, she knew it would. She was aware of him on a level that she had never experienced before. The last thing she wanted was him disturbing her concentration while she was operating.

At the end of the hall, she punched the down arrow and the elevator doors immediately slid open. The car was empty. Why couldn't it have been crowded? She stepped inside and turned to face the opening. Rob slipped in behind her. The doors closed, shutting them in together.

Music played softly overhead. She could see a blurred reflection of herself and Rob in the brightly polished metal panels. The simple white blouse and fitted navy skirt that she had picked out that morning made her look like a schoolgirl instead of a thirty-five-year-old woman with a demanding career.

The scent of his cologne tickled her nose. It was a brand she liked, and on him it smelled particularly good—spicy but not overpowering. She tried not to breath.

His reflection leaned toward hers. She tensed as he spoke; his breath tickled her earlobe and the nape of her neck. "I think you have to push the button."

Blood rushed to her face, staining it crimson above her white collar. She jabbed her finger into the button for the third floor so hard it hurt.

Rob leaned away from Nora and let his gaze skim over her trim figure. She was tall for a woman, maybe five foot eight or five foot nine. She wore her hair pulled back into a French twist today, and the style accentuated the graceful curve of her neck. She radiated cool grace.

"I have my patients to think of, Mr. Dale. I can't allow just anyone access to their information."

She was still fighting even after the battle was lost. A part of him admired her tenacity.

"Mr. Branson has made me aware of the patient confidentiality issues. Everything I see or hear regarding patients will remain strictly confidential."

While he might admire her determination to get rid of him in spite of the pressure Willard Branson put on her, Rob couldn't help but wonder why. He decided to try a direct approach.

"Do you have something to hide, Dr. Blake?"

Her head snapped around and she stared at him with wide eyes. For a second, he thought he saw fear in their depths, but it was quickly replaced by anger. She turned her back on him. "I have no idea why you would even suggest such a thing."

The elevator doors opened and she rushed off. He followed at a slower pace, but more intrigued than ever. She entered the second doorway on the left and slammed it shut behind her.

After pausing to read her name and the name of her partner stenciled in gold lettering on the glass panel, he made a mental note to look up her partner's credentials. Rob had already checked Nora's. They were impressive.

He opened the door and stuck his head inside. A middle-aged woman with impossibly black hair teased in a 1970s flip sat behind an immaculate rosewood desk centered between two identical doors. Nora stood beside her. Two additional open doorways at each end of the reception area revealed examination rooms that were currently empty.

Rob winked at the secretary. "You must be Carmen. I'm Rob Dale. Is it safe to come in?"

She hid a smile with difficulty as she glanced between Nora and him. "For the moment."

"Good." He entered the stark office with plain white walls and a half dozen reception-style maroon chairs lining the perimeter. "How's Harold getting along?"

"He's much better, thank you."

Nora's frown deepened as she glared at her secretary. "Do you know this man?"

Rob walked forward and grasped Carmen's plump fingers. He gave them a squeeze. "We've spoken on the phone so many times this week that I feel like Carmen is an old friend."

Carmen batted her eyes. "You're just as charming in person as you are on the telephone."

"Not nearly as charming as you are. I would have braved the dragon days ago if I had known how pretty you were. I'm so glad to hear Harold is doing better. I've been praying for him."

Nora's mouth dropped open. "Who are you calling a dragon and who is Harold?"

"Harold is Carmen's husband. He had a nasty bout of pneumonia. It's a good thing her daughter was able to come over and take care of him since Carmen couldn't get time off from work," Rob said, enjoying Nora's obvious confusion.

Nora folded her arms across her chest as she frowned at her secretary. "You didn't mention you needed time off."

Tilting her head to one side, Carmen said, "Actually,

I did ask for a few days off last week, but you said your schedule was full and that I was needed here."

"Oh, yes. I remember that. Well…you should have made a point of telling me it was a family emergency."

"I'll be more clear in the future, Dr. Blake."

"Carmen is not my regular secretary," Nora said, giving Rob a pointed look.

Carmen nodded. "I'm a temp. I fill in for Delia when she takes time off. She goes to Vegas every chance she gets. I think she has a boyfriend there."

"All right then." Nora's smile looked forced. "Carmen, Mr. Dale will be shadowing me for a few days. Please get him a set of scrubs."

Rising from her chair, Carmen said, "Dr. Kent has several sets in his office. I'll get one for you. You look about the same size."

Nora walked toward the inner office on the right and Rob followed.

Inside, a quick glance around the room revealed a large oak desk with two chairs facing it. They matched the chairs lining the outer office—none of which looked made for comfort. On the desk were an oversized paper pad and a computer screen. Several filing cabinets sat beneath a wide window with a nice view of downtown Austin in the distance. A tall, gray metal wardrobe took up the remaining space in the corner. There was a closed door on the near wall. Rob assumed it connected to the exam room. On the opposite wall was a small taupe sofa. He crossed the room and sat down.

Reaching out, he plucked several long blond hairs from a faint depression in the padded arm. A green-and-red plaid throw blanket lay draped over the other end of the couch.

"Do you sleep here a lot?" he asked, looking to where she stood pulling open the small wardrobe.

She withdrew a set of green scrubs on hangers. "Occasionally, when I need to remain in the hospital."

"Your home is in Prairie Springs, isn't it? That's only thirty minutes from here."

"Thirty minutes is a long time when a patient needs their chest reopened." Spinning around, she held the scrubs close to her chest like a flimsy cloth shield. "How do you know where I live?"

He rose from the sofa and crossed to stand in front of the wall behind her desk where a half dozen framed certificates hung in two neat rows.

"I do my research, Nora. You graduated from Albertville High School in Boston at the precocious age of fifteen and at the head of your class. You finished pre-med at Columbia in three years and entered medical school with top honors. You joined the army and studied at Walter Reed where you chose to specialize in cardiac surgery. After that, you did your peds cardiac fellowship at the Cleveland Clinic. You were married briefly—"

"I know my own history," she interrupted quickly.

"Of course."

He turned to study the silver-framed photo on her desk. Picking it up, he compared the young woman's face in the picture to Nora's. There wasn't a resemblance. The snapshot was of a smiling woman in her early twenties with thick brown hair that cascaded around a delicate oval face. "Pretty girl. Who is she?"

Nora took the frame from him and replaced it in the exact spot at the right-hand corner of her desk. "My stepdaughter. Since you seem to be so well versed about me, Mr. Dale, I think it's only fair that you reciprocate."

He held his hands wide. “My life is an open book.”

“Somehow, I doubt that.”

“What would you like to know? I graduated from high school in Dodge City, Kansas—not even close to the top of my very small class. I drifted between majors at the local junior college and finally ended up in the army. It didn’t take me long to realize that I wanted to be a ranger. Those guys do the fun stuff. Twelve years later, I decided I was getting too old to go jumping out of planes. A desk job or training new recruits didn’t appeal to me, so I opted to leave the service.”

“How does one decide that digging into other people’s lives makes a worthwhile second profession?”

“That was easy. I was sitting in a café in the busy capital of a small Middle Eastern country and relating the tale of how I met a pair of gunrunners to some friends. A man at the next table leaned over and asked me if I could help him get an interview with the unsavory duo. The guy turned out to be Derrick Mitchell, a senior reporter for *Liberty and Justice.* When my story panned out, he got promoted and asked me to come to work for him.”

“Just like that? You didn’t study journalism for years or work your way up from copy boy to the newsroom?”

Her sarcasm didn’t offend him. He rather enjoyed the way she lifted her chin and tried to talk down to him although she was a good four inches shorter than his six-foot frame. He sensed it was a ruse designed to put him off. It didn’t work.

“Nope. The job just fell into my lap. I believe the good Lord puts me where I am needed most.”

She looked down and smoothed the fabric she held with one hand. “Yes, I imagine you would have a simplistic outlook. I think a person should have to work hard to achieve what they want, otherwise it is meaningless."

"You don't believe that God led you to become a surgeon in Austin?"

She gave an emphatic shake of her head. "No. It took fifteen years of hard study, grueling clinical hours and painstaking attention to detail. I've earned my place here—it didn't fall into my lap. God had nothing to do with it."

Something about her answer intrigued him. At first he couldn't quite put his finger on what it was, then he knew. Her vehement denial of God's role in her life, like her sarcasm, didn't ring true. There was more to this woman than she allowed others to see. His sudden intense urge to understand her better caught him off guard.

This was more than his usual need to find the story behind the person. He studied her face for a long moment, noticing her high cheekbones and full lips, the stubborn jut of her chin and the delicate winged brows above her expressive eyes. And then it hit him.

He expected annoyance, even arrogance from her, but what he saw in Nora's eyes was infinite sadness—a longing for something precious that had been lost. In the war-torn countries where he had served he'd seen the same look all too often. It touched something deep inside him.

Gently, he said, "That doesn't mean God didn't lead you here. What made you stop believing?"

He watched the struggle on her face. For a second, it seemed as if he had connected with her, but the outer door opened and Carmen entered with a pair of scrubs over her arm.

The moment was lost and Nora turned away. Rob

moved to take the scrubs from Carmen and offered his thanks. She nodded and left without speaking.

Nora closed the door of her closet. "I don't have time to argue the existence of a higher power with you, Mr. Dale. I have rounds to make. If you'll excuse me, I need to change. You may use the exam room through that door."

Her cool tone conveyed in more than words that she was done talking to him. Rob touched one finger to his forehead in a brief salute and pulled open the door she indicated. As it closed behind him, he heard the lock click with a snap. Unbuttoning his shirt, he acknowledged that he'd uncovered more questions than answers in his brief time with Dr. Nora Blake.

He looked forward to the rest of the day with a growing sense of anticipation that he hadn't experienced since he'd arrived back in the States. Dr. Nora Blake presented an intriguing puzzle—one he found himself eager to solve.

Nora walked to her chair and sank onto the familiar seat. A second later, she put her elbows on the desk and dropped her head into her hands.

Why now? Why after all these years? The pain of her past never truly went away, but there were days that she didn't think about those difficult, sad hours and what she had lost. In the past year, there had even been times when she didn't think about Bernard and the terrible debt she had to repay.

How ironic that the charity work she was doing to make amends was the very thing that might shine a spotlight on things best left hidden.

Looking up, she focused on Pamela's picture. Her

stepdaughter had endured enough pain in her life. Nora wasn't about to let Rob Dale add to that burden.

He might appear cute and harmless, but so did a terrier puppy. It was only after one had turned your backyard into a crater-filled moonscape that you realized their true purpose. They had been bred to dig out vermin.

Rob Dale of *Liberty and Justice* struck her as the same kind of animal. He was no one's lapdog.

She needed to steer him away from anything that involved her personal life. As a plan it wasn't much, but it was all she had.

She rose and quickly changed out of her skirt and blouse and into her scrubs. She didn't have any surgeries today, but she needed to follow up on three of her patients who were still in the hospital.

At the door leading out to the reception area, she paused with her hand on the knob. Letting Rob or anyone on the staff see her rattled would only undermine what she hoped to accomplish at Mercy Medical Center. When she felt she had control of her emotions, she exited the room with brisk strides. Rob, already changed, hastened to follow her.

"Where are we going?" he asked, working to tighten the drawstring on his scrub pants while he tried to keep pace with her.

"We are going to the PICU. That stands for Pediatric Intensive Care Unit. I have three patients there."

"I thought we were going to surgery."

"Not today, but I have an AV canal repair scheduled for the day after tomorrow."

"AV canal. What kind of injury is that?" He finished

cinching up his pants and pulled a small notebook from his breast pocket.

"An atrial ventricular canal is a congenital cardiac defect, as are the vast majority of the patients I see at this hospital. When I work at the base hospital, I do mostly follow-ups on adult patients after bypass surgery."

They passed the elevators, but she didn't stop. Instead, she pushed open the stairwell door and headed up. Two floors later she opened another door and strode out onto the pediatric floor. Unlike the rest of the hospital, the walls here were brightly colored and decorated with oversized cutouts of cartoon characters.

Rob noticed she didn't seem winded by the rapid climb. "So you don't get many injures like Ali's?"

"To be perfectly honest, I have never seen a case like Ali's and I've only read about a very few in the literature. Most of them were adults involved in motor vehicle accidents. The vast majority of people who sustain enough trauma to tear apart an internal structure of the heart don't survive.

"The fact that Ali has is amazing. Two of the cases I studied healed on their own. Two required surgery to repair the tear when they began to show signs of fluid buildup in the lung. Three others died due to heart tissue death after approximately four days. However, Ali's operation will be the same as for a simple VSD repair."

"How can you operate on the kid if you haven't had a case like this before? What's a VSD?"

Nora paused outside a pair of wide double doors marked with PICU in large letters. "A VSD is a congenital cardiac defect."

"You said that before."

"And my answer was correct both times. We have

several good handouts that we give to parents explaining the defects in detail and how they are repaired. I'll make sure Carmen gets you some to study."

"When do you see patients in your office?"

"Consults and a few follow-ups are scheduled once a week on Mondays. Ninety-five percent of my patients are direct admits to the PICU. Heart defects in children often go undetected until they are in crisis. Unless they have need of a second surgery in the future, I don't normally see them after they leave the hospital."

"Doesn't that make it hard to get to know the families?"

"My focus is on my patients, not the families. There are social workers and others who deal with any issues that arise with them."

Pushing open the doors, Nora entered the unit and walked to the nursing desk. Theresa Mabley, a stout woman with short salt-and-pepper hair was dressed in her usual blue scrubs. Standing behind her were a collection of residents and nurses, all waiting to begin reporting to Nora on the patients.

"Good morning, Theresa. Mr. Dale, this is the head nurse in our PICU. Mr. Dale is a reporter, and he'll be rounding with me for the next several days. You may answer any questions he has."

Theresa nodded in his direction. "Nice to meet you, Mr. Dale."

He extended his hand. "Call me Rob. I promise not to get underfoot more than fifty times a day, Theresa."

His lopsided grin gave him the look of a charming rogue, and it was painfully clear to Nora that even the stalwart charge nurse wasn't immune as Theresa shook his hand and smiled back at him. "I doubt you'll be underfoot at all, Rob. Is this your first visit to a PICU?"

"My very first. Be kind to me."

Theresa chuckled. "Let me give you the tour. We currently have an eight-bed unit. However, thanks to a recent quarter-million-dollar gift made to the hospital in our name, we'll soon be resuming construction to expand to a fifteen-bed unit with all new, state-of-the-art equipment."

Nora held her breath thinking he would ask questions about the money, but Theresa was already on to her favorite topics—the need for more nurses and her grandchildren.

Nora stared at the two of them. How did he do it? How did he connect with people so easily? She didn't get it. It had taken months for Theresa to warm up to Nora, and even now they were far from friends. Yet Theresa was chatting away with this reporter like she had known him for ages.

Suddenly, the code-blue alarm rang. Glancing down the hallway, she saw the light flashing over Cara Dempsey's doorway. Rob Dale was completely forgotten as Nora raced toward the room.

Chapter 3

Rob watched Nora bolt down the hallway. Several people in lab coats came running into the unit and rushed passed him, closely followed by a security officer. Rob had no idea what was going on, but it didn't look good.

He moved to where he could look through the door and yet be out of the way. All he could see was a ring of people crowding around a warming bed. Theresa entered the room, but she didn't join the crowd. Instead, she went to stand beside a young couple huddled together watching the activity with wide frightened eyes.

Draping an arm around the young woman's shoulder, the nurse gently explained to them what was going on. Rob couldn't hear everything over the noise of the alarms, but it was clear that their baby was in serious trouble.

The young mother burst into tears and pressed her

hands to her mouth, then shouted, "Don't let her die! Please, God, I'll do anything, just don't let her die!"

Nora, at the side of the bed, looked up and motioned with her head toward the door. "Take them out of here, and someone silence that alarm!"

Theresa gently but firmly herded the couple out of the room. A tall, thin, young man with blond hair and dressed in a dark suit met them at the unit door and led them away. Rob noticed he was holding a Bible in one hand.

Theresa came back and stopped beside Rob. In a weary voice, she said, "That little one has been looking for the light ever since her surgery."

Sending her a puzzled glance, Rob asked, "What do you mean?"

"Her condition has been getting worse instead of better."

His heart dropped like a stone. "Can they save her?"

"They are doing everything they can."

The alarm stopped, and in the sudden silence he heard Nora calling out orders for medication and asking for a stat blood gas. Her face was calm, but her voice vibrated with intensity. After the requested drugs had been given, Nora studied the monitor intently, then turned to one of the nurses. "Why wasn't I paged?"

"I was told Dr. Kent was covering for you. I've paged him three times, but he hasn't answered."

"I want to be paged every time one of my patients is in trouble. It doesn't matter if Dr. Kent is covering or not. You call me. Is that clear?"

Meekly, the nurse nodded and said, "Yes, Doctor."

Leaning toward Theresa, Rob asked, "What's wrong with the baby?"

"She had what we call transposition of the great arteries. Think of the heart as two separate pumps fused together. The right side of the heart collects blood from the body and sends it to the lungs for oxygen. The left side of the heart collects blood from the lungs and sends it to the rest of the body."

"Okay, I get that."

"Early on, the blood vessels coming out of the top of Cara's heart began to grow incorrectly. The right side of her heart collects blood from the body but the blood vessel that should take it to the lungs lead out to the body instead. So blood leaves the heart without oxygen. The left side still collects blood from the lungs but then sends it back to the lungs again."

"Wait a minute. You can't live if your body isn't getting oxygen. How did she survive until now?"

"The same way all babies do. In the womb. Cara got her oxygen from her mother's blood. It wasn't until after Cara was born and had to breathe on her own that the trouble began."

"I take it Dr. Blake couldn't fix her heart?"

"From what I understand, Dr. Blake did a beautiful switch of the arteries. Cara's blood is now going exactly where it should."

He shook his head. "Then why isn't she getting better?"

"Because sometimes life isn't fair, Mr. Dale. Cara suffered a stroke. Her brain is damaged. It's one of the risks involved in being put on the heart–lung bypass machine during open-heart surgery. We see a lot fewer cases like this now than we did ten years ago, but it can happen to anyone who undergoes this kind of surgery."

"What can be done for her?"

Theresa gave a deep sigh and laid a hand on his shoulder. "If you believe in prayer, pray for her recovery. Everything *humanly* possible is already being done."

Rob nodded and breathed a silent prayer for the baby and for the men and women working to save her.

The unit doors opened. A distinguished-looking man with wings of silver in his dark hair and a deep tan walked briskly toward them. His white lab coat flapped open to reveal a gray silk shirt and a red tie above well-tailored slacks. He smoothed his sleek hair with one hand as he asked, "Did someone page me?"

Theresa left Rob's side to confer softly with the man Rob assumed was the missing Dr. Kent. After listening to what the head nurse had to tell him, Dr. Kent nodded and walked into the room.

At the foot of the bed, he thrust his hands in his coat pockets. "I see you have everything under control, Nora. Is there anything I can do?"

She was reading a slip of paper from one of the machines beside the bed and didn't glance up. "We have a stable heart rhythm at the moment."

He ran a finger between his neck and his collar. "The batteries were dead in this silly pager of mine."

Nora looked up but she didn't smile. "Yes, one of the nurses mentioned she paged you several times. I find changing the batteries on a regular basis prevents such problems."

She moved away from the bed and turned to the residents who had been watching her. "Let's get started on rounds, shall we? Dr. Dalton, perhaps you can give us an overview of this patient's neurological status, and Dr. Glasgow can give us fluid recommendations."

A nervous-looking young man with thick glasses

swallowed hard, then begin reciting a list of facts and numbers. Most of the nurses filed out of the room, leaving only one to answer questions posed by Nora and the other doctors. It was as if nothing special had happened. One minute Rob had been watching Cara Dempsey's life hanging by a thread and the next minute everyone had gone back to other duties. It was almost bizarre.

He turned his attention back to Nora. What kind of woman did it take to make life-and-death decisions for children like this on a regular basis? What did it take for her to do such a job? He wanted to know what kind of toll it exacted on her, how she handled the pressure, what made her tick. He wanted to learn a lot more about her—and not just for his story.

Nora clasped her arms across her middle as the adrenaline rush ebbed away, leaving her feeling weak and shaken. It took all her strength to maintain a calm, controlled demeanor. It was important for her students to see that panic had no place in a critical care setting. Getting them to focus on the details of their patient might very well prevent a crisis from occurring again.

Glancing down at Cara, Nora bit the corner of her lip. She had helped the baby cheat death once more, but would it be enough?

I want to fix her. I'm a surgeon. That is what I do. I fix broken kids.

Only some children couldn't be fixed. She knew that better than anyone. She had done all she could do for this one at the moment. She accepted it, but she didn't like it.

From the corner of her eye, she saw Rob enter the room and stand at the far edge of the group. As she listened to the young residents list the baby's treatments, she turned so that she could see Rob better without being observed.

What was he thinking? Was he looking for a story angle or was it genuine concern that she saw in his eyes when his gaze rested on the baby?

And why did she care what the man thought? Determined to put him out of her mind, she looked at the residents. "Who is next on our list?"

Rounds were accomplished in a relatively short time. As the group broke apart to attend to various other duties, Nora returned to the computer corner and started dictating her notes for the day. When she was finished, she looked over to see Rob straddling one of the office chairs nearby. His arms were crossed on the seat back and his chin rested on his forearms. He watched her intently.

"What?" she asked, growing uncomfortable with his scrutiny.

"Is Cara Dempsey going to be okay?"

"I don't know." The faces of the children who had died while under her care would never be forgotten. Their names crowded into her mind.

For a moment, she was tempted to share with him how truly difficult it was to do the job she loved. Fortunately, her pager began to beep. She checked the message. "It looks as if we are done for the day. I'll show you back to the office so you can change."

"Do you often have to save the day because Dr. Kent can't be reached?"

She scowled at him and began walking down the hall. "Of course not. We're a team."

"He isn't much of a team player if the nurses can't get ahold of him when he's needed."

As much as Nora didn't like Rob prying into her life, she wasn't about to turn him loose on Peter. Her partner had been going though a rough time of his own since his recent divorce.

"Dr. Kent's pager battery was dead. It happens. You may shadow me and ask questions about open-heart surgery or Ali Willis's care, but I will not discuss my colleagues with you. Are we clear on that?"

"Crystal clear."

"Good. I'm finished with my rounds for the day and I don't have any patients scheduled in the office. Unless you wish to sit and watch me sign insurance forms and wade through the paperwork waiting for me now, I suggest you leave."

"Okay then, I'll see you tomorrow."

"No, I won't be here." She stopped at the elevator instead of taking the stairs. Her legs were still feeling shaky. It opened quickly, and she punched the button for the third floor.

"You mean you actually get a day off? That's great. Perhaps we could get together over lunch and you could tell me more about your work with Children of the Day."

"That won't be possible. I'm working at the Fort Bonnell Medical Center tomorrow. I cover a few shifts a month there so that the army cardiac surgeons can get a little time off."

"What if there is an emergency with one of the kids in this unit?"

The elevator doors opened and she stepped out. "Dr. Kent will be covering here. My next surgery is scheduled for the day after tomorrow at 8 a.m. sharp. If you wish to join me, you should be here at six-thirty."

As they entered her office, Carmen looked up and

held out a stack of notes. "You have two requests for consults. One from a doctor in Waco and one from here in Austin. Oh, and Tarkott Pharmaceuticals returned your call."

"It's about time. Get them on the line for me again."

Walking into her inner office, Nora noted with relief that Rob chose not to follow. She didn't like feeling as if she were constantly on display.

Sitting behind her desk, she turned on her computer and waited for it to boot up. The welcome screen flashed on and Nora opened the files she needed to update. Typing quickly, she had finished her first case when the phone buzzed and Carmen's voice came over the speaker. "I have Tarkott's CEO, Mr. Sawyer, on line one."

Quentin Sawyer had once worked with her husband. His reputation for being a hard businessman was well earned. This wouldn't be easy. She pressed the button. "Good morning, Quentin. Thank you for returning my call. I hope you and Merilee are enjoying the cooler weather."

She engaged in a stint of small talk in spite of her discomfort at trying to do so. Quentin and his wife had been friends of her husband, but Nora never felt she belonged in their social circle. Still, her old contacts in the pharmaceutical world came in handy at times like this.

When Quentin paused for breath in his description of his latest classic car acquisition, Nora jumped in. "As you know from my messages, Quentin, my charity, Children of the Day, is in desperate need of antibiotics. Our doctors in one of our refugee camps have reported a severe outbreak of staphylococcus, and we are asking for your help. We need four thousand vials of penicillin, and I'm not going to take no for an answer."

* * *

Rob stood beside Carmen's desk and listened through Nora's partially open door to her side of the conversation. He might be guilty of eavesdropping, but she was talking about Children of the Day and that was his story. He smiled at the secretary and took a seat in one of the chairs just outside Nora's door as if he were waiting for her to finish.

"No," Nora said emphatically. "Five hundred vials isn't enough. We need four thousand. Your company's tax break on such a donation will more than offset the cost of sending us the drugs. We both know the drugs are sitting in your warehouse taking up space. Your newer generation antibiotics are in much more demand."

In the silence that followed as she listened to the person on the other end of the line, Rob caught Carmen's eye. "Does she do this often?"

"All the time. She knows a lot of drug people. I think that's what her husband did before he died."

Nora's voice cut in again. "You must be joking. I'm willing to take products with less than one year's shelf life but not something that is going to expire in two months. Six months is as low as I will go, and only because I know exactly where the drugs are going and that there won't be a delay in using them. I'm sure your company wants to be seen as ethical as well as charitable." Nora's tone was cool as ice. Rob didn't envy the person on the other end of the line.

He pulled out his notebook and began to jot down some notes.

"I have a reporter here from the paper *Liberty and Justice*. You may have heard of them," Nora continued. "I'm sure you don't want them doing a story about how

Tarkott Pharmaceuticals is giving away drugs that are worthless in exchange for a hefty tax break."

Rob's eyebrows rose in surprise. So she wasn't above using the power of the press when it suited her. He admired her nerve.

"Good. Send the drugs directly to me. I'll take care of the international shipping costs and the needed forms. I thank you, and Children of the Day thanks you. We'll make sure that your company is given the recognition it deserves for your kind gesture. Please give Merilee my best. Goodbye."

The sound of her receiver hitting the cradle signaled Rob that she was free. He rose to his feet, then stepped inside her office. At the sight of him, her expression hardened in a way that would have made most people turn tail. "I thought we were through for today."

"I have a couple more questions, but I couldn't help overhearing your conversation just now. Do you often solicit drugs for Children of the Day?" He flipped open his notepad and began writing.

"I help when I can."

"It must make it easier for you than for some since your husband was in the pharmaceutical business." He waited to jot down her comments, but when she didn't speak he glanced at her.

During his years in the army he had seen fear in the eyes of many people, but he certainly wasn't expecting to see that emotion on Nora's face at this moment. Her eyes were wide with alarm, her skin drained of color.

He lowered his pen and took a step toward her. "What's wrong?"

She recoiled and looked away. "Nothing. Nothing's wrong except that you are keeping me from getting my work done. I really have to insist that you leave now." Her voice trembled ever so slightly. She pulled a folder from the stack at the side of her desk and opened it.

He stood rooted to the spot, uncertain of what to do. "I'm sorry if I upset you."

"I'm not upset. I'm simply busy."

Her tone was stronger, but he didn't believe her. Part of him wanted to know what had caused her distress, and another part of him wanted only to reassure and comfort her.

"Good day, Mr. Dale!" This time the command was unmistakable. She didn't even glance in his direction.

"Good day, Nora." He walked out of her office with a dozen unanswered questions whirling though his mind.

Calling herself every kind of fool, Nora closed the file she was holding and rubbed her temples with the tips of her fingers. The tension headache building behind her eyes didn't ease.

She had overreacted to Rob's comment about Bernard's business. She had seen the look of speculation in the reporter's eyes when he left the room. Her hopes that he wouldn't look too closely into her past might have just flown out the window and *she* had thrown up the sash. What could she do? How could she fix this?

By giving him what he wanted.

The answer that occurred to her was surprisingly simple. Rob wanted an in-depth look at her work for Children of the Day. The more she resisted his attempts to do that, the more likely he was to wonder why she wouldn't cooperate.

If she decided to help him, would he think it was strange? Would it make him more suspicious?

She glanced at Pamela's picture. What choice did she have?

Rising, she hurried to her door and pulled it open. To her relief, he hadn't left yet.

"Rob, I'm sorry," she said quickly. "I shouldn't have snapped at you."

She didn't know who looked more surprised by her apology, Rob or Carmen.

He shook his head. "Don't give it another thought. Are you sure you're okay?"

She took a step toward him. "I'm stressed, that's all. With baby Dempsey's condition on my mind and then hearing a pharmaceutical company tell me they don't want to help sick children… I just lost it. You were a handy target. I'm sorry."

"I can see how you might feel stressed."

"That's no excuse for my behavior. I do understand what you are trying to do with your article. If you can raise the awareness of what Children of the Day does, then I'll try not to hinder you." She smiled broadly. "You said you had a few more questions. I'll try to answer them."

He waved one hand. "It can wait."

"Are you sure?"

"Absolutely. I'll get out of your hair and let you get back to work."

"All right then. Good day." Nora walked back into her office and sank into her chair. She hoped that Rob had accepted her explanation and would be satisfied with that.

He watched as Nora went back inside her office and wondered why she had undergone such a change of heart. Her explanation was reasonable, but it didn't feel quite right.

He nodded to Carmen. "I'll see you the day after tomorrow. I'm going into surgery with the good doctor."

"You won't see me. Delia will be back tomorrow."

"Then I look forward to meeting Delia."

"I'm not so sure you should look forward to it. Delia is a bit of a dragon. She runs a very tight ship."

"Then I look forward to taming the dragon."

Carmen tilted her head to one side. "If anyone can do it, I think you're the man for the job."

He touched his brow with one finger and gave Carmen a wink before heading out the door. In the hallway, he glanced at his notes. He had written the words *husband, company name* and *background check*.

After pulling his cell phone from his pocket, Rob scrolled through his contacts until he found the one he was looking for. He placed the call, and on the second ring it went to voice mail.

A man's gravely voice said, "Encore Investigations. Leave a message at the tone."

"Murray, this is Rob Dale. Call me when you get this. I have a job for you. Dig up anything you can on a charity called Children of the Day in Prairie Springs, Texas."

Rob paused as he considered his next request. Was he doing the right thing by prying into Nora's past? If she was no different than any other person he was writing about, why did he feel guilty about doing this?

Maybe it was because he already felt a personal connection to her that he couldn't quite explain. He needed the information for the piece, but he also wanted to get to know more about Nora for selfish reasons. He'd never met anyone as complex, as driven, and yet with an underlying vulnerability that touched something deep inside him.

If they were simply two people getting to know each other, he wouldn't invade her privacy this way, but she was part of a story. He'd let his personal feelings get in the way of good reporting only a short time ago and it had cost him. He wouldn't make the same mistake twice.

Finally, he said, "Murray, I also want you to do a background check for me. Find out what you can about a cardiac surgeon named Dr. Nora Blake, about her deceased husband and about the company he worked for. Something tells me Dr. Blake isn't exactly what she seems."

Chapter 4

The sun was just peeking over the horizon the next morning when Nora pulled into the nearly empty parking lot at the Prairie Springs park. Only a half dozen cars dotted the spaces. Five of them she recognized as other runners who preferred to exercise in the quiet of the early morning hours. The red SUV was one she hadn't seen here before.

As she opened her car door, the beast tried to get out first, climbing over Nora in his exuberance at the idea of a run in the park. Nora held on to the leash with grim determination as fifty pounds of Airedale terrier hit the end of the nylon strap.

"Conan, stop it. Sit!" Nora commanded, getting out and rubbing the bruise she knew she'd have on her thigh.

The russet brown, curly coated dog with a black saddle marking on his back dropped to his haunches and gave her a wide doggy grin. Once they were on the jogging paths, he would be the perfectly behaved running companion, but sometimes he was too eager to get under way.

"Good dog. Stay until I've done my stretches."

The big terrier lay down to watch her. Officially, he belonged to Pamela, but his preference for Nora began the minute they brought the wiggling puppy home from the breeder.

Getting a puppy had been Nora's idea, a fact Pamela reminded her stepmother of when Conan destroyed some piece of furniture or dug up the flower beds. The only way to keep his exuberance in check was to see that he got plenty of exercise. Hence, he had become Nora's running partner.

Nora looped the leash over her wrist and quickly warmed up. Conan managed to behave until she was ready. Once her stretches were done, she looked over the park.

There were a number of trails and paths to choose from. The easiest ones meandered through the flat areas of the park that skirted the river. For the adventurous runner, there were paths that traversed the steep hillsides and rugged woodlands on the other side of the water. A narrow footbridge offered an easy way across the river.

"Okay, boy, which way today? Shall we run down by the water or up on the hill trails?"

Watching her intently, the big dog whined and then barked once.

"The river it is," Nora said, checking her watch. She didn't have to report to the Fort Bonnell hospital until ten o'clock and it was barely after six-thirty. The thought of getting away from the stress of her job and enjoying the beautiful morning made her smile. There weren't enough days like this.

With her eager companion running beside her, Nora started off at an easy pace. The morning air was cool, but it didn't feel like October. There wasn't a nip in the air yet or the smell of autumn that she had loved in her native New England. This part of Texas could have its share of cold winter weather, but so far, summer was lingering in the hill country.

She decided on a circuit that took her two miles around the outside perimeter of the park before it cut back along the river near the footbridge. The path was wide and they came upon only one other person jogging in the opposite direction. For most of the first two miles, they had the place to themselves. That was exactly how Nora liked it.

Both she and the dog were hitting a good stride when they rounded a sharp curve in the path at the footbridge. Just then a runner came off the bridge and turned in front of them. Nora veered right to go around him. Conan veered left.

The second she realized what was happening, Nora tried to stop. Conan didn't. The man they attempted to mow down jumped lightly over the taut strap leaving Nora to gape at him in astonishment as she stumbled past. It was Rob Dale.

Recovering her stride, she looked back once, then kept going. Of all the people in the world, why did she have to run into him? She'd thrown on an old yellow jersey that had seen better days and her most comfortable running pants—the faded green pair that had a hole in one knee. Maybe he hadn't recognized her.

No such luck. Within a few dozen yards, he came up from behind her.

"Morning, Nora." Matching her stride, he fell into step beside her.

"Mr. Dale." She nodded once in his direction.

"Nice morning for a run," he said, grinning from ear to ear.

"It was." Her tone was dismissive, but as usual he didn't take the hint.

Glancing at him from the corner of her eye, it was plain that he had already been at this for some time. His gray T-shirt was soaked with sweat, and his shoes and the hems of his dark blue pants were coated with fine gray dust from one of the park's steep trails that zigzagged to the top of the bluffs, yet he didn't seem winded.

Her first impression about him had been correct. He carried himself like an athlete. Although she considered trying to sprint on ahead, she doubted she could outrun him. Loping beside her, Conan eyed the man and growled low in his throat.

Good dog, she thought, mentally promising him an extra dog biscuit when they got home.

"Do you run here often?" Rob asked.

"No."

It wasn't a complete lie. She didn't get out here as frequently as she liked. She certainly wouldn't come here again until after he had left town. "I really prefer to run alone."

"Usually I do, too." There was a touch of surprise in his voice. Looking over, she met his gaze. His smile did funny things to her stomach.

Staring straight ahead once again, she considered what to do next. It was nearly two miles back to her car. He was jogging in the same direction. Other than being outright rude, she didn't know how to get rid of him. She considered just stopping and letting him go ahead, but knowing him, he probably wouldn't.

The fastest way to get rid of him was simply to keep going. She increased her stride and tried her best to ignore him.

The path they were on curved in and out of the trees that covered a large part of the park. Their long shadows kept the air cool in the early morning. A small breeze rustled the branches overhead and brushed her cheeks. The leaves of the oaks and maples were just beginning to put on their autumn colors of burnt orange, gold and red. A few fallen leaves dotted the path and grass beneath the trees. It was a beautiful area.

Normally she would have slowed her pace to enjoy the scenery, but not today. The trail made another sharp bend that brought them within sight of the river again.

The morning sunlight danced as reflected diamonds glittering off the ripples in the shallow water. On the opposite shore, a whitetail deer was drinking. The doe raised her head and then bounded away into the trees with her tail held high.

"That is what I call pretty," Rob said, glancing down at Nora with a sweet smile.

After that, he didn't say anything else. They ran side by side with only the sound of their feet hitting the ground and Conan panting beside them. Nora's self-consciousness slowly ebbed away. Bit by bit, the joy she always felt when she ran crept back over her.

When the parking lot came into sight, Rob slowed to a walk and propped both hands on his hips. To his surprise, Nora did the same. They were both breathing heavily. As they walked to cool down, he studied her covertly.

He liked that she was a runner. Without the hospital scrubs or lab coat she looked like any ordinary woman out for a jog in the park. Her blond hair was pulled back into a ponytail. Her running clothes had been chosen for comfort not style. She wasn't out here in the early hours of the morning to impress anyone. She was out here because she loved it. He understood the feeling.

When he'd had a chance to catch his breath and he could tell that she had done the same, he asked, "What's your dog's name?"

"Conan."

"Like the barbarian?"

She smiled slightly. It was the first time he'd seen her do so. He liked the way it softened her face. She should do it more often.

"That wasn't what we had in mind when we named him, but it fits."

By now they had almost reached the parking lot and Rob found himself reluctant to end the chance encounter. He dropped to one knee to retie a shoe that didn't need adjusting. Nora stopped walking. Conan apparently decided Rob didn't pose a threat and came to nuzzle his hand in the hopes of getting some attention. Rob, happy to oblige, ruffled the dog's ears. "He's a friendly fellow."

"Not usually," Nora admitted, giving him a quizzical look.

"Then I guess I feel privileged," Rob said with a chuckle as Conan began licking his face.

Rising to his feet, Rob patted the dog's head one more time. A picnic table sat nearby beneath the wide spreading branches of an oak tree. Rob took a chance and walked over to sit on the rustic planks. He held out his hand to Conan, and the dog tugged on the leash trying to reach him. Nora stepped closer.

Rob kept his attention on the dog as if it didn't matter whether or not Nora was there. Scratching Conan's wooly head just behind his ears, Rob crooned. "You're a good boy, aren't you? I'll bet you play a wicked game of fetch."

Glancing up at Nora, but keeping one hand on the dog, Rob said, "So tell me about Prairie Springs. What brought you and the barbarian to west Texas?"

Nora glanced toward her car, then back at Rob, a look of indecision on her face. In the end, her dog's delight in his new playmate seemed to win her over.

"Mercy Medical Center made me an offer I couldn't refuse," she replied.

"If you don't mind my asking, what kind of offer was that?"

She sent him a suspicious look. "Reporter Rob Dale of the *Liberty and Justice* is asking my permission before he peppers me with questions?"

He held his hands wide. "I don't have a pen or paper on me, so you're safe."

Obviously skeptical, she said, "Hmm. Maybe, but I doubt it."

He leaned back and folded his arms across his chest. "Fine. You ask the questions."

"How did you get that scar on your arm?"

He glanced at the puckered red mark. "Sorry. That would be privileged medical information."

She raised one eyebrow.

"All right. A camel kicked me."

"Is that a joke?"

"Oh, how I wish it were. Nope, a racing camel kicked me and broke my arm. It didn't heal right, so my paper brought me back to the States for surgery to break it again and pin it in place." He wiggled his fingers. "I'm almost as good as new."

She crossed her arms over her chest. "You expect me to believe that you're a camel racer in your spare time?"

He shook his head. "No. I was doing a piece on the plight of child jockeys. Kids as young as five are forced to participate in a very dangerous sport. Some are even bought and sold as slaves."

"Yes, I've heard a little about the practice. Did you publish your article?"

"I managed to type it up with one hand."

"That's dedication. Do you think it did any good?"

"It brought some attention to the problem. I'm not sure I did much real good, but I tried."

She took a seat on the bench beside him. "That counts for something."

He was glad it did in her eyes. "My turn. Aside from money, what would make one hospital's offer better than the next?"

"Why do you think my move here wasn't about the money?"

"Your pro bono work for Children of the Day tells me money isn't a high priority for you."

"You assume that. I could have ulterior motives. Besides, until I moved here, I'd never heard of Children of the Day."

He leaned forward and propped his elbows on his knees. "Okay, I assume the best about people. It's one of my flaws, but it wasn't about the money, was it?"

"I was promised the chance to set up a pediatric cardiac program exactly as I wished."

"But?"

"Yes, there frequently is a *but* in the business part of any medical program. After I arrived, funds were not available to purchase new surgical equipment or to enlarge the PICU to handle more cases."

He frowned. "I thought the PICU head nurse told me they were planning an expansion."

"They are now. A private donation is making it possible. Given a little more time and money, I'm going to develop a pediatric cardiac surgical unit that will rival any in the country." He heard the determination in her voice and saw the resolve in her eyes.

"Is it important to be better than anyone else?"

"Austin is a rapidly growing city in a rapidly growing area of the United States. For any child born with a cardiac defect here, yes, it's important that this unit be the best."

"Then I'm sure it will happen for you. Who made the donation to your cause?"

"I don't know." Rising suddenly to her feet, she gave a gentle tug on Conan's lead. The dog moved to stand by her side.

"I'd think you'd want to find out, maybe ask them for more money."

"The money came from an anonymous donor. I really should be going," she added, looking down to avoid his gaze.

He wanted to stay awhile longer, but he knew their time had come to an end. He stood, too. At least he'd been granted the chance to get to know her outside of the hospital. "I'll see you tomorrow before surgery."

She had slipped back into her cool professional demeanor. "Yes, don't be late, Mr. Dale. I won't wait on you."

"I'll be there bright and early. You can count on it."

She walked away with her dog at her side. Rob hoped she would look back at him, but only Conan spared him a backward glance.

Chapter 5

Nora rolled over and switched off her alarm a minute before the buzzer was due to sound. Sleep had been hard to come by last night, and not just because she couldn't get Rob Dale out of her mind. Her late-night emergency surgery had driven away every thought of him for a time, but when she returned home he had crept back into her mind.

As much as she tried to tell herself that she didn't relish the idea of spending any more time in his company, some small part of her was looking forward to showing him her work. Surgery was her passion. She loved it and she wanted him to understand that.

If only she didn't have to be careful about revealing too much of herself. He was very good at his job and that made him dangerous to her peace of mind.

Rising, she pulled on a red chintz robe over her simple

white cotton nightgown. After making her bed, she padded barefoot down the polished wooden stairs. The smell of cinnamon toast and freshly brewed coffee reached her before she rounded the corner into the gleaming, ultramodern kitchen.

Pamela, her twenty-four-year-old stepdaughter, sat at the oval walnut table situated in front of a large bay window that overlooked the lawn and garden at the back of the house. She glanced up from the newspaper spread out in front of her and tucked a lock of brown hair back behind her ear. Conan was lying under the table, happily gnawing on a chew toy.

Nora walked up to Pamela, slipped her arms around her shoulders and hugged her tightly, then dropped a kiss on her head. "Have I told you lately how much I love you?"

"Every day and twice on Sunday. I'm sorry one of your patients died."

Nora swallowed the lump in her throat. "What makes you think I lost a patient?"

Pamela patted Nora's arms still entwined about her shoulders. "I know this fierce hugging and that tone in your voice. It's a sign things didn't…go well."

Nora straightened. With one hand she smoothed Pamela's hair. "I'm as transparent as glass to you, aren't I? You're up early. What's the occasion?"

"I knew you had surgery today and if I wanted to see you at all, it would have to be at breakfast. There's toast and coffee if you want some. Do you want to talk about what happened at the hospital last night?"

Nora tried never to burden Pamela with the unhappy side of her work. "No, but thanks for the offer. Did you need to see me about something special?"

"No, I just like to spend time with you, and the busier you get at the hospital, the harder that becomes."

"I know. I'm sorry." Nora moved to the counter and poured the dark brew into a thick brown mug. She added a hearty dollop of cream from the carton in the refrigerator and carried her cup to the table, where she sat down opposite Pamela.

"Don't be sorry," Pamela said quickly. "I know you're doing what you love and I'm happy your practice is growing."

Nora managed a smile but decided to change the subject. "How is your new job at the library working out?"

"Good. Margaret Porter is a dream to work for. She's really open to new ideas for the youth and children's section. When she found out that I sometimes volunteer for Children of the Day, she asked me to look into coordinating some of the library's services with theirs. Are you sure you're okay? You don't look like you slept at all."

Nora blew on her coffee and then took a sip. She didn't want to depress Pamela by discussing her work. Setting her mug down, she said, "I slept, but I'll sleep better when that reporter is gone. I still can't believe that he went over my head to get permission to go into surgery with me today."

"I need to meet this guy."

Frowning at Pamela's wide grin, Nora said, "Why on earth would you want to meet him? He is the most annoying, nosey, pushy, smug man on the face of the earth." She picked up a wedge of toast and took a large bite, preferring to ignore the fact that she hadn't found him annoying at the park yesterday.

"Any man who gets this kind of rise out of you is definitely worth knowing."

"And what is that supposed to mean?" Nora mumbled.

"It means that I had just about given up hope."

After swallowing hard, Nora demanded, "Hope of what?"

"Hope that you would meet a man who sparked some kind of interest from you. I know that you loved Dad, but he's been gone for six years now. Don't you think it's time you started dating again? You don't have to spend your life alone."

Nora had no intention of looking for another relationship. She wasn't willing to risk her heart again. The knowledge of Bernard's betrayal was a bitter memory, but one she would never share with her stepdaughter. Pamela had adored her father. After his death, Nora had done everything in her power to protect the grieving teenager, including keeping the truth well hidden. "I don't ever intend to marry again. I'm content with my life as it is."

"It's not like I'm going to be living here forever. I'd like to think that you'll have someone to look after you and to love you when I'm not around."

Nora opened her mouth and then closed it again. Shocked, she reached across the table to take Pamela's hand. "Honey, you don't need to stay with me. If you want to get your own place, I would miss you, but I would understand. I don't need someone to look after me."

Pamela leaned back and crossed her arms. "Really? What day does the trash get picked up?"

"I don't know—Friday—it gets picked up on Friday."

"Tuesday. How soon will the oil need to be changed in your car?"

"What difference does that make?"

"Fifteen hundred more miles. Your work is the whole focus of your life, Nora. You need someone who will notice the details outside of the hospital."

"I can learn to do those things."

Pamela arched one eyebrow. "You're thirty-five years old. If you were going to learn to do those things you would know how by now."

"You don't need to make it sound like I'm some decrepit old dog that can't learn a few new tricks."

Pamela smiled that pixie grin that had won Nora's heart the very first day they had met. "You aren't old, and I don't think that you're decrepit. I just know how you are. Even Dad used to say that if it didn't have to do with medicine, you didn't think it mattered. You have a one-track mind."

"I'll hire a housekeeper if that will make you feel better, but I'm not going to go looking for a husband just so he'll know what day to take out my trash."

Leaning forward, Pamela stretched her hand palm up. Without hesitation, Nora took hold of it. "Medicine matters, but there is more to life than work. I wish you could see that. I know you still grieve for Sondra and for Dad, but it's not too late to start another family of your own."

Nora felt her stomach drop. Sometimes she still dreamed about the sweet smell of her baby girl nestled in her arms, but when she opened her eyes, she faced reality with a grim determination. This was her life now.

"Pamela, you and Conan are the only family I want or need."

The younger woman squeezed Nora's hand. "Maybe that's true, but I can't help thinking that there is someone out there who will love you as you deserve to be loved. Not as a great stepmom, which you are, or as a great surgeon, but as a woman."

When Rob walked out of the lobby and into the parking lot of the Prairie Springs Inn, the eastern sky held only a hint of pink and gold on a few wisps of high clouds. The air was still cool but the day promised to be another hot one. October in the hill country of west Texas was a lot different than October in Washington, DC. As he drew in a deep breath of clean air, Rob decided that he liked it here better than he liked the congested capitol.

Stepping into his red Jeep Cherokee truck, he soon put the small town behind him. Past the city limits, the dawn highlighted the steep bluffs and hills with a clear golden light that was so beautiful he couldn't help being overwhelmed by the sight.

What a wondrous day You have made, Lord. Thank You for this gift. Help me to use it wisely.

Rob sped toward Austin with his windows rolled down, enjoying the brief sights of the country and a short conversation with God before the outskirts of the city began to clutter the view.

As he pulled into the hospital parking lot, he checked his watch and saw that he still had twenty minutes before presurgical rounds in the PICU were due to start. If he stopped by Nora's office he might have a chance to spend a few minutes alone with her before her hectic day got under way. He tried telling himself it was a good angle for his story, but the truth was—he simply wanted to see her.

In spite of their differences, Nora drew him in in a way no woman ever had before. She was special. He sensed it deep in his soul. God had brought them together for reasons Rob didn't understand, but he was eager to explore the feelings she evoked. Whistling a favorite old tune, he entered the building and took the elevator to the third floor.

The office door was unlocked. He knocked once and then walked in. A thin woman with sparse brown hair and garish red lipstick sat behind the reception desk. She scowled at him. "May I help you?"

He grinned. "You must be Delia."

"I am *Miss* Walden—and you are?" She arched one eyebrow, her frosty tone making him feel like an errant six-year-old.

He held out his hand. "I'm Robert Dale, reporter for the *Liberty and Justice.* Would you tell Nora that I'm here?"

She slowly withdrew a pencil from the holder at the front of her desk, ignoring his outstretched fingers. "*Doctor Blake* isn't in the office, Mr. Dale. Would you care to leave a message?"

He let his arm drop. "No, I'll just wait for her in her office."

"That isn't possible. No one is allowed access to either Dr. Kent or Dr. Blake's offices unless they are present."

"Of course. I'll wait out here, then. How was Las Vegas?"

"It was hot." She turned to her computer and proceeded to ignore him. He settled onto one of the chairs along the wall. He had rarely met a woman he couldn't charm, but Delia Walden was apparently made of stern stuff.

"Have you worked here a long time, Miss Walden?"

She continued to type. He listened to the rapid clack

of her nails on the keyboard. After a moment, he sat forward and spoke louder. "Have you worked here long, Miss Walden?"

She stopped typing and the printer began to spew out pages. When it finished, she gathered them together, rose and carried them into Dr. Kent's office. A minute later, she returned empty handed, sat down and started typing again.

Rob glanced at the clock. It was past time for rounds to begin. Nora struck him as a very punctual person. He hoped nothing was wrong. "Is it unusual for Dr. Blake to be this late?"

Delia didn't pause. "Dr. Blake is not late. She came in half an hour ago."

He rose to his feet. "She did? Then where is she?"

"She normally goes to medical records to review old charts first thing in the morning. She should be making rounds in the PICU now."

Great. Now he was the one who was late. "I wish you had told me that when I came in."

Delia stopped working and gave him a cold smile. "You didn't ask me where she was."

Pressing his lips into a tight line, he nodded, then said, "I'll be more specific in the future, Miss Walden."

She turned away. "I'm sure you will."

He left the office and hurried down the hallway toward the pediatric wing. At the PICU, he pressed the button on the wall and the doors swung open. A group of nurses and doctors were already clustered at the front desk. As Rob walked down the hall toward them, he glanced into Cara Dempsey's room and stopped short.

The bed was empty. The jumble of monitors and pumps were gone, leaving only the warming bed covered with a crisp white sheet sitting against the wall. A cold feeling settled in his chest.

The automatic doors opened behind him and Nora came striding into the unit. He turned to her and asked, “Where is Cara?”

“She’s gone.” Nora’s voice was so matter-of-fact that for a second he thought he hadn’t heard her correctly. She walked past him without pausing.

Stunned, he glanced into the empty room. Deep, aching sorrow rushed in to fill his heart. God had a purpose for every soul. Only He knew what purpose Cara had served in her short life.

With leaden feet, Rob followed Nora to where she stood reading through another child’s chart. He asked, “When did it happen?”

Nora didn’t look up. “Late yesterday. I’m going to see the patient with the AV canal and then I’m going to scrub in for surgery. Do you still plan on joining me?”

He reached out and grabbed her arm. “Are you really so cold hearted? A child died. A child you operated on. Don’t you feel anything?”

She glared at him. “What are you talking about?”

“I’m talking about Cara Dempsey.”

Her lips pressed into a tight line for a second, then she said, “Cara Dempsey didn’t die. Dr. Kent transferred her back to the hospital where she came from at her parents’ request yesterday evening. There wasn’t anything more that we could do for her here.”

Relief swept through him. “She didn’t die? I saw the empty bed and I thought…one of the nurses said she wasn’t going to make it.”

“No, she didn’t die, but if she had, what I *feel* wouldn’t matter, Mr. Dale.”

She pulled away from his grasp and pointed down the hall. "I have another patient depending on me. A family in that room is putting their baby's life in my hands in the hope that I can give their son what they can't—a chance at a normal, healthy life."

"I made a rash assumption. I'm sorry."

"Yes, you did. Every child I see deserves my complete and utter concentration. I can't afford the luxury of *feelings* when I'm working."

Quietly, he said, "That must be very difficult for you."

For the briefest instant, her mask of indifference slipped. He saw pain and sorrow in her beautiful hazel eyes. A second later, her implacable demeanor was back in place. She took a step away and said, "Please excuse me. I have rounds to make."

Rob stood rooted to the spot as she walked away. He had been a soldier. He'd had to suppress his emotions during the heat of battle and mourn his fallen friends later when no one was depending on him to make quick, sound decisions. He thought that mindset belonged only in the jungles and deserts where armed conflicts reigned.

As he watched Nora lead the group of doctors and nurses into a room at the end of the hall, he saw the truth with sudden clarity. Nora was on her way into yet another life-and-death battle. He had no right to judge her.

Rob knew how to blend into the background. His years in the army had taught him that skill, and he put it to use that morning. After changing into scrubs, he followed Nora, Dr. Kent and several other doctors into the hallowed halls of the operating theater.

He wanted to be at Nora's elbow, probing into the emotions and drive that made her choose this kind of work, but he held back. He didn't want to distract her.

He didn't want to add any pressure to her today. Instead, he watched in quiet amazement as she, along with Dr. Kent and several others, began the operation.

Dressed in bulky gowns with their faces covered by masks, it was only possible to tell the two physicians apart by their height. Both Nora and Dr. Kent donned long lenses on heavy-looking headsets that appeared awkward and cumbersome, but in his research the night before, Rob had read that the lighted magnifying loupes were essential to working on minuscule blood vessels.

There were three nurses in the room who were moving about but not directly involved in the surgery. When one seemed free, he asked her to explain what was going on.

"Dr. Blake is closing an abnormal opening between the two chambers on the left side of the heart. To do this she has to build a wall out of living tissue and make a valve that works."

"That sounds complicated."

"It's like working on the inside of a deflated ball smaller than an egg. What sounds complicated about that?"

Rob suspected that he amused the nurse, but he couldn't tell if she was smiling behind her mask.

"Would you let Dr. Blake operate on your kid?"

"In a heartbeat. She has the gift."

"What gift is that?"

"When she makes those tiny stitches with sutures finer than a human hair, she is able to know how they will look when the heart is full and round and pumping blood again. Believe me, it's a God-given talent."

"Dr. Blake told me she doesn't believe in God."

"Maybe not, but He believes in her."

The nurse was called away and Rob moved closer to where Nora was working. Even from only a few feet away he couldn't see much. The patient was simply too small, the incision even smaller. The numerous hands holding instruments, gauzes and needles obscured any hope of his getting to view Nora's actual work.

What he did instead was observe the way the people working spoke quietly back and forth. There was chit-chat between Dr. Kent and the anesthesiologist about Dr. Kent's new sports car and his upcoming trip to Grand Cayman. The nurses talked about their kids and complained about the extra shift they were being asked to cover. From time to time, a nurse left the room to update the parents waiting down the hall. Everyone seemed on friendly terms with everyone else. Everyone exchanged bits and pieces of their lives.

Everyone, that was, except Nora.

She didn't look up; she didn't join in the chatter. If she spoke it was to direct someone or to ask for another suture or to have the lights adjusted. She seemed to Rob to be literally alone in the room—as if she were in some kind of bubble—exempt from everything except the task of mending a tiny flawed heart beneath her hands.

Nora knew Rob was there at the edge of the room. Even when he wasn't in her line of sight, she felt his presence. He wasn't being intrusive and she was grateful for that. It was hard enough to concentrate with so little sleep and with her unsuccessful surgery last night on the terminally ill soldier at the base hospital still fresh in her mind.

She had only been covering a call for the base cardiac surgeon, as she occasionally did, to help the overstretched staff at the Fort Bonnell Medical Center. The patient, a sixty-four-year-old major, had been unconscious when she arrived. To her deep regret, she never spoke to him, only to his grieving family.

Now, exhaustion pulled at Nora but she willed it away. She couldn't afford the distraction. This patient, the one on the table, deserved her full attention. As the time passed, she eventually forgot about Rob, last night's surgery and how tired she was.

Each miniature stitch she placed with near perfection filled her with a wellspring of satisfaction. With all its stress and pain, this was her life's work and she loved it.

When the reconstruction was complete and she was satisfied that she had done her absolute best, she spoke to the perfusion technologist. "Warm him up."

As the temperature of the patient rose, she waited with bated breath for that first quiver that would signal the heart was working. It was only a few minutes, but it seemed like hours.

Then, there it was, the first contraction, followed by another and then another. Soon the tiny heart was beating briskly before her eyes.

Suddenly her exhaustion came rushing in. She stepped back from the table. "Dr. Kent, will you close, please?"

"Certainly. You've done the hard part. Take a break."

She arched her back, trying to stretch tight muscles that ached in protest. Unplugging her loupes, she walked out of the operating room and into the scrub area. After pulling off her gloves, mask and cap, she tossed them into the trash. Then she ran her fingers through her hair plastered to her temples with sweat.

"How did it go?"

She spun around, surprised to see that Rob was still there. “It went well. It was a good repair.”

“Are you finished?”

She turned to the sink and began to wash her hands. “Not until we get little Mr. Drake back to the PICU and stabilized and I’ve had a chance to talk to his parents.”

“You called him by his name. That’s the first time I’ve heard you refer to one of your patients by name. You usually refer to them by their diagnosis.”

“Do I?”

“You don’t want to become emotionally involved with your patients. You see it as a weakness.”

She would have to add perceptive to his list of personality traits. Pulling a paper towel from the dispenser, she leaned back against the sink and dried her hands. “I’m very tired. Can we continue this conversation some other time?”

“Sure. I just wanted to say that I admire what you do. Watching you today was awe inspiring.”

He seemed so sincere. She wasn’t sure exactly what to make of this about face. He had gotten her used to expecting wisecracks, not compliments. An uncomfortable silence stretched between them.

Finally, she said, “Thank you.” She didn’t know what else to say.

“No, thank you, Dr. Blake, for allowing me to see what it is you do. I hope I can convey even a small part of the amazing talent and patience I saw today to my readers.”

“I’m glad I could be of some help.”

“I’ll be interviewing other people who work for Children of the Day as well as Ali and his grandfather over the next several days, so I'll be out of your hair until the day of Ali's surgery."

"Oh." How could she feel disappointed? She should be delighted—only she wasn't.

He smiled and touched one finger to his forehead in that silly salute that he used so often. "See you around, Doc."

As he walked out of the room, Nora couldn't explain the sense of loss that weighed her down.

Chapter 6

Rob adjusted his rearview mirror to check that his tie was straight. He turned his face one way and then the other to make sure that his shave was close enough and that his normally unruly hair had been brushed into submission.

Satisfied that he would pass even the most stringent inspection, he stepped out of his truck and headed up the walk leading to a stately redbrick Georgian home just off Veteran's Boulevard in the historical district of Prairie Springs. He glanced at his watch when he reached the front door. It was ten o'clock. He was right on time. Lifting the heavy ring in the brass lion's mouth, he knocked twice.

The door opened to reveal a stern-looking white-haired man in a short-sleeved olive-green shirt and black pants. Repressing the urge to snap to attention and salute, Rob extended his hand instead.

"Good morning, sir. I'm Robert Dale from the *Liberty and Justice*. We spoke on the phone yesterday afternoon. I'd like to say how much I appreciate your sharing your grandson's story."

The older man's keen blue eyes seemed to make a quick assessment, then he nodded. "At first I thought it was a bunch of nonsense making such a fuss about it, but a lot of good men and women worked long and hard to get my boy here. They deserve the thanks, not me. I only granted this interview so that I could give credit where credit is due."

"I understand."

General Marlon Willis let out a deep breath and stepped back from the door. "All right. Come in and let's get this over with. Ali is on the sofa in the living room. He tires easily so if I say we're done, we're done. Is that clear?"

"Crystal clear, sir."

The general lead the way across the polished oak floors of the entry and into a sunny room filled with oversized and comfortable-looking furniture. Rob saw a woman with shoulder-length chestnut hair seated in a wooden ladder-back chair beside a beige couch. On the sofa, a small boy of five lay propped up with pillows. He was engaged in putting the pieces of a simple wooden jigsaw puzzle together on the low table drawn up close beside him.

The woman looked up and graced Rob with a warm and friendly smile. The general said, "Sarah, this is Rob Dale. Mr. Dale, this is my neighbor, Sarah Alpert. Sarah has been helping me keep Ali entertained."

Rising, Sarah held out her hand. "Howdy, Mr. Dale. It's a pleasure to meet y'all."

His big hand almost swallowed hers. "That accent tells me you aren't a military transplant."

"No, indeed. I'm a Texan, born and bred and mighty proud of it."

"Sarah was friends with Ali's father—my son, Greg—when they were younger." Rob didn't miss the catch in the old man's voice.

Sarah gave him a kindly smile. "He was a fine man. A bit pigheaded at times, but I have an idea who he inherited that trait from."

The general managed a ghost of a smile at her teasing. "It must have been from his mother's side of the family."

She chuckled. "Right. And pigs fly, too. At least Ali didn't inherit the family flaw. He's a perfect little gentleman."

The boy watched Rob shyly. With his dark hair and soulful dark eyes it was obvious he was of Middle Eastern descent. Rob already knew part of the boy's history. He knew that the boy's father had been an American soldier and that his mother had been a humanitarian worker for Children of the Day in her native land.

Their marriage had caused a rift between General Willis and his son that had never healed. After his son's death when Ali was three years old, the general still didn't acknowledge his grandson. It wasn't until after a roadside bomb killed Ali's mother that the general stepped in. With the aid of Children of the Day, he arranged for his injured grandson to come to the United States.

Rob moved closer to the boy and said, *"Sabah al-kair, Ali."*

Ali sat bolt upright, a bright smile wreathing his face. *"Sabah alnur."* He returned Rob's greeting and then launched into rapid Arabic.

Rob laughed and held up one hand. "You'll have to go more slowly. I'm a little rusty."

"I talk English okay good," Ali said proudly.

"Probably better than I speak Arabic," Rob conceded.

Sarah brought over a second chair. After nodding his thanks, Rob took a seat and pulled out his notepad. Smiling at the boy, he said, "Do you mind if I ask you some questions about your trip to America?"

Ali sank back against the pillows. The animation left his face, and Rob noticed how pale he looked. The general sat on the end of the sofa and patted the boy's leg. "It's all right if you don't want to talk about it."

Ali lifted his chin and Rob saw a likeness between the boy and his grandfather in the stubborn jut of their jaws. "I can talk now. After bomb kill Om…" He paused and cast Rob an imploring look.

Rob supplied the word the boy was searching for. "Mother."

"Yes, after bomb kill my m…mother, I go to hospital in big tent."

Pressing a hand to his chest, Ali continued. "I hurt here very much. I scared until I see Dr. Mike."

Rob looked from his notes to General Willis. "Dr. Mike?"

It was Sarah who spoke first. "Captain Michael Montgomery is a U.S. Army doctor. He and Greg served together. After Greg's death, Michael kept an eye on Ali and his mother."

Something in the way she said the name Michael made Rob look at her closely. Her eyes met his briefly, then slid away. A faint blush tinted her fair cheeks. He wondered what history she shared with the good doctor stationed so far from Texas. He didn't have a chance to speculate further because Ali spoke again.

"Dr. Mike, he say I must go America to fix my heart. He say my jadd…my grandfather, is here and he will take care of me."

He puffed out his little chest. "I tell Dr. Mike I can take care of me okay good. He say I fly in big helicopter with David and pretty nurse Maddie."

Marlon said, "Chief Warrant Office David Ryland and nurse Madeline Bright were returning to the Fort Bonnell after their tour of duty in the Middle East ended. I pulled a few strings to make sure that Ali had their company on the way back. It was the least I could do for the boy. If I had tried to do more for him and his mother sooner, perhaps none of this would have happened."

The general grew quiet as he became lost in thought. Rob caught a glimpse of the toll the old man's grief and regrets had taken on him. Compelled to offer what comfort he could, Rob said, "You are doing the best for Ali now. That's what's important. The past can't be changed."

The general nodded, then grimaced and rubbed his left arm. Sarah leaned toward him. "Are you all right?"

He straightened and glanced at his grandson. Ali's eyes were wide with worry. Marlon managed a smile as he reached out and squeezed Ali's big toe. "I'm okay good. You go on with your story."

Ali grinned and stretched his arms wide. "After I get off helicopter, I fly in big, big plane."

"You must have been scared to come so far," Rob suggested.

"A little—but not much. Nurse Maddie and David, they stay with me. They tell me everything be fine."

"And they were right," Sarah said. "God brought you to us to get well."

"And to bring a little bit of my son back to me," Marlon added.

Rob glanced at the general. "Can I ask why Ali hasn't had the surgery already?"

"Apparently this type of injury is extremely rare. The hope at first was that the tear inside Ali's heart might heal on its own, but Dr. Montgomery wanted him in the States if that didn't happen. He was right about that. It wasn't long before the boy began having trouble with fluid on his lungs."

Sarah leaned forward to ruffle Ali's hair. "Once he got here, Dr. Blake wanted his nutritional status improved before she scheduled his surgery. Then we had a delay because of an upper respiratory infection. Once that was cleared up and he put on some weight, the surgery was scheduled for the middle of next week."

Ali smiled at his grandfather. "Soon, Dr. Blake make me all better and we tell Nurse Tilda go away."

Marlon and Sarah laughed.

"Tilda is the home health nurse looking after Ali and me," Marlon explained. "She would have made a fine drill sergeant. She loves ordering us around."

Ali grimaced and made a sour face. "Her medicine taste very bad."

Rob chuckled, but in his mind he prayed that Nora would be able to fix Ali's damaged heart. The case of little Cara had driven home just how risky such a surgery could be.

Please, Lord, this boy has seen so much of sorrow.

Let Your light shine upon him. If it is Your will, bring health, comfort and joy into his life and into the lives of those who love him.

Nora, with Pamela beside her, climbed the steps of the converted slate blue Victorian house that had become home to the charity Children of the Day. The charity was the brain child of Russian-born immigrant Anna Terenkov and named from the Bible passage 1 Thessalonians 5:5, "Ye are all the children of light, and the children of the day: we are not of the night, nor of darkness."

The organization had grown from its humble beginnings in Anna and her mother Olga's living room into a business that employed a full-time staff and had taken over the entire lower level of the building.

As Nora and Pamela crossed the wide, welcoming porch that wrapped around the gracious old home, Nora said, "You don't have to come with me if you have other things to do, Pamela. I wanted to visit with Anna about the medicine I'm shipping overseas. I don't know how long I'll be. It depends on what Anna is involved in at the moment. You can go on and I'll call your cell phone when I'm done."

"I don't mind the detour. Besides, Olga wasn't at the church this afternoon. I'm hoping to find her here so we can firm up plans for the children's traveling book exchange at her grief center. Oh, there she is."

Nora followed Pamela's gaze to see Olga sitting on the cushion-filled porch swing at the side of the house. She wasn't alone. Laura Dean, the secretary, and Caitlin Villard, the care coordinator for Children of the Day sat beside her. Nora's stomach did a funny little flip-flop when she recognized Rob leaning against the porch railing, pen and notebook in hand as he faced the three women.

Just then, he looked over and met Nora's gaze. His face lit up with a grin that turned her tummy flutters into a full blown twister.

She bit her lip and looked away. Her reaction was absolutely irrational. She couldn't be excited to see him. The man was a nuisance, nothing more. But if that were true, then why was she standing here feeling like a high school freshman who had just been noticed by the captain of the football team?

"Whoa, who is the handsome guy smiling at you?" Pamela's curious voice cut into Nora's jumbled thoughts.

"He isn't smiling at me," Nora insisted sharply.

"Okay, then who is the handsome guy smiling at me?"

"That is the reporter I was telling you about. Ignore him."

"Not a chance. Come introduce me." Pamela tugged on Nora's arm.

"No. I have to speak to Anna. Besides, he isn't the kind of person you should know," she whispered, hoping he couldn't hear that they were talking about him. The man was conceited enough.

"You make him sound like an ax murderer. I'm more intrigued by the minute. He's coming this way. Why, Nora, I do believe you're blushing."

Her stepdaughter's amusement was more than Nora could bear. "I am not."

Pulling open the door, Nora escaped into the lobby and all but bolted through Anna's open office door.

Rob worked to overcome the pang of disappointment he felt as Nora disappeared into the building without even speaking to him. It was crazy, but he was hurt by her obvious rejection.

When the young woman with her came toward him, he recognized her from the picture on Nora's desk. Smiling, she held out her hand. "Hello, I'm Pamela Blake. Nora tells me you are exactly the kind of man I shouldn't meet."

Taken aback by her comment, he found himself at a loss for words.

She laughed at the look of confusion on his face. "I need to speak to Olga for a few minutes, then I'm going to grill you about your intentions toward my stepmother."

He found his voice. "My intentions are strictly honorable." His conscience gave a small twinge. That wasn't exactly the whole truth.

"Nora is usually a good judge of character, so why doesn't she like you?"

He shoved his hands in the front pockets of his jeans. "I'm doing a story about Ali Tabiz Willis and Children of the Day. Your mother doesn't like the idea of anyone profiting from the suffering of children. My boss and her boss see it differently."

Pamela gave him a long, hard look. He couldn't tell what she was thinking.

"Interesting. If you're busy with Olga, I can wait and speak with her some other time."

"Mrs. Terenkov and I were almost done."

They began walking back to the porch swing where the other women sat. The wide veranda, surrounded by towering magnolias and lush crape myrtles, overlooked the street but gave the illusion of being a quiet oasis.

"You promised to call me Olga," the older woman

chided in her lilting Russian accent. Dressed in a peasant blouse and full denim patchwork skirt over black and silver cowboy boots, the gregarious woman watched them with unabashed curiosity. "Hello, Pamela. How are you? How is the new job? How is your mother?"

"Fine, fine, and okay, I think." Pamela leaned back against the rail and tucked a windblown lock of hair behind her ear.

Rob sat on the wide porch railing beside her. From his spot he kept one eye on the door, hoping to have a word with Nora before she left.

Caitlin leaned forward, "Pamela, I see you have met Mr. Dale. He's doing an article on Children of the Day for the *Liberty and Justice* newspaper."

"Maybe more than one," he admitted. "I'm finding the charity has more facets than I first expected."

"My Anna-bug, she helps everywhere she can," Olga said with obvious maternal pride.

Caitlin patted Olga's knee. "She has her mother's boundless energy."

Laura, the slim young blonde, flashed him a wide smile. "Did we tell you that Olga runs the grief counseling center at the Prairie Springs Christian Church, helps here and still finds time to run the church's singles program?"

"Really?" He made a note of the fact.

Beside him, Pamela asked, "Are you married, Mr. Dale?"

"No," he replied slowly. He wasn't quite sure what to make of the outspoken young woman, but he suspected that given some time, he would come to like her.

Pamela's smile widened. "You should drop by our

singles meeting while you're in town. We meet every Thursday night. You would have a great time."

"You and Gary Bellman seemed to be having a great time together last week," Caitlin said with a wink. Rob had already learned that Caitlin, the newest staff member of Children of the Day, was the care coordinator and the woman responsible for getting Ali to the States.

Pamela blushed. "Thanks to Olga's matchmaking skills, I think I've found a winner. Now, Caitlin, I saw you and Chaplain Steve looking very cozy at the church social with the twins the other day."

"He's a wonderful man and the girls adore him," Caitlin replied with a soft smile.

Olga reached out and tweaked Caitlin cheek. "The girls aren't the only ones who adore him."

"Have you managed to get Pastor Fields to ask you out, yet, Olga?" Caitlin's deft turning of the tables impressed Rob who knew she had been a successful lawyer before returning to her home town of Prairie Springs to care for her recently orphaned nieces.

"Yes, he asked me out last night."

Laura's eyes widened in disbelief. "He did?"

Pamela squealed with delight and clapped her hands. "Tell us everything."

Clasping both hands to her chest, Olga closed her eyes and leaned back in the swing. "I was so stunned I think I said no, and then yes, yes, yes."

She pressed the back of her hand to her forehead in a dramatic gesture. "I was so nervous I thought I might faint."

She sounded more like a giddy teenager than a mature woman in her midfifties. Everyone, including Rob, laughed at her antics.

"When are you going out? Where is he taking you?" demanded Pamela, grinning from ear to ear.

Rob smiled as he glanced between the women all offering tips for the upcoming date. He had no idea that discussing what to wear and where to go could generate such enthusiastic conversations. After a few minutes he was feeling like a fish out of water until Olga turned to him.

"Mr. Dale, tell us, where do you suggest we go? I'd like to hear a man's opinion of what makes the perfect first date."

Suddenly, all eyes were on him. A fish out of water didn't quite cover the sensation creeping over him. A giraffe up to its chin in quicksand would be more like it.

He hadn't dated much in the past few years. His life as a covert scout for the army didn't lend itself to romantic evenings. After he'd left the army, there had always been another to story to uncover and deadlines to make.

Thankfully, the front door opened and Nora came out with Anna beside her. Anna carried a tray loaded with glasses of iced tea. "The weather is so lovely I thought we would join you out here. I have great news, everyone. Dr. Blake has been able to obtain the antibiotics so desperately needed in the refugee camp in El Almira. The drugs are on their way as we speak."

"Praise the Lord," Olga cried joyously.

"Amen," Anna replied. "He certainly knew what He was doing when He sent you to our organization, Nora."

After setting the tray on a small rattan table by the swing, Anna began handing out the glasses. "What was all the squealing and laughing about? We heard you clear into my office."

"Pastor Fields asked your mother for a date," Caitlin said with glee.

Anna's eyes widened. "Oh?"

"I was going to tell you this evening, Anna." Olga's eyes slid away from her daughter's and focused on Rob. "Mr. Dale was just telling us what a man thinks would be the perfect first date."

Rob glanced at all the women waiting for his nonexistent expertise. His collar seemed uncomfortably tight. He reached for a glass of iced tea while stalling for an answer. When his gaze met Nora's he saw the faintest trace of a smile tugging at the corner of her oh-so-kissable mouth. She was enjoying his discomfort.

What would the perfect first date with her be like? Suddenly, he could see them together with amazing clarity and he liked what he saw.

Pamela said, "Dinner and a movie are always a good place to start."

"I'd take her on a hike," he said softly.

"A hike?" Olga looked at him askance.

"We'd go somewhere up into the foothills just before dawn when the air is cool and clear. At the top of a high bluff I'd spread a picnic blanket on the ground. Then, we'd share a thermos of coffee and a loaf of French bread. The kind that has that wonderful thick crust but is soft as butter on the inside, and we'd cover our bread with big spoonfuls of strawberry jam.

"Then we would watch the sun come up. We'd sit in quiet awe and hold hands as God painted the sky and the hills with breathtaking colors and opened a new day for just the two of us."

As he stared into Nora's eyes the people and things around him faded away until all he saw was her. The afternoon breeze played with the few strands of her hair that had escaped from the silver clip at the nape of her neck. He didn't know much about fashion, but her bright pink blouse made her look young and carefree—something her white lab coat and scrubs never did.

Her eyes, so recently crinkled with amusement, stared back at him now filled with an emotion he couldn't read. The connection between them was real and powerful. She broke the contact by looking away first. The rest of the world snapped back into focus for him.

Rob realized the other women were watching him with varying degrees of puzzlement, and in Pamela's case, speculation.

Olga broke the silence. "Ya, I think dinner and a movie is the place to start."

Feeling more than a little foolish, Rob said, "Dinner is great as long as you pick a place that serves a good steak even if you're only getting a salad.

"As for the movie, don't choose a chick flick on the first date. A lot of guys really don't get them. Pick a comedy or a good action thriller. If you can stand it, go for the scary movie and hide your face against his shoulder at all the good parts. Nothing makes a guy feel more macho."

His eyes were drawn to Nora again, but she wouldn't look at him. Instead, she said, "I need more ice in my tea."

Once more she escaped from his sight into the building, but Rob knew she had to come out sooner or later.

Another thing he knew for certain—Nora Blake was definitely a woman worth waiting for.

Chapter 7

Nora hurried through the lobby and made her way straight to the small kitchen the staff used at the rear of the building. Once inside the swinging door, she put her glass down on the counter and pressed her palms to her burning cheeks.

How did he do that? How did he mesmerize her with his eyes? Try as she might, she couldn't deny that there was an attraction between them.

The bad thing was—she knew he felt it, too.

The notion that a man like Rob Dale might find her attractive wasn't beyond the bounds of belief. She'd had her share of interest from men, but other than Bernard, none of them had made an effort to get past her prickly defenses. Usually, all it took was for her to start talking about open-heart surgery to turn a first date into a final one.

So why was Rob so interested in her? Was it because he sensed she was hiding something? If he was a good reporter, and she suspected that he was, then she couldn't rule out the idea that he had ulterior motives.

If that was the case, she wouldn't fall for his obvious ploy to gain her favor.

And if that wasn't the case?

She bit her thumbnail. If she secretly longed for someone to share the joys and burdens of her life, was that wrong? She wasn't dead. Would it hurt to explore her feelings for him?

The rational part of her mind quickly squashed the glimmer of romance she felt blooming. There was no future for them. He would be gone soon. If she let down her guard where he was concerned, it would only bring her disappointment and heartache.

I need to avoid him until he finishes his story and leaves town.

Even as the thought occurred to her, she knew it wasn't going to happen. He would be at the hospital again next week when Ali Willis underwent surgery. Clasping her arms tightly across her chest, she paced the small confines of the kitchen.

At the hospital she could keep her contact with him strictly professional. She'd make sure that there wouldn't be any moments alone with him. Not in the elevator or her office or anywhere else. If they weren't alone together, he couldn't set her pulse to racing with his nearness or the tender look in his eyes.

She stopped pacing and leaned on the counter. That was all she had to do. She would avoid any time alone with him.

Grabbing up her glass, she pressed it against the ice

dispenser on the fridge and filled the tumbler to the brim. Closing her eyes, she pressed the chilled container to her temple and sighed.

The practical side of her mind quickly pointed out the obvious flaw in her plan. They hadn't been alone together out on the veranda just moments ago and he'd still managed to send her into a tailspin.

The cool glass against her face reminded her of his description of the cool morning air up in the hills. It was so easy to visualize walking hand in hand with him to the perfect spot to watch the dawn.

Her eyes flew open. What was she doing daydreaming about a date with the man?

She disliked everything he stood for. He and his newspaper were exploiting Ali's tragic story for material gain. The very idea made her sick to her stomach. His job was to snoop while there were things in her past she wanted to keep buried. Her gut instinct told her that if Rob ever suspected she was hiding something, he would go after it like Conan after a buried bone and dig up whatever dirt he could find in the process.

Exposing Pamela to the pain Rob might uncover was something Nora simply wouldn't allow.

Determined to remain resolute and unaffected by Rob's presence, Nora left the kitchen and returned to the porch. Everyone was laughing at something Rob had said. She smiled as she joined the group and took a sip of her tea.

In the sudden quiet that settled over the gathering, Nora felt his eyes on her. She was proud that she managed to swallow her drink without choking.

"Has there been any word about John and Whitney Harpswell?" Pamela asked.

Olga shook her head. "Nothing."

Rob tilted his head. "Harpswell? Aren't they the newlywed soldiers who are missing from their camp in the Middle East?"

Olga nodded. She reached over and covered Caitlin's hand with her own. "We are praying for them constantly."

"Are they relatives of yours?" Rob asked.

Olga smiled sadly. "No, although Whitney's brother lives here. After my husband, Anna's father, was killed in Afghanistan and we came to this country, God showed me a way to heal my own grief by helping others. It is through Him that true healing comes to us although it seems at times that life is so unfair."

"It does seem that way," Caitlin agreed. "My sister and her husband were killed not long ago, and I became the guardian of their twin daughters, Amanda and Josie."

"They are adorable girls," Pamela added.

Olga looked at Rob. "At the grief counseling center we have a program called Adopt-a-Soldier for the children. It's a wonderful way for them to feel like they are helping others. The twins adopted Whitney and John Harpswell."

Caitlin looked down at her hands. "The girls chose them because they reminded them a little bit of their mother and father. They have been exchanging e-mails with the couple, with my help of course because the girls are only kindergartners. Now, John and Whitney are missing in action. The girls are praying so hard for their safe return. I'm worried about what another loss will do to them."

"The girls are strong, and you are strong, too," Olga stated firmly. Caitlin looked at her and nodded.

Rob said. "I know the area well. The terrain is really rugged. The desert marches right up to the mountains there. It would be easy to be cut off from camp the way the fighting has been moving back and forth in the area."

"Were you stationed there?" Nora asked. It was frightening to picture him in the thick of battle half the world away.

"I was at the camp a few times. The majority of my time was spent with the local tribesmen. They are mostly nomadic herdsmen."

He gave her a lopsided grin. "A few of them do a little gunrunning and smuggling on the side. My job was to infiltrate enemy territory and spot potential strike targets. To move undetected by the enemy in that area can be done, but it's easier if you have help."

"I pray that someone is there to help John and Whitney," Olga added fervently.

"Amen," he said softly and bowed his head.

A shiver skittered down Nora's spine at the reverent timber of his voice. He made no secret of his belief but wore it openly. How did he reconcile the horror of war with his vision of a loving God? How did he hold on to his faith? She longed to ask him that question, but before she could, she heard a phone inside the building begin to ring.

"That's my cue to get back to work," Laura said. Setting her glass on the tray, she jumped to her feet and hurried away.

Anna rose and stretched her hand out to Rob. "I have a number of calls I need to make myself. Please let me know if you have any other questions, Mr. Dale."

He shook her hand. "I'll do that."

Turning to Nora, Anna said, "Thank you again for your help in getting the drugs we need. You are a true blessing."

"I do what I can."

"As do we all." Anna looked at Caitlin. "Do you have the e-mail address for the company that wanted to donate shoes?"

"I have their card on my desk." The two women walked into the building.

Olga rose as well and moved to stand in front of Nora. Reaching out, she grasped Nora's hand. "Major Jackson's wife came to the center this morning. She wanted me to be sure and thank you for all you did for her husband."

"It wasn't enough or he wouldn't have died."

"Don't be so hard on yourself, dear. Our Lord decides when we are called home and it was Major Jackson's time."

Nora raised her chin and shook her head. "I don't believe that."

Olga patted her hand. "Not now perhaps, but I have faith that you will in time."

Turning to Pamela, Olga said, "You wanted to talk to me about the library book exchange we have planned, didn't you?"

"I did, if you have a few minutes." Pamela picked up the tray with the empty glasses.

"I do, and inside I have a sketch of the area we'd like to use. Please excuse us." Olga nodded to Rob and Nora and led the way into the house, holding open the door for Pamela.

Suddenly, Nora found herself alone with Rob. It was exactly what she wanted to avoid.

So why am I still standing here?

Rob saw the uncertainty in Nora's eyes and knew just how she felt. This was unfamiliar emotional territory.

As a scout for the army he knew how to read the land, how to find the high ground, how to use the cover of hills and gullies to his advantage. None of that knowledge helped him now.

Why had he made such a fool of himself talking about picnics at dawn? The thought that she might have been laughing at him glued his usually glib tongue to the roof of his mouth like a spoonful of peanut butter would.

The silence stretched between them. At last, she said, “Don’t let me keep you if you have somewhere to go, Mr. Dale.”

“I’m free until dinner. I was hoping that we had known each other long enough for you to call me Rob.”

Crossing her arms over her chest, she stared at the ground. “Are you finished with your story on Children of the Day, Rob?”

He loved the breathless way she said his name and wished she would say it again.

“Not quite. I have a few more angles to check into.”

Wariness appeared in her eyes. “Angles? What kind of angles? I would think that the organization is very straightforward. They do wonderful and much-needed work.”

The indignation in her tone made him smile. Was she always so quick to defend those she considered friends? Would she ever see him in that light?

He settled his hip on the porch’s wide rail. “Every story has layers, Nora. Nothing is quite as simple as it seems. I’m sure it’s the same for the patients you see. None of them is simply a heart needing repair.”

Tilting her head slightly, she said, “That’s true. Every patient is unique. Some of them come with complex sets of problems.”

"Like Major Jackson?"

She sighed deeply. "Yes. His problems were more complex than most."

"The other morning you said *if* Cara Dempsey had died you still wouldn't have had the luxury of allowing your feelings to interfere with your work. You were actually talking about Major Jackson, weren't you? He was the one who died."

"Yes, but it doesn't matter."

He wanted to offer her comfort and reassurance. "It matters, but I understand what you are saying. It comes with the territory, doesn't it? Sometimes we have to go on no matter what. Do you ever feel like throwing back your head and howling at God in anger for putting you in that position?"

A small smile tugged at the corner of her mouth. "I don't believe in God, but sometimes I rage at the injustices I see."

"Who are you raging at?"

She shrugged. "Life. The universe."

"That is God," he said gently.

Meeting his gaze with a degree of speculation, she asked, "What about you? Do you ever rage at Him?"

"I have a few times in my life."

"Weren't you afraid that lightning would strike you down?"

He knew she was trying to sound sarcastic, but he could see an interest that she couldn't disguise. She was curious about his relationship with God, and that was fine by him.

"As I recall, I was more worried about the next incoming mortar round."

Her smile faded. "Was it terrible to be in the war?"

How to answer that? How could someone who hadn't been there comprehend what it was like? He searched for the words to explain it but couldn't find them.

"I understand if you'd rather not talk about it." The gentleness of her words surprised and touched him.

"Thanks. It wasn't always bad, but today is far too nice a day to talk about the times that were bad."

She stepped up to the railing and raised her face to the breeze. "Yes, it's too beautiful out today to dwell in the dark places of our past."

What kind of dark places haunted her eyes and filled them with sadness? He wanted to ask, but he knew it was too soon for that. He sensed that the fragile connection they had at this minute could all too easily be lost.

"Did I sound like a total moron telling Olga to take her Pastor Fields on a breakfast hike for her first date?"

She braced her hands on the rail and ducked her face. He knew she was smiling. He leaned forward and was rewarded with a glimpse of her mirth.

She sent him a sidelong glance. "Not a total moron," she admitted. "But did you notice the cowboy boots she had on? I can't see her hiking far in those."

"What about you? Do you like hikes and strawberry jam?" He waited with bated breath for her answer.

The laughter left her eyes as she stared at him. Her lips parted, but she didn't speak. Instead she suddenly drew back, and he felt the bitter pang of defeat. The tenuous thread between them had been broken.

She looked toward the house. "If you will excuse me, I have to see what's keeping Pamela. We have another appointment and I don't want to be late."

"Of course."

As he watched her hurry inside, he balled his fingers into a fist and tapped the railing in frustration. For a second, they had shared a closeness that he wasn't ready to abandon.

Which didn't make sense. He wouldn't be in town long enough to pursue a relationship with Nora, but illogical as it seemed, that was exactly what he wanted to do.

His musing on the subject was cut short by the ring of his cell phone. He pulled it from his hip pocket and frowned when he saw the number on the display. It was his private investigator. He glanced at the door where Nora had gone inside. A stab of guilt cut through him. Did he really want to hear about Nora's past from someone other than her?

The memory of his boss telling him he hadn't done a thorough job on his last assignment was as clear as the persistent beeping of his phone. He flipped it open and walked to the far end of the veranda. "Dale here."

"Rob, this is Murray. I got that information you wanted."

"Okay, go ahead."

"There isn't much to tell. Children of the Day was started by a woman named Anna Terenkov about five years ago. Her mother emigrated from Russia about a year after her husband was killed in Afghanistan. It looks like Anna was about thirteen at the time. The mother is some kind of counselor."

"She's a grief counselor at a church here," Rob supplied.

"Right. Anyway, the charity looks to be on the up-and-up from this end. I can try making a few calls to my overseas contacts, but I don't know anyone operating in the same areas," Murray admitted.

"The paper has a reporter near one of the places they have a refugee camp. I could ask him to check into it." Rob didn't like the idea of asking Carter for help, but if that was his only option, he'd use it.

"Are you talking about the guy who got your assignment?"

"Carter is covering my area temporarily."

"That's not the way I heard it, but you would know." Murray's tone clearly said he wasn't convinced.

"Anything on Dr. Blake?"

"Not much. She was born in Boston. She's from a working-class family."

Rob cut in impatiently. "I know all that. Skip to when she got married unless you have something unusual before then."

"Nope, she seems squeaky clean. Nothing but a traffic ticket when she was in college. She married into money. Bernard Blake was the owner and CEO of Hannor Pharmaceuticals."

"Hannor. That name rings a bell." Rob searched his memory but couldn't put his finger on why it was familiar.

"I'm not surprised. They had a stake in everything from aspirin to the latest heart drugs."

"No, it's not that. It'll come to me. What was his story?"

"His first wife died in a car accident when their daughter—"

"Pamela." Rob supplied the name with another twinge of guilt.

"That's it. The girl was only three at the time. Everyone I talked to said they were surprised when he married a woman half his age because he'd been a single father for twelve years. After he remarried, he and his new wife hit the social scene in Washington, DC, big time. People said he liked to show her off."

"I've met her and I can't blame him."

"People said it was his thing, not hers. She could dress the part but never really fit in. Too obsessed with her work."

That jived with the Nora he knew. "Anything else?"

"Blake and his company were in the news a few times with big charity donations. The bulk of it was overseas to really poor countries. Other than that, there isn't much. The company looked to be in some financial trouble about two years before he died, but he turned it around nicely. He died six years ago in some kind of skiing accident in the Swiss Alps."

"Anything funny about that?"

"Funny as in getting an old husband out of the way so the young wife could enjoy his money? Not that I can tell. The wife and daughter were here in the States at the time. The only odd thing is that she broke up the company and sold it off after he died."

"So she made a tidy profit there." Rob considered if that was something he needed—or wanted—to look into further.

"Not really." Murray sounded puzzled. "She actually took a loss on most of it. The lady might be a good surgeon, but she doesn't have a head for business."

Rob relaxed for the first time since the call started. He hadn't uncovered anything shady in Nora's past. Her husband's death was the reason for the lost and hurt look he saw in her eyes. It made sense if she were still grieving for him.

"Do you want me to keep digging?" Murray asked.

"Into Nora Blake? No, but dig a little deeper into Hannor Pharmaceuticals. I can't think why that name sticks in my head."

"You're paying the bills. I'll call you if I find anything."

Rob closed the phone just as Nora and Pamela came out of the building. Pamela waved, but Nora didn't look in his direction and he was relieved. He was afraid his guilt at prying into her past might be written all over his face.

Nora walked briskly down the steps of Children of the Day with Pamela at her heels. She wanted to put as much distance between herself and Rob as possible. The man possessed an uncanny ability to unnerve her.

"Nora, slow down. What's the hurry?"

"I want to see if my hairdresser can work me in today. This is the only day I have free this week and I need a haircut."

"Oh, that's a good idea. I'll go with you."

As they turned the corner at Veteran's Boulevard and Nora was sure she was out of Rob's sight, she slowed her pace. Now she could take a deep breath and relax.

The boulevard was the main street in Prairie Springs. In one direction it led to a bridge just outside the main gates of Fort Bonnell. In the other direction, it ran through the bustling two-mile-long business district of the community that thrived outside one of the country's largest military bases.

The town's sense of pride and patriotism was evident in the Texas and American flags displayed everywhere from storefronts to private homes.

"You don't have to keep me company." Nora gave her stepdaughter what she hoped was a normal smile.

"I don't mind. I can help you pick out a better hairstyle."

Giving Pamela a perplexed look, Nora asked, "What's wrong with this style?"

Reaching out, Pamela tugged on the hair below Nora's clip. "Nothing's wrong with it except that it isn't a style. It's a ponytail. You need something that's younger and bouncy around your face to make you look less severe."

Nora stopped. "You think I look severe?"

"A little."

Shaking her head, Nora began walking again. "This is ridiculous. Who cares what I look like?"

"But you have such pretty hair. There are women everywhere who pay large sums of money to get your gorgeous honey wheat tones. You're always scraping it back into a roll or a clip."

"I like to be able to get my hair out of the way."

"You don't like to look friendly?"

Nora's jaw dropped. "What kind of question is that?"

"Just because you're a brilliant surgeon doesn't mean you have to go around looking like a frump."

Nora stopped again and stared in amazement at Pamela. "Now you're telling me that I'm frumpy."

"Not today. The color of that shirt looks great on you, but how many outfits do you have that aren't black or gray?"

"Lots."

"Not counting the blue and green scrubs you wear."

Taking a quick mental inventory of her closet, Nora said, "Several."

"Three."

"Three is several." Nora started walking again.

"Three is not enough."

Grabbing her stepmother's arm, Pamela turned her toward the display window of a boutique. "That outfit would look delicious on you."

The mannequin in the window wore a long peach-colored tunic with wide, three-quarter-length sleeves over a pair of matching slacks. Nora studied it but shook her head. "It's too young for me. You should get it."

Pamela dragged her toward the store. "You make yourself sound like Olga's Russian grandmother. It is not too young for you. Humor me. Try it on and then tell me it doesn't look good on you."

Twenty minutes later, with two new outfits in a shopping bag on her arm, Nora followed Pamela out of the boutique, not quite certain how her stepdaughter had managed to talk her into buying both the pantsuit and a new dress. She had to admit that Pamela was right. Both outfits, but especially the simple red sheath dress, looked stunning on her.

What would Rob think if he saw her in it?

She tried to dismiss the idea by telling herself she didn't care what he thought of her wardrobe, but it wouldn't quite go away. Some small part of her knew he would like it.

Feeling more lighthearted than she had in months, Nora enjoyed Pamela's teasing as the two of them window-shopped their way toward the beauty parlor two blocks down the street. The little bell over the door jangled as they went in, and Nora was happy to see that her stylist was free.

"Thea, do you have time to give me a trim?"

"Dr. Blake, how nice to see you. Yes, I have time for you. Have a seat."

Pamela took the bags from Nora's hands as Nora sat in the empty chair. "She doesn't want just a trim, Ms. Thea. She wants a new style."

"Really?" Thea's face brightened. "I so glad to hear you say that. I know just what we should do."

Nora listened to the enthusiastic pair discuss her hair quality, face shape and style options with trepidation. There had been a time when she had been a bit vain about her hair. Bernard had always loved it when she wore it up. He used to say it made her look regal. She still wore it in a French twist when she wanted to present a poised front. In a way, it was part of her armor.

Armor? When had she stopped thinking of herself as a woman? Closing her eyes, she said, "All right. Cut it—but not too short."

She kept her eyes closed until Thea finished snipping, curling and brushing to her satisfaction. Turning the chair at last, Thea pulled off the plastic cape and said, "There. What do you think?"

Nora peeked cautiously, then opened her eyes wide. It was like looking at a different person. Styled from a side part, her hair now fell to a few inches past her jaw line in a soft, feathery cascade. The bangs that were swept to one side definitely made her look younger. She turned her face first one way and then the other. "It looks…"

"It look fabulous, Thea. You are a genius! Don't you just love it, Mom?"

Nora wasn't sure. "It's going to take a little getting used to."

"It's always that way with a new style. Take our word for it, you look great."

After paying Thea and adding a generous tip, Nora gathered up her belongings. She left the shop feeling the unfamiliar swing of her hair against her neck as she moved. Glancing at her reflection in the plate glass window, she decided it wasn't a bad style. It was kind of fun. Besides, it would grow out again.

Pamela glanced at her watch. "We still have to stop at the grocery store and it's already after four. We need to get going."

"What's the hurry? I thought we might go out to dinner."

"Oh, we can't tonight."

Nora detected a tone she hadn't heard in Pamela's voice since the girl had been a teenager. Something was up.

"Why not?" Nora asked. "Surly you aren't ashamed to be seen with your frumpy stepmother now that I have a new hairdo."

"It's not that."

"Okay, what is it?"

Pamela scrunched her face as she said, "We're kind of…having company for dinner tonight."

Nora's stomach did a flip-flop. "Who's coming to dinner?"

Pamela bit her lip, then smiled with false brightness. "I invited Rob Dale."

Chapter 8

Nora flinched when her doorbell rang a few minutes before seven o'clock that evening. She glared at her step-daughter.

"That must be him," Pamela said cheerfully as she laid a third place at the table.

"I can't believe you invited that man to dinner." Nora slammed the lid on the pasta simmering on the back burner of the stove. As much as she wanted to be angry, a quickening sense of excitement bubbled through her veins.

Pamela came up behind her and gave her a quick hug. "Relax. The guy has been eating takeout and restaurant food for days. I felt sorry for him. All I did was offer him a home-cooked meal and a chance to get out of his motel room for an evening. Anna is feeding him tomorrow night, so it isn't like this is anything special. Now stop pouting and behave."

As Pamela headed for the door, Nora called after her. "Who is the mother in this house, anyway? It's my job to tell *you* to behave, not the other way around."

Pamela's answer was an airy wave of her hand. Nora rolled her eyes and pulled the hissing pan off the burner. It was clear that Pamela had no idea what an awkward position she had placed her stepmother in.

I can do this. I can spend the evening being polite but cool. He is Pamela's guest, not mine. With any luck, he won't stay long.

She glanced toward the living room and frowned when she heard his voice followed by Pamela's laughter. She would have to warn Pamela that the man was a consummate flirt. Pamela was normally a level-headed young woman, but Rob Dale had a way of mesmerizing a person.

Nora pressed her hands to her midsection to quell her jitters. As her palms touched the sleek fabric of her new dress, she suddenly wished she hadn't allowed Pamela to talk her into buying, let alone wearing, the bright form-fitting outfit. Of course it was too late now to change.

She chided herself for being silly. He couldn't possibly know it was a new dress. He certainly wouldn't expect her to entertain in her scrubs.

Carrying the steaming pan to the sink, she strained the penne and transferred it to a waiting bowl.

"Is there anything I can do to help?" The sound of his voice close behind her made her jump.

"Whoa!" He grabbed the bowl of pasta as it skittered out of her grip to the edge of the counter.

She whirled around to find him only inches away. "You startled me."

"Sorry." His smile didn't look the least bit apologetic.

"That's quite all right." She hoped she didn't sound as breathless as she felt.

She sidestepped him, but not before she noticed how his cobalt blue crewnecked shirt outlined the athletic muscles of his chest. The color made his eyes seem even brighter. Or maybe it was just the humor that lurked in them.

He tilted his head slightly. "You've done something different with your hair."

She raked her fingers through her bangs and brushed them back self-consciously. "I got a trim today, that's all."

"I like it. The shorter style really suits you."

His flattery sent heat rushing to her cheeks. She struggled to replace her giddiness with cool politeness. "Thank you. Dinner is almost ready. Please have a seat. Where is Pamela?"

"She said she needed to powder her nose. This smells great. It was really nice of your stepdaughter to invite me. I hope I'm not putting you out."

"Of course not." It wasn't cooking an extra serving that was difficult, it was keeping her wits about her when he was so close.

Rob looked around. "Where's the barbarian?"

Relieved to be free of Rob's close scrutiny, Nora headed to the table and began straightening the silverware. "He's outside in the backyard."

"He hasn't been banished on my account, has he?"

"Conan doesn't have the best manners at mealtime.

I hope you like Italian cooking," she said in a rush to cover her nervousness.

"I do."

"Then you'll love Nora's chicken and pasta in her special creamy pesto sauce," Pamela said as she came strolling in. Nora relaxed a fraction.

Rob chuckled. "That's almost a tongue twister. It's a good thing you aren't cooking it. Pamela's chicken and pasta in special creamy pesto sauce would be tricky to say six times."

Pamela dissolved into a fit of giggles as Rob grinned at her. Nora stared at the two of them laughing together like they had known each other for years instead of hours. Abruptly, she turned away.

It wasn't jealously that made the sight painful. It was knowing that Rob Dale had the power to hurt Pamela as easily as he amused her. Nora wouldn't allow herself to forget that fact—no matter how much she found herself wishing she could.

Throughout dinner, Rob remained acutely aware of the woman seated across from him. Nora barely touched her food. She toyed with her salad and then with a small portion of chicken while he managed a second hearty helping. The food was good, but it couldn't sidetrack him from the question that had been plaguing him since he arrived. Why did Nora seem so uncomfortable? Was it just because he was here, or did she have something else on her mind?

Even distracted, she managed to look especially lovely. Her red dress accentuated her slender figure and put color in her cheeks. The soft way her hair curved around her face made her eyes seem bigger and more luminous. She certainly didn't look like the Dr. Ice Princess he had met that first day.

Had it only been a week ago? It didn't seem possible that he had become so drawn to a woman in such a short time. If only he could find a way to break through the barrier she used to keep him at arm's length. More than anything, he found himself wanting to know her better, to see where these budding feelings would take them both.

"Are you enjoying your time in Prairie Springs, Rob?" Pamela asked. Nora's stepdaughter had turned out to be an engaging woman with a quick wit and a ready laugh. To his amusement, he also found her to be a determined interviewer.

"It's a little quiet for my tastes. It reminds me of my hometown. The sidewalks get rolled up in Dodge City at sundown, just like here."

"So you prefer the big city?" Pamela lifted her glass and took a sip of water.

"I prefer to go where the news is. What about you? Do you miss the excitement of Washington, DC? It must have been hard to move to a small Texas town after growing up in the capital."

Looking taken aback, Pamela asked, "How did you know I grew up in DC?"

"I have my sources."

Nora's fork clattered to her plate. Her eyes widened, then her gaze slide away from his. He had pricked a nerve, but which one?

Pamela dismissed him with a wave of her hand. "Oh, you looked me up on Google, didn't you. I'm flattered, but I'm sure you didn't find much. I'm not exactly newsworthy. Now, Nora, on the other hand, has published dozens of articles and made the news a number of times for her work with children."

"Rob isn't interested in hearing about us. His story is Children of the Day. Isn't that right?"

Did he detect a challenge in Nora's eyes. "That was my assignment to begin with, but a good reporter is always on the lookout for the next big scoop."

Pamela laughed. "The only big scoop in Prairie Springs is the triple-decker ice-cream cone at the Creamery downtown."

"Speaking of ice cream, can I get you some dessert?" Nora rose and picked up his empty plate.

"No, thank you. I'm stuffed. The chicken was delicious."

She inclined her head ever so slightly. "I'm glad you liked it."

"It was the best I've had in a long time. You'll have to give me the recipe." There was a hint of a blush in her cheeks again and he smiled. Was she so unused to compliments?

"Do you like to cook?" Pamela asked.

He tore his gaze away from Nora's face. "I try my hand at it when I'm at home."

"And where is home?" Pamela inquired. "Still Dodge City?"

Nora interrupted. "We don't need to keep Rob here with our chitchat. I'm sure he has things he needs to do."

"I don't have anywhere else to be. I'm free for the whole evening."

Nora's smile in response to his comment appeared stilted, but she hid her chagrin well. Turning her back on him, she carried the empty plates into the kitchen.

"Home at present," he said, "is a tiny apartment in Washington, DC."

Pamela's eyes lit up. "Oh, what part?"

"Somerset."

Clapping her hands together, Pamela said, "We used to live in Brookdale. Is Mario's Pizza Palace still on the corner across from the park?"

He nodded. "It is."

"My dad used to take us there. Remember, Nora?"

"I remember." She came back to the table and gathered up the water glasses. "He loved their pepperoni. He always said it was the best pizza in or out of the country."

"Then he traveled a lot?" Rob posed the question he already knew the answer to. Nora kept her gaze down.

"When I was little I thought he traveled too much," Pamela said sadly. "After he married Nora, he stayed home more and I liked that, but then—"

"I'm sure Rob isn't interested in our ancient history, Pamela," Nora interjected.

"Of course." Pamela smiled at Rob. "I'm sorry. Would you like a tour of the house? My father collected some very nice artifacts from around the world, and I've kept a few of his favorite pieces. After that I'll show you Nora's studio downstairs. You'll be amazed by her talent."

"No!" Nora objected so quickly that both he and Pamela looked at her in astonishment.

"Forgive me." Nora picked up several more dishes. "It's just such a mess down there. Don't take him downstairs, but you really should show him your father's collection of Chinese carvings. I'm sure he'd rather see that than my crewel-work. I'll make some coffee for us and we can have it in the den."

"All right." Pamela gave her mother a puzzled look but led the way out of the kitchen. Rob followed, but he had very little interest in seeing an art collection. What he wanted was to find out why Nora didn't want him to see her studio.

As he followed Pamela into the large wood-paneled den adjacent to the living room, Rob took stock of Nora's home. It was certainly nice but by no means lavish. The furniture was solid, not trendy. It supported Murray's assertion that she hadn't made a lot of money after her husband's death.

As he looked over Bernard Blake's collection of delicate and intricately carved panels and pottery, he admitted silently that the man had an eye for beauty. Rob glanced up at Pamela. "This is impressive, but at the risk of sounding stupid, can I ask a question?"

"Certainly."

"What kind of torturous work does Nora do in the cellar?"

"Torturous?" The look she gave him questioned his sanity.

"She said I wouldn't want to look at her cruel work."

Pamela laughed out loud. "Crewel. C-r-e-w-e-l. It's a type of needlework."

He pressed a hand to his chest. "That's a relief. I was worried. I though the doctor was hiding a diabolical laboratory in the cellar."

She patted his arm. "You're so funny."

"I try. So tell me about your father. I know he was the CEO of Hannor Pharmaceuticals."

"How did you know that? No, don't tell me. You have your sources."

"That's right." He admitted with a small pang of guilt.

"My dad was a great guy in so many ways. I'm really proud of his legacy. Oh, not these artifacts, but the way he helped people. His company made major discoveries in the area of heart disease research, but even more than that—he was a great humanitarian. His company donated more drugs to third world countries than his next two biggest competitors combined."

"That is something to be proud of. Nora certainly seems intent on following his lead with her work for Children of the Day."

"She does a lot more than help Children of the Day. When Mercy Medical Center halted funding for the new PICU, Nora donated a substantial sum to get the project underway again."

"Really?" Rob filed the fact away for future reference. "No one mentioned that. In fact, she said the donation was made anonymously."

Nora's lifestyle didn't suggest that she had a quarter million dollars lying around waiting to be given away. Not that he was any judge of how the wealthy lived. His family had lived paycheck to paycheck when he was growing up. No doubt a cardiac surgeon pulled in a tidy salary—for sure more than a reporter.

Pamela bit her lip and looked as if she had said too much. "Please don't mention that I told you about it. She would hate it if that got out."

"Why is that?"

"Because she's a very private person." Forcing a smile, she continued, "Nor was my father one to brag. However, you mustn't think he cared only about his work. After my mother died, he raised me alone and we were best buddies. He always had time for my dance recitals and school plays. He never acted like a big shot. He was just, Dad."

"Did that change when he married Nora?"

She cocked her head to the side. "Why, Rob, I believe I see the nosy reporter rearing his curious head."

"Sorry. Force of habit. You don't have to tell me anything. We can talk about sixteenth-century jade dragons or the weather."

She regarded him silently for a moment. "No, I don't often get a chance to talk about my dad. When he died, Nora had a very difficult time, and I know she doesn't like to discuss it."

"I don't want you to do anything that will upset her."

"Nor do I, but it was my life, too, and I like to share my memories. Things changed a little after they were married. Dad spent more time socializing, but you know how Washington is. Big money is courted on a very grand scale there. I'm sure you've seen that for yourself."

"Occasionally. That must have been hard on you, seeing him with a new wife."

"I was fifteen and a royal pain at that stage of my life. The truth of the matter is that I *was* jealous at first, but once I saw how warm and genuine Nora was, I knew Dad had made the right decision. She was the best big sister-girlfriend-mother that any spoiled brat could hope to find."

"I can't see you as a spoiled brat."

"Oh, believe me, I was. If this is off the record, I'll tell you about the time I got four nannies in a row to quit their first week on the job."

"I'd love to hear the story, but the truth is, nothing is ever really off the record."

She laid a finger against her lips and tapped it several

times. “Hmm. I think I’ll take a chance and trust you. It involved my friend Greg and his pet rats.”

With Pamela and Rob out of sight, Nora sagged against the kitchen counter and crossed her arms over her middle. Pamela would quiz her later about her overreaction, but by then Nora would have a plausible excuse and her nerves wouldn’t be stretched to the breaking point the way they had been all through dinner.

She drew a deep, calming breath. It wasn’t as if she had done anything wrong. She had a right to her privacy. Her studio was her sanctuary, her escape from the madness and pressures of her work. She wasn’t ashamed of it, she just didn’t want *him* there.

The sound of Rob’s deep laughter and Pamela’s giggle reached Nora from the other end of the house. The thought that it might not be wise to leave the two of them alone spurred her into action.

Nora opened the fridge, then pulled out a bag of gourmet coffee. As she spooned the grounds into the maker, the pungent aroma helped to calm her jitters. While the coffee dripped its way into the pot, she brought out her seldom-used silver service. She quickly filled the sugar bowl and cream pitcher. A few minutes later she transferred the piping hot brew into the ornate urn.

Tray in hand, she left the safety of the kitchen and entered the den. Rob, standing beside the display case, hurried across the room. “Let me get that for you.”

His hands brushed hers as he took hold of the heavy tray. A fission of electricity seemed to arch between them. She met his gaze and couldn’t look away.

His usually merry eyes darkened with emotion and seemed to draw her in with a tenderness she had never experienced. She held her breath, afraid to break the cocoon of warmth that surrounded them.

Pamela cleared her throat. "I'll pour."

Nora let loose of the tray and rubbed her palms on the sides of her dress. Rob, for once seemingly at a loss for words, carried the platter to the low table in front of the burgundy leather love seat and pair of wing-backed leather chairs that faced the fireplace.

Nora sat on the edge of one chair and Rob sat in the other one. Pamela poured the coffee into the three gold-rimmed, delicate china cups. The silence grew. Nora racked her brain for something to say that wouldn't sound inane but couldn't come up with anything. She could feel his eyes on her. She licked her suddenly dry lips.

Pamela handed a cup and saucer to Nora and then one to Rob. He nodded his thanks and took a quick sip. He nodded again. "This is good. It beats the stuff they serve at the Prairie Springs Inn. I mean, the coffee there is okay, but this is…better. The service is good there. I've stayed at a lot worse places…and…at some better ones." He smiled and took another sip.

Pamela sat back on the love seat with a small smile just curving the corner of her lips. "How interesting."

Nora caught her stepdaughter's knowing look and wanted to shake her. Calling up the memory of the cool reserve and polite small talk that had surrounded her among Bernard's friends, she looked at Rob and said, "Where do you go after you leave Prairie Springs?"

"Hopefully, back to the Middle East." His eagerness to return was evident.

"Back to war?" A chill raised goose flesh on Nora's

arms. She tried to tell herself that she would feel concern for anyone going into harm's way.

"Back to covering the war and other stories there. After serving twelve years in that part of the Middle East, it's almost like my backyard. I know the people there. I respect them, and they respect me."

"What is keeping you from going back?" Nora asked, intrigued in spite of herself.

"I messed up on my last assignment. Another reporter did a better job. My paper sent him to take my place for the next month. If he does a good job he could earn a permanent assignment, but covering in-depth stories there requires contacts. I have them in the area, he doesn't. So I still have a shot at getting back there."

"I would have thought you had seen enough of war after your time in the army." Nora knew she sounded disapproving.

"There were times when I thought that, too, but then I'd meet some kid from Indiana who was using his army pay to buy books and pencils for a village school with only ten kids who'd never seen a book in their lives. Then there was this coffee merchant and his wife who smuggled arms to the freedom fighters in the hills at the risk of their own lives.

"The struggle for liberty has so many faces that we never see in the sound bites on the six o'clock news. I wanted to tell those stories."

Intrigued with this new facet of the man, Nora asked, "Do you believe what you write will make a difference in how people see the conflict?"

"I don't write stories to try and change people's perceptions. I write to shine a light on a subject or a person that may have otherwise gone unnoticed, because everything and everyone is important.

"That GI from the Midwest isn't a particularly important fellow except to his folks and maybe a girlfriend. I doubt he's going to become our next president. Well, who knows? Maybe he will someday, but what he did was important in a life-changing way to ten schoolkids who don't even speak his language."

"I think your profession sounds like a very noble one," Pamela said.

"It can be. I try to live my life with God's work in mind, but Nora thinks I'm exploiting little Ali by writing his story." He was grinning when he said it, obviously trying to bait her.

"I don't think you are exploiting the boy. I think your paper is exploiting his suffering for gain." She touched the locket at her neck but put her hand down when she realized he was watching her.

Rob held his hands palm up as if balancing her words. "There isn't much difference, but I can see your point."

She inclined her head ever so slightly. "Thank you."

"My paper is in business to make money, that's a hard fact of life that I can't change, but I'd like to point out the good we do. Thousands upon thousands of people will learn about Children of the Day from what I write."

"That's certainly true," she admitted, "but what angle will you use?"

"Angle?"

"You said you were checking all the angles. Will your readers learn about the difficult but important work being done by Anna and a dedicated few, or will they read that a nonprofit charity helped a three-star general pull strings to get his grandson into this country for heart surgery?"

Rob raised his eyebrows and cocked his head to one side. "Both stories are true."

Clearly appalled, Pamela said, "You aren't going to print that Anna or anyone at Children of the Day did something unethical, are you?"

"I would if that were the case."

"Of course they didn't do anything wrong. Why would you think that?" Pamela's indignation was an echo of Nora's feelings on the subject.

"He would think it because it would make a *sensational* story," Nora said with a pointed look in his direction.

"It would have been a *great* story if a former U.S. Army general had misused his position. I'm happy to say that wasn't the case. The general called in a few favors to get his grandson escorted here by an army nurse, but she was on her way here anyway, so that wasn't out of line. He's paying all the bills for the boy's medical care so it's not like charity funds were misused. Children of the Day merely assisted with expediting the needed paperwork because the boy's mother worked for the organization overseas. I didn't find anything questionable in that help."

"I'm sure you've learned how much good Children of the Day has done. In spite of all that, you would have printed a story that cast them in a poor light, anyway?" Nora asked.

"I've said before that I believe God puts me where I'm needed most. If He had wanted me to reveal corruption disguised as charity, then that is what I would have found. If He wants me to reveal the true charity of the spirit that exists here, then that is what I will do."

Nora allowed herself to relax. "So you do believe in the good that is being done here?"

"I haven't seen anything to suggest otherwise. Have you?"

"No," Nora declared, happy that she could answer with conviction. "I made sure that Children of the Day was on the level before I offered them my services."

"That's what I've found so far."

"Does that mean you'll be leaving soon?" Pamela asked.

A chill settled over Nora. On a deep level, Nora knew things would never be the same once he was gone. He had awakened something inside her that she had thought was long dead.

He nodded but didn't take his eyes off Nora. "After Ali's surgery, yes. Although, I must admit I like the country around here. I wouldn't mind coming back and spending some vacation time here."

Pamela looked hopeful. "Perhaps you could ask for another assignment in the area."

"A reporter doesn't often get to choose his assignments."

"I imagine not. This one must seem rather tame after the dangers of a war zone," Nora suggested.

"I didn't choose this one, that's true, but a mark of a good reporter is that he does an impartial job no matter how he feels about his subject matter."

Pamela nodded in understanding. "So you can't let your personal feelings interfere with your work. I think Nora has mentioned that about her work, too."

"I made that mistake recently and it cost me," he said with a wry smile.

"Everyone makes mistakes now and then," Nora said, knowing she had made her share.

"That's true," he admitted. "We're only human, but the smart thing is to learn from our mistakes."

Nora felt Rob's gaze on her and looked into his intense blue eyes. He said, "I'm trying not to let personal feelings interfere with my work here, although I'm finding that much harder than I expected."

He was talking about her. He had personal feelings for her. Nora couldn't decide if the idea pleased her or frightened her witless. In that moment, she realized she had been fighting a losing battle from the first moment he walked into her life.

She liked him. She liked him far more than she should. Against every ounce of better judgment that she possessed, she knew that seeing more of Rob Dale was exactly what she wanted to do.

Chapter 9

The next day, Rob interviewed several more volunteers who worked regularly with Children of the Day. They all said pretty much the same thing. The charity did desperately needed work in war-torn countries around the world. Anna Terenkov might be the founder, but she was inspiring dozens of men and women to take up the cause with her.

Many of those who gave of their time were civilians, but a large number were servicemen and women who wanted to help in any way they could. The fact didn't surprise Rob. During his time in the service, he had seen the generous nature of American military personnel numerous times.

His dinner with Anna and her mother turned out to be a pleasant enough evening. The Tex-Mex food was a little too hot for his taste, but there was plenty of it, and the women, especially Olga, provided lively conversation. While he gathered a little more insight into Anna and her organization, he knew he hadn't uncovered anything new.

Now, as he sat against the headboard of his bed at the inn and typed his notes into his computer, he knew without a doubt that his piece, while touching and filled with stories about the good individuals could do, was also bland. It wasn't the story that would wow his boss or earn back the assignment Rob wanted.

Shutting the lid of his laptop, he sat up on the edge of the bed and raked his fingers through his hair. He couldn't work tonight. His heart wasn't in it. Maybe what he needed was some fresh air to stimulate his brain. He rose and walked to the window of his second-story room at the Prairie Inn that looked out on the town square.

The street below was quiet now; the shops were closed. The street lamps made small lonely islands of light in the darkness. At the intersection just up the road, a traffic signal blinked a repeated yellow warning. Proceed with caution.

It was a sign he should heed, only his heart was speeding ahead and he was pretty sure it was steering him into trouble.

Picking up his keys, he shoved them in the pocket of his pants and let himself out of his room. A young couple walked past as he opened his door. The man had a sleeping toddler draped over his shoulder and the young woman was looking at both of them with eyes overflowing with love.

As he watched them pass, Rob knew a moment of jealousy. Would a woman who loved him ever walk at his side? Would he ever carry his own sleeping child? The questions had never seemed so important before.

After doing a few quick stretches in the motel parking lot, he broke into a jog and headed toward the quiet downtown area. Before long his feet fell into an easy, familiar cadence and he let his mind wander. It wasn't the story that had him itching to get out of his room and run through the empty streets. It was thoughts of Nora. He longed to see her again.

Until he'd sat across the table from her he'd rarely thought about settling down, about coming home to the same woman every day. He had four brothers, all with big families to assuage his parents' need for grandchildren. Rob had always used his army career as an excuse when his siblings or parents started pressuring him about settling down. It was true, but the real reason was that he'd never met a woman like Nora.

Was she at home tonight? Or was she at the hospital mending someone's broken heart with her capable hands and gritty determination? The more he learned about the subject of pediatric cardiac surgery, the more he was awed by what she did.

That she also chose to work at Fort Bonnell's hospital proved she cared about the military men and women stationed here. She seemed almost too good to be true, except that she didn't share his faith.

What had happened to make her turn away from God's love? He wanted to know the answer. His faith was as important to him as the air he breathed. He could only imagine how empty life must be for someone who didn't believe in God's salvation. He wanted to help Nora find her way back. He wanted to hold her hand and watch the sun come up.

Turning off the main street at the next corner, he soon found himself in a residential area. An occasional dog barked at his passing, but for the most part, the stillness of the night helped settle his restlessness.

His piece on Children of the Day was almost complete. Once Nora read his article about Ali and the charity, she might be less disapproving of his work. Perhaps then they could find some common ground and begin to explore the feelings they had for each other.

What if she didn't feel the same emotions, the same sense of rightness when they were together?

As he passed by the next house on the block he let his fingers tap the tops of white picket fence. His parents had the same kind of fence in front of their home in Dodge City. The love and happiness he had known there had shaped his entire life. He stopped to gaze at the light pouring out of the large bay window of the two-story Victorian. If he ever had a family, he would want a house like that one with an inviting front yard and lots of character.

Suddenly, the light snapped off. He stood, drawing in deep breathes of the cool night air and staring at the home's dark facade.

He took a step back. What on earth was he thinking? He and Nora didn't have a relationship or any hope of a relationship. Dr. Nora Blake was way out of his league. Besides, he wasn't a picket fence type of guy. It was okay for his parents and his brothers, but he had always needed more adventure.

Besides, he'd be gone soon, back to reporting from inside a war zone if he got his wish. That was what he wanted, wasn't it?

Of course it was. Turning around, he started jogging back to the motel, but the peace of the night was gone.

Once inside his room again, he plopped on the bed and picked up the remote. Pointing it at the TV, he switched it on. A commercial was playing for a local Italian restaurant. It looked like a decent place. With another week of eating out looming in his future, he decided he might have to try it. He scribbled the name and address on the notepad by the phone.

Nora's Italian cooking had certainly been to his liking, but then almost everything about Nora seemed to be to his liking.

Giving himself a mental shake, he tried to dismiss her from his mind. He wouldn't see her again until Ali checked into the hospital for his surgery, and that was a good thing. Time away from her was exactly what he needed.

Except it wasn't what he wanted.

He crossed out the restaurant name on his notepad. He didn't need to be reminded of her when he was eating alone, either. He'd ask around and get some recommendations for places to eat. In west Texas it should be easy to find a place that didn't serve pasta and pesto sauce. On the other hand, it might be hard to find a place that didn't have jalapenos in every other dish.

He smiled as he wondered if Olga had decided where she wanted Pastor Fields to take her on their date. He'd give a day's pay to be a fly on the wall for that. During Rob's brief meeting with the pastor that morning, he'd found himself wondering exactly what the lively Russian lady saw in the man. To Rob's way of thinking, the minister was far too reserved for the gregarious and lovable woman.

Still, only God knew the ways of the heart. Perhaps the two were made for each other.

Rob clicked between the major news channels to catch the latest headline and finally switched the television off. He glanced at his watch. It was almost midnight. That would make it early morning in where Carter was in the Middle East.

Picking up his computer, he sat back against the headboard and typed in the e-mail address he'd gotten from the paper's Web site. He sent a brief note asking the reporter to check into Children of the Day's refugee camp in the area. Rob knew that not all supplies and funds raised for charity actually found their way to the needy. Often a hefty percentage found its way into the pockets of unscrupulous managers, greedy middlemen or criminal elements at both ends of the operations.

He had no idea how soon Carter might reply, but Rob decided to wait up. He was rewarded with the ding of incoming mail a half hour later. Scanning the note, he saw Carter was willing and eager to give Rob a hand with the investigation. The unwritten part of the message was that Carter would be able to ask Rob to reciprocate in the future.

The last thing Rob wanted to do was to help the rookie reporter succeed at the job that should have been his.

Late the next morning, Nora left the PICU and walked toward her office. As she reached her door, it opened and she came face to face with Rob. She froze as she stared at him in surprise. Her heart skipped a beat and then sped into overdrive. She couldn't believe how happy she was to see him. "Rob, I didn't think I'd be seeing you until Ali's surgery."

He looked embarrassed and unsure of himself. She found it endearing.

"I thought I'd stop by and get those information pamphlets on what parents can expect during their child's surgery that you told me about. You know, for background stuff for my piece."

"Oh, yes, of course. Was Delia able to get them for you?" Her irrational bubble of happiness deflated. He hadn't come just to see her.

He glanced over his shoulder and let the door close. "She did, but I don't think she liked doing it for me. She made a point of saying several times that I didn't have an appointment or a child that needed surgery."

"Delia runs a very tight ship. She doesn't like things that vary from the norm. Sometimes I'm afraid to tell her I'm going to be working late. She takes it as a personal insult if she doesn't get to lock up."

"Carmen mentioned that the woman was a bit of a dragon. I thought she was exaggerating. Look, I don't mean to keep you. I'm sure you have work to do."

"Actually, I'm caught up for a change." Was she being blatantly obvious? The smart thing would be to excuse herself and hide out in her office until he was gone, but today she didn't want to hide.

Maybe it was her new hairdo that made her feel brazen. She'd gathered several compliments on it that morning. Or maybe it was because she'd been thinking about him and now that he was here, she didn't want him to leave.

He relaxed and stuck his hands in the front pockets of his jeans. "I was just on my way to the coffee shop downstairs. If you aren't busy, I'd like to buy you a cup."

She nodded, hoping she didn't look over eager. "Sure. I have a little free time."

His engaging grin reappeared. "That's great. After you." He gestured for her to proceed him.

At the elevator, they stepped on and she tapped the button for the main level. It didn't light up. She pushed it again and nothing happened.

"Do I have to worry about you in elevators?" Rob started to reach around her.

She held up her hand. "I've got it."

She pressed the disk firmly one more time. It lit up and the car began descending. Meeting Rob's eyes in the reflection of the polished metal doors, she saw the humor sparkling in them and smiled back.

He said, "I have a confession to make. The pamphlets were just an excuse to see you again."

She couldn't hide her surprise. "They were?"

"I hope you don't mind."

Although she knew it was foolish beyond measure to admit as much, she smiled shyly and said, "I'm glad you thought of it."

"You are?"

"I am." She was still smiling when the elevator doors opened. Rob had come to see her. Bubbles of delight made her almost giddy. She hadn't felt so happy in years.

Two of the surgical nurses were waiting to get on with tall foam coffee containers in their hands. Nora nodded at them. "Good morning, Traci. Hello, Emily."

Traci's eyebrows shot up. Emily looked taken aback but managed to say, "Hello, Dr. Blake."

Nora continued across the lobby into the trendy coffee shop that occupied a small room beside the hospital's gift shop. She noted with relief that the half dozen booths were empty. After giving their order at the counter, they sat down and waited for the teenage girl to bring them their drinks.

When they were alone, Rob said, "I wanted to thank you for dinner the other night. You and your stepdaughter were exceeding nice to open your home to a stranger."

"It was nothing."

"Oh, but it was something. Not everyone would do that. Especially if they feel about reporters the way that you do."

"I don't have anything against reporters in general,"

"So it's me in particular you don't like."

She stared at him, aghast. "Oh, no!"

Tilting his head, he said, "I'm kidding."

She relaxed. "Sorry. I don't get much levity in my day-to-day life here. Mostly I get one crisis after another."

"I can't imagine doing what you do."

"You could with the right training."

"No, I can't even mend my own socks let alone stitch an artery to the heart."

"Well, that's your problem." She nodded sagely.

He cocked his eyebrow. "What is?"

Shaking her head sadly, she said, "Many men suffer from sock-sewing phobia. I can recommend a good therapist."

Rob leaned forward to look at her more closely. "Nora Blake, did you just make a joke?"

"What? You thought I didn't have a sense of humor?"

Shaking his head, he said, "I should have realized that anyone who keeps a dog like Conan can't be completely devoid of the emotion."

Her eyes narrowed. "I was wrong about you, too."

"How do you mean?"

"I apologize for accusing you of trying to exploit Ali. I believe you sincerely want to be helpful."

Relaxing, he said, "That's good, because between you and Delia, I was beginning to think I'd lost my touch."

"Don't think I've fallen for your charms just because I've revised my opinion of your work."

He leaned toward her with a grin. "Do I have charms?"

The waitress arrived with their drinks and saved Nora from having to answer. She took a quick sip of her sweet, hot concoction.

Rob sat back in the booth. "So what made you change your mind about my work?"

"After you left the other night I searched the online archives of *Liberty and Justice* for some of your articles. I was impressed with both the pieces you talked about and some of your others. You have a knack for finding the motivation behind what people do when faced with terrible circumstances."

"I like to think so."

"I do disagree with your article assessing the military's role during natural disasters overseas."

"Really. How so?"

Rob listened to Nora's opinions with interest. She had a good grasp of international politics, and that surprised him. She was always surprising him and he enjoyed it. Now that he was with her, he couldn't remember why he thought he should stay away.

She stopped talking to take a sip of her coffee. He said, "Would you allow me to repay your dinner invitation with one of my own for tomorrow night?"

He saw her hesitation and added, "For both you and

Pamela, of course. I was hoping you could suggest a local restaurant that isn't quite so… Texan."

"La Primo Bistro is good if you like Mediterranean food, and it's only a few blocks from here."

"That sounds great." Anywhere sounded good if she accepted his offer. His hopes rose.

"I'll have to ask Pamela if she has any plans."

"Of course, but if she can't make it at least let me buy dinner for you."

A reticent expression crossed her face and she stared down at her coffee. "You don't have to do that."

"I know I don't have to, but I'd like to. What do you say?" He held his breath willing her to say yes.

Later that same evening, Nora glanced at the Swiss cuckoo clock on the wall of her studio when it began to chime. The miniature bird darted out of his house and chirped with wooden wings fluttering. It was eleven o'clock at night.

"Why aren't you in bed yet?" Pamela asked as she came halfway down the stairs.

"It's about time you got home," Nora said, setting her magnifying loupes aside and rubbing her eyes.

"I'm sorry I'm late. A few of us stopped at the Creamery for hot fudge sundaes after the singles meeting. I hope you weren't worried."

Turning around in her chair, Nora smiled at her stepdaughter. "Worrying is part of a mother's job."

"Which you take too seriously. I'm a big girl now. What are you working on?"

"The daughter for my newest house."

Coming to stand beside Nora, Pamela picked up the miniature doll. Only two inches tall, the girl wore a blue satin dress with delicately embroidered red roses and green leaves on the hem. "This is lovely."

"I like the way it turned out, but I think the room needs something else, I'm not sure what. I thought about a dog."

Pamela bent to peer into the interior of the two-story dollhouse. An Edwardian family, resplendent in the dignified clothing of the era, sat in a parlor on the first floor. "A dog would be good. Oh, is that a teddy bear? He's so cute."

Pamela carefully picked up the tiny stuffed toy. "You've sewn a heart on his chest."

"Not just a heart," Nora said.

Pamela looked more closely. "I see. It's two halves of a broken heart sewn together. I don't know why you didn't want Rob to see this. You are so talented and clever."

Nora shrugged and began to put her tools away. "This is just a hobby. It's not like he would be interested in it."

"Oh, I think he would."

"I saw him today," Nora said, hoping she sounded nonchalant.

"Really?" Pamela was examining the papa doll. "I adore this fellow's smoking jacket."

"Rob wants to repay us for dinner by taking us out to eat at La Primo Bistro."

"That's nice. I hear they have good food. What day were the two of you thinking of going on this date?"

"It isn't a date," Nora insisted.

"Sounds like it to me."

"You were invited, too. I know it's very short notice but he asked if we could make it tomorrow night. I told him I would have to check with you."

"Tomorrow?" Pamela caught her lower lip between her teeth.

Nora swallowed her disappointment. "You have other plans."

"I do, but you can still go."

"I'm certainly not going if you can't make it. Inviting him to dinner was your idea in the first place."

"Okay, I think dinner at La Primo Bistro sounds like a wonderful idea. Call him and tell him it's fine with me."

"Are you sure?" Nora didn't want Pamela to feel like she was being pressured into going.

"I'm sure. I'll just call my friend. We can see a movie some other time. After all, Rob isn't going to be here that long."

"No, he isn't." Some of Nora's excitement dimmed. Rob would be leaving next week. She should be glad. Only, she found herself wishing he would stay.

And if he could? What then?

Chapter 10

Rob had to admit that he hadn't felt this nervous before a date since high school. Probably not even then. As he held open the restaurant door for Nora and Pamela, he hoped it didn't show.

Inside, he glanced around at the elegant decor. Frescos on the walls depicted scenes from the different provinces of Italy. Small tables with white linen tablecloths were grouped around a large fountain in the center of the room. Candles in red glass globes in the center of each table added to the ambiance.

As a waiter with an authentic Italian accent led them across the room to a table in a small alcove, Rob decided that if the food was as good as the setting, he was in for a treat.

As he pulled out Nora's chair, he couldn't help but admire the way she looked in her stunning black dress.

The waiter seated Pamela. She murmured her thanks but kept looking toward the entrance.

"What's good here?" Rob asked, checking out the menu with difficulty instead of feasting his eyes on Nora.

"I can recommend the calamari and the scallops." Nora lifted her fan-folded napkin from her plate and spread it on her lap.

When the waiter returned to take their order, Pamela said, "Nora, Rob, I know this is going to sound rude, but I'm not staying for dinner. My date just arrived."

"What?" Nora demanded, clearly stunned.

As the waiter retreated, Rob glanced in the direction Pamela was looking. A young man in his midtwenties stood just inside the entrance. He was dressed in a dark gray jacket over blue jeans. A string tie at his throat and the cowboy hat in his hands completed the outfit.

Pamela stood and dropped a kiss on Nora's cheek. "I knew you wouldn't come without me, but I really didn't want to change my plans with Gary. The two of you have a great evening. Rob, perhaps we can grab lunch sometime before you leave Prairie Springs."

He rose to his feet. "I'll make a point of it."

Pamela left and made her way between the tables toward the door. Her date broke into a wide beaming smile when he caught sight of her. Both of them waved as they headed out the door.

Rob glanced at Nora. Her cheeks were rosy red with embarrassment. She said, "I am mortified by my stepdaughter's behavior. I can't believe she would do this. I'm going to have a serious talk with her when she gets home."

"I'm sorry she upset you, but don't let it ruin your

evening." He opened the menu. "You said the calamari is good. Let's start with that for an appetizer, shall we?"

"You're being very gracious about this."

He didn't feel gracious at all. He was positively delighted to finally find himself alone with Nora.

"Here's how I look at it. Pamela just cut my bill by a third. We can splurge and get the lobster."

A ghost of a smile curved her lips. "I thought you liked steak."

"No, I told Olga to choose a restaurant that served a good steak for her first date," he corrected. "I enjoy a good steak as much as the next guy, but I prefer seafood."

Nora, who was looking toward the door, drew in a sharp breath. "It seems Olga didn't take your advice."

"What makes you say that?"

"Because she just came in with Pastor Fields."

Rob twisted around in his chair. Sure enough, the Reverend Frank Fields, dressed in somber shades of black, was standing beside Olga Terenkov as they waited to be seated. Olga was wearing a bold pink-and-white flowered dress. She had a bright pink shawl edged with foot-long fringe draped over her arms. A large starburst necklace glittered at her throat. She looked like an exotic bird standing beside her date as she chatted away.

Rob turned back and leaned toward Nora, his eyes brimming with amusement. "Don't you think he looks nervous?"

Nora knew exactly what the minister was going through, but he couldn't possibly be more nervous than she was at this minute. While she wanted to be angry with Pamela for running off and leaving her alone with

Rob, she had to admit she wasn't. Pamela had been right. Nora wouldn't have had the courage to come alone.

Rob would be leaving soon, and this might be her last opportunity to spend time alone with him. Determined to enjoy the evening, she was nonetheless glad to focus on Olga's situation instead of her own. She said, "Olga has a good heart, but she can be a bit flamboyant."

Rob leaned closer to Nora. "How does it look like it's going for them?"

Sending a covert glance over his shoulder toward Olga and Pastor Frank, Nora knew what Olga was feeling, too—excitement and nervous energy.

"They're just being shown to their table. Should we make ourselves known?"

"Not unless they notice us. Let them enjoy each other's company without thinking they're being watched. What's happening now?"

"Robert Dale, stop being a nosy reporter," she chided.

"I can't help it. Act nonchalant and tell me what they're doing. Better yet, trade places with me."

"No, then I couldn't see. They're being shown to a table by the fountain." Quickly, she raised her menu in front of her face. "Olga is looking this way."

Nora giggled, feeling daring and silly at the same time, but for once she didn't care. She wanted to enjoy an evening in Rob's company and forget that they didn't have anything in common or any kind of future.

"Don't keep me in suspense. What's going on?" he demanded in a low voice vibrating with suppressed laughter.

Nora raised up to peek over her menu. Her eyes widened with surprise. "Olga is hugging another man."

Rob raised both eyebrows. "Whoa. That can't be good."

* * *

Rob wasn't as interested in how Olga's big date was going as he was in watching Nora. He'd never seen her so carefree and relaxed. She looked genuinely happy as she delved into their game of make-believe espionage. Someday, he would have to tell Olga how indebted he was to her for this evening.

"I'm sure the man is an old friend or someone from her church—although he looks like a pro wrestler," Nora whispered.

"Maybe he's an old boyfriend trying to steal her away from the good minister."

Nora lowered her menu and leaned forward, a perplexed frown on her face. "What on earth is going on?"

Rob turned to look. Olga and a beefy-looking man with bleached blond hair combed straight back were still toe to toe, but they had their hands at their throats. He couldn't imagine what they were doing. "I have no idea."

Soon, the pastor and a nearby woman customer joined the pair, all with their hands working on something between Olga and the unknown man. It wasn't until the woman stepped behind Olga that Rob realized she was trying to unlatch Olga's necklace. A second later, Olga stepped away, leaving her starburst necklace dangling from a thick gold chain that encircled her friend's neck.

Rob and Nora looked at each other and both tried to stifle their mirth behind their hands.

"We shouldn't be laughing." Nora gave him a stern look, but neither of them could keep a straight face.

Working hard to keep his chuckles contained, he opened his menu and pretended to study it. "For the main course I'm going to have the lobster. What about you?"

"I'm thinking of having the sea bass." Her voice quivered, but she managed to suppress her amusement. "Poor Olga. How embarrassing."

"Did she get her necklace back yet?"

"I'm afraid to look." She leaned slightly to the side to look around him. "They made it to their table. Let's hope things go smoothly for them for the rest of the evening."

"Amen." Rob looked over his shoulder. Olga, intent on speaking to her date, had leaned toward him at the small, intimate table. She was toying with the ends of her shawl and didn't seem to notice how close the fringe was to the candle until the dangling trim made contact and burst into flames.

Olga shrieked and dropped the fabric on the tables. She shot to her feet and spun away as Pastor Fields beat at the burning material with his napkin. Olga stumbled backward into the low rim of the fountain. She teetered and flailed wildly for an instant. A passing waiter tried to grab her and missed, losing control of the tray he balanced overhead in the process. As Olga fell into an undignified heap in the shallow water, the tray with several loaded plates crashed to the floor, sending the sound of shattering china reverberating through the restaurant. Rob and Nora both leaped up to help.

Rob's heart went out to Olga as he and Pastor Fields assisted the dripping woman out of the fountain, ignoring the crowd gathering around them. Pulling off his jacket, Pastor Frank draped it over her shoulders.

"Are you all right?" Nora asked, clearly concerned about her. "Did you hit your head?"

Olga straightened and pushed her hair out of her eyes. "Nothing's hurt except my pride."

Glancing down at her sodden clothes, she gave Pastor Frank a wry smile. "It's a good thing this dress is wash and wear."

Her friend, the jewelry-wearing bodybuilder, muscled his way through the crowd. "Olga, darling, are you injured?" he demanded in a thick Russian accent.

"I'm fine. Really. Everyone, I'm okay. I'd just like to go home."

"Of course." Frank took her elbow and began steering her gently through the crowd.

By now the restaurant management had arrived and order was restored quickly as the broken plates were swept up and a fresh tablecloth replaced the charred one.

Nora and Rob returned to their table, but their easy laughter had dissipated. He could only hope that Olga's mishap hadn't ruined his evening as well.

Olga's first-date disaster put a damper on Nora's mood and forced her to take a closer look at what loomed in store for her. Pastor Frank and Olga's romantic future didn't look bright, but at least there was still a faint glimmer of hope for them. They lived and worked in the same town. They shared common values. She and Rob had nothing in common. There was no future for them beyond the next few days.

Trying to pretend that tonight would be enough had been foolish. All she was doing was courting heartache. Resolving to remain detached and guard the wall she had built around her heart, she bit down on her lip to stop its quivering.

Suddenly, Rob reached across the table and covered her hand with his own. "What's wrong?"

His touch made her heart contract with longing. Why did he make her wish for things she knew would never be hers? Tears threatened, but she blinked them away. "I'm just feeling sorry for Olga. She was anticipating tonight with such happiness and look how it turned out."

"I'll grant you that isn't the way I'd like to end our evening, but every relationship is filled with ups and downs. If the pastor is a brave, wise man, and I think he is, he'll see that Olga is a woman of great faith and fortitude. She certainly showed grace under pressure here tonight. If she wanted to make a lasting impression on him, I think she managed that."

"I hope you're right."

"I am. Now, let's order, and to make sure our evening doesn't end in disaster, I'm going to blow out this candle." He leaned forward and extinguished it with a single puff.

Nora smiled, but she knew it wouldn't be a candle that spelled disaster for her. Her growing feelings for Rob could only lead to pain. Sharing those feelings wouldn't be possible. A strong relationship had to be built on trust and honesty, two qualities she was sadly lacking.

After the waiter took their order, Rob sat back in his chair. "Tell me about yourself, Nora."

Oh, how she wished she could. She picked up her water glass and took a sip before she answered. "What is there to tell that you don't already know?"

"A million things. Are you a Cowboys fan? Do you like buffalo wings? Do you like Texas?"

They were all safe topics, and she relaxed a fraction. "Texas is…big. It takes a little getting used to, but yes, I like it. I'm not a sports fan and I don't care for buffalo wings. What about you?"

"I like all kinds of sports, I'd rather have buffalo

wings than a burger and I think Texas is growing on me. I certainly like Prairie Springs."

Did she really want to know why? Wouldn't it be better to skip even this casual exchange of personal information? Still, she couldn't help asking, "Why is that?"

"I like the small-town atmosphere. I like the patriotism and the feeling that our men and women in the service are accorded the respect that they deserve here. I like that people show pride in their country here. I also like that a lot of people here do more than pay lip service to their faith. They put it into action."

"Your faith means a lot to you, doesn't it?" Setting her glass down, she used her napkin to dab at the corner of her mouth. What would it be like to believe so strongly in something other than herself?

"Yes, it does. It could mean a lot to you, too, if you gave God a chance."

"I gave God a chance once."

"What happened?"

Suddenly his question wasn't casual but deeply private. Going back to that time in her life was so painful, yet she suspected that he would understand.

"I prayed once for Him to save someone I loved. Praying didn't make a bit of difference. Besides, if He is such a loving father, why do I see so many children with defective hearts?"

"I'm sorry for your loss, Nora. It's true that there is suffering in this world. I won't deny that, but once we accept God's love and His forgiveness, we can bear anything. He doesn't promise us that we won't have pain. He only promises that He will be there to comfort us no matter what."

"But as a soldier, how did you face death and suffering and not question that belief?"

"You give me too much credit. I've had my share of doubts. I'm only human."

"How did you get past those doubts?" She wanted to understand him. To do that meant understanding how he saw his faith. Her resolve to remain detached began slipping away.

"I guess I kept my heart open to Him."

"What do you mean by that?"

"We can't see God's love any more than we can see the radiation that produces the X-rays you use, but the love is there the same way your radiation is there."

"We have film that provides the proof that X-rays exist. There is no proof that God exists." Her sarcasm sounded hollow, even to her own ears.

"There's no proof that He doesn't. Sometimes I see proof of His love more when I'm not looking for it. Take Ali as an example."

Scowling at him, she asked, "How can you use that child's tragic life as an example of God's plan? The boy lost everything."

"At first glance it does seem that way, but widen the picture. General Willis and his son never reconciled before his son was killed. If Ali hadn't been orphaned and injured, Marlon Willis would never have known his only grandson. Now, Ali's bright eyes and shy smile have helped an old man find comfort and closure to his son's death. We have no idea what other gifts Ali has to bestow on those his life will touch now."

Nora fingered the locket she always wore. She had been grief stricken after losing Bernard and her baby girl. Her focus then had been her own heartbreak and on

Pamela's suffering. Later, she had allowed bitterness to creep in and replace the love she had known. Exploring the possibility that God was using all of them for something greater was a hard concept to take in.

"It would be comforting to think that some good will come out of Ali's sad experience, but I'm not sure I see how it can."

"Because you only see with human eyes. The good that comes out of this may not even be in our lifetime, Nora, but it is there. Faith makes it possible to believe that. God can heal anything."

"I hear that all the time. Usually before someone is depending on me to fix their child's bad heart. God should do His own repairs."

"He is, Nora. You are the tool He uses whether you admit it or not."

She wanted to accept that what Rob said was true, but she was afraid. She was afraid to give up her grief. She was afraid to admit that she wasn't in control of her life.

"Is it so hard to accept that you are an instrument of God's love?" Rob asked gently. "That you have been placed here, exactly where you are needed the most, with exactly the right skills?"

She shook her head. "If that were true I would be able to save every child. I believe in science and in the things I can see and touch."

"Pamela said that you do needlework."

Taken aback by his abrupt change of topic, she sent him a puzzled look. "What does that have to do with religion?"

"Then you know what a tapestry is."

"Of course. It's a woven picture or pattern made to hang on a wall."

"Exactly. I once saw one of a lion. It was full of beautiful colors of gold, blacks and browns and only two small dots of white. Those white dots were in the eyes of the lion and it made him seem to be staring straight at me."

"I'm not following you."

"Think of our lives as threads in a tapestry of infinite size. Your life, my life, everyone's life is a colored thread being woven into a great cloth. As the thread we can't see the pattern. Only the weaver, God, knows what the picture will look like."

She'd never thought of her life as part of a greater whole. "You're saying our individuality doesn't matter."

"No. I'm saying that without those two dots of white thread the lion would have been pretty, but it wouldn't have seemed alive. They changed everything."

Nora touched the locket she wore. "Even a brief life has a purpose," she said quietly.

"I believe that with all my heart. Nora, why don't you come to church with me on Sunday?"

She shook her head. "I don't know. It's been such a long time. It wouldn't feel right."

"Give God a chance. If you don't feel comfortable, you can leave. Take my word for it, they don't lock the doors to keep the flock in."

"I'll think about it."

"Good." He sat back with a satisfied grin. "I'll pick you up at nine."

"If I decide I want to leave or I get paged to the hospital, then you would have to leave, too."

"I won't mind, honest. Fair enough?"

"You're persuasive, I'll give you that."

"Each of us seeks God in our own way, so it really

isn't me. It's your heart looking to find answers. Maybe the Lord just put me here as a sort of signpost to point you in the right direction."

Was he right? There had been times in surgery when she felt as if some greater force were guiding her hands. She had known patients that survived and thrived against all odds.

Nora wanted to believe that she had a purpose beyond the successes and failures of her own life, but how could she ever really be sure?

A small voice at the back of her mind whispered, *By faith.*

Whistling happily, Rob let himself into his motel room later that night after taking Nora home from the restaurant. The evening spent with her would have to qualify as one of his most memorable, and not just because of Olga's mishap.

Tossing his keys on the dresser, he kicked off his shoes and dropped onto the bed. Crossing his arms behind his head, he lay and stared at ceiling.

He couldn't stop thinking about the way Nora looked tonight—how pretty she was when she smiled, the way a small furrow creased her forehead when she was concentrating. She had an adorable giggle.

It seemed like he discovered something new and special about her each time they were together. He'd known a lot of women in his time, but he'd never met anyone who made him feel the way she did. He might never grow tired of watching her eyes light up when she was happy.

Even though she hadn't given him a yes or no answer about attending church with him, he was still hopeful.

Faith was the path to true happiness. Rob wanted to help her discover that for herself.

He glanced at the red numbers of the clock radio beside the bed. It was late, but sleep was the last thing on his mind. Sitting up, he pulled his laptop from the bedside stand and opened the lid. The message that he had new mail prompted him to open the program. One of the messages was from Carter. Rob tapped the mouse to open the e-mail.

Scanning the brief note quickly, Rob saw that the young reporter had done a good job talking to everyone he could find who was involved with Children of the Day on his end. His list of contacts was impressive. He might be new to the area, but he was methodical. Carter had gotten statements from aid workers, clergy and medical personnel all praising the work done by the small Texas charity. It wasn't until Rob reached the end of the missive that he frowned and reread the sentence.

The doctor here is particularly grateful for the case of antibiotics that arrived yesterday. He says one thousand vials of penicillin will help stem the spread of a serious infection among the infants and children. He sends his thanks and prayers for more medicines.

One thousand? Rob distinctly remembered Nora negotiating for four thousand vials of antibiotics. What had happened to the rest of it?

He tried to think if Anna or anyone else had mentioned how many drugs had been sent. All he could recall was Nora saying she would handle the shipping herself. Had Tarkott Pharmaceutical sent less than promised? Wouldn't Nora have mentioned it if that were the case?

Rob typed a quick question. Are you sure he only received one thousand vials?

He hit Send and bit his thumbnail as he waited for an answer. He glanced at the clock as the minutes slowly ticked by for almost an hour. At last, the incoming mail chime sounded, and he clicked open Carter's answer.

The doctor definitely said one thousand. Why?

An uneasy sensation settled in Rob's stomach that had nothing to do with the lobster he'd had for dinner. He typed another note to Carter.

Four thousand vials were shipped. See if you can discover where the holdup is on your end. Call me when you get an answer. I don't care what time it is here. Rob typed in his cell phone number and hit Send.

The most likely explanation was that the cases of drugs had simply become separated during the overseas shipping process. They would probably show up in a day or two. If they didn't, Rob would take a much closer look to find out why.

Chapter 11

Rob's cell phone started ringing just as he was opening the motel room door on Saturday afternoon. He tossed his pillowcase full of clean laundry on the bed and pulled the phone from his pocket, knowing it was his boss by the ring tone he had set. He wanted it to be Carter calling to tell him the rest of the drugs from Children of the Day had arrived. It was irrational to expect an answer in less than twelve hours. Rob knew he had to be patient awhile longer.

"Dale here," he mumbled, balancing the phone between his ear and his shoulder as he dumped his clothes onto the bed and began sorting them to put them away.

"Are you still at Fort Bonnell?"

"Hello to you, too, Derrick."

"Yes or no?"

Rob raked a hand through his hair and sat down on

the edge of the bed. His boss obviously wasn't in the mood for humor. "Yes, I'm still here."

"Great. There's a story coming in over the wire about the newlywed soldiers that have been missing for the last few months."

"The Harpswell couple?"

"Right. The husband has been found."

"Alive?" Rob held his breath.

"Yes, alive. Amazing, isn't it? I thought for sure they were both dead."

"What about his wife?"

"No sign of her. The guy was in pretty bad shape, but the word is that he's going to make it."

"Thank God. There are a lot of people praying for him here."

"Here, too. I want you to get local reaction to the news. Interview people the couple served with, you know the drill. The wife has family in the area, doesn't she?"

"Yes, a brother."

"Great. Get an interview with him."

"I'll try."

"Don't try. Do it."

"Where is John? I'd like to give the brother and the people at Children of the Day as much information as I can."

"He's being medevaced to Germany. From what I gather, the guy doesn't remember anything that happened. They're hoping it is temporary amnesia, but who knows."

"That's rough. His wife is still missing and he's the one person who might know what happened to her."

"It isn't the news everyone is praying for, but it's good news nonetheless."

"Where did they find him?"

"Some local herdsmen found him wandering in the foothills about fifty miles north of where the convoy was ambushed."

Rob already had a mental picture of the area. It was rugged, nearly inaccessible terrain. He had crisscrossed the area on horseback and on foot two years before while following leads on a terrorist training camp.

"I'll get a story to you ASAP," Rob promised.

"That's what I'm paying you for." The line went dead and Rob closed the phone.

Leaving his laundry on the bed, Rob grabbed his keys and headed out the door. Anna and Olga deserved to know about John Harpswell as soon as possible. Ten minutes later, Rob pulled up in front of the Children of the Day offices and hurried up the steps to ring the bell.

Olga answered the door dressed in jeans and an oversized chambray shirt with the sleeved rolled up past her elbows. By the look on her face, Rob knew she had already heard the news. From the lobby he could hear the sound of the television playing. Over her shoulder she called out, "It's Rob Dale."

Anna appeared quickly from the other room. To Rob's surprise, Nora was with her. Olga grasped Rob's arm. "Have you heard that John Harpswell has been found?"

"I got a call from my boss a few minutes ago. What are they saying on the news channels?"

Anna answered him. "Only that John is injured and being flown to Germany for medical care. They aren't saying anything about Whitney. Do you know more?"

He followed the women inside where several staff

member were clustered in front of the small television in the corner of the lobby. "I don't know much more than you do. The call I got said John Harpswell had been found wandering alone, that he had a serious head injury but he is expected to recover."

"And?" Nora prompted, studying him closely.

"He doesn't remember what happened."

Olga pressed a hand to her heart. "How awful, but thank God he is safe now. I'm sure the army is searching the area for signs of Whitney, too."

"It's a very rugged and remote area." Rob tried not to sound discouraging, but he didn't want to hold out false hope.

"I should call Evan Paterson," Olga said suddenly. "He's Whitney's brother. He has been in limbo not knowing what happened to her, and now he has to face more uncertainty. I'm going to see if there is anything we can do." Olga quickly left the room.

"Amnesia is not uncommon after head trauma," Nora said quietly. "Did they say what kind of injury it was?"

"No. What are you doing here?"

"I stopped by to make sure Olga was okay after her disaster of a date last night."

"Is she?" he asked, glancing toward where Olga stood with the secretary's phone pressed to her ear. The other staff members, including Anna, were still watching the latest on the television.

Nora nodded. "I would have been in tears, but she's as chipper as ever. She says it will make a great story for them to laugh about in years to come. The big man she was hugging is actually a distant cousin, by the way."

"It was nice of you to come."

Nora had surprised him yet again. The cool, detached

doctor he'd met less than two weeks ago wasn't the caring friend he saw today. Was it Nora who had changed or was it his perception of her? Every time he learned something new about her it made him want to know more.

The realization that he was falling hard for her stuck him with sudden clarity.

Nora glanced at the others and then at Rob. "Are you going to stay here for a while?"

He forced his mind back to his job. "My paper wants me to interview people who know or have served with John and Whitney and get their reactions to this news. What about you?"

"I just got back from making rounds at the hospital. I was thinking about taking Conan for a run in the park. I was going to ask if you wanted to join us, but I see that you have to work."

"Would you like to tag along with me instead?"

"On interviews?"

"Yeah. I've been into surgery with you. Now is your chance to see me doing my job."

She hesitated and he was afraid she would say no, but after a moment, she smiled and said, "Okay. Where are you going to start?"

Just then, Olga came back into the room. "Evan is on his way here. He wants to talk to you, Rob. I told him you were familiar with the area where John was found."

"I'll be happy to talk to him, but I don't know that I can add anything to what he already knows."

Olga sighed heavily. "Evan needs to feel that he is doing something—anything—to help find his sister. He has a ranch just outside of town. He'll be here as soon as he can get someone to stay with his daughter.

In the meantime, can I get you some iced tea or something to drink?"

Rob glanced at Nora. She shook her head, so he said, "No, we're good."

"All right then, I'll be with the others if you need me."

Twenty minutes later, there was a loud knock at the door. Leaving his seat in front of the television, Rob walked to the entryway. He quickly assessed the man Anna showed into the room.

Evan Paterson was tall with sandy-brown hair and the rugged features of a man who spent his days outdoors. He came toward Rob with purposeful strides and held out his hand. "Thanks for seeing me, Mr. Dale."

"Not a problem."

"I understand that you're a reporter for the *Liberty and Justice*."

"That's true, but I hope you won't hold it against me. I'd like to do an interview with you about your sister, but I know this may not be the best time."

"You're the first reporter I've met that cared whether it was a good time or not. Most of them just pepper me with the same questions over and over again. Olga tells me that you know the area where John was found."

"Please, have a seat," Rob suggested, leading the way back into the lobby. "Yes, I've spent time in the area. It isn't an easy place to search."

Evan sank onto the edge of a chair and leaned forward, his blue eyes searching Rob's face. "I'll give you an exclusive interview if you'll tell me what you know about the area."

"The closest thing to the terrain that we have in this country is the badlands. It's rugged and harsh. It's an easy place to get lost."

"But you found your way around it."

"I was trained to survive in that kind of environment, and I had local tribesmen to guide me."

"Will they help the army?"

"Maybe. The problem is that the people there distrust strangers."

"You must know someone who will help. Please, I'm begging you."

The odds of finding anything about the missing woman after all this time were slim to none unless John Harpswell recovered his memory. Rob did know men who crisscrossed that hostile region, but they were gunrunners and smugglers. They wouldn't talk to just anyone.

If he gave Carter access to his Middle East contacts and the young reporter uncovered something about Whitney Harpswell, Rob knew he could kiss his hopes of reassignment goodbye. Carter would be able to keep the Middle East post for as long as he wanted.

Rob drew a deep breath and let it out slowly. "I might know someone. Let me make a few calls."

Nora waited for Rob as he shook hands with Evan on the steps of the building. As Evan walked to his truck parked on the street, Nora moved to stand beside Rob. "Do you really think your friend can find her?"

"Honestly, I doubt it, but it's worth a try."

"What are you going to do?"

"Our paper has a reporter in the capital. If I give Carter the names of some of my old contacts and vouch for him, he may be able to uncover some new information."

"Is he the man who got the job you wanted?"

"That's the one. I may be helping him keep the job I want, but what choice do I have? Even the remote possibility that I could help discover the fate of that woman is worth more than any job. You saw the look in Evan's eyes. He'd do anything for his sister."

"What if your reporter friend doesn't turn up anything?"

"Then Whitney Harpswell's fate remains in God's hands and we've done everything humanly possible."

Nora reached out and took his hand. She had been wrong to be afraid of him. Lacing her fingers through his, she gave a gentle squeeze. "You're a good man, Robert Dale."

His eyes met hers and darkened with deep emotion. "I'm glad you think so."

"I'm going to miss you when you leave."

A grin tugged up the corner of his mouth. "Is this the same woman that wouldn't give me the time of day two weeks ago?"

"No," Nora answered sincerely. "I'm not the same woman at all, and I have you to thank for that."

To her delight, he leaned down and kissed her.

The world dropped away, leaving the two of them alone as a feeling of rightness engulfed her and sent her heart spinning. Gently, he cupped her face in his hands and drew away. Gazing into her eyes, he whispered, "I like the new Nora."

"The new Nora likes you, too."

His grin widened. "I'm in unfamiliar territory here. What happens next?"

The buzzing of her pager brought her back to earth with a thump. She pulled the device from the pocket of her jacket and scrolled through the message all the while wishing that Rob would kiss her again. Her bubble of happiness subsided when she saw she was needed back at Mercy Medical Center.

"I'm sorry, Rob, I have to get back to the hospital." Oh, how she wanted to stay with this man and share the happiness skipping through her veins.

"I hope it's nothing serious."

She forced herself to smile. "Serious is what I do best."

He stroked her cheek with his fingers. "I believe it is. Will I see you at church tomorrow?"

She hesitated. So much had happened so quickly. Was she willing to let God back into her life? Rob, Anna and Olga, they all made living their faith look so easy, but it wasn't. Giving her life over to God was a step Nora wasn't sure she knew how to take.

Rob seemed to sense her indecision. He reached out and drew her into his arms. She rested her cheek against his chest and listened to the strong beat of his heart beneath her ear. The tension in her body melted away.

"Nora, God is there for you whenever you need Him. I'm not trying to push you into doing something you aren't ready for."

"Thank you." She closed her eyes and inhaled the spicy, warm scent so uniquely Rob's own.

She felt him kiss the top of her head, then he said, "I have phone calls to make and interviews to do and you have to get to the hospital."

"I know," she admitted, but she didn't move.

For the first time in years, she permitted herself to give and to receive comfort from someone other than Pamela. Allowing her small universe to expand and include Rob meant trusting him. The prospect was as scary as it was exciting.

After several seconds, he slipped a finger under her chin and lifted her face to his. “Sweetheart, are you all right?”

Hearing him call her sweetheart sent a thrill of pleasure zinging to her core. The concern she saw in his eyes touched her deeply. Could she really be falling in love with this man? She barely knew him. It was all happening so quickly. Uncertainty reared its head. How could this be real?

Unbidden, the memory of Bernard’s first kiss crept into her mind. She had trusted him and believed that she loved him. She had been convinced that he was a good man, too. It wasn’t until later she found out how wrong she had been.

Taking a step back, she tried to gather her scattered wits. It was foolish to dream of becoming involved with Rob. As wonderful as it felt to rest in his arms, it could never be anything permanent. The fear of risking her heart again overshadowed the peace she found in Rob’s embrace. She wasn’t strong enough to take a chance on love again.

Brushing her hair back, she said, “Forgive me. I don’t know what came over me.”

She turned away, but he caught her arm in a gentle but firm grasp. “Nora, there are so many things I want to say to you, but this isn’t the right time or the right place.”

She managed a smile. “I don’t think there is a right time or a right place for us.”

“What does that mean?” The look of confusion on his face mirrored her own emotions.

“Why don’t we just agree that we like each other and

not look for anything more. I'm sorry if I gave you a different impression. I'll see you Monday when Ali checks into the hospital for his surgery."

As she hurried down the steps toward her car, she didn't know was if she was running away from or running toward a broken heart.

Chapter 12

Shortly after nine o'clock on Monday morning, Rob accompanied Ali, General Willis and Sarah Alpert to the pediatric floor at Mercy Medical Center. All of the adults bore worried expressions. Only Ali, walking beside his grandfather and holding the old man's hand, seemed unaware of the seriousness of the situation. Although his surgery wasn't until tomorrow, he would undergo more tests today to make sure he was strong enough to have it done. Under one arm, he clutched a brown teddy bear wearing a cowboy hat and boots.

When they had been shown to a room and Ali had changed into his pajamas, Marlon Willis sank into the recliner at the bedside with a deep sigh. His face was flushed and he seemed to be breathing hard. Sarah paused in the process of showing Ali how to make the head of the bed go up and down. She reached over and touched the general's shoulder. "Are you okay?"

Marlon's eyes flew open and he patted her hand. "I'm a little tired, that's all."

Rob settled himself into one of the chairs in the room and kept glancing toward the door. He knew Nora would be here to see Ali soon.

After a few minutes, two nurses entered. One said, "General Willis, we have some papers for you to sign at the nursing station. While you are doing that, we'll get Ali admitted."

Marlon heaved himself out of the recliner. He tousled Ali's hair. "I'll be back in a few minutes. You do what these ladies tell you to do."

Ali's eyes grew suddenly serious. "Yes, Grandpa."

The nurse looked at Rob and Sarah. "You'll have to step out as well."

Rob followed the general and Sarah to the main desk where another young nurse explained in detail the plans for the next day. When she was finished, the general asked a few questions, then signed the documents she slid across the desk to him.

Rob glanced down the hall and saw Nora walking toward him. She looked as beautiful as ever. He smiled when she met his gaze, and he walked toward her. Stopping in front of her, he said, "I was hoping to see you."

There was a wariness in her eyes that troubled him. Her smile was tight as she asked, "How have you been?"

"Not bad. And you?"

"I've been…okay. Is Ali and everyone ready for his big day?"

"He's the only one who isn't scared. Is there somewhere you and I can go to talk?" Rob wanted to speak to Nora alone. He wanted to tell he how much he had missed her the past two days.

"I'm really very busy. Perhaps another time."

The door of Ali's room opened and the nurses came out. Nora avoided looking at Rob and said, "I'd like to see Ali alone for a few minutes. Please tell his grandfather that I'll be out to talk to him shortly."

Rob nodded. "Sure."

He took a step back and shoved his hands in his hip pockets. She seemed so distant. He wanted to reach out and take hold of her hand, but she entered Ali's room before Rob could think of anything else to say.

Walking back to the desk, Rob told Sarah and Marlon what Nora had said. Together, they waited in the hall until Nora came out of the room. She avoided meeting Rob's eyes as she approached the general. "Do you have any questions about what we'll be doing tomorrow?"

He shook his head. "I just want to know that my grandson is going to be okay."

She clasped the chart tightly to her chest. Looking down, she said, "The statistics are certainly in his favor, but I can't make that promise. I'll see you before the surgery tomorrow."

She walked away quickly to confer with one of the nurses and together they entered another room. Rob watched her go with a sinking heart. Could she dismiss him so easily from her life? He didn't want to believe that any more than he wanted to believe that she was involved in stealing drugs.

"Maybe we should have found a doctor with more of a bedside manner," General Willis said, an unhappy scowl on his face.

"Nora is the best at what she does," Rob assured him.

"She had better be."

They reentered Ali's room to find him sitting up in bed with a big smile on his face. "Doctor Nora say she fix my heart tomorrow. She tell me good story."

"What story?" Rob asked, intrigued by Ali's lack of nervousness.

"She tell me how she fix my heart with little, how you say, oh, stitches. She show me Mr. Bear with broken heart and how she fix him. She fix me just the same."

Rob picked up the bear Ali kept beside him. "You mean this bear?"

"No. She keep her Mr. Bear to show other kids."

Rob and the general exchanged puzzled glances. Nora hadn't been carrying a toy.

Taking his teddy from Rob, Ali sat the toy on his lap. "She is nice lady, but I think she is sad, too."

"Why do you think that?" Rob asked gently.

"She asked me if I'm scared. When I tell her no because God and my mother will take care of me, too, she get tears in her eyes."

Nora finished her rounds in the PICU by eleven o'clock and walked toward her office. Her few patients were all doing well. If only she could say the same about herself.

Outside she might have appeared as calm as ever, but inside she waged a constant battle with her aching heart. Seeing Rob today only made her more aware of the depths of her feelings for him.

Yesterday, she had tried to shake thoughts of him by taking Conan for a run through the quiet streets of the town. It wasn't until she found herself outside the Prairie Springs Christian Church that Nora knew she hadn't succeeded.

As she stood looking at the steeple silhouetted against the bright blue Texas sky, she knew Rob would be inside, but she also knew that wasn't the only reason she was there. She wanted to go in.

She wanted to know the kind of peace and love that Rob talked about when he spoke about his faith. Rejecting God out of grief and anger had been easy when the pain of her loss was fresh. Now, she was afraid that God wouldn't want her in His house after all these years.

Having the dog at her side had kept her from stepping into the church. When she turned away, a heavy sense of loss had settled in her chest and it hadn't gone away—until she had been alone with Ali this morning.

The little boy's bravery and unshakable faith made her ashamed of her own behavior.

Pushing open her outer office door, Nora saw Delia coming out of Peter Kent's office. Sitting quietly in the chairs along the wall was a young couple with a baby sleeping in a carrier at their feet. They held each other's hand tightly.

Delia said, "The Pelletier family is here to see you."

"Thank you, Delia. Please show them into the exam room." Turning to the parents, Nora said, "I'll be with you in a few minutes."

She had already reviewed the findings of the baby's cardiologist. What she had to do now was give the waiting couple the surgical options open to their child. They had already been to two other surgeons, neither of whom would attempt the complex repair.

Inside her office, Nora leafed through the chart Delia had prepared. As usual, her secretary had included all the information she needed. Delia was nothing if not meticulous.

The outer door opened and Delia came in. "I need your signatures on a few things, Dr. Blake."

"Of course." Nora took the stack of papers and began signing beside the red flags Delia used to mark all the places that needed Nora's name. The amount of paperwork the office generated was staggering at times. Nora didn't envy Delia and Carmen the job of keeping it straight.

When she was finished with the papers, Nora handed them back to Delia. "Is that all?"

"For now."

The woman turned toward the door, but Nora called after her. "Delia, wait a minute."

Pausing with her hand on the doorknob, Delia looked at Nora over her shoulder. "What is it, Doctor?"

"I just wanted to tell you how much I appreciate the work you do for Dr. Kent and myself. We couldn't run this office without you."

Her usually implacable expression changed to one of surprise. "Why…thank you, Dr. Blake."

"You're welcome."

A mild puzzled expression remained on Delia's face as she left the office.

The next chart Nora picked up belonged to Ali Tabiz Willis. Glancing through the preoperative laboratory reports, Nora was satisfied that Ali was well enough to undergo open-heart surgery. There was no sign of the upper respiratory infection that had plagued him in the last few months. Keeping the buildup of fluid off his lungs with the use of potent drugs had been a delicate balancing act, but it was only a stopgap measure. He needed the tear in the membrane between the two large chambers of his heart repaired, and soon.

Unlike the baby in the next room, Ali's repair would be a simple one and the boy should be out of PICU in less than a week. He could be out of the hospital and home in less than a week and a half. Once Ali was home, Rob would leave, too.

Closing the file, Nora glanced around her office. Rob's presence was everywhere. She could see his cocky grin and the gleam of humor in his eyes as plainly as if he were standing in front of her. She could still hear the tenderness in his voice the first time he'd stood in this room and asked if she believed that God led her to become a surgeon in Austin. Was it only two weeks ago? That day she had denied God's role in shaping her life.

Now, she would tell the family in the other room that she could repair their child's defective heart. What if the course of her life had not been a set of random events but a series of circumstances meant to place her exactly here on exactly this day to save this baby?

The thought was mind-boggling and humbling.

Rising, Nora walked through the exam room door. Inside, she greeted the parents. "Hello, I'm Dr. Blake."

Moving directly to the small sink, she thoroughly washed her hands and dried them before turning around. The couple, both in their early thirties, looked tired and fearful. The baby began to fret and the mother reached down to lift him from his carrier. Smiling up at Nora with a mixture of hopefulness and maternal pride, Mrs. Pelletier lifted him to her lap and said, "This is our son, Jason."

The little boy, now four months old, was thin with a pale, mottled color to his skin that Nora saw all too often. He stopped fussing when his mother began bouncing him and opened his eyes. Large and dark with thick lashes rimming them, he focused on his mother's face and opened his mouth in a sweet smile.

Nora held out her arms. "May I?"

"Certainly." The mother handed her child over, and Nora gathered the baby into her arms.

He was so light. Nora had forgotten how small and yet how perfect an infant could feel in her arms. Usually, she had the mother place the child on the exam table. This was the first baby she had held since Sondra's death. The pain of her loss was still there, still a part of her past, but this child belonged to the present and to the future if she were skilled enough.

With enormous wide eyes, Jason studied Nora and then decided she wasn't the one he wanted. He puckered up into a frown, but Nora cooed and rocked him until he settled.

Blinking back the tears that stung her eyes, she managed a smile for the worried couple staring at her. "I've looked at Jason's X-rays and echocardiograms and I believe I can do a repair. Does next Tuesday work for you?"

Leaning on the railing outside his motel room that evening, Rob turned his jacket collar up against the chill in the air. He glanced at his watch. It was ten o'clock.

He should make an early night of it, but he knew he couldn't sleep. Thoughts of Ali and his surgery scheduled for the morning kept Rob's mind racing. That and thoughts of Nora.

What was she doing tonight? How was she preparing? Or had she done so many of these operations that they no longer bothered her and she simply took them in stride? Somehow, he didn't think that was true.

For Rob, the waiting had always been the hard part. He wanted to get on with the action, get into battle, confront the bad guys or get to the bottom of the story. Now, he was discovering exactly how difficult waiting really was.

A light drizzle began falling. The wind blew the cold moisture against his face. It was a brisk reminder that October was almost gone and winter was just around the corner.

And Nora was just across town.

Straightening, he shoved his hand in his jacket pockets. His time here was drawing to a close but he wasn't ready to leave. His feelings for Nora were something that he wanted to explore. He didn't want a next assignment if it took him away from her. He stared out into the half-empty parking lot.

Half-empty, the same way his heart felt. He'd finally met a woman who might fill that emptiness and he didn't know what to do about it. His feelings for Nora had quickly become more than friendship on his part, but he faced the fact that she had never really opened up to him. He always felt she was keeping something back. Why? How could he reach her?

He glanced over his shoulder into his room and decided it would be useless to call it a night. Instead, he walked down the steps at the end of the landing and over to his truck. Getting in, he started the engine without any real plan in mind. He didn't know where he was going, but he knew where he wanted to be.

A few minutes later, he turned his vehicle onto the

street where Nora lived and pulled up in front of her house.

The lights were on, and the sight made him bold enough to approach. Shoulders hunched against the drizzle, he rang the bell and waited.

Pamela opened the door, a look of surprise on her face. “Rob, what are you doing here?”

“That’s a good question. I’ll let you know when I have an answer. Is Nora here?”

Pamela stepped back from the door, inviting him in. “She’s downstairs in her studio. Go on down. I think she’ll be glad to see you.”

As he took the steps to the lower level, he paused on the last step in surprise at the sight spread out before him. He hadn’t known what she did in her retreat, but the long tables with a dozen dollhouses down the center of the room was the last thing he expected to see.

Nora was seated with her back to him and her loupes on. He couldn’t see what she was doing. Conan lay on the floor beside her with his head resting on her foot. He looked up at Rob and wagged his stump of a tail, then yawned and lay down again.

Rob suddenly wondered if he should be here at all. He started to turn away when one of the figures in the dollhouse nearest him caught his attention. It was a little boy with dark hair and dark eyes. He was seated on a rocking horse with a teddy bear riding in front of him.

Rob picked up the miniature bear and stared at it in awe. There were tiny patches on his fur as if his owner had been too hard on the toy. A brown cloth patch covered the sole of one foot and a red patch had been sewn on his chest. Rob looked closer. The red patch was in the shape of a broken heart with both pieces mended together with incredibly fine stitches.

He glanced at Nora and found she was looking at him with an odd smile on her face. She said, "I call him Mr. Bear."

"Ali mentioned meeting him." Rob walked toward her and gestured around the room. "This is quite a collection you have. Did you make them all?"

"I buy the people and the houses, then I decorate the homes and make the clothing for the dolls to portray different eras."

"I've never seen anything like this."

"It's a hobby."

"I thought your hobby was crewel embroidery."

"If you'll take a look at the sofa and footstool in this house you'll see examples of my crewel-work."

He moved to stand beside her, and she handed him the pieces she was talking about. The intricate, tiny stitches were amazingly complex.

He glanced at her. "Have you always done this?"

She turned away and placed the doll she was working on into the bright yellow kitchen of the house beside her. "Pamela and I bought the first house together when I was pregnant. She wanted to give it to her new baby sister, but her sister never made it home from the hospital."

Stunned at the pain in her trembling voice, Rob knelt beside her chair. "What happened?"

Nora touched the locket she wore. "Sondra was born with a heart defect. One that couldn't be fixed. She died when she was three days old."

"I'm so sorry."

She looked into his eyes. "Thank you. I've been wanting to tell you about her, but the time never seemed right."

"Tell me now. I'm listening."

"She's the reason I became a pediatric heart surgeon. She's my constant reminder of how easily a child can slip away. Each time I talk to parents about what might happen to their son or daughter in surgery, I'm really trying to prepare them for the heartbreaking, soul-killing pain they might have to face, but my words never come out right." She bowed her head. "Why is that, Rob?"

He gently swept her hair back her from her face so that she would look at him. "I don't know. Maybe because you weren't born with the gift of gab the way I was?"

She gave him a tentative, grateful smile and his heart went out to her. "I've looked at your surgical outcomes, Nora. You save ninety-eight out of every one hundred children that come to you."

"No, I lose two lives out of every one hundred that I'm trying to save. That's two families destroyed forever."

He glanced at all the houses and the figures inside. "So that's why you do this. You're making families that will last forever."

She held up the dress she had made to fit one of her dolls. "You're right. I come here to create perfect families frozen in time. The little boys will ride their tricycles or rocking horses forever. The little girls will play with their dolls or their puppies. Fathers will read their papers in their favorite chairs and mothers will be cooking in the kitchen. No one down here dies. No one ever has to grieve."

He took the dress from her hand and laid it aside, then he grasped her fingers. "None of them ever sees the beauty of a sunrise. They may not know sadness, but they don't know joy. None of them love and are loved in return. They don't have perfect lives. They don't have life at all."

She looked away. "I know."

Putting one finger beneath her chin, he lifted her face until she met his gaze. "We can only make the best of what we are given, Nora. I've been given the chance to know you and that makes me blessed. I find myself wanting to share everything beautiful with you."

Biting her lip, Nora stared at Rob without speaking as tears welled up in her eyes. Having him here was so right. Having him learn about her secret retreat and about Sondra gave Nora a sense of peace that she hadn't known in many years.

He understood what she had gone through, and someday soon she would tell him the rest. For now, knowing he cared was enough.

"I feel the same way about you, Rob. I never thought it was possible, but you have changed my life."

"Tell me you'll give what we have a chance to grow."

"I'd like that."

The relief on his face made her smile. He gripped her hands more tightly. "Nora, I love your spunk and the way you've dedicated your life to caring for children. I even like your dog, although he's chewing on my shoe at the moment."

Her eyes widened and she looked down. "Conan, don't do that."

Conan looked up as if surprised that he wasn't allowed to have expensive running shoes for a snack. He still had one white shoestring dangling from his mouth.

Nora met Rob's eyes and both of them began to chuckle. Taking her face between his hands, Rob said, "It's a small price to pay for a chance to kiss you."

She smiled sweetly. "Since you've paid the toll, I think you'd better collect your prize."

He leaned forward and covered her lips with his own. Nora gave herself up to the joy racing through her veins.

Chapter 13

As Rob entered Ali's hospital room on Tuesday morning, the sight of all the people clustered around the boy's bed took him aback. Besides General Willis and Sarah Alpert, he recognized Anna and her fiancé, David Ryland. With them were Caitlin Villard, army chaplain Steve Windham and Pastor Fields, all of whom he had met while doing his interviews about Children of the Day, and of course Olga.

Ali was holding the hand of chestnut-haired woman who stood beside his bed. With his free hand, the boy motioned Rob over. "This is my pretty Nurse Maddie."

Walking up to Ali, Rob leaned down and whispered, "You're right. She's very pretty."

"Pretty, but taken." A middle-aged man with a cane came to stand beside Maddie and lay a hand on her shoulder. "Hello, I'm Jake Hopkins. I'm the general's attorney and a friend of Ali's."

"A pleasure to meet you," Rob said, returning Jake's strong handshake.

Rob glanced around. These people, from all walks of life, had banded together to see that one little boy from a village halfway around the world had a chance at a new life. God's work was truly being done here.

The door to the room opened and Nora walked in with a chart in her hand. She looked up and her eyes widened at the sight of such a crowd in the room. Looking apologetic, she said, "I'm sorry, but I'm going to have to ask all of you to step out. Everyone but immediate family should go to the surgical waiting area."

"Of course, Doctor," Pastor Fields said, "but before we go, we would like to offer a prayer for Ali's recovery."

"Certainly."

Rob reached for Nora. She smiled softly as she laid her hand in his. Olga came to take Nora's other hand, a gentle look of happiness shining in her eyes. Pastor Frank and Chaplain Steve laid their hands on Ali. Around the room, the others joined hands and bowed their head.

"Heavenly Father," Pastor Frank began. "We are gathered here to ask for Your blessings on this child. Make him whole and well again if that is Your will. Give us the strength to face what is to come and lend us Your comfort. Through Your Son, Jesus, our salvation is secured and all things are possible. Be with this child today. Hold him in the palm of Your hand. Lend Your strength and wisdom to his doctors and nurses. Let them become the instruments of Your healing power. We ask this in Jesus' name. Amen."

A chorus of amens filled the room. Rob looked up and found Nora watching him intently. His heart expanded with love. If the room hadn't been full of people he would have told her that very instant that he wanted to be part of her life forever.

General Willis's cell phone rang and he stepped away from the bed to answer it, but then quickly turned back to his grandson. "Ali, I have someone special here who wants to talk to you. Does anyone here know how to turn up the volume on this thing so we can all hear him?"

"I do." Chaplain Steve took it from him and after a few seconds said, "That should be it."

"Thank you." The general took it from him and set it down on the overbed table in front of Ali. "Go ahead, son. You're on speaker now."

"Ali, can you hear me?" A man's deep voice came over the line amid a few crackles of static.

Behind him, Rob heard a quick indrawn breath. Looking over his shoulder, he saw Sarah press a hand to her chest. She caught his eye and managed to quickly compose her face, but not before he saw that she clearly recognized the caller.

"Dr. Mike, is that you?" Ali demanded in disbelief.

"It's me, little buddy." The army surgeon's voice reverberated with emotion. "Sorry I can't be with you today, but I'm thinking about you and wishing you the best. I know you'll do fine."

"I'm thinking for you, too, Dr. Mike."

Rob smiled at the boy's mangled English. This call would need to be included in his story. That Dr. Michael Montgomery was calling from a war zone half the world away to wish the boy well proved how much Ali had touched his life.

Rob looked around the room. This child had touched so many lives. He prayed Nora's gift would allow him to touch many more in ways only God knew.

After the call ended, everyone filed out to make their way down to the surgical waiting area. Rob stepped aside, hoping for a few minutes with Nora before she left to get ready. He didn't have long to wait.

She came out with one of the nurses. After giving some additional instructions on what she wanted done before Ali left for the pre-op area, Nora closed the chart she held and handed it over. When the woman walked away, Nora turned and smiled at Rob. The sight warmed his heart.

"Everything looks good," she said.

"You look good," he said, reaching to take hold of her hand and pulling her toward the open door of an empty room. Inside, he turned to face her. Gathering both her hands in his, he smiled and said, "In fact, you look great."

Grinning widely, she rolled her eyes in amusement. "Flattery will get you nowhere."

"I beg to differ. It got me a few minutes alone with you, didn't it?"

"I'm working, Rob." She tried to sound stern, but all he heard was a huskiness in her tone that sent his heart into overdrive.

Sighing heavily, he said, "I know. Just promise me that we can continue this later."

Rising on tiptoe, she planted a kiss on his cheek. "Later, I promise."

"I'll walk you down to surgery," he offered, not wanting her out of his sight.

"I have other patients to see. Ali won't actually go

into the surgical suite for another hour or so. I'll meet you down there. Until then, get a cup of that caramel coffee you like so much."

He squeezed her hands. "All right, but you can't get rid of me for long."

"I was hoping you would say that."

His cell phone began ringing. Nora raised one eyebrow. "You'll have to release my hand to answer that."

"It can go to voice mail."

Tugging free, she gave him a rueful smile. "It might be important."

He shook his head. "More important than spending a stolen minute with you? I don't think so."

"You really do know how to flatter a woman. Answer your calls while you can. You'll have to turn your phone off before you go into surgery. It can interfere with some of our equipment."

She gave him a quick peck on the cheek and walked out of the room. It amazed him how happy he felt just being near her, but he wanted so much more.

He pulled the phone out of the clip on his waistband. Flipping it open, he said, "Talk to me."

"I hope I didn't catch you at a bad time." Carter's voice sounded young, fresh and eager.

"You have no idea. What do you have for me?"

"I checked with the doctor at the camp and with InterAir Express, the shipping company on this end. Your missing drugs never made it into the country."

Rob walked to the large window at the back of the room. He suddenly had a very bad feeling in his bones. "Are you sure? It wouldn't be the first time officials in that neck of the woods skimmed supplies for the black market."

"I thought of that, too, but the invoice and papers are all in order. If the rest of the drugs left Austin, they didn't come here."

"It doesn't make sense. I know the woman who arranged the donations."

The silence on the other end of the line spoke volumes. After drawing a deep breath and blowing it out through pursed lips, Rob said, "You don't need to say it. I knew the guys at Memdelholm, too, but this isn't like that."

"If you say so." Carter's doubt was plain.

Rob didn't want to hear it. Didn't want to think it.

"Thanks for your help with this, Carter. I'll see what I can find out from this end. Any information over there about Whitney Harpswell?"

"Not yet, but I met with the coffee merchant you sent me to. He's agreed to take me to meet some of his—associates in the region. Thanks for getting the old guy to talk to me. He's a gold mine of information."

"Don't believe half of what he tells you. I mean it, Carter, be careful."

"For what it's worth, I know you wanted this assignment and I'm almost, but not quite, sorry I got it instead."

"Don't forget you're on *temporary* assignment there."

"Not if I can help it." Carter hung up and Rob closed his phone.

Raking a hand through his hair, Rob began pacing the small room. Only a portion of the drugs Nora had obtained in the name of her charity had reached their destination. Where were the rest?

He didn't like where this train of thought was leading him. Why would Nora siphon medical supplies away from Children of the Day? Why would anyone?

For money. The obvious answer made him sick to his stomach. He didn't want to admit that it might be true. His first instinct was to find Nora and ask her if she knew what had happened, but a growing uncertainty held him back.

He knew the hospital had stopped financing the state-of-the-art unit she wanted so desperately. Where had the money come from that she donated to get construction started again? Could her determination to build the best pediatric cardiac unit in the southwest have prompted her to get the money by illegal means?

No. It wasn't possible. He couldn't be in love with someone capable of doing such a thing.

I've only known her a couple weeks. How can I be so sure? Please, God, help me. I don't know what to think.

He hated the doubts piling up in his brain, but he couldn't stop them. He had been duped before.

Men he called friends, men he had fought beside and bled with had made a fool of him—for money. His respect and admiration for them had blinded him to the truth.

He glanced at his watch. Before he confronted anyone or revealed what he had leaned, he had some serious investigating to do. This time, he wouldn't allow his personal feelings to keep him from getting to the bottom of what was really going on.

After leaving the pediatric floor, he took the elevator to the third level. He walked down the hallway and entered Nora's office. To his relief, Carmen sat behind the receptionist's desk. She looked up and gave him a wide smile. With one hand she patted her dark hair into place.

"Mr. Dale, how nice to see you again. I thought you were going to be in surgery with Dr. Blake."

"I'm on my way there in a couple of minutes. There are a few facts I wanted to check out first. Maybe you can help me so I don't have to bother Nora."

"Sure. What do you need?"

He tried to sound nonchalant as he parked his hip on the corner of the desk, but his heart was racing. "I know Nora sometimes receives medical supplies for Children of the Day. Do they come through this office or through her home?"

"Through the hospital. Children of the Day has a large storage area here. It wouldn't be possible to keep such a volume of materials at her home. Besides, there are federal regulations regarding handling of medical supplies that are very strict. Children of the Day receives thousands of pounds of supplies from hundreds of different companies and organizations each year."

"It must be difficult to keep track of it all. Do hospital employees have access to the area?" He wanted his investigation to lead him away from Nora's involvement.

"We keep the keys here in the office. If I'm working and things come in for Children of the Day, Delia has very specific instructions for me to follow. All the paperwork is handled by her or by Dr. Blake."

"What about Dr. Kent?"

"He sometimes oversees donation arrivals when Dr. Blake is busy, but he uses our key. What is this about?"

He didn't want to lie so he settled on a half truth. "I'm just looking for a little more background information in case I need filler for a piece. Do you know which shipping company Nora uses when she sends donated supplies and drugs overseas?"

"She uses InterAir Express." It was the company Carter had mentioned.

He needed to know who had arranged that shipment. "Are they a reliable carrier?"

"I've never heard any complaints, but I can tell you that if Delia thought they weren't doing their job, she'd go elsewhere."

"Is there a way to see when the last two or three shipments were sent and when they arrived? That would give me an idea of how reliable and prompt they are."

Carmen clicked through to the company's Web site and logged on. "It looks like it took five days to get five cases of antibiotics to the Middle East, but it only took two days to get twenty cases of antibiotics to the Dominican Republic."

Quickly Rob jotted down the name of the clinic where the drugs had been delivered in the Caribbean. He said, "You can't beat that for good service. How is it all paid for?"

"Children of the Day has a corporate account and so does Dr. Blake, but I'm not sure I should be looking this kind of stuff up for you."

"I'm sorry. I get carried away sometime. You've been a big help, Carmen. Could you do one final little favor for me?"

She bit her lip. "That depends."

He reached out, lifted her hand from the computer mouse and planted a kiss on her knuckles as he gave her his best hangdog look. "I'm late for Ali's surgery. Could I borrow another set of scrubs from Dr. Kent?"

She blushed as she slowly drew her hand away. "Of course. I'll get them for you." She rose from her chair and went into the next room.

Leaning down, Rob grabbed the mouse and clicked through several more shipping files. His heart sank when he saw a dozen recent shipments to Mexico and the Dominican Republic had been charged to Nora's account and not to Children of the Day. Everything kept pointing back to Nora's involvement. There had to be something he was missing.

Why had she sent the drugs somewhere other than the refugee camp in the Middle East? There had to be a simple explanation. Maybe the charity had a branch operating in the Caribbean that he didn't know about. Perhaps the need was simply greater there and Nora had responded by dividing the shipment.

He heard the door to Dr. Kent's office open. Clicking the files closed, he rose and took the uniform from Carmen. "Thanks, sweetie, you've been a great help."

Carmen smiled at him. "Little Ali will be in my prayers this afternoon."

"Mine, too. I'd better get going. I'll see you later. Be sure and tell Harold I think he's a blessed man to have a wife like you."

She waved his compliment aside. "Honey, I tell my husband that every day."

Rob grinned and said goodbye, but outside the office his smile faded. He took the elevator to the fifth floor and made his way to the surgical waiting room. It was nearly full. Seeing Anna and Olga across the room, he crossed to where they were sitting and dropped into an empty chair beside them.

"Have they brought Ali by yet?" he asked.

"Just a few minutes ago."

Glancing around, Rob noticed Marlon's absence. "Where's General Willis?"

"He and Pastor Fields have gone to the chapel."

"That's good. I'd better get going or I'll miss the surgery." He rose, but paused, then asked, "Anna, does Children of the Day have an operation in the Caribbean?"

"Not at present, although we've talked about starting one in Haiti. Why?"

He didn't want to upset her until he knew more. "I'm just trying to get a better sense of how widespread your organization is."

She smiled sadly. "I wish we could do more."

"You're doing great work," he assured her. "God will bless your efforts."

Olga covered Anna's hand with her own. "I believe that He will. Look after little Ali in there for us, Rob. We'll be out here praying that He blesses Dr. Blake's efforts. She has our little boy's life in her hands."

Rob nodded. Nora might have all the answers to the questions racing through his mind, but he couldn't ask her about it now. She needed her full concentration on the delicate surgery she was about to perform.

Rob left the waiting room but paused outside the surgical suite doors. Pulling his cell phone out, he placed a call to Encore Investigations. He got the usual recording. When it was done playing, he said, "Murray, this is Rob Dale. I need you to check into a clinic in the Dominican Republic. I'm going to be out of touch for the next four hours, so leave me a message if you find out anything."

Rob recited the name and address from the shipping company records and then hung up and turned off his phone. Somehow, he was going to have to stand beside Nora for the next several hours and not ask her what she knew about the missing drugs. He prayed for patience.

Nora scrubbed in, donned her operating garb and backed through the operating room door with her wet arms curled in front of her. The electric cord for her electronic magnifying loops hung down her back from the headpiece like a long tail. One of the nurses came forward with a sterile towel, and Nora used it to dry her hands.

Ali was already asleep on the table. His eyes were taped shut and a white tube protruded from his mouth. At the head of the table the anesthesiologist had already connected the boy to a ventilator. An array of machines stood close by, and Nora looked to the perfusion technologist who would be managing the heart–lung bypass machine. "Are you ready?"

"We're good to go, Doctor."

Nora looked around the room. Rob hadn't yet arrived.

Dr. Kent came in behind her and accepted a towel from the same nurse. "This is going to be short and sweet, right? I've got a golf game scheduled this afternoon."

"That's my plan, Peter. It should be a straightforward repair."

The door to the scrub room opened again, and Nora relaxed as Rob came in.

Turning to one of the nurses, Nora said, "Would you please place a footstool behind me after I'm in position so that Mr. Dale can view the procedure, then we can get started."

Nora stepped up to the table. When Rob was in position behind her, she looked over her shoulder. "Can you see all right?"

"I'm fine," he answered quietly. His voiced seemed strained, but perhaps it was only the surgical mask making it sound distorted.

She turned back to the patient. Playing out the steps

of the procedure in her mind, a calmness settled over her. Rob's solid presence behind her gave her an odd sense of comfort. She had wondered if he would prove to be a distraction, but it seemed that he had just the opposite effect.

She held out her hand and said, "Scalpel."

Twenty minutes into the operation, Nora realized Ali's surgery was going to be anything but routine. One problem after another cropped up. His blood pressure dropped without warning, prompting adjustments in the anesthetic being use. After that, she found unexpected scar tissue over the front of his heart. A result, no doubt, of the force of the blast that had torn the inside of his heart. It was something she hadn't anticipated and it slowed the pace of the operation while she gingerly worked her way through it.

When it came time to cool his body and stop his heart, the perfusion technologist announced there was trouble with the heart–lung bypass machine. It wasn't cooling the blood circulating through Ali's small body properly.

While the tech and another nurse worked to discover what was wrong, Rob spoke quietly behind Nora. "What does that mean?"

"It means I have to use another method to stop his heart."

"Like what?"

"I'll use iced sterile saline and pour it over the heart to stop it instead. It is just as effective, but I'll have to be much quicker." It was another problem that plagued what should have been a simple repair.

With Ali's small heart open at last, Nora studied the jagged tear in the thick membrane between the ventricles of his heart. "What do you think, Peter? Would it be better to trim tissue and make a neat hole I can close with a Dacron patch or spend additional time stitching this up?"

When he didn't answer, she glanced up at him. "Peter?"

He blinked. "Sorry. I was a thousand miles away for a second."

"Were you in Cancun again, Dr. Kent?" one of the nurses joked.

"Santo Domingo…or I will be in two days, thank goodness. What's the problem, Nora?"

She indicated where she was working. "Would you trim and patch this hole or stitch it?"

He bent his head to peer through his loupes. "I say trim and patch."

She nodded in agreement and set to work.

"We're cooling now," the perfusionist announced.

Nora relaxed. "That's good to hear. Now I won't have to rush."

Twenty minutes later she had a neat patch in place and was satisfied that it would restore Ali's heart to normal function. She looked at the perfusionist. "Can we warm him now?"

"Yes, all the systems are working."

"Good. Warm our little boy."

Nora watched the heart, waiting for the first sign that it would begin beating on its own. Minutes passed.

"We're there," the perfusion technologist announced.

Nora frowned. "I don't have any activity. Are you sure he is warm enough?"

"Yes," the perfusionist was frowning over his machine.

"Better shock him," Dr. Kent suggested.

Nora looked at the closest nurse. "Give me the paddles."

The nurse handed her the internal defibrillator paddles, two foot-long wands with silver-dollar-sized discs on the ends. Nora gave the nurse the settings she wanted and then called out, "Clear."

She checked to make sure no one was touching Ali's body or the table he lay on, then she placed the paddles on either side of his heart and hit the button. The current made his heart jump, but it didn't keep going.

"What's the matter?" Rob asked.

Nora had almost forgotten he was there, but the sound of his voice steadied her. "His heart is proving to be a little stubborn. It doesn't want to restart."

After calling out a higher setting, Nora positioned the paddles again and delivered a bigger shock. Still nothing.

Fear settled in the pit of her stomach. Putting the paddles aside, she placed her hand around Ali's heart and began compressing it.

"Come on," she bit out through tight lips. "Don't do this. Don't die on me."

Chapter 14

Nora stopped massaging Ali's heart and called for drugs that would help. When they had been given, she picked up the paddles and shocked him again. Still nothing. Beneath her mask, she could taste blood where she had bitten her lips.

"What do you want to do?" Dr. Kent asked.

"He's okay for a while longer on the heart–lung machine, but you know as well as I do we can't keep him on it forever. This shouldn't be happening."

"Don't give up on him." She heard the pleading in Rob's voice, and it doubled the pain she was already feeling.

"Give him another dose of epi." She started massaging the heart again. Another round of shocks followed.

"Come on. Come on." As the minutes ticked by, her

hand began to ache. A nurse called out the time and Nora's heart sank.

Suddenly, she felt a Rob place his hand gently in the center of her back. Softly, he said, "The Lord is my shepherd, I shall not want. He maketh me to lie down in green pastures: He leadeth me beside the still waters."

"He restoreth my soul," she continued with reverence. She knew the passage from her childhood. Deep in her heart, she felt God's presence as a vital living thing within. Ali's life was in God's hands. Her life was in God's hands. Her baby daughter was safe and loved with Him in Heaven. She could let go of her grief and pain.

Tears filled her eyes and she swallowed hard, then whispered, "I'm not giving up on you, Ali. God, help me to save this child."

With his hand on Nora's shoulders, Rob could feel the renewed strength fill her body. She called out for more drugs and then lifted the paddles and placed them on Ali's heart again. "Clear!"

Rob heard a tiny blip and glanced at the monitor. There it was again. He sucked in a deep breath as the wavy line became a strong, even beat. Collective sighs of relief echoed around the room, and Rob felt weak in the knees.

"Okay, let's get our boy closed up and out of here," Nora said. She started back to work, but Rob heard the clear relief in her voice.

"I can close," Dr. Kent said.

Nora shook her head. "No, this is one case I want to finish myself."

Thirty minutes later, Rob watched as Ali, still asleep, was wheeled out of the operating room. Nora pulled off her mask and her bulky surgical gown. She looked ready to drop, but there was an air of peace about her as she smiled up at him. "I need to talk to Ali's grandfather and make sure Ali is settled in PICU, then I'd like to buy you a cup of coffee. What do you say?"

"That sounds good. I'll come with you."

Once outside the OR, Rob followed Nora to the waiting room. Marlon rose to his feet when he saw her. "How is he?"

"He's fine now." Nora smiled. "He's fine," she called out loudly so that everyone in the room could hear.

"Thank the Lord," Marlon said, and sat down abruptly. A cheerful buzz broke out as people patted each other on the back and hugged one another.

Nora sat down beside Marlon. "It was touch and go for a while. He may need to spend a little longer in the hospital than I originally said. You can go up and see him in another thirty minutes."

He took her hand and shook it. "Thank you, Dr. Blake."

"You're welcome, sir."

Rising she looked at Rob. He saw such happiness in her eyes that it stole his breath.

As they rode up to the next floor on the elevator with a half dozen other people, Nora reached over to take his hand. Leaning toward him, she whispered, "Thanks."

"For what?"

She smiled softly at him. "For being there today."

The elevator doors opened and they stepped off together. Even after she let go of his hand, the warmth of her touch remained. When they reached the PICU, she stopped at the desk while Rob continued into Ali's room.

There were several nurses at the bedside, checking

IV fluids and giving medications. Ali was still asleep. He looked so small in the bed. His thick, black eyelashes lay like dark crescents against his pale cheeks. Rob stepped up and laid a hand on the boy's head and whispered a prayer for his recovery. He knew that Ali wasn't out of the woods, but he felt in his heart that the Lord had great plans for the little man.

Nora came in with the head nurse at her side. As the two of them continued to confer, Rob stepped out of the room and turned on his cell phone. He had two messages. They were both from Encore Investigation. Rob hit Okay to play the first one.

"Rob, Murray here. I couldn't find anything on the clinic you gave me so I checked with my contacts at Interpol. The clinic is bogus. The place is a front for black market drugs throughout the islands. The local authorities moved in on it an hour ago but the place was empty. These guys never stay at one location for long. Whoever shipped your drugs had to know exactly where and when to send them. It was no accident."

Rob leaned against the nearest wall and balled his free hand into a fist. Someone involved with Children of the Day had deliberately misdirected desperately needed medication into illegal hands. It couldn't have been Nora. She wouldn't do that.

He walked to the doorway and looked in. She was listening to Ali's chest with a stethoscope and peering intently at the monitor over his bed.

Rob turned away and opened his phone to listen to the next message. Maybe Murray had found out the shipment had been a mistake.

"Hey, Dale, I almost forgot. I uncovered why you might have heard the name Hannor Pharmaceuticals.

The World Health Organization was investigating Bernard Blake before his death. There were accusations his company relabeled outdated measles vaccines then donated tons of it to poor villages throughout Indonesia. U.S. tax breaks on donated drugs are equal to their fair market value. The money kept his company going long enough to recover and prosper in the next few years.

"No one would have been the wiser except that there was an outbreak of measles in Indonesia a year later. A lot of kids died who had been vaccinated. After Blake's death, his wife broke up the company and sold it off, so the investigation was dropped. That's all I've got for you."

At the end of the message, Rob snapped his phone shut. Pressing his fingers to his temple, he struggled to hold on to his self-control. He wanted to drag Nora out of Ali's room and demand answers. No wonder she had evaded his questions about her husband and his business. He paced the hall until she appeared, a welcoming smile on her face.

"Are you ready for that coffee?" she asked.

"Nora, I need to talk you. We've got a problem."

Her smile faded. "You look so serious. What wrong?"

He stepped closer. "Three thousand vials of antibiotics were shipped from your office to black market drug dealers in the Caribbean instead of to the refugee camp in the Middle East. What do you know about it?"

Nora stared at Rob in complete shock. She couldn't believe her ears. "I don't know anything about it. Are you sure?"

"My source is positive."

"How could such a thing happen?"

His eyes never left hers. "Nora, the shipping invoice has your signature on it. It was paid for with your credit card."

A sick sensation settled in her stomach. "Rob, are you accusing me of stealing the medicine?"

His silence hurt like a physical blow. She said, "I didn't do it."

"I want to believe you."

"Then why don't you?" she snapped.

He stepped closer until he was looming over her. Softly, he said, "I've had the feeling since we met that you are hiding something from me. What is it, Nora?"

Unable to meet his gaze, she looked down. "I'm sorry. There are other people I have to consider."

"Now is the time for the truth."

"You really think I'm involved in this, don't you?" Tears pricked her eyes, but she had spent years putting her emotions on hold while she did her job. She called up that willpower now and crossed her arms over her chest.

"I want to believe you, Nora, but how can I when you won't be honest with me. I know about the outdated measles vaccines."

Her heart dropped like a stone as her worst fear materialized. Pamela would be devastated. Nora couldn't protect her anymore.

She glared at Rob. "So you've been investigating me from the start. Was your story about Children of the Day and Ali's surgery just a ruse to get close to me?" Shaking her head, she answered before he could. "Of course it was. All of this—us—it was nothing but a means to an end."

"That's not true. My assignment was Children of the

Day and Ali. I admit I had someone look into your background, but that was before we became involved."

Her mind was spinning, making it hard to focus. "What a fool I've been."

"Nora, a lot of people are going to start asking for an explanation when this story gets out."

"You mean when *your* story hits the press."

Spinning on her heel, she marched down the hallway unable to see for the tears that burned her eyes. She had been about to tell Rob that she was falling in love with him. How could she have been so mistaken? He didn't love her. He had only used her.

She didn't wait for the elevator, but took the stairs down to the third floor. Rob followed close behind her.

Nora yanked open her office door and stormed inside as she worked to get a grip on her emotions.

Carmen looked up, her eyes wide. She quickly closed the e-mail missive on her computer. "Dr. Blake, you startled me. Is something wrong? Did the surgery go okay?"

"Ali Willis should make a full recovery."

"That's good. Well, if you don't need me, I was just getting ready to leave."

Nora heard the door behind her open but she didn't turn around. She knew who was there.

"You may go home, but before you do, will you get me the files for the all of the medical shipments I've made for Children of the Day for the past year?"

Carmen looked from Rob back to Nora. "Certainly, but can I ask why?"

"Because Mr. Dale thinks I'm a thief." Her throat closed around the words and she couldn't speak.

Rob said, "Part of the last antibiotic shipment has gone astray and we want to find out how that happened."

Carmen glared at him. "Is this why you were asking questions earlier?"

"I had a suspicion and I wanted to check it out before I said anything."

"You used me to pry into Dr. Blake's private business. Dr. Blake, I am so sorry." Carmen's anger boiled over. "Do you want me to call security and have this jerk thrown out of the hospital?"

Nora raised her chin. She wouldn't cry even if her heart was breaking. "Yes. That is exactly what I want you to do."

The next afternoon, Rob sat at the small table in his motel room and stared at his blank computer screen with a sick feeling that he was sure would never go away. He had a story now that would wow his boss. It was the kind of story most reporters dreamed of uncovering...but he couldn't find the words to tell it. He forced himself to type the headline that would ensure his promotion back to the Middle East.

Prominent Pediatric Heart Surgeon Uses Charity to Cover Black Market Drug Deals.

Holding down the delete key, he watched the words disappear letter by letter from his screen. If only there was some way to make them disappear from his mind.

"Lord, why did You bring me here? Why let me fall in love with this woman? What lesson am I supposed to learn? Please, I don't know what I'm supposed to do."

The only answer that kept coming to mind was that he should believe Nora. He loved her. He knew in his heart that she couldn't have done this—but he had been fooled before.

A knock at the door forced him to get up. He expected it to be housekeeping making their daily rounds, but when he pulled open the door he saw Pamela Blake standing in front of him looking angry and determined.

"Pamela, what are you doing here?" Rob glanced behind him at the laptop lying on the table.

"I was coming here to punch your lights out, but my cooler side has prevailed." She fisted her hands on her hips. "Nora didn't do this, and I can't prove it by myself. Rob, I need your help."

He sighed. "I don't want to believe it myself, but everything points to her involvement."

Pamela took a step closer. "Then someone is making it look that way."

He turned aside. "I know that you love her."

"At least consider the possibility that she didn't do it," Pamela insisted, following him into the room.

He sat down at the small table and closed his laptop. He hadn't slept, couldn't eat, couldn't think of anything but the look of pain on Nora's face. "I want to believe that she is innocent."

Pamela sank to her knees beside him and gripped his arm. "Then *believe* her. Listen to your heart."

"A heart can be fooled—and broken."

"That's your excuse for not helping her? Your heart is broken? Get over it. So what if she kept a painful part of her past a secret? It's her life. Now that life is about to be destroyed."

He raked a hand through his hair. "I used to think I was a good judge of character, but I found out just how wrong I could be. I have to look at the evidence now."

She shook him. “This isn’t about you, Rob. This isn’t about how wrong you’ve been in the past. This is about Nora’s reputation. It’s about her future. I thought you cared about her.”

“I do.”

“Then why are you sitting here feeling sorry for yourself instead of getting out there and *proving* she didn’t do anything wrong.”

He stared into Pamela’s angry eyes and saw the truth in what she was saying. He *had* been feeling sorry for himself. He’d been wallowing in self-pity. The only thing making a fool out of him this time was his own doubt and insecurity.

The reason he couldn’t write the story was because he didn’t believe it.

So he had been wrong about his friends Benny and Drake. He wasn’t responsible for the bad choices they made. It didn’t mean he had to give up trusting people. Perhaps that was what God wanted him to discover.

He forced his tired brain into action. “Who could do it?”

“I don’t know. That’s why I came to you.”

“Okay, who could physically do it? Who has access to her files, the storage, shipping information, her credit card?”

“Does that mean you’ll help her?”

“Yes. Where is she?” He grabbed his car keys and started out of the room.

“At home, crying her eyes out and telling me that everything is fine. She always tells me everything is fine.”

Rob stopped and looked at Pamela. He saw a young woman in charge of her own life, and he had to admire her. Nora was blessed to have Pamela as a friend and as a daughter.

"Pamela, if this gets out, you are going to hear some things that will be hard to accept."

"You're talking about my father."

"Yes."

"I know that he was being investigated if that's what you mean. I also know that he made a terrible mistake when the company was in financial trouble and he tried very hard to make up for it later. His decision haunted him."

"Did Nora know about it?"

"Not until the investigation started. When she found out, they had a terrible fight and Dad left. I may have lost my father in that skiing accident, but Nora lost her husband and then her newborn baby all in the same week. I let her think she was protecting me by keeping the information and the press away from me because she *needed* to do that."

"You're a remarkable woman."

She smiled. "I know a great guy who thinks the same thing. His name is Gary. You should meet him."

"I'd like that."

Rob followed Pamela back to her house and parked his truck behind her car. She hurried up the front steps and opened the door, but he hesitated. How could Nora ever forgive him for doubting her?

Pamela looked at him. "What?"

"I don't know what to say to her."

"*I'm sorry* is a good start. If you want to add that you've been a complete jerk, that's entirely up to you. She's downstairs. Watch out for the dog. He gets cranky when she gets upset."

"Thanks for the warning."

Rob walked down the steps to Nora's workshop with his heart pounding harder than it did when he finished a ten-mile run. He didn't have a chance to plan what he would say because Conan suddenly appeared at the bottom step with his teeth bared. He growled with convincing menace.

Nora came to stand behind the dog. She had pretty much the same expression in her eyes. "What are you doing here?"

Nora couldn't believe that Rob had the nerve to show his face in her own home. "Have you come to smear more mud on me?"

"I came to offer my help."

"You've helped enough. You've got your story. Now, get out."

Conan growled louder. Rob slowly sank to his haunches and extended his hand to the dog. "Nora, I'm sorry. I'm a complete idiot. You are brave and caring woman, and I know you didn't do this. I doubted you because I had lost faith in myself, in my ability to believe wholeheartedly in others. You're innocent and I want to help you prove it."

Nora wanted so badly to believe him. She took a step closer and laid her hand on Conan's head. "How?"

Conan stopped growling and sat. Rob rose to his feet. "I need to get back into your office."

"Why?"

"Because my gut tells me that's where the answers are."

"Why should I trust you now?" Her voice cracked and she bit her upper lip.

"Trust me because I'm a good reporter."

"Ha!"

"Look, I know I made a big mistake. I'm asking you to forgive me. I don't blame you if you can't. I will never doubt you again as long as we live. I love you, Nora. I don't deserve you, but I can't help loving you. Maybe we've only known each other for a couple weeks, but God put you right in front of me for a reason."

There was no doubting the sincerity of his words. His eyes pleaded for her understanding more eloquently than his words. He took another step closer, holding out his hand to her.

She sniffed once. "You really hurt me."

"I know I did. I can't begin to tell you how sorry I am."

"I thought you were a good man."

He descended another step. "I need to keep working on that. I could use your help."

"I thought my husband was a good man, too, but he…he chose money over…over the lives of children."

Rob reached the bottom step and pushed Conan out of the way with his knee. "I know what he did, but I'm not him. You and I can make a fresh start, together."

He wrapped his arms around her. She leaned into him, letting go of her last burden. "I love you, too, Rob. You have no idea how much."

"I love you enough to let your dog chew my shoes while I'm wearing them."

She laughed through her tears as she looked down at Conan and back up at Rob. "You and Conan are going to have to work that out between you."

"We'll come to an understanding. Now, let's go to your office and see if we can figure out who wants to frame you."

Chapter 15

Rob sat at the computer in Nora's outer office and stared at the screen, determined to find the answers he was looking for. "Let's start with who could do this. Who has access to everything regarding medical supplies for Children of the Day?"

"Myself."

"Honey, I think we've ruled you out."

"Okay, someone in housekeeping or security? They have keys to everything at the hospital."

"But how would they get access to the shipping account? It's password protected."

"Anna Terenkov can get into the account, as can Delia and Carmen."

"Didn't you notice the unusual charges on your statements?"

"The money comes out of a special bank account. My

financial adviser handles everything to do with those specific funds. As long as the money was being used for Children of the Day, he wouldn't question the withdrawals. I only used part of the money for myself once."

"Why is that?"

"It's from my husband's life insurance. I swore I would only use it to make a difference for children. I was trying to make amends for what he did. I wanted to make sure the money was going for something worthwhile, something that would last."

"That's where the donation for the PICU construction came from."

"Yes. That is the one selfish thing I've done with the money."

"Building a state-of-the-art medical facility for children is hardly selfish. Who knows about the account?"

"Anna and my accountant. That's it."

Rob highlighted the screen and hit Print. "Okay, let's take a look at the dates of all the shipments over the past year and see if we can discover which ones didn't go where they belonged."

"These." Nora pointed out seven shipments. "Nothing should have gone to Mexico or to the Caribbean."

"Good. Now, do you have Carmen and Delia's work schedules?"

"I think so. Delia does the payroll." Nora moved to the filling cabinet and after a few minutes of searching pulled out a folder.

Rob took it from her and began to compare the dates. After double-checking them, he heaved a sigh. "I don't see a pattern. Delia was here most of these dates, but not for the last two shipments. Unless she and Carmen are in it together, I think we can rule them out."

Nora tilted her head to the side. "Let me see those shipment dates again."

Rob handed her the paper. "What is it? Do you see something?"

"Yes. And if I'm right, we need to hurry. Come on." She turned and left the office. Rob raced to keep up with her.

Once they reached the parking lot, Rob unlocked the door of his truck and Nora slid into the passenger's seat. After hurrying around to the driver's side, he got in and said, "Are you going to share what you know or keep me guessing?"

"I'm hoping that I'm wrong." She gave him directions, and a few minutes later they pulled up in front of a high-rise apartment complex a few blocks from the hospital.

Inside the building, they took the elevator to the twelfth floor. Rob followed her as she walked down the hallway to Apartment 1209 and knocked.

After a few seconds, the door opened. Peter Kent looked at them in surprise. At his feet were two large suitcases. "Nora, what are you doing here?"

"We have a problem at the office, Peter."

"Can't it wait until I get back from my weekend off?"

"Where are you going?" Rob asked.

"Santo Domingo."

Rob crossed his arms over his chest. "That's in the Dominican Republic, isn't it?"

"Yes, and I need to get to the airport."

Nora carefully watched her partner's face as she said, "Mr. Dale has discovered that someone has been stealing medical supplies from Children of the Day."

Peter frowned. "No kidding?"

"Yes," Rob added. "And that someone has been trying to make it look like Dr. Blake was responsible."

"That's terrible. Who at Children of the Day would do such a thing?"

"According to these shipping invoices, it's someone at Mercy Medical Center."

Peter shoved his hands in his pockets. "What shipping invoices?"

She held out the papers. "Each one of these shipments was made on days that I worked at Fort Bonnell."

"That's interesting, but I don't see what it has to do with me. I have a cab waiting downstairs and I need to get going or I'll miss my flight."

"The other odd thing about these dates," Nora continued, "is that each one of them happens to be exactly one week before your minivacations this year. You've been to Mexico and to the Caribbean a total of seven times in the last twelve months."

Peter took a step backward. "That doesn't mean anything. I like the beach scene."

Rob stepped forward and pulled his cell phone from his pocket. "I imagine a check of your credit card receipts will show that you visited the same locations where these supplies went on every occasion. What better way to make sure you get your money than to go in person?"

Nora closed her eyes. "Peter, how could you?"

He dashed toward the door, but Rob blocked his way and easily overpowered him by locking one of Peter's arms behind his back. "You're not going anywhere. Nora, call 911."

"Nora, please," Peter pleaded. "We can work this out."

"Tell me why you did it," she demanded.

"My ex-wife is still getting half of everything I make because of our stupid prenuptial agreement. I needed money that she couldn't get her hands on. The drugs and supplies are all still going to poor people."

"Made poorer by the prices they are forced to pay on the black market while you get richer on the side," Rob hissed. "How did you get access to Children of the Day's account information?"

"I saw Delia giving instructions to Carmen in the office when she was first hired. Carmen wrote them down. She keeps them in a notebook in the bottom drawer of her desk. I made a copy one day when she went out to lunch. After the first time it was easy and you never caught on."

"Oh, but we did catch on. Thanks to Rob. I never thought you would stoop so low, Peter." Nora gave him a look of disgust, then pulled her cell phone from her purse and dialed the police.

A few days later, Rob walked out of his motel room and pulled the door shut. He paused with his hand on the knob. He was closing the door on an important chapter in his life. One that had changed him forever.

He glanced over his shoulder. It was still dark out, but the first faint light could be seen touching the hills and buttes to the east. He smiled as he headed for the stairs at the side of the building. A new day was dawning. A new chapter of his life was just starting.

He carried his suitcase down the wide steps at the end of the wing. As he approached his ride, he extended his electronic key and pressed the button, and the rear hatch opened. He threw his suitcase in, slammed the hatch and walked toward the driver's side door. He had a hand on the handle and was about to open the door when he saw her standing a few feet away.

She looked so beautiful that it took his breath away. She took a step toward him. "I know you're leaving today."

"I was on my way to see you first." He walked toward her and held out his arms. She flew into his embrace, and he relished the feel of her safe in his arms. Was there any man in the world who was more blessed?

"I miss you already," she whispered.

He drew away to cup her face between his hands and gaze into her eyes. "I'll be back as soon as I can get things settled in Washington."

"I can't believe you're really moving here. We don't have much armed conflict in Prairie Springs. You might be bored out of your skull."

"You will never bore me."

"You can go on overseas assignments if that's what you want. You know I would never stand in your way."

"I know that. I also know that all I care about is right in front of me. I don't need anything else. Besides, Fort Bonnell is the largest military base in the United States. I think a good investigative reporter like myself can dig up a few stories for the Midwest bureau of *Liberty and Justice*. If not, I can always freelance for the Austin papers."

"I hope this is what you really want."

"I want to be where you are. You make me happy."

"Oh, Rob. You've given me so much. You brought God back into my life, and you've shown me that forgiveness is so much better than bitterness. You make me happy, too." She threw her arms around him.

"I'm glad," he whispered against her neck.

Drawing back, she brushed the tears from her face.

"You still have to stop by the hospital and see Ali. He was moved out of the PICU last evening."

"That's great news."

"And you need to stop by Children of the Day. Everyone wants to thank you for uncovering Dr. Kent's sad scheme."

"At least he is making restitution for his crimes. The money will go a long way in helping other children."

"We are all praying for him. He needs our forgiveness as much as anyone. Have you heard anything from your friend about Whitney Harpswell?"

"He called late last night. All he has come up with are dead ends. I'm going to stop by Evan's ranch and let him know before I leave town."

"Tell him not to give up hope."

"I will."

She tucked her hands in her jean jacket pockets. "So, have you had breakfast?"

"Not yet."

Nora grinned, happy and grateful to be able to spend a few hours in his company. God willing they would spend many more hours, days and years together, but she would never take her time with him for granted. She said, "I have a picnic basket with coffee and bread and jam. I know a place with a great view of the sunrise. Are you up for a hike?"

"With you? Always."

* * * * *

We hope you enjoyed reading

REUNITED IN WALNUT RIVER

by *New York Times* bestselling author

RAEANNE THAYNE

and

A MATTER OF THE HEART

by *USA TODAY* bestselling author

PATRICIA DAVIDS

Both were originally Harlequin® series stories!

From passionate, suspenseful and dramatic love stories to inspirational or historical, Harlequin offers different lines to satisfy every romance reader.

New books in each line are available every month.

Harlequin.com

BACHALO0819

SPECIAL EXCERPT FROM

Love Inspired®

On her way home, pregnant and alone, an Amish woman finds herself stranded with the last person she wanted to see.

Read on for a sneak preview of Shelter from the Storm *by Patricia Davids, available September 2019 from Love Inspired.*

"There won't be another bus going that way until the day after tomorrow."

"Are you sure?" Gemma Lapp stared at the agent behind the counter in stunned disbelief.

"Of course I'm sure. I work for the bus company."

She clasped her hands together tightly, praying the tears that pricked the backs of her eyes wouldn't start flowing. She couldn't afford a motel room for two nights.

She wheeled her suitcase over to the bench. Sitting down with a sigh, she moved her suitcase in front of her so she could prop up her swollen feet. After two solid days on a bus she was ready to lie down. Anywhere.

She bit her lower lip to stop it from quivering. She could place a call to the phone shack her parents shared with their Amish neighbors to let them know she was returning and ask her father to send a car for her, but she would have to leave a message.

Any message she left would be overheard. If she gave the real reason, even Jesse Crump would know before she reached home. She couldn't bear that, although she

LIEXP0819

didn't understand why his opinion mattered so much. His stoic face wouldn't reveal his thoughts, but he was sure to gloat when he learned he'd been right about her reckless ways. He had said she was looking for trouble and that she would find it sooner or later. Well, she had found it all right.

No, she wouldn't call. What she had to say was better said face-to-face. She was cowardly enough to delay as long as possible.

She didn't know how she was going to find the courage to tell her mother and father that she was six months pregnant, and Robert Troyer, the man who'd promised to marry her, was long gone.

Don't miss
Shelter from the Storm *by* USA TODAY
bestselling author Patricia Davids,
available September 2019 wherever
Love Inspired® books and ebooks are sold.

www.LoveInspired.com

Copyright © 2019 by Patricia MacDonald

LIEXP0819

Love Inspired®

Save $1.00
on the purchase of ANY Harlequin Love Inspired or Love Inspired Suspense® book.

Available wherever books are sold, including most bookstores, supermarkets, drugstores and discount stores.

Save $1.00

on the purchase of any Harlequin Love Inspired or Love Inspired Suspense book.

Coupon valid until December 31, 2019.
Redeemable at participating outlets in the U.S. and Canada only.
Not redeemable at Barnes & Noble stores. Limit one coupon per customer.

Canadian Retailers: Harlequin Enterprises Limited will pay the face value of this coupon plus 10.25¢ if submitted by customer for this product only. Any other use constitutes fraud. Coupon is nonassignable. Void if taxed, prohibited or restricted by law. Consumer must pay any government taxes. Void if copied. Inmar Promotional Services ("IPS") customers submit coupons and proof of sales to Harlequin Enterprises Limited, P.O. Box 31000, Scarborough, ON M1R 0E7, Canada. Non-IPS retailer—for reimbursement submit coupons and proof of sales directly to Harlequin Enterprises Limited, Retail Marketing Department, Bay Adelaide Centre, East Tower, 22 Adelaide Street West, 40th Floor, Toronto, Ontario M5H 4E3, Canada.

U.S. Retailers: Harlequin Enterprises Limited will pay the face value of this coupon plus 8¢ if submitted by customer for this product only. Any other use constitutes fraud. Coupon is nonassignable. Void if taxed, prohibited or restricted by law. Consumer must pay any government taxes. Void if copied. For reimbursement submit coupons and proof of sales directly to Harlequin Enterprises, Ltd 482, NCH Marketing Services, P.O. Box 880001, El Paso, TX 88588-0001, U.S.A. Cash value 1/100 cents.

® and ™ are trademarks owned and used by the trademark owner and/or its licensee.

© 2019 Harlequin Enterprises Limited

BACCOUP46996

SPECIAL EXCERPT FROM
HARLEQUIN®
SPECIAL EDITION

After escaping her abusive ex, Cassie Zetticci is thankful for a job and a safe place to stay at the Gallant Lake Resort. Nick West makes her nervous with his restless energy, but when he starts teaching her self-defense, Cassie begins to see a future that involves roots and community. But can Nick let go of his own difficult past to give Cassie the freedom she needs?

Read on for a sneak preview of
A Man You Can Trust,
the first book—and Harlequin Special Edition debut!—in Jo McNally's new miniseries, Gallant Lake Stories.

"Why are you armed with pepper spray? Did something happen to you?"

She didn't look up.

"Yes. Something happened."

"Here?"

She shook her head, her body trembling so badly she didn't trust her voice. The only sound was Nick's wheezing breath. He finally cleared his throat.

"Okay. Something happened." His voice was gravelly from the pepper spray, but it was calmer than it had been a few minutes ago. "And you wanted to protect yourself. That's smart. But you need to do it right. I'll teach you."

Her head snapped up. He was doing his best to look at her, even though his left eye was still closed.

"What are you talking about?"

"I'll teach you self-defense, Cassie. The kind that actually works."

"Are you talking karate or something? I thought the pepper spray…"

"It's a tool, but you need more than that. If some guy's amped up on drugs, he'll just be temporarily blinded and really ticked off." He picked up the pepper spray canister from the grass at her side. "This stuff will spray up to ten feet away. You never should have let me get so close before using it."

"I didn't know that."

"Exactly." He grimaced and swore again. "I need to get home and dunk my face in a bowl full of ice water." He stood and reached a hand down to help her up. She hesitated, then took it.

Don't miss
A Man You Can Trust *by Jo McNally,*
available September 2019 wherever
Harlequin® Special Edition books and ebooks are sold.

www.Harlequin.com

Copyright © 2019 by Jo McNally

HSEEXP0819

Love Harlequin romance?

DISCOVER.

Be the first to find out about promotions, news and exclusive content!

Facebook.com/HarlequinBooks

Twitter.com/HarlequinBooks

Instagram.com/HarlequinBooks

Pinterest.com/HarlequinBooks

ReaderService.com

EXPLORE.

Sign up for the Harlequin e-newsletter and download a free book from any series at **TryHarlequin.com.**

CONNECT.

Join our Harlequin community to share your thoughts and connect with other romance readers!

Facebook.com/groups/HarlequinConnection

ROMANCE WHEN YOU NEED IT

HSOCIAL2018

Reward the book lover in you!

Earn points on your purchase of new Harlequin books from participating retailers.

Turn your points into **FREE BOOKS** of your choice!

Join for FREE today at **www.HarlequinMyRewards.com.**

Harlequin My Rewards is a free program (no fees) without any commitments or obligations.

MYR18